"She's cute. She's a redhead. She's got that killer little body. What's wrong with her?"

"You have no idea."

"Don't be an idiot," Karen stated flatly. She'd always had little patience for what she called Stieg's "weirdo belief system," a term she applied to anything that went against what she was saying. "Ask her out."

"She called you a hooker."

"No. She asked if you were a pimp."

"What's the difference?"

"It's the fact that you can't tell that bothers me." She slapped his bicep with the back of her hand. "Come on. What's the problem? Really? She's sweet. She's funny, and God knows, you need some funny. I can't be around to entertain you all the time with my effervescent personality."

"You do not have an effervescent personality and—"

"Shit!" Erin barked before stumbling out of the bathroom, still holding a towel to dry her hands on. She spread her arms out wide and demanded with obvious glee, "Engstrom, you need to explain to me why there's a goat in your bathroom. And you need to do it right now!"

THE
UNYIELDING

SHELLY
LAURENSTON

k

KENSINGTON BOOKS
www.kensingtonbooks.com

KENSINGTON BOOKS are published by

Kensington Publishing Corp.
119 West 40th Street
New York, NY 10018

All Kensington Titles, Imprints, and Distributed Lines are available at special quantity discounts for bulk purchases for sales promotions, premiums, fund-raising, and educational or institutional use. Special book excerpts or customized printings can also be created to fit specific needs. For details, write or phone the office of the Kensington special sales manager: Kensington Publishing Corp., 119 West 40th Street, New York, NY 10018, attn: Sales Department; Phone: 1-800-221-2647.

ISBN-13: 978-1-61773-515-8
ISBN-10: 1-61773-515-9
First Kensington Trade Edition: April 2017
First Kensington Mass Market Edition: May 2018

eISBN-13: 978-1-61773-514-1
eISBN-10: 1-61773-514-0

10 9 8 7 6 5 4 3 2 1

Printed in the United States of America

ACKNOWLEDGMENTS

So many thanks to Kody Cushman. The *best*, most amazing tattoo artist this side of the Pacific. Not only for your invaluable knowledge about art and life and tattooing, but for giving me what I waited twenty years to get—my magnificent dragons and crows.

You are the absolute best, Kody. Thank you!

And big thanks to my editor, Alicia Condon, who has the patience of a saint. So I've decided to rename you Saint Alicia of the Kensington. Heh.

PROLOGUE

"Up. Now."

Harvold immediately woke at his mother's words. She already held the baby. His sister who could barely walk. And she roused his younger brother with the same words.

She led him and his brother to the secret exit at the back of the house. It was there in case of raids. It was the middle of winter. Who would raid now?

"Go," she ordered, pushing his sister into his arms. "Go and don't look back."

"But—"

"Do not ask questions!" It was her biggest complaint about him. He asked too many questions. He needed to know "too much."

But he was nearly thirteen years. He was almost a man. It was time he received answers.

"Just go." She suddenly hugged him, tight, his sister trapped between them.

It was a fierce, terrified hug. Then she hugged his brother the same.

"Go, Harvold. Protect your brother and sister. And *don't* look back."

The latch was unhitched and he and his brother snuck out of the house and ran through the forest and up the hill, their sister in his arms. But Harvold stopped. He would look back. He always did.

"Harvold!" his brother whispered.

Harvold ignored the desperate plea and instead found a place for his siblings to safely hide. A large boulder would do the trick and he planted them there.

The hiding place was perfect. Big enough to keep them out of sight, but located so that he had a perfect view of the village.

After handing their sister to his younger brother, Harvold eased around the boulder and looked down on the village that had been the home of him, his father, his father's father, and back and back for generations.

Those he'd known all his life were forced into the center of the village square, their elders and warriors shoved to the ground by men he'd never seen before. Large men. Harvold had never seen people such a size before. The women and children were kept from leaving, the entire village encircled by these large, terrifying men.

One of those terrifying men stepped forward, glaring down at Eindride the Patient. The stranger had long hair and a big beard so that all Harvold could see, even from this safe distance, was his fierce eyes.

"Tell me," the large man growled. His words, although low, carried on the crisp winter wind so that it was as if Harvold stood next to them. "Where is it?"

"I told you before . . . we don't know what you're talking about!"

The big man crouched in front of Eindride, one arm resting on his knee. "Do you know who I am?" he asked.

Eindride glared up at the man, because even crouching, he still towered. "You are Holfi Rundstöm."

Harvold's brother gasped at the name and Harvold quickly covered the boy's mouth with his hand.

Even though his brother was only nine, he'd heard of the Rundstöms. Everyone had. Their reputation went back for generations and they were feared for good reason.

"Yes, I am Holfi Rundstöm." The big man stood, lifted his blade and brought it down at a brutal angle. Not on Eindride, but across the neck of his oldest daughter.

Poor Eindride cried out in rage. He had seven daughters and he adored them all.

Rundstöm must have known this. Harvold guessed it was no accident he'd killed Eindride's eldest.

Rundstöm grabbed the next eldest of Eindride's girls and pressed his blood-covered blade against her throat. "I will ask one more time, old man," he growled. "Tell me where—owwwww!"

The hammer seemed to come out of nowhere, ramming into Rundstöm's giant head and forcing him to release Eindride's daughter and stumble back several feet.

It shocked Harvold that Rundstöm didn't fall to the ground dead. Because that was not a normal Warhammer. Its head was a thousand times bigger than anything Harvold had seen before from any blacksmith. Who had that much iron to work with and put into a single weapon?

Rundstöm's men, who appeared unarmed, grabbed nearby weapons from the blacksmith's stall, and snatching up anything available. Like a chopping axe.

"You dare come here, Holfi Rundstöm?" a bare-chested man demanded as he walked from the woods. He wore fur pants and boots but no shirt. The image of the large hammer he wielded was branded on his chest, a gold torc around his thick neck. "This town is under my god's protection."

"Fuck your god," Rundstöm growled back. "Fuck you."

Another hammer was tossed to the leader and he swung

it a few times as he walked. The head on the weapon was so large, Harvold had no idea how he managed not to beat himself in the face with it.

As those with hammers approached, Rundstöm and his men jerked their shoulders back, big black wings exploding from their flesh. Like the wings of Odin's ravens, Huginn and Muninn, except much larger.

"It's true," Harvold couldn't help but whisper over the panicked screams of his neighbors. "It's all true."

"What is?" his brother asked. "What's happening?"

Harvold motioned to his brother to stay in place, while he continued to watch.

He'd heard the old women of his village talking about this, but few had believed them. The stories of warriors chosen by one god to represent him or her in this world. To do his or her bidding. His parents worshipped any god they needed at any time, but these men, they only had one god they listened to, whose orders they followed, whose power they worshipped.

Those with the hammers must belong to Thor. And the men with the wings . . . their god had to be Odin.

Harvold felt his very bones grow cold. *Odin*. So feared, his parents rarely called on him for anything except during a time of war. And something told Harvold that the men Odin chose to wear his wings would be no better. Reason and talk would mean nothing to those who worshipped at the blood-soaked feet of Odin.

"Hold your weapons, ridiculous men," a woman called out. She wore long robes, and a hood covered her face. There were others with her, all women, Harvold thought, based on the way they moved. They came from the east. They had no weapons of their own from what he could see, but they also showed no fear as they strode toward the male warriors.

"Holde's Maids," the hammer wielder snarled. "What are you heinous bitches doing here?"

"Hold your tongue, Giant Killer, or I'll tear it from your mouth with my teeth."

"He's right, Alvilda," Rundström cut in. "Why *are* you here?"

The hooded woman stopped and stared beyond the men, toward the lake of the village. "Perhaps that is a question we should all ask," she said, waving her hand toward the water.

From the cold depths of the lake they appeared, naked and beautiful. Men and women, swords at the ready.

A woman led them, her hair in thick braids down her back. She gazed at the different groups, wide blue eyes slowly blinking. Even though she was naked and soaking wet, with snow under her feet, she didn't seem the least bit cold.

"What's going on?" the naked woman asked.

The two male leaders began to speak, but the hooded woman cut them off with a quick swipe of both her arms. "Why are you here, Eerika?" she asked.

"We heard you and the Ravens were planning an attack on our god's temple, not too far from here."

"Why would we ever bother attacking your god's fish-covered temple?"

From the north, bursting down from the nearby mountain, came another group. This one also all women. They cut through the snow easily by using long sticks attached to their feet and pushing with long poles held in their hands.

They each jumped from the high mountain ledge, some of them easily flipping in midair, before landing near the other groups.

And from the northern woods charged a pack of white

wolves. They growled and snarled and bit at each other until they stopped near the others and turned from animal to human. Easily, with no more than a thought.

The six groups stared at each other for several long moments.

"I don't understand," Holfi Rundstöm said to them. "Why are we all here? At the same time?"

"We've been lured here, idiot," the Holde's Maid snapped from behind her hood.

"Who would do that?"

"The Silent aren't here," another of the winged warriors suggested.

Holfi sneered. "They wouldn't dare."

"And Loki's Wolves are no longer part of the Nine," one of the Maids said.

"But we should be," a man who'd been a wolf laughingly suggested.

"But you *aren't*."

The leader of the Maids raised her hands to silence everyone and practically yelled, "Then *why* are we here?"

Harvold was wondering the same thing when another woman—a very *different* woman—silently landed on the boulder he and his siblings hid behind.

He looked up at her, knowing instantly she had not been born in these lands. Her skin was brown, as if she'd been in the sun for a thousand years, her eyes almost black. She still had the brand of her master on her arm. Harvold remembered her. She'd been hanged from a tree by her master for trying to escape. She'd been a slave. She still had the scars from where her master had beaten her. He'd left her still-bleeding corpse hanging from the tree near his hall, but it had suddenly disappeared.

Most of the villagers assumed a necromancer had taken

her for his dark works. But if a necromancer had brought her back, he'd have brought back a corpse that would have continued to rot for however long it roamed the land.

But the woman who now stood over him and his siblings . . . she was young, healthy, and well-armed.

She was *alive*.

She glanced down at Harvold, studying him closely. She was sizing him up, judging whether he was a threat to her. Much to his relief, she finally raised her finger and pressed it to her lips. "Shhhh."

Harvold shrank back and nodded.

Smiling, she raised her bow, nocked an arrow, and aimed. After a few seconds, she let the arrow fly. It struck Rundstöm through the neck, the huge man looking shocked before he fell to the ground.

More arrows flew from the trees and mountains surrounding Harvold's village, tearing into warrior and villager alike. Once the rain of arrows stopped, the woman on the boulder dropped her head back and unleashed a war cry that tore across the land.

"*Crows!*" one of the gods' warriors screamed out in warning and the slave women seemed to appear from everywhere. Women not born of these lands, some still wearing the brands of their masters on their arms or faces, bursting from trees, leaping from the mountain ledges, or just dropping down into the middle of the village.

Women with large black wings and a rune branded on their necks or right on their faces.

Harvold recognized that rune. It represented Skuld, one of the Fates his grandmother had been talking about lately.

"Treat your slaves well, my young Harvold," his grandmother would often say, "for if they die poorly at your hand, Skuld may send them back to tear you apart."

He thought she spoke of something rising from the grave. Something decayed and desolate, to reap revenge before being swallowed back into the hole it had sprung from.

But he'd been wrong.

These thriving, angry foreign women attacked without hesitation. Some lashing out with long, thin blades, impaling necks, thighs, and spines. Others wielded swords and shields, using crushing blows to decapitate, dismember. Battling anyone who would take their challenge.

Many of the villagers were struck down as they tried to escape, unable to avoid the battle that had exploded around them.

It was a brutal thing, no one spared. Even the winged women had suffered heavy casualties. But those who still breathed had no pity. They walked among the bodies, killing those—whether gods' warrior or innocent villager—they felt might still survive, slashing throats with their thin weapons.

One large, very brown winged woman grabbed one of Odin's warriors by the back of his throat, lifting him so he sat up a bit. He'd lost one of his wings and a leg below the knee during the battle, but still he breathed.

"Why?" he asked the woman. "Why have you done this?"

"Did you think the Crows would ever forget what you and the others did? That you killed our sisters? You cut them down while they slept. All of you attacking at once."

"That was—"

"Ten winters ago. Yes. And we did not forget, Raven." She leaned in. "We *never* forget."

She rammed her thin but strong edged weapon into the warrior's eye, forcing it in deep, and yelling over his screams, "*And now you can be like your god!*"

When the warrior's screams died off, the slave women raised their blood-covered weapons and roared in triumph.

Harvold didn't realize he was crying until he was forced to wipe his face. The entire village gone . . . even his parents.

His brother was resting on the boulder with him, also watching. Also crying. Harvold didn't make him look away. No point in protecting him anymore. Then Harvold remembered their sister.

"Where is she?" he asked, looking where she should have been, but wasn't.

The brothers scrambled from the rock and turned, both halting in surprise.

Men stood behind them. Men with wings. Not the black wings of Odin's warriors but large white wings. And the rune of Tyr burned into their biceps. They gazed down at Harvold's sister as she reached up to them with her fat arms.

"No!" his brother snapped, but Harvold covered the boy's mouth with his hand to silence him.

As one, the men looked at them. They had large eyes that didn't move. Just their heads moved and they blinked at Harvold. Like owls. Their heads and eyes moved like owls.

Harvold pushed his brother forward, and the young boy scrambled to pick their sister up. He returned quickly to Harvold's side, their sister tight in his arms.

After another minute of staring, the men walked around them in two lines before taking to the skies and launching an attack on the remaining slave women.

"*Protectors!*" one of the slave women screamed. "*Prepare yourselves, sisters!*"

Harvold decided not to watch. He'd seen more than enough this day.

Pushing his brother ahead of him, their sister still in his arms, they headed toward their grandmother's hut hidden deep in the woods, where they would hopefully be safe.

As they walked, his brother finally asked, "Why do you

think they killed each other like that, Harvold? Why are they still killing?"

Harvold shrugged and replied, "Guess they didn't get on . . ."

Centuries later . . .

Hel, goddess of the Underworld, paced back and forth in front of the dark, dank cave her father had been condemned to so long ago.

It was the one place she could not enter, nor send any of her Carrion warriors. The other Aesir gods knew well that if she could enter, she would release their captive. How could she not? He was the great Loki, trickster god and her father.

But she'd found the one god who could release him—Gullveig.

She was not of the Aesir line but Vanir, and there was no binding that would keep her from entering the cave.

Hel heard footsteps and quickly turned to face the cave opening, her hands clasped tight, her lips pinched together as she waited to once again see the father she loved so very dearly.

Gullveig walked out first. She was no longer sheathed in that weak human body she'd chosen to reenter the human world. She shone like the gold of the Rhine. Hair, eyes, skin—all of it gold and glistening even in this darkness.

Gullveig stopped at the cave entrance and leaned against the left side of the stone opening.

"Well?" Hel pushed when she didn't see her father.

"He's not there."

Hel's entire body became rigid. "What? What do you . . . what?"

Gullveig shrugged, already bored by the entire conversation. "He's not there."

"That's . . . that's not possible."

Gullveig turned and walked back inside the cave. When she returned, she held heavy chains, tossing them at Hel's feet.

Hel knew those chains. They were made from the intestines of her half-brother Narfi. An additional punishment for Loki because of what he'd done to everyone's favorite god, Baldur. The gods had changed Loki's son Váli to a wolf, who'd turned and killed his brother Narfi. They then bound Loki in his son's intestines, which turned into iron.

Why all this? Because Odin was a sick, vindictive fuck and it had always amazed Hel that so few mortals remembered that about the Allfather.

"What about Sigyn?" Hel asked desperately.

"Who?"

"His wife! Is she in there?"

"No one is in there. It's empty except for this gross snake that hissed at me. And when I went to rip its head off, it tried to bite me! Me! *Does it know who I am?*"

Hel stepped away from Gullveig's complaining. For the first time in eons, she felt something. Deep, *deep* inside her gut. *Panic.* By all that was Hel herself, she felt panic! And she knew why.

Hel pointed at one of her Carrion.

"Lock down everything. And get us back to *Eljudnir*. Now."

"What is going on?" Gullveig demanded, snatching her arm away from the Carrion who'd grabbed her to take her back to *Eljudnir,* Hel's hall. "Why are you so afraid?"

"Loki's free."

"So? You were about to free him yourself."

"I was. But that would have been *me*. He would have owed me. If nothing else, I would have been safe from his wrath. But now . . ."

"And what does any of this have to do with me and *my* plans?"

"It's not all about you, you know?"

"No. I don't know. *My* plans are already in play. Are you telling me you're going to change everything because your *daddy* might get pissy?"

Hel stepped close to Gullveig, one finger pointing in her face. "You don't know what you're talking about."

"And you need to balls up and keep your commitment to *me!*" Gullveig snarled back, slapping Hel's hand out of her face.

Hel reached for Gullveig's throat with both hands, but one of the Carrion quickly pulled Gullveig out of reach and another gently offered to Hel, "My lady, we should get you to safety. At least until we know *where* your father is."

Hel curled her hands into fists and lowered them to her sides. She gritted her teeth together as they briefly turned into fangs.

She took a moment to get control of her anger. "Fine," she finally said, keeping her eyes on her loyal soldier. After so much time together, the Carrion knew how to keep their ruler calm.

The Carrion smiled, his leather wings slowly moving behind him. The sound soothed Hel's angry, decaying heart.

Until she heard, "*What about me?*"

Her Carrion's lip curled and his jaw clenched.

Gullveig continued to forget that the Carrion were loyal to Hel and no one else. Not Odin. Not Thor. Not even the beautiful Freyja who easily swayed the hearts—and cocks—of weak-willed men to her side with no more than a charming glance.

At only a twitch of her finger, Hel's men would pounce on Gullveig and tear her apart.

But, as she had before, Gullveig would only come back,

and it was best not to remind the idiot that she was basically indestructible in this universe.

So, instead of twitching anything that would set her loyal soldiers off, Hel asked, "Where is Önd?" She watched—amused—as what little color was in her soldier's dead cheeks faded away, his eyes widening a bit.

"He is . . . he is not here, my lady."

"Where is he?"

"He is in the pits of the Christian hell . . . tormenting the demons."

Hel smiled. "Call for him. Tell him he is needed here by me."

"But, my lady—"

"Do it. Now."

The soldier briefly bowed his head. "Of course, my lady."

Hel leaned around the Carrion to look at Gullveig. "I have someone, dearest friend, who will happily help you with any of your needs. If you want the human world destroyed to pain Odin and the others . . . Önd is your man."

"Good," Gullveig replied, wonderfully oblivious as always. Completely missing the fact that at the mere mention of Önd's name, the other Carrion appeared . . . uncomfortable. "I look forward to meeting him. I'm so very tired of waiting."

CHAPTER ONE

"Why aren't you dead?"

As Erin Amsel slowly woke up, her head, face, and throat throbbing from where she'd been repeatedly hit, she realized she should have gotten much more of a clue when that question had originally been tossed at her earlier in the evening.

Especially since it was not a common question, definitely not the kind of pickup line one got in a hot LA club. But she'd been busy. Doing something she probably shouldn't have been doing, too bad it was kind of late for regrets now. Sitting in the second row of seats in a big SUV, with two large men on either side of her. Three men in the row behind. And two in the front.

She could almost hear her father jokingly reminding her, "You never pay attention!"

And she hadn't paid attention. Having some random guy talking to her was kind of par for the course in any club or bar. Hunting around for a piece of ass they could nail was what guys did. So she really hadn't paid any attention to his actual question. She just knew he'd been in her way. Blocking her from her target.

Because while everyone else in that overpriced joint had been drinking, getting high, and trying to be seen in the hopes of getting their picture in a tabloid or attracting the attention of a talent scout, Erin had had a very specific goal. To prove that the woman she was trying to get a closer look at was the high priestess of a goddess determined to destroy the world. To bring about the Viking end of days— Ragnarok. The goddess Gullveig.

The first time Erin and her sisters had dealt with Gullveig, they'd thought they'd stopped her from entering this world. They'd been wrong.

The second time, they'd been forced to shove her into some distant plane of existence just to give them time to come up with a plan to stop her for good.

This upcoming third time . . . would be the last time.

No matter how it all came down.

Yet even now her sisters worked to stop Ragnarok.

Her sisters. The mighty Crows. The human warrior clan of the goddess Skuld. Since before the days when Vikings terrorized Europe from their longboats, Skuld had chosen from the dying those she felt worthy to fight in her name. She didn't choose from pure Norse stock the way the other gods did. No. She chose from those who'd been dragged to the northern shores in chains. Always women. Always slaves. And always filled with rage.

Now, in this day and age, Skuld chose from the descendants of those women. Or from those mistreated in *this* time.

She gave them a choice upon dying. Go to the god they were raised to worship or join her. Get a shot at a second life and a chance to use all that rage and need for revenge they had stored in their souls to help prevent Ragnarok.

There were those who refused to take the offer, but many others did. And those women were now Erin's sister-Crows.

Women she lived and died for, who at the moment had no idea Erin was in deep trouble.

It was her own fault. In the weeks since they'd pushed Gullveig out of their world, Erin had known that somewhere in Los Angeles, there had to be a priestess who worshipped the crazy bitch. There had to be. Gullveig, like all gods, fed on the worship of humans.

So, while the rest of her Crow sisters and the members of the other Viking Clans—the Nine, as they were called—desperately searched for a way to stop Gullveig, Erin did her own research. She read every trashy gossip rag. Scoured every gossip Web site. Listened to the incessant babble of her sister-Crows who had dreams of being a "star" one day. She listened and she researched and she obsessed until she came down to just one.

Jourdan Ambrosio.

The hottest "it" girl on both coasts and in Europe, Jourdan was the quintessential "do nothing megastar."

She was attractive—although it was kind of hard to tell with all the makeup she wore no matter the time of day or where she was or what she was doing—single, rich, and had lots of famous friends. Her father was an infamous Italian director whose work got Erin thrown out of a college film class once because she spent most of the initial movie screening mocking it. The man was pretentious—her film professor just needed to deal with that.

Now his daughter, instead of becoming an actress like her equally famous Belgian mother, or a director like her father and older half brother, did nothing except "set the style" for everyone else and spend lots of money.

When Erin spotted her, she'd been sitting in the VIP section of the club, surrounded by desperate sycophants, and obscenely covered in gold and diamond jewelry.

If she wasn't a priestess for Gullveig—a name that translated into "gold drink" or "gold power" or "gold trance" depending on what you read—she should be. She was everything Gullveig seemed to love. Beauty and tackiness all in one slim, sexy package.

In the end, Erin was so sure she was right about Ambrosio, so obsessed . . . she hadn't really noticed the big guy hitting on her.

Of course, he hadn't been hitting on her, had he? Hitting on a woman didn't usually involve asking her why she wasn't dead.

Now Erin was trapped here, with her wrists zip-tied together, and her body throbbing from the short beating she'd taken when they'd forced her into the SUV. She had no idea where she was, but they were turning onto a dirt road.

Yeah, that couldn't be good.

Dirt roads and women in zip-ties never ended well.

The SUV stopped and the men got out, pulling Erin with them. She struggled, trying to pull away, but two of the men kept an easy grip on her.

So, like she did that first time, all those years ago, she brought her elbow up and back. Only this time, she didn't just break the man's nose—she crushed his face, forcing in his nose and cheekbones.

Blood splattered across Erin's face and that's when she remembered. That's when it hit her. This wasn't a replay of the last time she'd been killed. It couldn't be. She wasn't the same woman who'd been taken before.

She was no longer the Staten Island loudmouth and tattoo artist who'd found herself on the wrong side of mobsters. Who'd made the oh-so-Erin mistake of talking to federal agents like it was no big deal. Because she'd just been a tattoo artist. A nobody. And Erin had continued to believe that—at least in the back of her mind—until the day those mobsters blew her brains out.

But now she was a Crow, one of the nine recognized human clans that represented the Nordic gods on this plane of existence.

She'd fought Vikings, demons, and Helheim's Carrion. She'd been hit on by Odin and hit *at* by Thor. One time, Idunn threw an entire basket of her golden apples at her and another time Bragi—the god of poetry and eloquence—called her a "fucked up little twat that I would love to beat the unholy shit out of with my harp!"

And after all that, the one thing that remained was her. Erin Amsel had survived all of it. So was she going to let some low-life gangsters actually—

A bullet slammed into Erin's forehead and she fell back against the hard ground.

Stieg Engstrom thought his friend and fellow Raven brother Vig Rundström was just being an asshole when he'd insisted Stieg "watch Erin Amsel tonight. See where she goes. What she does. Keep her out of trouble."

He'd really thought Vig was just being a massive dick. Why else would he make Stieg, of all the people in the universe, follow Erin "I'm a pain in *everyone's* ass!" Amsel around Los Angeles?

When he'd seen her go into an LA club, one of those "latest hotspots in the LA area" as they were called on the local news, he thought the whole Raven brotherhood was just tormenting him.

They all knew he hated the LA club scene. Hated actors and models and rich people who thought their money alone made them important. Hated Hollywood assholes who thought their ability to get a movie off the ground made them kings of the world and the rest of humanity their bootlickers. He disliked those people so damn much, if he wasn't so loyal to his brothers, he'd have joined the Colorado Ravens just so he didn't have to live in Los Angeles anymore.

But what he disliked most of all was Erin Amsel. The most irritating, frustrating, rude, ridiculous woman the gods had ever placed on earth.

Following her, it seemed, was a complete waste of time. Because in Stieg's mind, how much trouble could one small redhead with an ego the size of Norway get into in a boring club?

Apparently a lot.

One second, she was obviously stalking that model chick he had seen on the cover of some men's magazine in the Raven house bathroom—why Erin was doing that, he had no idea—and the next, some big mountain of a guy was dragging her off into a back hallway.

Normally, Stieg would let Erin handle some pushy guy on her own. It wasn't like she didn't have the skill. He'd seen the woman lay waste to a whole line of demons once. Literally, she'd just gone down the line, slitting throats and setting some on fire until there was nothing left but bones and demon blood.

And yet . . .

So Stieg, against his better judgment, had followed—through the hallway, out the back door, toward the SUV. That's when he'd unleashed his wings and followed from above until they'd left the 101 Freeway and ended up going down some dirt road.

When they parked the black Escalade, Stieg hovered above them. He didn't really know what he'd expected. Maybe some tough talk. Maybe some threats.

People loved to threaten Erin Amsel, he just didn't know

why. Because threatening her was a sure way of getting her to focus on you. Making you part of her life's work, which was tormenting people beyond all reason.

That's what Erin Amsel did well.

But these men didn't even bother with tough talk. They dragged her out of the SUV, her hands zip-tied in front of her, stood her up—which was when she'd smashed one guy's face in with her elbow—stepped away, and a guy pulled a gun and shot her in the head.

Without a word. They didn't even seem angry about their buddy bleeding to death at their feet.

Who the fuck does that?

Christ, maybe this world needed to burn. Some days he really wondered if Ragnarok would be such a bad thing.

Yet Stieg didn't need to go all "Raven destroyer" on these assholes, because these men had no real idea what they were dealing with.

Tommy aimed his gun at Erin Amsel's chest. He hadn't checked to make sure she was dead the last time when he'd *thought* he'd killed her. Two bullets to the back of the head. What else was he to think? But this time he would end it. One to the head and two to the chest. That was always the best way to take a person down and make sure they stayed down.

But before he could pull the trigger again, the ground beneath his feet shook and he turned, his weapon instinctively raised.

Surprised, he gawked at the man standing behind them, partially shielded in the dark. The headlights of their vehicle showed only a bit of his face . . . and his size.

"Who the fuck are you?" Tommy demanded, not sure how stupid this man could be.

The man didn't say anything. He just pointed.

Behind Tommy.

Tommy looked over his shoulder, his eyes widening. Horror coursed through his bloodstream as he watched Erin Amsel getting to her feet. Digging into her forehead until she pulled the bullet out.

"I am," she growled, "so sick of being *shot in the head*!"

Her scream snapped Tommy out of it. "Kill her!"

The men raised their guns, but the SUV suddenly spun to the side and he briefly wondered if that man had moved it. With his bare hands.

No one was that strong.

They were both gone. Amsel and that man.

Tommy and his guys looked around, trying to see in the dark, the headlights illuminating a different part of their surroundings.

"Where are they?" Tommy barked. "Where the fuck are they?"

Feet hit Tommy in the head and he realized that Tesco was disappearing up into the sky.

They could hear Big Tessy's screams before he came back down, landing hard on his face. Blood poured not only from where he'd landed but from his back and inside thighs. Damage he wouldn't have suffered from a straight fall.

Their SUV spun, crashing into several of Tommy's men, sending them flipping into the dark. Tommy could hear bones shattering, the groans of his men.

But there was no one behind the wheel of the SUV. It was like someone had pushed it. Again.

Backing up, feeling terror for the first time in decades, he held the gun out in front of him, flanked by the last two of his men.

Until they were gone, too, dragged off into the night.

Their screams . . . God, their screams.

"Hi, Tommy."

He whirled around at Amsel's voice, ready to fire, but her hands—now free—caught the weapon, turning it away. Pulling back her right hand, she rammed it into his forearm and he felt the bone shatter from that one hit.

Tommy dropped the gun and fell to his knees in the dirt.

Amsel kicked the gun aside and rested her hands on her hips. "Tommy, Tommy, Tommy." she said, smiling, despite the bruises and blood on her face from the beating she'd taken. And that shot to the head. "You do know I'd forgotten about you, right?"

"You know him?" another voice asked. The big man from earlier.

He came out of the darkness looking really pissed off, Tommy's last two men gripped tight by their throats. He tossed them aside like they were nothing.

"I do. From a long time ago. This is the man who killed me."

"Don't you mean *tried* to kill you?" Tommy asked, cradling his broken arm against his body.

Amsel crouched in front of him, one finger stroking his cheek. "No, no. You actually did kill me. But before my last breath, she came to me. A goddess named Skuld. And she made me an offer. Gave me a chance at a new life. A Second Life."

The woman was insane. Tommy knew that now, but he could play along. "You just had to give her your soul, right?"

"Aww. It's sweet you think I actually have one. But no." She traced the line of his jaw and it felt weird.

He glanced down and saw that the tip of her finger no longer looked like a finger. Not a human one. Black and dangerously sharp, it reminded him of . . . a talon?

Why did this woman have a talon?

"She promised me," Amsel went on, "that I'd never have

to be scared again by assholes like you. And she didn't lie to me." She flicked that talon and pain seared his cheek, blood poured down his jaw. "If you'd just left me alone, Tommy, this wouldn't be happening."

The man with Amsel took a knee behind Tommy and grabbed a handful of his hair, yanking Tommy's head back. "Why is he still alive?"

"Are you in a rush?" Amsel asked, laughing a little. "Got something else to do?"

"He shot you in the head."

"Again."

"And yet you haven't wasted him."

"Death is so final." She looked at Tommy and added, "Usually."

The man growled and she threw up her hands, revealing that all her fingers were black talons.

"What?" Amsel snapped. "What is wrong?"

"I don't understand why you're letting him live."

"I don't understand why you're so uptight. My God, man, *loosen up.*"

"He shot you in the *head*. I'd think you'd be a little angrier."

Amsel shrugged. "I don't let the little things bother me."

"*He shot you in the head,*" the man repeated. "How is that a little thing? And then he did it again!"

"You are not making friends, Tommy. He so wants to kill you," she mock-whispered.

"I so really do."

"But I'm not going to kill you." She grabbed Tommy around the throat with both hands and stood, taking Tommy with her, the man forced to let go of Tommy's hair. "That would be too easy. Because you don't deserve the quick exit of an honorable death. You deserve to suffer." She smiled. "And I'm going to be the one to make sure you do."

* * *

Stieg waited for Erin to do what she had always done so well. Make someone's life hell.

But, while still gripping the throat of the man who'd shot her in the head *again*, she abruptly looked at Stieg and asked, "How does my face look?"

Shocked at the question, considering the timing of it, Stieg answered, "What?"

"I asked how my face looks?"

"Why?"

"Is it bruised?"

"Of course it's bruised."

"Then I'll need to crash at your house tonight."

"You can't afford a hotel?"

"Wow, dude. I've been shot in the head and you're going to make me stay at a hotel . . . alone? All by myself?"

"Oh, please," Stieg scoffed, disgusted she was trying to force herself to cry. "And why don't you just go home?"

"Looking like this?"

"It wouldn't be the first time you've gone back to the Bird House looking like that, so why does it matter now?"

Erin started to reply, but then she stopped, shrugged, and said, "You're right. I'll just . . . just . . . you're right."

Erin Amsel never told Stieg he was right. About anything. She went out of her way to never tell him he was right about anything because it amused her to torment him.

Torment was what she was good at.

"The Crows don't know what you're doing, do they?" Stieg accused.

"What am I doing?"

"I don't know, but it's something. You're up to something!"

"What do you care? Why are you even here?" She stared at him a moment and asked again, "Why *are* you here?"

"I thought you were going to kill this guy?"

"Don't try and distract me with this idiot. Just tell me what you're doing here."

"You tell me!"

They stared at each other for a moment until Erin shook her head and offered, "How about we let that lie . . . and you let me crash at your place, because I heard you have an apartment now."

"And the hotel's out because . . . ?

"Betty has spies at all the hotels."

Betty Lieberman, an Elder Crow and fulltime Hollywood agent, was odd but she didn't seem that odd.

"Why the hell does Betty have spies at all the hotels?"

"What? You think she keeps movie moguls under control with her charm?"

"Oh. *Oh.*"

"And if she finds out I was there, it'll make its way through the Crow Phone Line."

A phone line that Stieg knew from experience was the fastest on the planet. "And you don't want that because . . . ?"

"I won't ask you any questions and you don't ask me."

Stieg figured that was for the best. He knew that if his Raven brothers felt the need to follow the woman, it must be for a reason. Probably. Maybe.

Who the hell knows what those idiots are up to?

"Fine."

"Fine."

Stieg motioned to Erin's current prey. "And what about him?"

She smirked. "You thought we'd forgotten about you, didn't you, Tommy?" She shoved him into Stieg's arms. "But we didn't."

She slapped her hand against Tommy's face, her long fingers going from right above his eye, down one nostril, and across his mouth to his chin. She unleashed enough heat from her hand to melt all that was under her hand, ignoring Tommy's screams as he writhed between them, desperately trying to get out of Stieg's grip.

Not that Stieg blamed the man. He, too, had faced Erin's "special gift" from the goddess Skuld. Not every Crow received a gift, but the ones who did gave their enemies much to contend with.

For Erin her gift was a mighty flame. So that when she finally pulled her hand back, the damage was complete. No plastic surgeon could fix what she'd done to that man's face. It went past skin and muscle and right into bone.

Attempts would be made to fix the damage, Stieg was sure, but that would simply add to the man's suffering—and Erin knew it.

"This way I'll probably forget you again," Erin told Tommy—*still* smiling—with one finger tracing what she'd done to his body, "but you'll never forget me. Ever."

"Are you done?" Stieg dropped the Crow's prey. Honestly, she should have just killed him.

"Yes. I'm done. You're so uptight."

"Yeah, yeah, yeah, whatever."

"Oh, come on!" she insisted. "This is a good night. I'm alive and well. You're the big he-man who helped. Isn't that what matters?"

"That would depend on who you talk to."

"That's very nice."

"You could, however, be a little less cheery. You did just disfigure a man."

Erin stared down at her victim a few seconds before casually giving her standard reply. "He started it."

CHAPTER TWO

Inka Solberg-Bentsen, Head Priestess of the Los Angeles Holde's Maids, stared across the table at Freida, leader of the Giant Killers.

The Giant Killers were the human warriors of Thor, or as Inka's fellow sisters called the Nordic god, "The idiot."

She stared and she stared until Freida finally screeched, "*Why do you keep staring at me?*"

"Probably because it irritates you so."

That's when Freida tried to climb over the diner table but Chloe Wong, leader of the Crows, yanked her back with one arm. "Sit down, crazy woman."

"Kera hasn't figured out this isn't a good idea, has she?" Inka asked Chloe, amused as the poor all-night diner staff kept a close eye on the table of people who didn't look like they belonged together.

Because they *didn't* belong together. They never had.

For centuries, each of these groups had not merely *tried* to kill each other, but had succeeded several times over. More than once, the Claws of Ran had wiped out the Silent; the Silent had wiped out the Maids; the Maids had wiped out the Claws; the Ravens had wiped out the Crows and the Crows turned right around and wiped out the Ravens; then the Protectors came along and wiped out the Ravens *and* the Crows. Then there were the Isa, who had been in several blood matches with almost all the Clans since they seemed to hate anyone who wasn't a wild animal. Only the Valkyries managed not to be involved in any of the drama. Favored by all the gods, they took the souls of warriors to Valhalla, and no Clan would risk ending up on the wrong side of their favor.

So this gathering of the Clan leaders in a diner in the wee hours of the morning was just asking for trouble.

But the woman who'd arranged this little get-together was new. She'd only been part of the Crows for a few weeks. Not even three months, but she'd been chosen as War General in this latest battle. Because she was so new, she had no long-term hatred of anyone. Add in that she'd been a United States Marine and she came to the table with skills some of them didn't have.

War General Kera Watson walked into the diner with the Raven she called "boyfriend," a term that made Inka laugh. Clan males didn't really make good boyfriends. Once they locked onto a woman, they were in it for the long haul. Otherwise, a girl or guy was just a one-night stand. Of course, this attitude sometimes led to stalking charges and restraining orders, but only when they insisted on latching onto the Unknowing, the humans who knew nothing about the Viking Clans and the gods who'd created them.

Within the Clans, however, breakups were much easier. They sometimes involved bloodshed and the occasional bar fight, but were much more containable in the end since Clan members rarely brought lawsuits against each other, and proper Viking funerals were paid for out of an All-Clan funeral fund.

"Stop smirking," Ormi whispered against Inka's ear. "You're making Freida nervous."

"I'm not even thinking about her," she whispered back.

"It doesn't matter. She *thinks* you are." Ormi slid his hand onto her thigh under the table. "Let's just try to make this as painless as possible. For all of us."

Ormi, the Protector leader and a good man—*her* good man—was right. If things turned ugly here, chances were the Clan members would suffer the least. There were innocents in this diner and despite Inka not caring as much as she probably should, she knew that Ormi cared. He always did. It was what she liked about him.

"I'll be good," she promised, squeezing his thigh under the table.

"That's my vicious girl."

Stieg's apartment wasn't far from Raven territory.

An apartment in a nine-unit building that looked out over the Pacific would cost the average renter a small fortune. More than five to six times as much as a monthly mortgage payment for a house in the Valley. But most of the properties around Stieg's building were owned and managed by Ravens; the Vikings had gobbled up a good chunk of this territory long ago. So Erin was sure that Stieg was only paying a fraction of what non-Ravens were paying in the same location.

Of course, that's where Ravens made most of their Clan's money. Through real estate. Something they'd learned long ago from their Viking ancestors . . . it was all about territory.

They landed on the roof and Erin paused to take in a deep breath of ocean air. She always loved being close to the ocean. She found it relaxing. She loved relaxing.

"It's really nice—" she began, only to realize that Stieg had already gone through an unlocked door, disappearing into the building.

She let out a sigh. It was going to be a long, painful evening.

Of course, Erin would never say that Stieg was the worst of the Viking men she knew. For instance, the Giant Slayer who'd been moved to another state because Erin had burned the flesh off his arm after he drunkenly groped her tit during a party.

Still, Stieg was not the easiest man to deal with. She'd never met anyone so young who seemed so bitter. Something about him just radiated "old man ordering kids off his lawn."

Pulling in her wings, she ran after Stieg, catching him on the second floor as he lumbered his way to the last apartment at the far end. He dug into the front of his black jeans and pulled out a set of keys.

He unlocked his door and walked into his pitch black apartment. Tossing the keys onto the table beside the door, he turned on one light—and one light only—before grabbing the remote from the coffee table, turning on the big flat-screen TV, tossing that remote onto the couch, going into the small, open kitchen, grabbing a Norwegian beer from the fridge, walking back into the living room, dropping onto the couch, putting his feet up on the coffee table, and proceeding to watch "American Greed." A show about white-collar crime and the rich people who ripped middle-class people off so they could buy sixteen six-figure cars that they ended up never fully paying for and, once sold by the government to recoup losses, could never pay back those who'd been ripped off.

And the whole time, Erin stood in his doorway, watching him.

When Stieg continued to ignore her, she finally asked, "Aren't you going to invite me in?"

He slowly looked away from his show, dark gray eyes locking on her face. "Are you a vampire?"

"Not that I'm aware."

"Are you polite?"

"We both know the answer to that."

"Then why would you need to be invited in?"

Deciding it would be a waste to argue that with him, Erin stepped into the apartment and closed the door behind her.

It wasn't a bad place at all. Clearly the Valkyries had helped him decorate. Erin couldn't imagine Stieg Engstrom purposely buying the gorgeous painting of a horse that was on a far wall near the sliding glass door that led to the balcony. Or the very expensive espresso machine she could see in his open kitchen.

His apartment wasn't large at all, but she bet the view of the ocean made up for all that.

She walked across the living room, barely glancing at the one bathroom and one bedroom she passed.

Pushing open the sliding door, she stepped outside and took in a big breath of the lovely ocean-scented air. There was no moon tonight, but she could see plenty. The pit fires locals had made on the beach, the well-lit tankers out in the Pacific, and the street lamps that dotted the walking path that separated the apartments and the beach.

And what she couldn't see, she could hear. Like the waves rolling onto the sand.

The Crow house—or, as the other Viking Clans called it, the Bird House—sat on an enormous bit of Malibu property, too, although you had to walk a while before you actually hit the ocean. Much to the annoyance of every multimillionaire actor and director, billionaire entrepreneur and sheik; and European royal who had a title but no real cash to their name, the Los Angeles Crows would *never* give up their Southern California home, even if they didn't have a bird's-eye view of the Pacific.

Why would they when their sister-Crow elders had been so smart?

Those ladies had bought the property back in the early twenties when it was *still* considered pricey for any land at that time.

Since then, many had tried to buy them out. When that didn't work, they tried force.

But the Crows never took well to any of that. They would go the legal route first. Yet if that wasn't effective . . .

Back in the thirties, the first head of the Los Angeles Mafia family had tried to get his hands on the Crows' territory. He wanted it to "retire" to after he and a friend were shot in what Chloe liked to call "the first drive-by shooting in the LA area." His men tried money first and when that didn't work, they sent some hitters to the house in the middle of the night.

When the Crows finished burying the bodies, they tracked down the mobster and dealt with him personally, forcing his wife to have him declared legally dead so she could deal with his estate. The cops believed it was a rival crime family that made the man "disappear" but no. It had been the Crows. And those old-school girls had made him suffer before they were done with him.

Crows today, though, avoided unnecessary torturing . . . unless a guy was really asking for it. Like Tommy. Tommy had asked for it. He should have just left Erin alone.

Someone knocked at Stieg's door and he barked, "Yeah?"

Erin had to laugh. He was just so dang unfriendly. Everyone thought that Ludvig Rundstöm was the unfriendly one, but he was just painfully shy and looked incredibly terrifying. But it was Stieg who was the archetypal Viking at heart. Rough, gruff, and of little patience.

The door opened and a very tall, very beautiful woman strutted in. She was lean with exceptionally large breasts that pretty much screamed *stripper*.

Erin rested against the sliding door frame and watched

the woman walk over to Stieg and toss a *thick* stack of bills at him that had been wrapped together with a rubber band.

"Who's this from?" Stieg asked, holding up the money.

"Joel."

"When did we start taking cash?"

"When they hand it to us."

"I don't—"

"Are you a pimp, Engstrom?" Erin had to ask. She walked back into the room. "Is she giving you your cut for the night?" She pointed at him. "Do you have a street name? Like Whitey-Tuff, spelled with two *F*s, of course. Or White-Boy, White-Boy? I think the repetition gives it a nice ring, don't you?"

"Look at you," the woman said to Stieg, "finally making friends. I'm so proud."

"You, shut up." Stieg looked over his shoulder at Erin. "And you shut up, too."

"So is that a yes?"

"That is not a yes!"

"But I think we can all agree it's not a no, either."

Stieg growled and his best friend since he was fourteen quickly cut across the room toward Erin, her hand out. "Hi. I'm Karen."

"Erin. Now is your name *just* Karen?"

"Oh, my stage name is Sharelle."

"Of course it is!" Erin replied, sounding truly gleeful.

"She does not have a stage name!" Stieg barked. "And both of you, stop it. You're freaking me out!"

"Everything freaks you out," Karen said, winking at Erin. "And Stieg . . . why don't you offer your guest some refreshment?"

"There's beer in the fridge."

Karen rolled her eyes and Erin laughed.

"Give me a minute, would you?" Karen said to Erin before walking over to him and whispering, "Why are you being such an uber-asshole to this girl? She's cute."

"You wouldn't understand."

"Wouldn't understand or wouldn't care?"

"Both."

"She's here. She must like you."

"Nope. The last thing she'll ever do is like me."

"So she comes to your house? Alone?"

"She needed a place to crash for the night."

"Is she a heroin addict?"

"What? No!"

"Then crack? Meth? The ponies?"

"No. She's not an addict of anything except making me miserable."

"Then trust me. Girls don't go to guys' homes unless they like 'em. At least a little. Not unless they're full-blown addicts. Besides, she seems really sweet."

"She called you a hooker!" he finally barked, fed up with the conversation.

"I'm sure she meant escort. Right, uh . . ."

"Erin."

"Yes. Erin. Right, Erin?"

"Exactly right."

"There's a difference?" Stieg asked.

"Between a twenty-dollar-a-blow-job hooker and a fifteen-hundred-a-night escort? There's a huge difference."

"Huge," Erin insisted.

"I don't like you two getting along," Stieg finally admitted. "So both of you stop it."

Erin laughed again. She did love laughing at him.

"Why is it so dark in here?" Karen demanded, flicking a switch near the kitchen. Her eyes widened when she looked at Erin.

"Oh, honey, your face! What happened?"

"I fight hobos for cash."

"Make a lot of money with that work?"

"More than you'd think."

"I'm getting irritated," Stieg complained from the couch.

"Ignore him," Karen said, dismissing Stieg with a wave of her hand. "He's being bitchy. You stay here; I'll get my first aid kit. We'll get ya cleaned up."

"Thank you."

Once Karen was out the door, Erin quickly walked over to the couch and flipped over the back, landing beside Stieg. She rolled her way onto his couch like she did it every day.

As a man, he enjoyed the way her lean, gymnastics-and-ballet-trained body found its way beside him, but as Stieg Engstrom, he just wanted to shove her out the front door. Or off the balcony.

"Your girlfriend's hot," she told him. "I can't believe you're pimping her out."

"I am not pimping . . ." Why was he defending himself to this crazy woman?

"She's not a hooker. You're not a pimp." She lifted the large stack of money that Karen had given him. "But you've got all this money lying around your house. Pimp money."

"It amazes me that more people haven't shot you in the head."

"That's mean! People love me."

"Imaginary people?"

"They *talk* to me and tell me I'm pretty and inform me when the neighbor's dog is stalking me in the name of the high god Satan . . . so how imaginary can they be?"

"What bothers me is that I really can't tell if you're joking."

She grinned. "I know."

Karen walked back into the room. She held her ridiculously sized first aid kit—she had enough equipment to do open heart surgery if she needed to—and a magazine.

She shook the magazine at Erin. "I *knew* I recognized you!" She placed the kit on the couch and flipped through a recent issue of *Rolling Stone* that had Erin's sister-Crow Yardley on the cover. When she found the page she wanted, she pointed at it and exclaimed, "This is you! Isn't it? Isn't it?"

"You need to calm down," Stieg told his friend.

But Karen was in a zone. "You should see the people she's tattooed. Movie stars. Rock stars. Those people who don't do anything and have no obvious talent, but are stars anyway. She's huge." She pointed at the front of the magazine. "She knows Yardley King. *The* Yardley King."

"So?" Stieg asked. "*I* know Yardley King."

Karen snorted. "Yeah, Stieg," she laughed and winked at Erin. "Sure you do."

"Yeah," Erin mocked him. "Sure you do."

"Your work is amazing," Karen babbled on to Erin.

"Thank you."

"So . . . discounts for friends?"

"Subtle, Karen," Stieg muttered.

"What? She can say no. She's not required to help me even though I'm taking time out of my evening to help her painful-looking wounds. And knowing I'm doing it with loving care . . . she could still say no. If she wants."

Erin didn't answer, but her smile was ridiculously wide. She was clearly enjoying herself, despite the obvious sympathy-pumping going on.

"I need to pee," Erin announced, chuckling and heading off to the bathroom.

"I didn't need that information," Stieg let her know.

Erin went into the bathroom, closing the door behind her.

Karen sat down next to him and asked, "And what's wrong with her?"

Stieg stared at his friend. "What?"

"Come on," Karen pushed, "she's cute. She's a redhead. She's got that killer little body. What's wrong with her?"

"You have no idea."

"Don't be an idiot," Karen stated flatly. She'd always had little patience for what she called Stieg's "weirdo belief system," a term she applied to anything that went against what she was saying. "Ask her out."

"She called you a hooker."

"No. She asked if you were a pimp."

"What's the difference?"

"It's the fact that you can't tell that bothers me." She slapped his bicep with the back of her hand. "Come on. What's the problem? Really? She's sweet. She's funny, and God knows, you need some funny. I can't be around to entertain you all the time with my effervescent personality."

"You do not have an effervescent personality and—"

"Shit!" Erin barked before stumbling out of the bathroom, still holding a towel to dry her hands on. She spread her arms out wide and demanded with obvious glee, "Engstrom, you need to explain to me why there's a goat in your bathroom. And you need to do it right now!"

Kera stood in front of the table with Ludvig "Vig" Rundstöm standing behind her. Like most Ravens, he towered over everyone, but he wasn't nearly as devious as his brethren. He was, Ormi knew, one of the most dangerous Ravens. It was often said that if the Clans ever wanted to take out the Ravens, the first to go would have to be Rundström.

"He can't stay," Brandt Lindgren of the Silent mouthed

off to Kera. A woman who obviously hated him with every fiber of her Skuld-committed soul. "Clan leaders and War General only."

Sadly, the Silent weren't actually silent. Although, as Inka always pointed out, they clearly should be.

"You should sit over there, Rundstöm." Brandt pointed to the other side of the diner. "Far, far away from us."

"What is wrong with you?" Kera asked in that way Ormi loved. She wasn't being mean or sarcastic. She really wanted to know what was wrong with Brandt Lindgren. And if it was something that could be managed with medication.

Brandt had no answer for her, so Kera looked back at Vig and said, "I won't be long."

The man grunted and, with a glare at Brandt that should have had him wetting himself, the Raven went to a table nearby and sat down . . . and stared. At Brandt.

Inka's grip on Ormi's thigh tightened, because they both knew she was loving this. She loathed Brandt, too.

"Thanks for meeting me here," Kera began. "Now to start—"

"In the future," Brandt cut in, sounding as condescending as he possibly could, "we usually have these sorts of leaders-only meetings at a more secure location."

"Chloe told me we couldn't use the cave again. That was only for All-Clan meetings."

"And Miss Wong is correct. But for these kinds of meetings we use churches. Or temples. Or synagogues."

"For meetings involving Nordic gods? That seems . . . rude."

"It's not. We all have an understanding."

"But why do it in any one of those places?"

"Because," Inka explained to the confused girl, "the priest, imam, or rabbi always makes us promise not to kill each other on their hallowed ground."

"And you guys stick to that?"

"Mostly," they all said in unison.

Ormi watched Kera struggle to understand the logic, but it was all due to agreements centuries old. When things were different. "I'll keep that in mind for next time," she finally muttered, going through her messenger bag.

"You do that."

Josef Alexandersen, leader of the Ravens, locked his eyes on Brandt. "Okay, now you're starting to piss *me* off. You keep using that tone and I'll let Vig over there tear your head right off your body."

"Why are we here?" Rada Virtanen, leader of the Claws of Ran, asked. In a few hours, her people would be out surfing in Malibu and she was not about to miss that.

Kera grabbed a chair from another table and sat down in front of them, dropping her messenger bag onto the floor near her feet. "The research that the Protectors and Jace Berisha have been doing . . . they may have found something. Something we can use to destroy Gullveig."

Mist Falker of the Isa pushed her half-eaten sandwich away. "Has she come back to this world?"

"Not that we know of," Kera admitted. "But she will return. I think we can all agree on that."

"So they have a way to kill her," Rada said. "I don't know why we needed a meeting for that bit of information. Why don't the Crows just do it already? You started this."

"*We* started this?" Chloe Wong snapped back.

Before either woman could tear into each other across the table, Kera calmly laid her hands down and sternly ordered, "*Ladies*, that is enough. So let us retract our talons"—she pointed at Chloe and then Rada—"and whatever those things are."

"They're *claws*."

"*Whatever.* And to your point, Rada, there's no just doing it. It won't be that easy."

"I think we all knew that," Inka suggested, "when even Odin and Thor couldn't kill her. Even Loki tried and he has quite the god-heavy body count."

"So then what's the plan?" Freida asked. "What do you think will work?"

"We think . . . Surtr's sword will do the job."

Mist shook her head. "Surtr? Surtr who?"

Rada, however, was quicker. She leaned forward. "Surtr *the fire giant*? The giant who will destroy the world during Ragnarok with that fucking sword?"

Kera shrugged. "That's the one."

"So you want to unleash him on us? So he can bring Ragnarok *before* Gullveig can?"

"Not him. His sword. We use the sword on her."

"Do you know how big that sword must be? The man's a *giant*."

Inka held up her hand. "We can make it smaller. It's a spell. It makes giant things tiny. Well . . . normal sized for us, tiny for them. So it's doable, but . . ."

"But?" Brandt demanded. "But what?"

"It's the sword's location that's the problem."

Rada shoved a fry into her mouth. "If it's in Muspellheim with Surtr, we're all screwed. No human can walk through the land of the fire giants."

"The sword is not with Surtr," Kera told them.

"Oh," Brandt said, relieved. "Then maybe—"

"It's with Nidhogg."

Freida fell back in her seat. "The *dragon*?"

Kera cringed a bit. "Yeah, that's the one."

"That sounds like a suicide mission," Rada muttered.

"But," Mist reminded them, "Nidhogg lives at the roots

of the World Tree. A human can walk around there. Maybe sneak past him to get the sword . . . ?"

"Nidhogg lives *near* the roots," Inka explained. "But the place he calls home is actually Náströnd."

"Corpse Shore?" Josef's lip curled. "Gross."

"That's not the only problem," Sefa Hakonardottir added, the leader of the Valkyries finally saying *something*. "To get that sword, someone's going to have to go into eight of the Nine Worlds, where none of us are actually welcome anymore. Rada is right. That's a suicide mission."

"The Valkyries can go," Brandt insisted.

"We go to Asgard. We come home to here, AKA Midgard. That is the extent of where we can go in the Nine Worlds."

"Since when?"

"Since the twelve hundreds. And that's not going to change now. Trust me."

Mist asked, "Can't the Maids summon the sword?"

"From the other worlds? No. We got cut off from them in the *sixteen* hundreds."

"Excuse me," Kera interrupted. "This has all been discussed, analyzed, everything. We've done all this work already."

She was right. They had. For hours, days. They'd discussed, argued, and dealt with all this.

"And?" Rada asked.

"And we think there's only one person with a chance in hell who can go to Nidhogg's domain and get that sword. Physically touch it and bring it back here."

"Who?" Josef asked.

Kera opened her mouth to reply but the pause . . . that pause said it all.

"Oh, God," Mist gasped, her entire body recoiling in her seat. "Not *her*."

"*Anyone* but her."

"Have you lost your minds?"

"Stop." Kera held up her hands. "Everyone, stop. Look, we have been over this. And we're still looking for another way. Any other way. But I don't think there is one. Erin Amsel is our one and only shot at getting this sword. She has the power of flame at her disposal. She can also be touched by fire without being harmed. And to be quite blunt with all of you—she's the only one with the *guts* to do this."

"Sweetie," Rada said, leaning forward, "that's 'cause she's *insane*."

CHAPTER THREE

"The goat?" Erin pushed when Stieg didn't answer her. She wanted to know. She had to know!

"Do I come to your house and ask you stupid questions?" Stieg asked.

"Yes," Erin replied. "All the time. And yet I'm kind enough to tolerate it."

"No, you don't."

Karen got up, turned on more lights in the apartment, and set up a little station on the kitchen counter so she could tend Erin's wound.

Erin leaned over the back of the couch and softly taunted Stieg with, "You get freaky with that goat, don't you?"

His jaw clenched, which was amazing to watch, because Stieg's jaw was so cut in the first place.

"Admit it," she went on, trying to get him to loosen up. Just a little. "She's a good-looking goat. I'm not sure I blame you."

"I do not get freaky with the goat, I am not a pimp, and Karen is not a whore. You, however, are kind of a pain in the ass."

"Just kind of? I must be off my game tonight."

"Why are you torturing me? I did a nice thing tonight. I didn't have to, but I did. And now I'm getting hell for it."

Erin hated to admit it . . . but he was right. And it wasn't fair. Especially since she wasn't loosening him up at all, but making him ridiculously tenser. Besides, it wasn't nearly as much fun messing with him when Kera wasn't around to get all defensive and protective of Vig's brothers.

Erin reached for Stieg's remote. There was a few seconds of struggle over it before she managed to get it away from him—or he just gave up—and she turned up the sound on his TV show.

She tossed the remote back into his lap and patted his shoulder before joining Karen in the kitchen.

Karen smiled at her. "You two would make such a cute couple," she whispered.

"Aww, sweetie. You're so clueless. But that's what makes you adorable."

Stieg tried to focus on his TV show, but he found his gaze constantly straying over to Erin and Karen.

Karen was, as Erin had pointed out, extremely beautiful. She was also the closest thing he'd ever had to a big sister. From the time he was fourteen, Stieg had been on the streets—after years of bouncing in and out of the foster care system due to his mother's ill health and eventual death and his father's asshole behavior—and it had been Karen, two years older, who'd watched out for him. Had taught him the rules. Introduced him to the locals. Told him who to watch out for. Who to avoid. She had always been tough, brutal and, when necessary, heartless, but she'd always had his back.

So, when Odin had tracked him down—after Stieg had

told the first Raven elders who'd found him to "fuck off"—
Stieg had told the god "no deal . . . unless you take care of
Karen, too."

In usual Odin style, the god had thought Stieg was asking
him to set Karen up as his on-demand whore, but that was
the last thing he wanted for her. He simply wasn't about to
leave her alone on the streets of LA while he was living it
up in Malibu.

Of course, "living it up" turned out to be wildly inac-
curate. The first four weeks, the Ravens did nothing but
beat the shit out of him, but that turned out to be part of the
training and not some annoying hazing ritual by a bunch of
rich dude-bros. If it hadn't been for Karen, Stieg would have
bailed after the very first attack. He'd never been a glutton
for punishment and he'd dealt with more than enough beat-
ings at the fists of his old man. Why take it from strangers?
Yet he knew that part of his deal with Odin was that he'd
stick out the training for six months and the god would make
sure Karen got what she needed.

And what had she needed? More than Stieg needed. She
was amazingly smart and just a good person. She simply
needed a chance and an education. Odin gave her both. He'd
kept his promise, so Stieg had kept his.

Stieg didn't regret that decision, though. He eventually
enjoyed being a Raven. He was good at it, and the jobs they
gave him were a solid outlet for his rage.

And Stieg had a lot of rage. He couldn't help it. His father
had treated him like shit.

There was a burst of laughter and he realized it was Erin
Amsel. God, that woman confused him.

The first time he'd ever seen her, she'd been sitting in the
backyard of the Bird House, feet up on the patio table, *Vogue*
magazine open on her lap, and one hand constantly touching
the back of her head. He'd found out later that's where she'd

been shot, in the back of the head, so it was probably bothering her at the time.

Right away, he'd noticed those long legs on her surprisingly small body, her red hair, and dark green eyes, and he wanted to start talking to her right away. He'd assumed a girl like that would be scooped up pretty quick by one of his smoother brothers. Especially since she was "the new girl" as every Raven and all other Clans called recently arrived Crows.

Raven brothers knew the time to make a move on a new Crow was when she first arrived at the Bird House. That's when they were the most confused and, to be honest, kind of needy. They'd just been killed and were starting their new life among a bunch of women they knew nothing about. The Ravens wanted to move in before the new Crow realized how little they actually needed a man in their Second Lives.

So Stieg had automatically assumed the pretty little redhead would be no different from any of the others. She'd be just as confused and shell-shocked as all the Crows who'd come before her.

But he'd been wrong.

He'd watched her glance up at him and Vig, walking by on their way to retrieve their leader, Josef, after a previous evening's party. And, with a completely straight face, "Hey, Hitler Youth. Are Himmler and Goebbels showing up soon, too?" Then after chuckling at her own appalling joke, she'd gone back to her magazine.

Stieg had stopped walking and glared down at her, no longer blinded by her pretty face and long legs. He didn't even know this woman and she was already attacking him?

Well, yes and no.

Erin attacked nearly everyone who came into her line of sight, but it would be wrong to say she was being cruel or vicious. She was just being kind of . . . well . . . a . . . smart ass.

The Crows seemed to like her, though. And some of the Ravens. A few of the Valkyries. One of the Isa, but no one knew why. None of the Giant Killers. Definitely none of the Silent or the Claws of Ran. But more than a few of Holde's Maids tolerated her, and the Protectors had learned to like her recently but refused to have her anywhere near their precious books, as they were the Keepers of the Word. What "word," though, Stieg didn't really know. Or care.

What did interest him was that it seemed Karen liked Erin, too. He just couldn't figure out why. Karen liked so few people.

"There," Karen finally said. "That should do it."

"Thanks."

Stieg glanced over in time to see Karen pull some of Erin's red hair down around her face.

"You need bangs," she told her.

"Why is that?"

"To hide the hole in your head." Karen lowered her hands. "Speaking of which . . . why do you have a hole in your head?"

"Birthmark."

"That's still bleeding?"

"Uh . . ."

"No, no." Karen shook her head. "Don't bother. I can already tell you're lying."

"How? I'm really good at lying."

"You don't survive as long as I have if you don't know how to spot liars. And you've got a tell."

"I do?"

"Yeah."

"Was it the pause?"

"No."

"The 'uhhhh'?"

"No."

"Tell me."

"Why would I? So you can learn to control it? You don't survive as long as I have if you—"

"I can't listen to this anymore," Stieg barked and threw the money Karen had given him earlier back at her. "Take this. Put it in the safe."

"Don't throw things at me! You know I hate that."

"I hate that you're still in my apartment. I hate that you're talking to her. But no one cares about that."

"It must be late," Karen complained, swiping the money off the floor. "He's getting bitchy." She headed to Stieg's bedroom. "Bitchy!"

"I adore her," Erin informed Stieg.

"Why? Because she sucked up to you?"

"I've liked people for less."

Karen returned. "All right. I'm out of here. Nice meeting you, Erin."

"You, too. And thanks for the medical aid."

"No problem . . . and maybe I can call your shop about an appointment . . . ?" Karen always had a lot of gall, but damn.

Erin didn't seem to mind, though. "I won't be in for a few weeks, but they'll set up an appointment for you."

Karen clapped her hands together. "Thank you!" She stopped by the couch and, as she'd done every night for more than a decade, she kissed the top of Stieg's head. "Talk to you later," she murmured before walking out and closing the door quietly behind her.

Stieg again tried to focus on his TV show, but the air around him shifted, and suddenly Erin was sitting next to him on the couch. She'd leaped over the back of it, landing with her legs comfortably tucked up under her.

"So you can't date her because she kisses you good night like my grandmother used to kiss me?"

"We're not having this discussion anymore."

"Because you fear love?"

Remembering he had a TV in his bedroom, Stieg stood. "You'll sleep out here," he ordered. "There's sheets in that closet over there."

"Don't you want to stay up and talk all night and eat ice cream? I can braid your hair," she said in an annoying sing-song voice.

"No."

Erin watched the Viking lumber to his bedroom.

"Karen was right . . . he is being cranky." If she wasn't so tired from her long night, she'd probably follow him into his bedroom, just to torture him a little more with general chitchat and platonic affection. Things he seemed to hate so much.

Unless it was coming from Karen.

Erin didn't understand that relationship but it wasn't really her business. She'd only brought it up because it seemed to bother Stieg. And she did love bothering that man.

The bathroom door—which she'd left partially ajar when she'd run out—opened a little bit more and the goat stuck its head out. It took a quick look around the room, spotted Erin, didn't seem to care, looked around for a bit longer, then charged out into the living room.

That was . . . strange. What was it looking for? What was it afraid of? Had it been hiding in the bathroom all this time? Erin had assumed the animal was in the bathtub because Stieg didn't want it shitting all over his apartment. Logic she could totally get behind.

The goat made a crazy turn toward Stieg's bedroom door and rammed it with its head. She backed up and rammed it again. Stieg opened the door and let the goat in, then closed it.

She opened her mouth to say something but quickly decided not to bother. Because really . . . what was there to say about Stieg and his goat?

Erin laughed. Who was she kidding? There was just *so much to say* about Stieg and that goddamn goat!

Kera stood outside the diner, Vig beside her.

"That went poorly," she finally remarked when most of the other leaders were gone. The sound of Freida's Harley-Davidson bike put her teeth on edge.

"There was no bloodshed," Vig reminded her. "So we all call that a win."

She faced him. "Who knew Erin freaked them out so much?"

"Erin has a way of getting under people's skin. If she likes you, it's funny and cute. But if she doesn't . . ."

"I am well acquainted with Erin's ways. I still have scars from her ways, but it's not like we have much of a choice." Kera scratched her forehead with her thumb. "I still don't know about not telling her any of this."

"Don't," Inka said as she came out of the diner with Ormi right behind her.

Kera immediately felt defensive of her sister-Crow, her arms crossing over her chest. "You think Erin Amsel will run?"

"Not in a million years. If she does run, it'll be headlong right into the thick of everything. The girl has no sense whatsoever. But from what Ormi and I can already tell, timing will be everything in this battle."

"Timing?"

"Yes. Timing. *When* we send her. *When* she has to return. Plus, you can't just send that girl into the Nine Worlds. We'll have to prepare her. Give me some time to do the research.

We have books about the other worlds; I'll see what I can find. But unless you *want* Erin Amsel jumping the gun, as she's been known to do, you'll wait. At least a little while."

Kera didn't realize she'd dropped her head, her gaze locked on the ground, until Inka grabbed her chin and forced her to look in her eyes.

"Don't let them get in your head. You're doing what you have to do. And Erin Amsel, of all people, will be totally on board."

"She's my friend."

Inka's hard face softened just a bit. "Then treat her like the Viking warrior she is. Erin chose this life and, from what I've seen, she hadn't regretted a moment since. Don't doubt her commitment now."

"I don't, Inka. I doubt mine. Sending my friends into the unknown? I . . ."

"What did you think this would be? A cakewalk? We're Vikings. Death is what we do. If she goes and fails, she'll die with honor. Nothing means more to us. And no matter what any of you think about her, that includes Erin Amsel." Inka patted Kera's cheek. "Now, what about our little ace in the hole?"

Kera frowned, confused. "Ace in the hole?"

"The false prophet who shall bring the battle with Gull-veig's minions to us."

"Oh. Him." She sniffed. "Handled."

"Excellent. He's more important than you realize. We can't have him slipping through our fingers."

Kera smiled for the first time. She knew it wasn't one of her friendly ones, either. "Don't worry," she said, taking Vig's hand and walking off. "I doubt that will be happening."

* * *

Davis Henry Braddock knew the other psychiatrists were coming tonight and he was ready for them. He wasn't about to let those demonic women get the better of him. He would not be *used*. He was the Great Prophet. He would sit at the right hand of God.

And if he had to lie to get his way and get out of this hell-hole, he would do it.

He took in a deep breath and closed his eyes, working to relax his nerves and his soul.

Davis wasn't too worried, though. He'd been working on the other doctors for a while now. They were slowly becoming convinced of his sanity.

His only problem, really, was *her*. Not his ex-wife—whom he no longer thought of as his wife because she was pure evil—but that *other* woman.

Dr. Annalisa Dinapoli, forensic psychologist and the person blocking him from his freedom.

But not today.

Today she would not—

"*Daaaaaaaaavissssss.*"

—she would not stop him—

"*Daaaaaaaavisssssssssssss.*"

—from getting the freedom he deserved. Because it was up to him to defeat the evil—

"*Davis. I know you hear us. Join us, Davis. Join us.*"

Davis shook his head. He wouldn't listen to these whispers. He wouldn't listen to them.

Hands gripped the bars on the windows high above, where he could not reach; faces appeared.

Davis quickly turned from them. They weren't real. They couldn't be real. He was seven floors up! No balconies or stairs on the outside of the facility on this side. There was no way anyone could be up this high unless—

"Davis! Look at me! Look at ussssssss!"

Davis shook his head. To look would be to say they were real. That the wings were real. The women were real. That they were hanging from the bars on his windows like demons from the very pits of hell. Calling to him. Trying to lure him into their darkness.

They began chanting in a unified sing-song voice, "Dav-is! Dav-is! Dav-is! Dav-is!"

He covered his ears. He wouldn't listen! He didn't hear them. He couldn't hear them!

Annalisa let her colleagues stare into the room that Davis Henry Braddock, cult leader and murderer, now called home. The Pacific Mental and Rehabilitation Center.

There'd been a few doctors—well, one asshole specifically—who felt that Braddock had perhaps been misdiagnosed by her. He said he didn't see any signs of delusion or violent outbursts. True, Braddock had attacked his wife and buried her . . . but she'd survived. And, for her colleague, that meant he hadn't been trying *that* hard to kill her. Instead, Braddock had had a small breakdown that he was long over. And therefore should be handed over to the proper legal authorities.

Hearing that line of reasoning, Annalisa had to call on all her skills not to openly roll her eyes and let out a loud, "Oh, puh-leeze!"

The others might not know what her colleague was up to, but she did. *He* wanted to be the one to "heal" Davis Henry Braddock. To bring the cult leader back from the brink of insanity. And normally, Annalisa wouldn't care. She'd let the two idiots ride off into the sunset together. But Braddock was an idiot with a purpose. Her people needed him and she wasn't about to release him to the "proper legal authorities," which she had no control over.

Thankfully, Annalisa had help. She always had help.

Crows never fought alone.

"Good Lord!" her colleague gasped. "How long has he been like this?"

"Just started a few minutes ago," one of the nurses said. "Don't know what brought it on."

The nurse had to talk loudly to be heard over Braddock's screams of "*I can't hear you! I can't hear you! I can't hear you!*" He just kept screaming the same thing again and again. His hands over his ears; his body rocking back and forth on the balls of his feet.

Annalisa let out a long sigh. "This is *so* sad. So much progress . . . gone." She motioned to the nurse and gave an order for medication to calm him down.

Not just for the benefit of her colleagues but because she didn't need Braddock suddenly deciding to ram his head into the wall until he was dead.

They had plans for this boy!

"Doctors," Annalisa said, waving her hand to indicate they should leave the room.

Together they finished their rounds for the night and headed out.

Braddock had been calmed down and was heavily drugged and secured to his bed.

After waving at her colleagues, a perfectly acceptable "see you tomorrow!" smile on her lips—she'd had to practice to get that thing to look friendly and not "predatory and absolutely terrifying," according to their leader, Chloe—Annalisa walked to her Jaguar and remotely unlocked her doors.

She tossed her briefcase and purse into the backseat and,

after taking a breath, she glanced up at the very high protective gates that enclosed the hospital property. Perched on top of the deadly razor wire were the sister-Crows from two Strike Teams that she didn't belong to. It had been decided early on that their fellow sister—and Annalisa's team member—Jacinda, aka Jace, shouldn't be involved in the tormenting of Davis. Not simply because he was her ex-husband and the man who killed the sweet Crow, but Jace wouldn't enjoy doing such a thing to the man. Any man. Unlike Annalisa and many of their other sisters, who enjoyed this work way more than they should.

She'd do it *for her sisters*, because she was loyal to the Crows. But she wouldn't *enjoy* it.

Not like the rest of them did.

Grinning her more "predatory and terrifying" smile, Annalisa got into her Jag and headed home. She owed drinks to her helpful sister-Crows and she wasn't about to hit some hot bars with overpriced drinks dressed like a college professor who hadn't had sex since the Bush administration.

CHAPTER FOUR

"You know, I think that's my goat."

Stieg forced his eyes open and glared at the woman staring down at him. "What?"

Erin yawned, stretched, and then insisted, "I think that's my goat."

Stieg looked over. The goat was under the covers with him, her little head resting on his chest.

"No, it's not."

"I'm pretty sure it is. The one I got for Kera's pre-welcome party."

"What the fuck is a pre-welcome party?"

"The party she *thought* I was throwing her but wasn't. Her real party was outside. You were there. For the real party anyway. Not the pre-welcome party."

"And what was the goat for?"

"She thought I was going to sacrifice it. But I wasn't. I was just doing it to torture her." She sat down on the edge of his bed, very near him. "Personally, I don't understand blood rituals. They are so goddamn messy."

"Why are you still talking?"

"Don't worry. I'm not asking for her back or anything.

She kept eating Chloe's expensive sheets anyway . . . so . . .
yeah."

"You're *still* talking."

"Wanna go get breakfast? I'm hungry." And healed.
Her wounds and bruises were almost completely gone. The
woman healed faster than most of the Clan warriors. "If
you want, I can give you a platonic kiss on the forehead like
Karen does to get your day started."

"*No.*"

"Bitchy to bed, bitchy to rise, I see," she teased. "Come
on." She tapped his arm. "Let's haul it out!"

Stieg watched Erin walk out of the room before looking
at his goat and asking, "It's going to be a long day with her,
isn't it?"

Tessa Kelly returned to the hospital where she'd once
worked, in the heart of Korea Town.

It hadn't been an easy job, but it had taught her everything
she knew as a nurse. That had been her First Life, though,
when she'd had simple plans and simple dreams. That was
a long time ago. She was into her Second Life now but she
hadn't had to change who she was to enjoy her new existence. She'd managed to keep all her old contacts, which
helped at times like this.

"Candy."

Candy Yun came from around the intake desk and pulled
Tessa into a big hug. "How have you been doing? How's life
with the rich and famous drug addicts?"

"Fabulous as always," Tessa replied, laughing. "So what's
going on?"

"Did you happen to catch the news yesterday? Because I
think this one's right up your alley."

"What are you talking about?"

Candy led her down the hallway. "Two females came in yesterday after they fell off an overpass."

"What?"

"By all rights, they should be dead. Or at least new tenants of our long-term-care ward."

"But they're not?"

"Broken arms and that's about it."

As they reached the end of the hall, Tessa stopped and gazed at Candy, her mouth slightly open.

"Yeah," Candy said when she saw Tessa's expression. "That's what we're saying."

"Why didn't you—"

"Separate them? Yeah, we tried that. We've separated them . . . six times? They keep finding each other."

They turned the corner and at the second room, the yelling became impossibly loud. Candy pushed the door open and Tessa stepped inside.

One female was trapped on her hospital bed, her right arm in a cast, and a pillow pressed down on her face. The other female was on top of her, holding that pillow in place with her good arm. Her other arm was in a cast.

"I think they're yours," Candy said.

It wasn't something they'd ever discussed. That Tessa was a Crow and often the one who greeted the new girls. Hell, Candy probably didn't even know about the Nine Clans or the Nordic gods or any of it. But when a nurse worked in a hospital long enough, she learned things. Picked up things.

Apparently Candy had picked up that Tessa seemed to be drawn to women who managed to survive the unsurvivable, which was true. But she was usually given a heads-up by Chloe that there was a new girl to get. But not this time. And two at once? That was super rare.

Tessa watched the women fighting on the bed. "What makes you think they're mine?" she asked as the one being pinned down managed to get her foot under her assailant and shove her across the room. Both women scrambled to their feet and squared off, growling at each other like wild animals.

That's when Tessa noticed something interesting . . . they were twins.

Identical twins.

Twins who apparently hated each other.

"Come on, bitch!" one screamed at the other. "*Come on!*"

They charged, meeting in the middle of the hospital room, ignoring their casts as they each dragged the other to the floor.

Tessa let out a breath before looking back at a smirking Candy. "Yeahhhhh," she reluctantly admitted, "they're probably mine."

Erin was pouring two glasses of orange juice when she heard a woman scream. She spun around, ready for battle when she realized it wasn't a woman screaming . . . it was the damn goat.

She stood in front of Erin, staring up at her with those odd eyes, and made that sound again.

"Why is she screeching at me?" Not a lot put Erin on edge, but that sound was doing a damn good job.

"She's hungry," Stieg said as he walked out of the bedroom wearing black sweatpants and no shoes. "And probably needs a walk." He grabbed a leash and held it out to her. "Can you walk her while I get cleaned up?"

Erin looked at the leash and back up at the man. "Seriously?"

"I don't want her shit in my house."

"Ewww." Erin took the leash just so they could stop this conversation. "You know you can't *keep* her, right?"

"Why not?"

"She's a herd animal. She needs other goats to keep her company. And when she goes into heat, she's going to get really loud on you."

Stieg stared at Erin a long moment before he asked, "How the hell do you know that?"

"My father's cousins had a dairy farm in Wisconsin and we'd go to visit in the summer." She put the collar and leash on the goat. "I can't believe I'm about to walk a goat." She gazed at him. "Is this my life now? Goat walking?"

"For once you're doing a nice thing for someone other than yourself. You should roll with that."

"I do nice things for people." When the Viking gave a grunt that sounded dangerously close to a laugh, Erin turned away from him and headed toward the door. The goat followed behind, without Erin having to pull on her leash.

"And if one person complains to me about this goat, I'm sending them to you," she yelled back at him before slamming the door closed.

Out into the hall, into the elevator, and down to the first floor. Erin was just walking out the door as Karen was about to step in. The pair smiled at each other, but Erin quickly noticed that the goat ducked behind Erin, like she was afraid of Karen.

"Hey," Karen greeted, sifting through her mail, not even noticing. "Sleep all right?"

"Yeah. Stieg's couch is surprisingly comfortable."

Karen lowered her hands, the mail slapping against her thighs. "He made you sleep on the couch? I swear! That man!"

Erin had to laugh. She knew that Karen didn't understand the relationship not only between Erin and Stieg, but between Crows and Ravens.

There had been a time when Ravens and Crows went to

war with each other constantly. After several failed truces and some necessary alliances through the centuries, though, they'd learned to tolerate each other. Sort of.

That still didn't mean a Raven gave up his bed to a visiting Crow. Not unless there was fucking to be had.

Karen gazed at Erin's face, blinking hard. "You heal fast."

"Oh. Yeah. Genetics. The Amsels are a fast-healing people."

Karen frowned. "Really? I figured someone as pale as you would be bruised for days."

"Makeup helps."

"Makeup? It doesn't look like you're wearing makeup."

"It's the natural look. Wearing makeup so that you look like you're not."

"You can do the natural look on bruises and a hole in your head?"

"Uh-huh. Well, I better get going," Erin quickly said, floundering.

"I can't believe he has you walking his goat." Karen shook her head. "I can't believe he *has* a goat. He picks up the weirdest strays. Why can't he just get a dog or a cat like everyone else?" She shrugged. "I used to have a lizard that I found in the trash. But nope . . . he's gotta be . . . Stieg."

With a sigh, she moved toward the elevator and Erin continued down the building's front steps, the goat now pulling her until they were outside.

Once they were on the street, the goat seemed to calm down and walked beside her with no problem. She was like a well-trained dog on the leash.

It was weird.

The walk took longer than Erin thought it would because the goat continued to make stops to graze on bushes and plants along the way. When she dove headfirst into someone's rose-bushes, Erin decided it was time to take her back to Stieg's place.

A few hundred feet from the apartment building Erin stopped walking, her senses alive, in tune to everything around her. The goat stopped, too, gazing up at her.

Erin crouched down and petted the animal's head. "You are such a good girl," she told her, unclipping the leash from her collar. "So good that if you get scared, you're going to run back to Stieg's building, and not just run away. Because Stieg is very attached to you. I can tell these things." She wrapped the leash around her hand. "But you don't have anything to worry about, because I'll protect you. Okay?"

Smiling, Erin stood, breathed in . . . then took two steps and swung her leash-covered fist through the passenger-side window of the black car parked on the street. Her hand went through the glass and she punched the man several times before grabbing his throat.

She hadn't just attacked randomly. They'd been watching her.

As Erin choked the passenger with one hand, the man on the driver's side reached under his leather jacket.

"Ah-ah!" she barked, making a grab for him with her free hand.

But before she could get hold of him, the goat rammed the car door, startling all of them. Erin, however, recovered first, slamming the driver's head against the steering wheel.

The man she was choking tried to get his hands around her throat, but someone else grabbed her by the waist and yanked her away. With her grip still on the passenger's neck, he was forced to go with her out of the car window. Stieg was beside her, yanking the man away from Erin and lifting him off his feet with one hand while holding her back with the other.

"What are you doing, Crow?" Stieg demanded, sounding awfully pissed.

How was this her fault? "He started it!"

"By existing?"

"By being from the Vatican." She stepped back to get Stieg's hand off her shoulder. "Aren't you, mother—"

"Hey!" Stieg cut in. "A little respect."

"What kind of Viking are you?"

"One that respects a long-standing truce."

"The Crows don't have a truce with these people." She pointed at the passenger, his face bloody and swelling from the pummeling she had given him. "So keep that in mind when you think about *lingering* around me."

Erin grabbed the goat's collar and led her back toward the building with her blood-and-leather-covered hand.

Once inside Stieg's apartment, the door closed firmly behind her, she looked down at the very helpful goat, gently stroking the horns that had left a deep depression in her stalkers' door.

"You are such a good girl. Yes, you are." She crouched down and used both hands to rub the animal's neck and shoulders. "But you need to talk to your boy about wearing a shirt when he's out of the house, because he's really hot without a shirt."

The goat leaned against Erin's knee and Erin took that as a tacit agreement.

Stieg stared down at the man holding a handkerchief to his broken nose. "Have you decided that life's not worth living?"

"She attacked us."

"You were stalking her. You're lucky that all that happened to you was bird shit on the roof of your car."

"What?" He turned to see that a load of bird shit decorated their immaculately cleaned, four-door, late-model sedan. "Oh, come on!"

"Be grateful. They could have pecked your eyes out."

"Stieg?" Mr. Matucka called out from his store front. "Everything okay?"

Matucka had been great to Stieg since he'd moved in. Probably because every time Stieg went into his general store—which was several times a week—he didn't buy just one quart of milk, but four quarts of milk, a few pounds of fruit, an entire display box of candy, a case or two of beer . . . you know, staple supplies.

"Everything is fine, Mr. Matucka. Thanks."

"Okay. Let me know if that changes."

Stieg waited a few seconds until the old man went back into his store before he asked, "Want to explain to me why you are here?"

When neither man answered right away, Stieg pulled his phone from the back pocket of his jeans. "Fine. I'll just call Chloe Wong and let her know the Vatican was coming after one of her sister-Crows."

"If we were going after her," the driver snapped through the broken passenger-side window, "we'd have sent the nuns."

The driver was right. The Vatican never would have sent these honorable men if they wanted the Crows challenged. They would have sent the Sisters of St. Mary Magdalene Convent of All Saints. Or, as the Clans knew them, the Chosen Warriors of God.

It was because of the bloody and brutal War of the Sisters that the Nine Clans had agreed to a truce with the Vatican. But that truce had been signed centuries ago and the Crows had joined the Nine only recently. So as far as the Vatican was concerned, the Crows were still a dangerous enemy with a vicious past.

"Then what do you want?" Stieg asked.

"We were asked to check on her. Make sure she's safe."

Stieg started laughing, something even he admitted he rarely did.

"I'm not lying," the man argued, defensive. "We were asked to ensure she was still breathing."

"You want me to believe that someone's not only coming after a Crow . . . but *Erin Amsel*? Seriously?" He laughed more. He couldn't help it!

That was like someone saying they were purposely trying to enrage Jace. No one purposely enraged Jace, the Crow's resident Berserker. No one who wanted to live anyway.

"Why would anyone tell you to check on Erin Amsel?"

"We don't ask why. We just do."

"How sad for you," Stieg said sincerely.

"You can keep your pity, pagan. You people have brought us all to the brink of End Times with your dead religion and you have the nerve to—"

Stieg stepped into the man, towering over him, cutting off his next words. He briefly wondered if this was what it was like for the monks that met the first Vikings on the shores of English land. "We ain't that dead. Not yet, *priest*. And we can take care of our own."

"Your own? You still call the Crows *slave*."

"Not to their faces."

"You want us gone, we're gone. But do yourself a favor, pagan. Keep an eye on your friend. For her sake as well as the sake of the world."

Erin looked up from her phone when Stieg walked back into his apartment. "Hey, we got new Crows at the House. Twins. Weird, huh? We've never had twins before." She glanced off. "Wonder how they died."

Stieg stood in the doorway, staring at her.

"What?" She rolled her eyes. "What did those priests say? They started it," she quickly accused . . . again. "I was just walking your goat. And your goat needs a name. Something cute . . . but regal." She thought a moment. "Daphne." Erin nodded. "We'll call her Daphne."

"I'm not calling her Daphne."

"What's wrong with Daphne? It's a perfectly—"

"Hilda."

"Hilda? What kind of name is Hilda?"

Stieg closed the door and moved toward her. "A good Norse name."

"Is there such a thing?"

He stood in front of her . . . still bare chested. Only among the Nine had she seen men so cut. Not just their abs, either, but their shoulders, arms, and God, their necks. Thick like the base of ancient tree trunks. She could hang off that man's neck like a monkey and be perfectly happy.

The damn thing was distracting. Stieg Engstrom was distracting.

Erin had never noticed that before. Yet as he stood so close, she couldn't ignore it now. Heat came off him in soothing waves while his dark gray eyes glared at her.

"You need to tell me what you did," Stieg ordered.

"And you'll need to be *way* more specific than that."

"Who were you following last night? And why?"

Not in the mood to answer—because she knew it would get right back to her sister-Crows—Erin tried to step around Stieg, but he blocked her with his big body and stopped her from moving by placing his arms on either side of her, hands gripping the kitchen bar behind her.

"You've got the *Vatican* keeping an eye on you. The priests don't normally do that. They know better. So you need to talk to me."

"Actually," Erin said, "I don't. That is the beauty of being me."

"You're hiding something."

"Probably."

Stieg leaned in closer, their faces nearly touching. "Tell me," he ordered.

Erin couldn't help but smirk a little. "Make me."

His frown deepened and she thought for sure that he was going to kiss her.

"Come on, Amsel," he abruptly whined, eyes rolling in his head. "I don't want to fight you." He glanced at Hilda. "Not in front of the goat."

"Not in front of the . . ." Disgusted, Erin pushed her way out of Stieg's hold. "I'm canceling breakfast. I need to get back to the house. Meet the new girls. Now, before I go, we need to get our stories straight."

"Our stories? About what?"

"About what I was doing here last night."

"Hiding from the truth and lying to your friends?"

"Are you going to be a dick about this?"

"Only if I need to be. And since you're not telling me the truth . . ."

Sighing, Erin looked at her phone again and found the app to call her favorite car service. "I'm leaving," she said once the app told her the car was on its way.

"I can take you back."

"No thanks." She walked toward the door. "But heads up. I'm telling everybody we slept together."

"Why would you do that?"

"Because you're my alibi for last night and no one would believe I was just hanging out with *you*."

"You tell them that, and it will not go well for you."

Erin stopped at the door, her hand on the knob. She looked back at Stieg. "Why would you say that?"

"Because you're *you*."

A little insulted, Erin faced him. "What does *that* mean?"

"You tell everybody you slept with me, they'll just think you took advantage. That will not go well for you. Trust me on this."

"Are you high?"

"Honest." When Erin just gawked at him, Stieg explained, "I'm the former street kid who is considered sensitive because of my tough upbringing and abusive father. You're the Crow that every Clan male is warned to avoid. You tell your sisters that you slept with me, and it will *not* go well for you."

She laughed right in his face. "Okay. You believe that." Rolling her eyes, she walked out the door.

"Don't say I didn't warn you!" Stieg yelled after her.

CHAPTER FIVE

Stieg walked into the main house on Raven territory.

When he'd first arrived here, all those years ago, he'd hated this place. Hated everything about the Ravens. And told them so as often as he could manage. Every time he opened his mouth he told them. His first three months here he was called nothing but "the little asshole."

Honestly, he had no idea how he'd lasted as long as he had. The Ravens were rivaled only by the ancient Spartans when it came to training their brothers. And, over the centuries, they'd been accused of being abusive by other Clans like the Isa and Holde's Maids. Even the Giant Killers. But Stieg had learned from his first brutal battle against demons that the Ravens had been preparing their young brothers for what they would face when they were old enough.

Because of his training with the Ravens, Stieg had been able to survive a fight with a nine-foot Minotaur and beat a lesser fallen angel into a messy pulp of blood, brain, and shattered bones.

Stieg no longer hated his brothers. He loved them and trusted them with his very life every day. He was grateful that they'd found him and that Odin had convinced him to join the Clan when the elders couldn't. Taking his rightful place among the Ravens had been the best decision he'd ever made. Because now he was no longer some faceless street kid the beat cops were terrified of. He was no longer just the "idiot son of Agnarr Engstrom" as he was described by Agnarr Engstrom.

Eventually, Stieg had made a name for himself among his brethren beyond "the little asshole." Now he was Stieg the Always Angry. A title he'd gladly accepted without a smile because it had been true.

He knew well that he was rude, cranky, short-tempered, with little patience for stupidity, and almost painfully stubborn.

So stubborn, he'd refused to see his father when he'd come to the door looking for him, drunkenly yelling from the front of the house. Agnarr had thought he was still a Raven, although his wings had been torn from his back by his own fight team and he'd been left bleeding on the streets of downtown Los Angeles. Of course, Agnarr blamed everyone for his troubles but himself and his weakness for drink. It had been bad enough living with the man when his mother lived, but once she'd died, Stieg knew his time at his father's San Fernado Valley home would be short. Not willing to go back into the foster system—as he knew he would—Stieg had bailed at fourteen, unable to stand a moment more of the bastard.

He'd lived on the streets until Odin came. He offered the usual. Women. Fights. Drink. A really nice car. All the things Ravens loved. Stieg had turned him down, too. But Odin was, among many things, smart. Or, as the Maids called it, devious. He found Stieg's weak spot—Karen—and exploited it. A move that worked.

And, all those years ago, as Stieg had stood on the second-floor landing of the Raven House, listening to his father bellow and curse and demand he "come down here and face me, you little pussy!" his brothers never moved. They never let the man in. Agnarr was no longer a Raven. He had no honor, and he no longer had a son.

But Stieg had brothers. Loyal to him and to Odin unto death.

He also had a fight team he'd been part of since he'd been ready for battle. His Elder brothers had placed Stieg with those whose temperament fit him perfectly.

Vig Rundstöm. The nicest, shyest six-foot-seven-inch man Stieg had ever met who could lay waste to an entire battalion of demons without much effort.

Siggy Kaspersen. Stieg's best friend and drinking buddy who wasn't as stupid as everyone thought, but didn't really try hard to be smart, either. The guy loved a good beer, a good video game, and gods, he knew how to dance. Not easy for a six-four, three hundred and twenty pound man raised by a single-mom Valkyrie with a dance studio.

Rolf Landvik. The brains of their team and the smallest, at only six-three and two hundred and sixty pounds. He could read runes, hear the dead speak, and found the Crows "charming." He also loved a good bottle of wine and knew languages that weren't Germanic in origin.

As a team, they were awesome. With them as friends and Raven brothers, Stieg couldn't be happier.

Stieg walked down the marble halls of his Raven home but, as he neared the normally unused library—the books they had in there came with the original house—he slowed his gait, finally stopping right outside the open doors.

He stopped and he listened.

"Of all the people we have to count on . . . why is it *her*?" complained Josef, their leader.

"The gods have always been cruel. Why should things

change now?" That came from Vestarr Claesson. One of the oldest local Elders. When Stieg had first seen him out in the practice ring, he'd made the mistake of taking his age for a weakness, wondering why his trainer was forcing him to fight some old man.

When Stieg woke up from his coma a day later . . . he knew why.

Just hearing the man's voice made Stieg's right eye throb. That was the eye a healer had to force back in because it had popped out during the fight. There had been a worry Stieg would never see out of that eye again, but so far . . . you know . . . so good.

"Should she be told?"

"What if she runs?"

"Crows don't run."

"No. But they protect their own," another Elder said. "They'll die before they let anything happen to her. And we can't even hope to win this without the Crows. So we wait and let them handle it."

"Fine. But . . ."

The voices faded off and Stieg realized he now stood in front of the doors, watching the men he respected so much, with an intense distrust he hadn't felt in years.

"Stieg." Josef glanced around at the others, wondering how much Stieg had heard. "Need something?"

"Yes. I need a house. With a yard."

"We just moved you into that apartment."

"Yeah. But now I have the goat. And the goat needs a yard."

"You have a goat?" Josef asked. "Why do you have a goat?"

"I don't know. I came home one day . . . and there was a goat. Her name is Hilda. So I need a house."

Josef let out an annoyed sigh. "Fine. We'll get you a house. I'll talk to Danny. He's got some local properties that might work."

Stieg nodded. "Okay." He stood there and waited.

Finally, Josef asked, "Why are you just standing there?"

"Why *can't* I just stand here?"

Josef took in a breath and looked down at the ground, which meant he was getting angry. So Stieg wasn't surprised when he suddenly barked, "*Siggy!*"

Big steps charged down the stairs and Siggy slid to a stop in front of Stieg. "Hey!" he greeted Stieg. "What's going on?"

But when Siggy looked over at Josef and the Elders, his happy grin faded, and he took Stieg's arm. "Come on, brother. Let's go . . . away."

"So, what do you know about them?" Erin asked her team leader and the LA Crows' second in command, Tessa.

They stood right by the open sliding doors that looked out over their enormous backyard with the Olympic-size pool.

The twins, Ailey and Aisling O'Reily, were very pretty, tall, thin twenty-year-old girls with long blond hair and big blue eyes. Even with opposite arms in casts, they looked like something out of a "Come to Ireland" tourist ad. They sat at one of the round, metal picnic tables that dotted the back-yard. Several of the sister-Crows sat around them, explaining their new life.

As the girls listened, they had that stunned expression new Crows often had. As if seeing the world for the first time.

In a way they were. They were no longer average women going about their average day. Simply worrying about the bills, the kids, the husband. Now they had to worry about those sorts of things *and* the end of the world. About the gods and their wars. About hatred and revenge and the desperation of those who feel they're losing their power. Because all those things were part of the eventual destruction of the existence they all knew.

Or, as Erin liked to call it among her sister-Crows, "What happens when men become assholes."

"So I heard Betty's going to be their mentor," Erin said.

"Yeah."

"Why?" Erin thought their leader had been prepping her to become a mentor to the new Crows.

Betty Lieberman had done it for many years, but she was an Elder Crow now, semi-retired, and spent less time at the Bird House and more time keeping her creative agency flying high. Plus, Betty had been out of her gods-induced coma for only about three weeks now. It seemed she'd need a bit of rest rather than jumping in with two new girls.

"I thought I did okay with Kera."

"You did great, Erin. Kera's already a War General. The fastest in Clan history."

Erin knew she was feeling a little sensitive after her conversation with Stieg, but she still had to ask, "Then what's the problem?"

Tessa shrugged. "They are."

Erin didn't understand what Tessa was talking about. The twins were just sitting there, listening to everyone as Jace placed a tray of fresh-squeezed orange juice and Danishes on the table. Without looking at each other, the twins reached for the same glass, their fingers barely grazing—that's when twin number one suddenly hauled off and punched twin number two, sending the girl flipping back off the bench.

Twin number two hit the ground hard, but she was up and on her sister in seconds, the pair knocking over the big table, sending the other sister-Crows scrambling to get out of their way. Juice and Danishes flew every which way.

"Holy shit!" Erin yelped, laughing out loud. "*What the fuck?*"

"Yeahhhhh." Tessa sighed. "Yeah."

Erin watched the bloody brawl, her fellow sister-Crows trying to haul the twins apart, but neither girl was having it.

"Are they always like this?" Erin had to ask.

"Apparently so. That's how they died."

"Wait . . . what?"

Tessa nodded. "It somehow started off as a brief knife fight—involving bread knives—at their mother's house, which led to a car chase, which led to a car accident, which led to road rage, which led to them fighting on the 101 over-pass near Studio City, which led to them fighting *off* the overpass before the cops and fire department could get to them. They died on scene but Skuld brought them back. Now they're being called 'lucky' in the news that they only had a few scrapes and broken bones. They just got out of the hospital. Found out from one of my old nursing buddies they had to separate them during their recovery. A lot. And they've had their casts replaced twice, I think."

Loving this, Erin asked, "Is it over some guy? It's over some guy, isn't it?"

"Apparently no." Tessa watched their sister-Crows at-tempting to pull the O'Reily twins apart, but now that they had their newfound strength, they were determined to kill each other all over again. "Chloe called their mother—of-fering the services of our wonderful rehab and our skills at managing those with anger issues blah blah blah—and ap-parently they've been like this since they were *inside* her. She actually has no desire to see them again. Not when she has six other kids who are normal and have children of their own and everyone is happier without the twins around."

"Damn. Dude . . . *damn.*"

"I know, right?"

Two Crows fell into the pool when one of the twins shoved them off so she could wrap her hands around her twin's throat and attempt to choke the life out of her.

"Huh," Erin said, her mind turning.

"What? What's that look for?"

"Well . . . I could be wrong, but you know how we can't die the same way we died in our first life?"

"Yeah."

"I'm just wondering if for them, it isn't just a matter of not being able to die falling off another bridge . . . or if no matter what they do to each other . . . they can never kill each other again."

Tessa gawked at Erin. "Why would you say that?"

"Because it's kind of true. It wasn't the fall that killed them as much as it was each other. I mean, they could have died in the car accident. They could have died during the knife fight in their mother's house. So it's not just the manner of death, but what actually *caused* it. Which would be . . . them."

Tessa buried her face in her hands and Erin could hear her whispering "Fuck" over and over again.

Not that Erin blamed her.

One twin got the better of another and had her in a brutal headlock; the other began to turn blue, but it was competing with the red hue of her rage.

Erin was completely enthralled by all this. She couldn't look away! Watching twins battling each other for what appeared to be no real reason was like watching professional wrestling. Or a documentary on two wild animals trying to survive life on the African plains.

"What are we watching?" a voice asked from behind them, causing both Erin and Tessa to let out yips of surprise.

It wasn't easy to sneak up behind Crows, but they'd been so distracted by the twins. . .

"Vig," Tessa greeted the dark pile of hair and muscle standing behind them.

One of the first things that had impressed Erin about Kera was that she saw past the terrifying visage that was and always would be Ludvig Rundstöm. Before any of them even knew Kera Watson existed, Kera had met Vig at the coffee shop where she worked, and had been kind to him when most everyone else avoided the man. Not surprising. He looked like a mass murderer waiting to happen.

But he wasn't. He simply came from a long line of brutal Vikings who raped and pillaged their way up and down the European coasts. And that was before any of them were chosen as Ravens for Odin. Although he battled like his ancestors, Vig had managed to avoid the raping and pillaging pretty well for most of his life.

"We're watching the two new girls," Erin explained, motioning to the battling twins.

"Huh," was all Vig replied as he watched the fight, not saying another word for about two full minutes. Finally, he turned to Erin and asked, "What were you doing at Stieg's place last night?"

Tessa's head snapped around, dark eyes locking on Erin. "What? You were you at Stieg's last night? Why? Why were you at Stieg's last night?"

While Vig was calm with his question—more curious than anything—Tessa sounded panicked.

Erin just didn't know why. "Well—"

"Oh, Erin . . . you didn't sleep with him, did you?"

"Uh—"

"Did you take advantage of that boy?"

Erin blinked, not even bothering to hide her smile. "Pardon me? Take *advantage* of Stieg Engstrom? Seriously?"

"Erin. You know he's been through a lot." Tessa sounded so disappointed in her.

"Why are you whispering? He's not here." Considering all the crap Erin had pulled over the years, sleeping with a Raven wasn't something she thought she'd ever get in trouble for. "It wasn't a big deal."

"For you, maybe. But what about him? What about *Stieg*?"

"What about him? He got laid. Do you really think anything else matters to a guy?"

Sadly tsk-tsk-tsking, Tessa turned away from Erin and walked past the sliding doors to help get control of the twins.

"Is she really mad?" Erin asked Vig.

"I don't know if I'd say that she's mad as much as disappointed in you as a fellow Crow and disgusted by you as a human being."

"Wait . . . *what?*"

"I think they're hiding something from us."

Siggy looked up from his plate of food, a fork in one hand, a piece of bacon in the other and blinked at Stieg. "Hiding what?"

"No idea. But it's something."

Siggy rolled his eyes and went back to devouring his food. "You accuse everyone of being up to something. You're completely paranoid."

"I am *not* completely paranoid. You should have seen their faces when they noticed I was standing there. Like they'd been caught doing something."

"So? What if they are hiding something from us? So what? They're our Elders. I'm sure they wouldn't put us in any situation we couldn't handle."

"You poor, delusional fool."

Siggy shrugged rather than trying to speak with the half a roll he had in his mouth. The man ate like he was still on the Viking boat and hadn't seen food in days.

Rolf sat down at the table, placing a copy of the *Wall Street Journal* beside his empty plate before asking Stieg, "You slept with Erin Amsel?"

Stieg frowned. "What?" Then he remembered the psychopath's plan to get away with whatever she'd been up to. "Oh. Yeah," he lied. "I, uh . . ." He made a loose fist and sort of jabbed at the air. "I gave it to her good. Or something." *That should be convincing, right?*

Although Rolf didn't look convinced and Siggy only seemed concerned.

"Do you want to talk to my therapist?" Siggy asked, patting Stieg's forearm.

"No, I do not want to . . . wait. You see a therapist?"

"It was court ordered after the, uh . . . incident."

"That was like five years ago. Why are you still seeing a therapist?"

"I don't know." He looked down at his nearly empty plate. "I just like having someone to talk to that's not you guys."

"*You* slept with Erin Amsel?" Rolf asked Stieg again. "And lived to tell the tale?"

"What does *that* mean?"

"It's Erin. She can take most guys down with a thought. But you . . ."

Stieg glared at his friend. "But me what?"

"Nothing." Rolf picked up his paper and began to read it.

Siggy continued to focus on what was left to eat on his plate.

Stieg let them ignore him for another few minutes while he ruminated on the last three minutes of conversation. Then he slammed his fist on the table and yelled, "Both of you are complete and utter assholes!"

* * *

Erin sat at the kitchen table while her Strike Team stood over her . . . disgusted.

"How could you?" Kera demanded.

"Poor little Stieg," Maeve sighed out, shaking her head.

Leigh pointed a damning finger at Erin. "Did you even think about him? When you were taking advantage of that poor defenseless boy?"

Annalisa kept her hand pressed against her mouth and nose, trying to keep her laughter in.

And Alessandra asked, "How was he?"

The only one missing was Jace, but she was outside trying to help with the twins.

"Are you all done?" Erin asked.

"You can stop smirking," Kera snapped at her.

"Okay." She grinned instead and Annalisa walked out of the room, unable to handle another moment, her laughter echoing back to them from the hallway.

"We expected more from you," Kera told her.

Leigh frowned a bit at Kera. "Did we? Really?"

Maeve scratched her arm, then informed them all, "I think I have a flesh-eating bacteria in my hand, spreading up my arm."

"You do not," Erin informed her as strongly as she could without hitting, "have a flesh-eating bacteria."

"How do you know?" Maeve held her arm out for Erin to look at. "They could be eating me alive inside!"

"You don't even have a rash!"

"Can we focus on one psychosis at a time?" Tessa asked before informing Erin, "You should apologize."

"To Kera?"

"*To Stieg!*" they all yelled at her, which made Erin burst into a fit of giggles.

She couldn't help it. They were all being so—

"Why don't you make yourself useful," Kera ordered her, "and deal with the twins."

"I thought they were Betty's problem."

"She's not here! So get out there and assist!"

"Okay. Okay. No need to get hysterical."

Still laughing, Erin walked out of the kitchen and went into the backyard. As the twins rolled by her on the grass, she reached down, grabbing each woman by the back of her long blond hair. She yanked the pair apart and proceeded to shake them—still using their hair—until they both calmed down. "*That is enough!*" she bellowed.

When their arms hung limply at their sides, Erin tossed the pair in two separate directions. Smiling, she wiped one hand against the other and said, "See? Not so hard."

"What's this?" a sister-Crow asked, shoving a cell phone close to her face.

"I have no idea. You're holding it way too close."

"You slept with Stieg Engstrom?"

That's when even the birds in the trees went silent, and Erin realized that all her sister-Crows were now staring at her.

Then Jace's soft voice said, "Oh, Erin. You didn't!"

"He—"

"Do *not* say he started it," someone barked at her.

Erin threw up her hands. "Then I have no response."

CHAPTER SIX

Stieg walked into the Bird House kitchen to find Jace getting together a bunch of ingredients for something he was sure would taste great. Since she had connected with her father's side of the family, she'd been cooking more, and absolutely everything she'd made so far was amazing.

But as soon as Stieg stood next to her, he had a feeling he wouldn't be getting whatever she was making. "Hey."

"Shut up," she snapped back.

"How could I have made you angry already? I just got here."

Without even looking at what she was doing, Jace cracked eggs into a bowl. "I can't believe you slept with Erin and that you then ran around telling everybody."

"No, I didn't. *She* ran around telling everybody."

"Erin is not one to brag. Not about that. I know her."

"You don't know her that well."

"What does that mean?"

"I can't talk about it." He leaned over, trying to see what Jace was putting together. "What are you making?"

"Nothing for you!" she snarled.

"I didn't do anything!"

"Taking advantage of my friends is not doing anything?"

"I didn't take advantage of anyone. I—" Stieg remembered his promise to Erin to keep her stupid lie going.

"You . . . what?"

"Can't talk about it."

Jace stopped putting ingredients into the bowl and faced Stieg. "What are you two up to?"

"I'm not up to anything."

"Implying that Erin *is* up to something?"

"I didn't say that. I can't talk about it."

Jace threw up her hands. "All right. Fine. But you have to let everyone know you're not the poor abused boy here. That whatever you two did was mutual and consensual."

"And how do I do that?"

"By saying that it was *mutual and consensual.*" She shook her head and grabbed a small bottle of vanilla. "I don't want Erin hurt."

"Can she be?"

Jace slammed the bottle down on the counter. "*What kind of question is that?*"

"A very non-hysterical one. Unlike your question." Stieg finally took a step back and asked, "What's going on with you?"

He knew that Jace was at the forefront of the Clans' work on finding a way to destroy Gullveig for good. Every day and many nights, she worked alongside the Protectors, researching very old books in a vast number of languages. And he was beginning to worry she was getting burned out, unable to find anything that could help.

Because, at the end of the day, even Odin and the other gods couldn't stop Gullveig. And they'd tried. Three times they'd stabbed, impaled, and burned her. And three times she'd come back.

If the gods couldn't kill her, what could some humans with a lot of books do?

"What? Nothing," Jace said too quickly. "Nothing's wrong."

"Come on, Jace. It's me. Don't lie."

She spun on him, one finger angrily pointed at him. But before she could say anything, two blond women Stieg didn't recognize head-locked their way through one end of the kitchen and toward the other side. They occasionally stopped to punch each other in the face. One punched her twin in the breast, which seemed . . . an unusual fighting choice. Then they released each other from the headlock so that they could shove each other out the other side of the kitchen through the swinging door.

A few seconds later, a group of Crows followed after them, begging them to, "Stop! Stop! *What the hell is wrong with you two?*"

"New girls?" Stieg asked Jace once they were alone again.

"Yeah," Jace said, her anger forgotten in the distraction of two women brawling in the kitchen. "Twins. Very sweet."

"Clearly."

Betty Lieberman had been in a coma for weeks before an old Albanian witch helped her snap out of it, and ever since then, she had been making up for lost time. She opened the front door to her palatial mansion and led the very young actor into her home.

"I really appreciate this opportunity, Mrs. Lieberman," the twenty-three-year-old gushed.

"Oh, sweetie, call me Betty," she purred, taking his hand. "Everybody does." She walked down the marble hallway toward her home office where she could give the young man a chance to read for a part she was sure he was right for.

Then some fine dining ordered in and . . . they would take it from there.

As she neared her sunken living room, she heard the TV playing. She stopped outside the wide open entryway and released her prey . . . er . . . potential client.

She walked until she stood on the other side of her very long, specially made leather couch, which could fit her entire original Strike Team from her battle days. The ladies still loved to get together once a month, drink, watch movies with hot men, and talk shit about *everybody*.

It was what they still did best.

But it wasn't one of her Strike Team sitting on the couch, pouting. It was Erin Amsel.

Erin looked up at Betty with those big green eyes, her red hair in two adorable ponytails, and such a look on that puss.

The pair of them had had a similar upbringing. Betty had been born and raised in Queens. Her early training came from the world of New York TV news, where she found out from a very direct and rude boss that, "You'll never get on camera with that nose, sweetheart. You better get it fixed."

Betty never got that nose job, but she did decide that if she was going to work behind the camera, she was going to *own* the industry. And she did. And the man who gave her that unsolicited piece of advice? She'd crushed him. Not physically. But she'd pushed him out of the business, made sure he never worked in the industry again.

And she'd made sure he knew who'd destroyed his career.

The bitch with the big nose.

Erin Amsel was originally from Staten Island. A nice, middle-class girl with real artistic talent and a big mouth. Her sense of humor reminded Betty of her own, and they'd both entered their Second Lives at the end of a bullet. So Betty had been more than happy to be the kid's mentor.

And now, she was getting ready to pass on that torch.

But first Betty had to do what she had always done best . . . deal with an upset artist.

Erin hadn't realized she'd be interrupting Betty and one of her, uh, "recruiting" sessions, but she also hadn't been thinking too clearly. Too baffled to call first, she'd done what she'd always done. Stop by 7-11, pick up a Big Gulp and a large bag of chips, and crash on Betty's couch, watching favorite shows on Betty's giant TV.

Betty stared at her for a long moment.

Erin was about to tell her she was going, when Betty looked at the extremely handsome young man and said, "Get out."

"But I thought we were going to—"

"Out. My assistant will set up another appointment for you."

Unable to hide the frustration on his face, the young man stomped out, and Betty dropped on the couch beside her.

"You didn't have to tell him to go."

"You know my rule, sweetie."

Erin grinned. "Clits before dicks."

"Always." Betty shoved a handful of chips into her mouth and leaned back into her shockingly expensive couch. "Now tell me what you've fucked up today, kid."

"Wait." Jace put the brownie batter in the oven, set the timer, then grabbed Stieg Engstrom's arm, and dragged him out the sliding glass doors from the kitchen and into the yard. She kept walking, taking the big man with her. She knew he was letting her "drag" him. Unless she was in one of her rages, her strength was just regularly enhanced. Not majorly enhanced.

But she had to make sure she'd heard Stieg right.

Once they were a good distance from the Bird House, she faced him. "You didn't sleep with her?" She needed to make sure she understood what she'd gotten him to tell her with the promise of licking the brownie batter–covered spoon.

Happily cleaning that spoon, he said, "Uh-uh."

"Then why did you say—"

"I didn't say anything." He licked brownie batter off his bottom lip. "She's the one running around telling people. She insisted. But don't say anything. I'm not supposed to tell anybody."

"Why?"

Stieg looked off and Jace knew he was debating whether to break Erin's confidence more than he already had, but Jace was already worried. Her friend tended to go off on her own sometimes. Take risks she shouldn't. At least risks she shouldn't when her fellow Crows weren't around. When they were too far away to come to her aid.

"Tell me, Stieg. It'll be between us. I need to know what she's doing."

He shrugged. "She went to a club last night."

"Erin?"

Erin hated clubs . . . and club people. If she felt the need to dance or whatever, she went to the gay clubs with the lesbian Crows, knowing that she'd get to dance to great house music with the certainty that the gay men dancing next to her would have absolutely *no* interest in her whatsoever.

"Yeah. And while she was there . . . some guy from her past came along and took her."

"What guy?"

"The guy who killed her in her First Life."

"Oh my gosh!"

"I know. He and his thug friends took her to some dirt road and shot her in the head."

Good Lord. How many times does that make that Erin has been shot in the head?

"And then?"

"Well . . ."

Jace nodded. "Okay." That "well" meant Erin did what she did best. Most likely killed everybody involved and went about her day. "That still doesn't explain why she didn't come back here. What's she hiding?"

"I'm not sure. She wouldn't even tell me, and I helped save her."

"Uh-huh."

"I did. I was very helpful."

"Sure you were. Erin always needs help during a fight."

Stieg growled a little.

"So, how did this guy find her?" Jace asked.

"I guess he saw her at the club and was worried she'd recognize him. Probably a little surprised she was still breathing. You know . . . after the head shot and all."

"One does not usually walk away from two shots to the head." Jace shook her finger. "But you can't tell me the man who killed her just *happened* to be in the club Erin was in. A Staten Island mobster isn't going to move to LA and not have every mobster in LA trying to kill him. It doesn't work that way."

"Get that kind of criminal knowledge from your family?"

"They're not criminals." And when Stieg did nothing but stare, "They're not *all* criminals." Jace began to pace. "So first, we have Erin's past coming back to haunt her. That's weird. And we still don't know what Erin Amsel, of all people, was doing at an LA club."

"Looking for a date?"

"Erin doesn't go to clubs to find dates."

"Where does she go?"

"Is that important now?"

"I'm just curious!"

"I need you to focus. She's looking for something. Or someone. We just need to figure out who." She blinked. "Or whom. One of those."

"Why?"

"To protect her."

"From herself?"

"Someone has to do it, and you're not busy."

"I could be busy. I have a life now."

"Is this about that goat?"

"I'm getting her a house."

Jace blinked. "You're getting a house for a goat?"

"Well . . . I'll be living there, too."

"Why?"

"Erin said it needs a herd. But I'm pretty sure I can't have a herd of goats in my apartment."

"Soooo . . . because of what Erin said, you're getting a house?"

"She seems to know goats so . . . yeah." Stieg frowned. "Why are you staring at me like that?"

Jace shook her head. "No reason."

"Jourdan Ambrosio, huh?" Betty reached for Erin's Big Gulp and took a sip, then she gazed down at the giant cup in her hand before sighing, shoving it back at Erin, and leaving the room.

When she returned, she had a very expensive bottle of wine and two glasses.

"It makes sense, don't you think?" Erin asked. "About Ambrosio."

"It does." Betty filled the two glasses, handed one to Erin, and dropped onto the couch beside her. "I know Ambrosio.

She's a horrible person. Petty. Vapid. Shallow. I tried to get her as a client, but my nemesis got her first."

"You tried to get her as a client? The woman has no talent."

"No. But she makes lots of money being a talentless ho. And I love making money off people who don't deserve what they're getting. It makes me feel like I'm accomplishing something when I take my percentage."

"You're not."

"But if anyone is going to be a priestess for Gullveig, I bet it's that nasty little slit. But so what? So what if she's Gullveig's priestess? What are we supposed to do with that information?"

"I'm hoping she can let us know if and when Gullveig is returning. We can't just sit around waiting for her."

"We're not. Battle plans are being readied. The geek Clans are doing their research. The Vikings are on this."

"I still want to see this thing through."

"Then do it. I seriously doubt your tracking Jourdan Ambrosio is going to adversely affect the current situation. It's already the end of the world."

"Not necessarily. We could still pull this out."

"That's the difference between you and me, sweetie. You're always so hopeful." She patted Erin's knee. "And don't worry. I won't say a word to anybody. It'll be between you and me."

"Good. I don't want to hear it from Kera when she finds out what I'm up to. 'You can't do this alone,'" Erin said in a high mocking voice. "'You're not an army of one. We're a team. We have to do all things together. I used to be a Marine.' Blah, blah, blah, blah, blah! She'll drive me nuts."

"She will. And don't get me wrong. I do like Kera but . . . whoa. My father was former military and I've been having flashbacks since she became a Crow." Betty picked up her wineglass and took a sip. "So I hear you're fucking Stieg Engstrom."

Erin shrugged, not really in the mood to lie, but not in the mood to explain anything, either.

"That's kind of some low-hanging fruit, isn't it? Poor little street kid."

Erin rolled her eyes and fell back on the couch, making Betty laugh.

"God, calm down. I know you didn't fuck Stieg Engstrom."

That surprised Erin. Everyone else who'd heard assumed that "of course" she did and "of course" she'd somehow managed to use the big bastard. "How do you know that?"

"Because if you had, you'd be walking bowlegged."

"Thanks for that visual."

"I call it like I see it, and that man is a Viking's Viking. So why are you telling everybody you did?"

"He's my cover for last night."

"Because of this thing with Ambrosio?"

"No. I met up with Tommy in one of the clubs I hit."

"Tommy who?"

"The guy who killed me."

Betty reared back. "*What?*" She placed her wineglass on the coffee table. "What the hell, Erin?"

"I was stupid. I wasn't paying attention . . . things got a little out of hand."

"Are you all right?"

"Yeah. I'm fine. Stieg actually was there. I kind of think he was following me, but I don't know why, and he won't tell me. Then again, I'm not sure he knows why. Ya know?"

Betty studied Erin for a moment before guessing, "You got shot in the head again, didn't you?"

Erin threw up her free hand. "How many times, Betty? Seriously. How many? It's starting to give me a complex."

"Awww, sweetie." Betty patted her knee. "It should. It *should* give you a complex."

"I need you to do me a favor."

Stieg immediately replied, "No."

Jace got that look on her face that he was sure she reserved just for him. "Stieg Engstrom!"

"No. I'm not following that crazy woman around. She attracts trouble."

"I need you to protect her."

"Why do you say that? Have you been talking to the guys from the Vatican? I know you're on better terms with them than I am."

"No. Have you been talking to the Vatican?"

"It's kind of complicated."

"You know what . . . don't tell me. As we're speaking, I can feel the rage building. Just do me this favor. Watch out for her."

"I'm not getting involved in this! She is not my problem. She will never be my problem!"

"Do this for me."

"No."

"Please."

"No."

"Please."

"*No.*"

"*Pleeeeeeeeeeease!*"

"*All right!*" Stieg briefly rubbed his eyes with his fists. "And I hate you."

"No, you don't. You *love* me."

"Shut up."

* * *

Danski "Ski" Eriksen was sitting in the kitchen of the Protectors' home. A mansion that held the largest private library of its kind anywhere on the West Coast. He'd been spending days reading through old Norwegian text—one of the few languages he knew well—desperately trying to find something that could help them in the upcoming war when a plate of brownies was placed in front of him.

He looked at the woman he loved and smiled. "Hi, Jace."

She sat down next to him. She tried to smile but it didn't happen.

"What's wrong?"

"I was talking to Stieg."

"I'm sorry. That's a lot of dumb to deal with in one day." When she stared at him, her bottom lip sticking out in a sweet little pout, he said, "Sorry. I didn't mean it."

"Yes, you did."

"I did, but I love you, so I will continue to lie and tell you that your Raven friends aren't stupid."

"Thank you." She glanced over at the book he was going through. "Bear is going to lose his mind when he realizes you took that book out of the library."

"Everybody and their mother are in the library right now. Protectors. Holde's Maids. Even the Silent have deigned to grace us with their annoying presence in a show of support. There's just too many people for me at one time in one place." He took her hand, kissed the back of it. "Tell me what's wrong."

"Based on what Stieg just told me . . . I don't think we have enough time to keep looking. For another option, I mean." She stopped speaking, taking a moment to get herself under control. Fighting back tears.

He'd been afraid of this. Jace's idea of a way to destroy Gullveig was brilliant, but it would require almost a sure sacrifice of whoever undertook the quest. But the one thing all Clan members knew that is when they took what their god offered and were branded with their god's rune . . . sacrifices would have to be made.

And sometimes those sacrifices would be their very lives.

"So," he said, realizing how hard this was for Jace, "Erin is our only option?"

Tears freely rolled down Jace's cheeks. "Yes," she said, nodding, her voice still strong. "Erin is our only option."

CHAPTER SEVEN

After a long, relaxing shower, Erin sat outside in the Bird House backyard and spent some time drawing on a white pair of Converse. A future birthday gift for one of her sister-Crows.

She'd become infamous among the Clans for her painted and drawn-on Converse. But Erin simply used her talents as an artist and her knowledge of each of her sister-Crows to make them something she knew they'd like. When she'd started doing it, she hadn't thought much about it, but she'd actually gotten a request from one of the Claws who owned an art gallery near the Santa Monica Pier to do a display of her "work."

Erin had laughed when she'd gotten the offer, thinking it was just a joke, until she realized the Claw was very serious. He seemed pretty sure he could sell her work for a lot of money.

And if they could put off the end of the world, she could always use the extra cash, so yeah, why not? She had never had a show of her work before. Mostly because people walked away with her art on their body, but it would be nice to know that side of the art world. Or, if not "nice," at least different. She enjoyed different.

Finishing up the Converse with her signature, Erin saw the squirrel sneaking down from the tree. He glanced back and forth several times before he started to make his careful way across the yard. Of course, if this was just any squirrel, she wouldn't care. She had no problems with squirrels as a species. They were actually kind of cute, despite the fact that they were part of the rodent family and could carry plague.

But this wasn't just any squirrel. This was Ratatosk. Messenger for the gods. His entire immortal squirrel life was spent causing problems, running back and forth between the eagle at the top of the World Tree and the dragon at the bottom, spreading rumors and insults.

That was one of the reasons Erin was watching him so closely. Yes. He often brought messages to the Clan leaders when information had to spread quickly, but what was he doing now?

Ratatosk wasn't there to give Chloe an important message. He was up to something. Nothing major. Just being a little dick. Erin should know. She spent most of her days being a little dick and she knew the signs. The furtive eyes. The creeping pace. He was looking to start some shit between Clans.

Something they couldn't afford right now.

Erin knew she could just go over there and scare him off with a hand wave and a stern, "Get out of here, Ratatosk!"

But, from one little dick to another . . . that seemed unimpressive. So, softly, very softly, Erin gave a whistle.

Not even five seconds later, Kera's dog came trotting through the open sliding glass doors. Her name was Brodie Hawaii. At one time she'd been a battered and beaten fifty-pound pit bull with half her muzzle gone and her teeth ground down to nubs or pulled out completely. She'd been used for fighting and mating when Kera found the poor animal tied up and left to die in her old neighborhood. Kera had taken Brodie in and had given her the best life she could at the time. Then Kera died and Skuld gave her a chance to become a Crow. Kera said she'd take the offer but not unless Brodie could come with her to her new life.

Poor Kera, at the time she still didn't understand how gods worked and that the old saying "be careful what you ask for" was invented *because of them*. Skuld gave her what she asked for. She let Brodie come with Kera into this new life, but not before killing her and remaking her into the first and perhaps only Crow-Dog.

So the pit bull standing beside Erin was no longer the fifty-pound disfigured wreck of an animal that she'd once been, but a one-hundred-pound beautiful pit with all her teeth and fangs and the addition of retractable wings and a steel-enhanced muzzle.

Petting the back of Brodie's neck, Erin leaned in and whispered, "Look. Look over there. What do you see, girl?"

Brodie's ears shot up straight, as did her tail. Then she was moving so fast, Erin instinctively leaned back so she didn't accidentally get hurt.

Ratatosk took off but Brodie was on him in seconds, scooping the little bastard up in her mouth and running all over the yard with her new prize.

Laughing, Erin carefully wrapped the Converse in white tissue paper and returned them to the box they came in.

Kera came outside as Erin got up from the table, the box under her arm.

"Hey. Have you seen—Brodie, *no!*"

Erin laughed harder.

"You did this, didn't you?" Kera accused.

"He'll be fine. He's immortal. I think."

"You think? Erin, why? *Why?*" Kera snarled at her before running after her dog, begging Brodie to drop the squirrel but . . . yeah . . . that wasn't going to happen unless Kera had something better to offer. And what was better than a struggling, squealing squirrel that no one particularly liked?

Erin was on her way back upstairs when she passed the TV room. Things had been pretty quiet the last few weeks since they'd managed to shove Gullveig out of this world, so the room was packed with her sister-Crows hanging out and killing time until they had something specific to do. As Erin passed, she realized that one of those annoying celebrity news shows was on. She only watched those if everyone was in the mood for mocking, because she always felt the need to mock celebrities. They made it so easy with their bullshit.

But she suddenly stopped when she heard the blond, spray-on tan, Botoxed talking head go on and on about some new club in LA that had just opened and how everyone who was anyone was going to be there. "Tonight."

Erin thought about that a moment. An opening like that . . . if the owners wanted it to be successful they'd pay someone like Jourdan Ambrosio to be there.

Tucking the box under her arm, Erin pulled out her phone and quickly texted Betty. If there was one woman in Hollywood who could get Erin on a "list," it was Betty.

As she patiently waited for a response, Brodie charged by with Ratatosk still in her mouth. If Erin didn't know better, she'd swear that squirrel shook his tiny fist at her in a show of hatred.

A few seconds later, Kera charged by now with several other Crows in tow, all of them trying to help her wrangle her dog.

"Dammit, Erin!" Kera yelled as she ran by.

"What?" Erin asked, taking a step back when she thought Kera was about to circle around just so she could slap the crap out of her. But, thankfully, Kera kept going and Erin got her return text.

> You're in, bitch.
> Muchos gracias, senorita!
> God, girl! Your Spanish is the worst. Go back to Staten Island!

Laughing, Erin headed up to her room to find the right kind of ridiculous clothes to wear to a stupid club opening so that she could snag the bitch who would worship at the altar of Gullveig.

Stieg went looking for Erin that night because he knew—deep in his bones, he knew—she'd be out again.

And he was right.

It actually wasn't as hard to track her down as he'd thought it would be. Karen always talked about the hottest clubs—even though he didn't care—and he knew Los Angeles like the back of his hand. Especially Hollywood. So, after checking with Karen, he found out about a new club opening and knew—he *knew!*—that's where he'd find her.

And that's exactly where he did find her. Stomping up the street in a cute dress, ridiculous high heels that she was not comfortable walking in, and a tiny black backpack.

He knew the club she was heading for. It might be under new management, but it was one of those joints that had been around for years and years, changed owners more times than he changed the oil in his car, and had seen quite a few rising and current star overdoses in its time.

If Erin was looking for someone famous and in demand with the news rags, this was the place to go.

Stieg made a U-turn and parked his truck on the street. He took big strides to catch up to her and was a few feet away when he saw another car slowly pass from the opposite side of the street. He only noticed it because of the sound. He'd always loved cars and he knew a perfectly maintained but seriously souped-up engine when he heard one. He then noticed the darkened windows. Too dark to be remotely legal.

Once the car passed an oblivious Erin, it went up a little farther then made its own U-turn.

That's when Stieg began to run, pushing past people in his way.

The car neared Erin and the windows lowered just enough for all those automatic weapons to be trained on the Crow.

Stieg picked up speed, and just as he reached her, Erin spun around. Her eyes widened at the sight of him and her fists jerked up to defend herself. Stieg ignored that and wrapped his arms around her waist, used his body to block hers, and then yanked both of them up and over a seven-foot high wood fence.

They hit the hood of a piece-of-shit car on the other side. One of many since they'd apparently landed in a junkyard. He rolled them off the hood and used the car to block them from the onslaught of gunfire.

When it stopped, he gazed down into Erin's face and asked, "Is there anyone in the world that's *not* trying to kill you?"

It was really starting to irritate Erin that the man kept saving her. What was happening? What was going on? She was a Crow, goddammit! She should be able to save herself! "I dealt with the only one from my First Life who wanted me dead," she replied to his stupid question. "And anyone from *this* life would never come after me with guns. They're all demons."

"Not all of them."

"The nuns don't count. They hated me long before I had wings."

Big sausage fingers suddenly covered Erin's mouth. "Shhh. I think they're coming back." Erin rolled her eyes and Stieg removed his hand from her face. "What?"

"You act like you're so impressive right now. Like you've got super hearing. But with that goddamn muffler on their piece-of-shit car, people in China probably can hear them."

"That's a finely tuned—" He stopped himself. Growled. "Instead of arguing, why don't we try to answer the question of why they're coming back?"

"To make sure I'm dead?"

"Drive-bys don't work that way. They shoot, they go. If they miss, they come back another time to finish the job. What you don't want to do is sit around waiting for the cops to come."

"Is this knowledge from your previous thug life?"

Stieg growled again and got up until he was crouching over her. "Let's find out why they're after you."

Erin sat up. "And how do we do that? It may be Hollywood, but I'm sure people will notice when a couple of winged warriors come swooping in to deal with the local gangbangers."

"You're right." Stieg stood and Erin followed. "That's why we need bait."

"What bai—heyyyy!"

He tossed her back over the fence with an ease Erin found highly disturbing, but she effortlessly landed on all fours, her body used to safely landing from much higher positions. As soon as her body hit the ground, she heard the brakes of her assailants' car screech and the tires tear up the asphalt as they spun around, cutting off other drivers.

Erin slipped off the high heels she'd worn to help her

get into the club and started running. She pushed past all the tourists and the crazy locals running for their lives during the attack or filming on their cameras until she hit a street that led into an alleyway. She turned and a few seconds later heard squealing tires. She turned again, but saw a dead end up ahead. Before she could unleash her wings and take to the skies, she was snatched up and held aloft by a Raven with absolutely no respect for personal boundaries.

"Put me down."

"Shut up."

Erin laughed. She didn't know why, but she was finding this whole thing weirdly entertaining. Maybe it was seeing how Stieg Engstrom handled things out on his own. No backup from his Raven brothers. No Rolf handling the more subtle refinements of negotiation. Or Vig terrorizing everyone without saying a word, just standing there . . . being horrifying. Or Siggy being the goofy entertainment.

This was all Stieg.

Erin was impressed and startled at the same time.

Below them, the car pulled to a stop. To the men inside, Erin had just disappeared, so she was assuming confusion.

Then something shocking happened.

The doors opened . . . and women came out. All gang members if Erin was to go by their tattoos, but still. She'd automatically assumed it was men trying to kill her. Look at that. She was guilty of reverse sexism or . . . whatever.

"Uh-oh," Stieg mumbled.

"What?"

"They're women."

"So?" When he didn't answer, she knew he'd have a problem fighting these broads simply because they *were* women. "They tried to kill me," she reminded him.

"Yeah. I know."

"*You've* tried to kill me. *I'm* a woman."

"Yeah, but you're like me. You don't need a gun."

"So?"

"It just feels weird and wrong."

"Oy," Erin muttered. Then she unleashed her wings.

"Ow! *Bitch!*" Stieg roared as the power of her wings sent him flipping back several feet.

The women below heard him, but before they could look up, Erin dropped to the roof of their car.

Shocked, two stumbled back. Two others gave a small horrified squeal. And a fifth, spotting Erin's wings, wisely made a run for it.

Once the shock wore off, the women attacked. They raised their guns, but Erin moved to the car's hood and caught the closest arm to her and twisted until the bone cracked and splintered. She yanked the gun away and used it to bash in the woman's face, sending bone into brain.

To stop the others from firing, Erin extended her wings, shoving two of the women away. And then brought her wings down and up. That made the dirt in the alley swirl like a tiny tornado, temporarily blinding the attackers. With her body still on the hood of the car, she placed her hands down and kicked out with one leg, her foot crushing the windpipe of one woman. She side kicked another across the jaw, so that her neck snapped at the base.

Erin bounced off the car and caught one of the last two women by the throat. She yanked her close and wrapped her other arm around her neck, lifting and twisting at the same time until she'd separated head from spine. She dropped the body and caught hold of the gun aimed at her by the last female.

The Nine Clans were not allowed to use guns. Their gods thought it was a sign of weakness. They preferred edged weapons or hand-to-hand, so Erin didn't take the gun. She simply twisted it around and made the woman pull the trigger herself. The first two bullets hit her in the gut. Eyes wide, she helplessly watched as Erin readjusted the weapon until it was under her chin—then Erin made her pull the trigger one more time.

Stepping back, Erin tried to wipe the splattered blood from her face. Finding that futile, she went into the car to see if she could find a cloth to do the job.

And that's when she saw it.

She was running blindly. No idea where she was going. She just knew she had to get away.

Christ almighty, what had they done? She'd not been okay with killing a woman in the first place. Maybe beating the hell out of her. They'd done that before. To teach a girl a lesson. She was okay with that.

But their orders had been clear and the money too good to ignore. So they'd gone to do the job. But she'd never expected this. How could she?

She turned blindly down a street, her tears making it hard to see. And yet she felt him. Even before he landed in front of her. She knew he was coming for her.

As soon as he slammed into the ground, black wings out, big body in a crouch, she dropped to her knees and prayed to God for forgiveness for all her sins.

So many sins.

Slowly, he stood. He was so big. Massive. And terrifying.

"Please," she begged, holding her hand up, arm out. "Please."

He walked toward her, towering over her—and, shaking, sobbing, she waited for death.

* * *

Erin turned the corner and saw Stieg speaking to the last gang member. The one who'd made a run for it.

But that's all he was doing. *Talking* to her.

So, Erin charged her. To be honest, she didn't really have a plan or intention of killing her. The woman looked kind of young. Not quite a kid, but not a seen-it-all, done-it-all broad either.

Still, Erin shot toward her, just to teach her a lesson, but Stieg turned in time to see her.

"Run," he ordered the little gangbanger, then he faced Erin and came at her, taking her out like a goddamn right guard protecting the quarterback.

They didn't hit the ground, though. Instead he lifted Erin up and held her in his arms in order to give the murderous little bitch a chance to get away.

Instead of trying to get out of his grip, Erin moved toward him, wrapping her legs around his neck and her arms around his head.

"Hey! Cut it out!"

Laughing, she used her chest to smother the big Viking.

He tried to swat her off, trying not to hurt her, which she appreciated. Still, she didn't let him go.

Finally, Stieg grabbed her waist and yanked her off. "Stop it, you crazy—hey!"

She maneuvered out of his arms and climbed over his head until she was wrapped around his back with her arms around his ridiculously thick neck and legs around his chest.

"*What are you doing?*" he bellowed.

To which she replied calmly, "I don't have shoes."

Stieg twitched a bit, confused by her response. He'd been worried he was in a fight for his life with an out-of-control Crow, but Erin wasn't like her sisters. She didn't lose control. Why should she? She didn't let shit bother her. She left the rage to everyone else.

"What?"

"I don't have shoes. I took them off on the street near the club so I could run from that car." She stretched out her legs so he could see her feet. "See? No shoes. And I'm not a hippy. I'm not walking around goddamn Hollywood without shoes if I don't have to."

"There had to have been an easier way for you to tell me that without attacking me."

"I'm sure there was . . . but this was more fun." She tapped his shoulder. "To the car, James!"

"Shut up." But he did start walking.

"What did that little twat tell you anyway?"

"There's a hit out on you."

"Oh. Well that explains it."

"Explains what?"

"This. I found it in the bangers' car." She handed him a picture.

Stieg stopped walking and stared at it. "What the fuck is this?"

"My picture from that dating site."

He glanced back at her. "You're on a dating site?"

"Yes. But not to find a date."

"Because that would be too normal for you?"

"That and it was a test."

"For?"

"Me and my sister-Crows wanted to test something. So I was chosen to set up a profile on the site. We wanted to avoid the models and the actresses because we didn't want anyone too pretty. But we also wanted to avoid Rachel and her crew because we didn't want guys with a fetish for large muscular women who could twist them into pretzels. I was right in the middle."

"What were you testing?"

"To see how many guys would send pictures of their

penises without prompting." She leaned in and added, "Short answer . . . *all of them*."

Stieg sighed. "Is that what the Crows get up to when you don't have anybody to kill?"

"Yes."

"Come on," he said, walking and still holding the picture.

"Where to?"

"To find the guy who may be able to give us an idea of what the fuck is going on with you."

"Going on with *me*? I didn't do anything!"

"God, Amsel, you're such a liar."

Erin laughed. "Yeah . . . I know."

CHAPTER EIGHT

Craig heard the knock on his office door and frowned. His protection knew he didn't want to be bothered when he was counting money. Thinking maybe the cops were coming into his club—not a big deal since he had a secret way out of there—he walked to the door with his .45 held tight in one hand.

He threw open the small sliding piece that allowed him to look out into the hallway. When he saw who was staring back in, he quickly closed it, and stumbled away, his weapon raised.

The reinforced steel door was torn off its hinges with one hit of that ridiculous shoulder and before Craig could get off a shot, the big bastard was standing right beside him rather than in front of him. But Craig had no idea how that was possible. No one was that fast.

"Hi, Craig." Stieg Engstrom smirked at him. "How's it goin'?"

With the much bigger man still next to him, Craig rested his ass against his desk. "Did you kill all my guys?"

"Nope," a short redhead replied as she leaned against the now door-free opening. "They're still breathing."

She sucked on a red lollypop until Stieg snarled, "That's a pot-pop. It's probably filled with THC."

The redhead lowered the pop to study it a moment before shrugging her shoulders and tossing it back into her mouth.

"Erin!"

She pulled the lollypop out again and tossed it into the trash while sighing dramatically. "Such a goody two-shoes."

Engstrom put his massive arm around Craig's weak little shoulders and held up a picture. "That idiot over there"—he motioned to the redhead walking around Craig's office and being goddamn nosey—"is this idiot." He held the picture closer to Craig. "So what do you know?"

"There's a hit on her," Craig admitted. "Million bucks. They want her dead."

"And they're sending out local talent? Why not professionals?"

"Don't know. Something to do with her. Professionals won't go near her."

The redhead gave a little twirl and announced, "It must be my adorable charm."

"Quiet," Stieg snarled. "Who put the hit out?" he asked Craig.

"Have no idea." Craig tried to stand up at that point, but Engstrom pulled him right back down to the desk with a slight tug of that arm.

"I don't believe you."

The redhead sat down on the other side of Craig. "I don't believe you, either," she said, resting her cheek on Craig's shoulder.

Craig had known Engstrom for a long time. He'd hired him back when he'd been just an oversized kid. Gave him a few bucks off the books to bring in deliveries or work the door. He was so big, the cops never questioned his age but he'd had to be watched. He used to have a bad temper. The slightest insult and he'd take a guy down, putting him in the hospital for days. One time weeks, when he thought the guy was getting a little too "handsy" toward the girls in the club.

Then Engstrom had disappeared. It happened all the time with street kids. Sometimes they went home. Sometimes they moved to another city like Seattle or Portland.

Sometimes they ended up dead.

That's what Craig had expected. That the kid had gotten physical with the wrong guy and gotten his head blown off. He'd believed it until a few years back when Stieg Engstrom had walked into Craig's club again. He'd been even bigger, meaner, and for once, not alone. He'd come in with a small group of equally large white guys who looked like extras from that Nazi propaganda film *Triumph of the Will*.

They'd come in for drinks and Craig had made sure his staff took care of Engstrom and his friends. Keeping him happy had seemed like a prudent thing to do.

And now, with Engstrom's arm around Craig's shoulders and the redheaded woman on his other side, Craig understood why.

These were people trained in the art of terrifying others. They knew they were strong. They knew they were willing to do things others weren't. And Craig knew that no matter what happened tonight, no matter what they did to him, they'd wake up in the morning and feel nothing about it, one way or the other.

So Craig's problem wasn't in telling them the truth. His problem was whether they'd believe him. Because the truth had sounded ridiculous when he'd first heard it.

"It's some religious group out of Riverside."

"The Catholics?" Engstrom asked, startling Craig.

"The Protestants?" the redhead asked.

"The Muslims?"

"The Sikhs?"

"The Evangelical Christians?"

"The Jews?"

Engstrom leaned forward a little and the redhead shrugged at his unasked question. "My people have had some issues with me in the past."

"I sense almost everyone can say that about you."

"Well?" the redhead pushed, leaning in close to Craig. "Which is it?"

"I have no idea. I just know they're religious and out of Riverside."

"Maybe a cult," Engstrom suggested.

The redhead sighed. "I've already been shot in the head by a cult once." She shrugged. "This can't keep happening."

"Seriously," Engstrom asked, "is there *anyone* who doesn't want you dead?"

Sister Theresa Marie Rutkowski stared at the two men from the Vatican and she didn't bother to hide her disdain. "You couldn't stay out of sight of one tiny Crow?"

"She blindsided us."

"We didn't even ask you to do anything. Just watch her. How hard is that?" Disgusted, she looked over the men.

One had gotten his face broken—nose, jaw, forehead, eye socket. The other was wearing a collar around his abused throat, the Crow's fingerprints still visible on his skin where his neck was bare.

"I don't even know what to say," Theresa admitted.

"We should have gone ourselves," one of Theresa's girls mumbled behind her. Girls who weren't nuns but who trained to be the sisterhood's eyes, ears, and fists on the streets.

"No, no," Theresa argued. "That would not have gone well. Especially when it comes to Erin Amsel."

Sitting across the room, Sister Mary Marie leaned forward, her cell phone in her hand. "We have a problem."

"Another one?"

"Amsel's heading over to that cult."

"Please tell me it's not Braddock's cult."

The man that even the pagans referred to as the "false prophet" had tried and failed to do what the sisters of the Chosen Warriors of God had attempted more than six hundred years ago—to wipe out the Crows.

Of course, at that time, it hadn't gone well for the sisterhood, either, and led to repercussions that the Chosen Warriors still cringed over although they were never publicly discussed.

"No. The one in Riverside. It's just her and some Raven."

Theresa spread her hands out. "Do you see, gentlemen? What happens when you can't do your job?"

"You're blaming this on us?"

"This won't go well." Mary Marie looked down at her phone again. "That cult is out of control and well-armed. Should we—"

"We're not doing anything," Theresa said.

"If she dies—"

"I know. But if the world ends . . . we're golden." Theresa pointed at the two men. "I don't know about you two, of course, but the sisterhood is golden."

Theresa grabbed the salad she'd been meaning to eat all day from the far side of her desk, moved it to a spot in front of her and opened the container. "We'll use this as a test," She dug out a fork from her desk drawer and took the bottled water handed to her by one of her girls.

"A test of what?" the useless man asked.

"If she dies . . . she dies. But if she doesn't . . ." She shrugged. "Then we see if the sisterhood can assist her in other ways. Perhaps with the help of our friends since we know the Crows won't trust anything directly from us." She pointed her fork at the men. "But we won't be using any of you. In fact, your job is over. Let the Vatican know we no longer need your services."

"But—"

"You've proven yourself useless. Let's just leave it at that." She glanced at Mary Marie. "But help from our more"—she shrugged—"valuable and less-seen friends. That those pagans might accept."

"You think our friends will help?" Mary Marie asked. "The Crows may have quite the reputation but Amsel . . . oy. She has enemies in nearly every pantheon."

"I know," Theresa said with a sigh, sadly choosing the low-fat dressing to put on her salad.

Honestly, it wasn't just actresses who felt the judgy-ness of this town.

"Although I have to admit, if she weren't a pagan *and* a Crow, I would kind of love her. She's such an unabashed dick."

CHAPTER NINE

Erin stood in front of the makeshift sign that led into the rundown but expensive property of the church that had put out a hit on her. "Nice to know that while they're busy trying to have me killed, they still have time in their hectic schedules to openly disparage homosexuals with their fancy signs."

Stieg grunted, his usual response to most of her observations.

But then he suddenly added information. And used words! "When I lived on the streets, Karen and I ate at a lot of church soup kitchens. Most just wanted to help, make sure we ate. But we learned to actively avoid some. . . . because their bologna sandwiches came with a huge side helping of indoctrination and hatred."

"Did you ever deal with these people?" Erin asked.

"No. But they're all alike. The names may be different, but the hatred is always the same."

They walked down the long road toward the church, passing more signs with horrible, hateful slogans every few feet until the church itself came into view. The shitty, barely standing wood building looked like it had been pieced together by the original American settlers.

"Something tells me they don't have that million to pay for my death."

"They're doing this for their Lord, so they think it's okay to lie. You know . . . to murderers." Stieg suddenly looked at her. "I guess it's not worth it for me to ask you to wait here while I deal with this?"

"No."

He rolled his eyes and started toward the church, but Erin stopped him.

"Or we can compromise," she suggested.

"Compromise? You compromise?"

"Yeah."

"I don't."

"Oh." She took his arm and led him off to the side. "Well, it's time to try something new."

The thing that Stieg loved about every human being on the planet, the one thing they *all* had in common no matter the race, religious belief, or political ideology . . .

They all had to pee.

And when the preacher was coming out of the port-a-potty—because the ramshackle church apparently didn't have indoor plumbing, which was the most horrifying thing about all of this as far as Stieg was concerned—Stieg grabbed the man from behind, quickly covered his mouth and dragged him off to a shed a few hundred feet away.

Erin let them in and closed the door

"Scream and I'll snap your neck," Stieg warned. "Understand?"

The preacher gave one nod and Stieg released him.

Stieg had honestly thought he'd spend the short amount of time they'd have with this man trying to drag information out of him. That was usually how such things worked.

But as soon as the preacher saw Erin, his eyes lit up. "It's you!" he exclaimed, sounding ridiculously happy. "God has sent you straight to us!"

Erin playfully clapped her hands together and replied with great sarcasm, "Praise the Lord and pass that dag-gum ammunition!"

Stieg kind of enjoyed how she had no patience. It was almost like she had no fear. Or, at the very least, she was determined to find the humor in any given situation. Stieg's mother always considered that a gift. Humor was what she'd used to handle dying of cancer.

Shame his father didn't have the same set of skills.

"You're trying to kill her," Stieg said to the preacher. "Why?"

"Because if she succeeds in her quest, she will stop the End Times. She will prevent our Lord's second coming." The preacher's eyes were wide and wild, suggesting he believed everything he was saying. So desperate to shed this world that didn't treat him right, he was willing to sacrifice everyone else.

A philosophy Stieg could never truly get behind. "Quest? What quest?"

"To stop the End Times."

"Yeah, yeah, I get that," Stieg said. "I'm asking for specifics."

The preacher smiled and Stieg knew that now the struggle would come. Whatever the man knew about the how, what, and why of what Erin needed to do—if he knew anything—he was not about to give up easily.

Stieg reached out to grab the preacher's throat to start the coercion when Erin stopped him, placing her hand on his wrist.

"What?" he asked.

She lifted her nose, sniffed the air. "Smell that?"

"Smell—?"

Erin suddenly kicked the shed door open and shoved Stieg and the preacher out of the hut. But before she could follow, two women slammed the shed door closed and another man placed a metal bar across it.

Stieg ran toward the shed, but a chain was thrown around him and he was yanked back by four, then five men. Once they had him on his back, chains were wrapped around his throat and arms.

But these were just humans. The Unknowing.

Stieg immediately began to toss his captors off. He used the chains to yank others to him and, once close, knock them out.

The preacher quickly saw that Stieg couldn't be contained and screamed at the women still pressed against the shed. "*Do it! Do it now!*"

Ignoring the sounds of Erin on the other side trying to beat her way out, the women stumbled back and one took out a lighter.

That's what Erin had smelled—turpentine. They'd doused the area surrounding the shed with turpentine.

"*No!*" Stieg shouted, but the shed was already in flames and Erin was still inside.

Then the preacher and his flock began to cheer and sing hymns.

Stieg's rage slid through his body like blood through veins, and he got to his feet. Ready to take vengeance. Ready to destroy.

But before he could begin, the fire began to . . . pull back. Pull back and *under* the walls of the shed. Pulling back until it was completely gone.

The cheering and singing faded away. The banging from the inside of the shed also stopped.

Stieg's rage slipped away as well and he began to move back.

"Run," he told the idiots. They were stupid. Had no idea what they were doing. They'd all have to meet their Christian God eventually and when they did, he'd impress upon them the error of their ways.

But this . . .

"*Ruuuuuuun!*"

Some of them seemed to snap out of it and did as Stieg ordered, but others were still standing there when the first line of flame snaked from under the door and wrapped itself around the preacher's waist. The heat cut through flesh easily and sliced the man in half.

The line of flame slipped back under the shed walls. A brutal moment of silence followed until the shed exploded out, the roof, flipping fifty feet away, leaving only Erin standing there.

Calm, quiet Erin.

And that told Stieg that Erin was angry. Not a little angry. *Crow* angry. The kind of angry that had started wars between countries. The slaughter of entire villages. The decimation of entire armies. The onetime near destruction of all the Clans.

Stieg lifted his hand toward the Crow. "Erin . . ."

Her green eyes cut toward him, and at that point, Stieg just dove for cover. He had no other choice.

He landed behind a tree and watched as Erin lowered her arms to her sides and opened her fingers, palms up. Her lips curled and thick lines of flame burst from her hands, sending a wall of fire straight into the preacher's flock.

The flames were so high and thick that Stieg could see nothing else, but the screams of the victims filled the air, along with the smell of burning flesh.

The wall of flame moved across the land, burning everything in its path, including the church, and leaving nothing behind but scorched earth. Once the fire had finished feeding, it died. The surrounding trees and the town several miles away left untouched.

Amazing, really. It didn't take much for a wildfire to start in California, and Erin had started a few in her time. But she'd clearly gotten control over her flames. He just hadn't realized until now exactly how much.

He stepped out from behind the tree and went to her.

She was still in the remnants of the shed, on her knees, her head bowed, her chest rising and falling from her hard panting.

Stieg crouched beside her, ready to comfort Erin as he'd often done for Jace since they'd become friends. Her berserker rage sometimes led to bouts of hysterical tears.

But he didn't expect tears from Erin, just remorse. He placed a hand on her shoulder. "Erin—"

Stieg didn't know what happened. One second he was trying to comfort Erin, and the next . . . she had her tongue down his throat.

She dug her hands into his hair, leaned into him.

Stieg grabbed her around the waist with every intention of pushing her away.

You know . . . that was his intention. But instead he yanked her close, lifting her up a bit so that he could pull her in tight.

Then, as suddenly as it started, it stopped.

Erin pulled away, stood, and Stieg followed. She let out a breath. "Come on."

She took a step but abruptly stopped and turned to face him. She pressed her forefinger into his chest and leaned in close.

"I . . ." She took in a deep breath. Let it out. "I *fucking* love being a warrior for a Viking god."

Grinning, she turned and walked away, heading back to the car.

The thing was . . . Stieg couldn't argue with her. He loved it, too.

The acolytes stripped the priestess of her robes and carefully handed over the gold-and-diamond-handled knife, placing it directly into her palm.

The priestess folded her fingers around the hilt and walked past the kneeling acolytes, chanting in an ancient language she'd taught to them. As she approached the jewel-covered altar, her victim yelled for help, trying desperately to get loose from the leather bindings.

She leaned over the young man, stroking her hand down his face, before kissing his screaming mouth. Raising the blade high above her head, she brought it down on the sacrifice's chest, burying it up to the hilt, deep into his heart. She yanked the blade out, splattering blood across the chanting acolytes. She did it over and over until the blood touched them all.

She lifted her hands and chanted loudly along with the others, backing away from the altar.

There was a sound like something tearing and she watched the body, waiting to see the sacrifice split open. But the mystical doorway opened behind the altar and she quickly realized why. There wasn't just one, there were many.

It was the leader she focused on. He came through the doorway first, forced to crouch a bit in order to get his entire body through. He was at least seven feet tall, the leather wings extending from his back double that.

Long blond hair braided loosely swung across his right shoulder. His thick beard covered the lower half of his face. Cold blue eyes looked over everything and everyone as he moved around the altar.

He saw her and came forward until he stood in front of her.

With her head forced all the way back, she looked up at him and smiled. He did not smile in return. His hand wrapped around her throat and he lifted her off the floor. She pawed at him, desperate to be free, while the worshippers panicked at her shocked squeal and made a run for the doors in the large hall of the private mansion.

Still holding onto her, he turned toward each exit and she watched the doors slam shut before her people could reach them. They tried to pry them open but the exits were magically locked.

He wasn't just a warrior, he had strong magical powers as well. "I am Önd. These are my men. Our great lady Hel has sent us here to help your Gullveig in any way she may need. But first"—he pulled her close so they were eye to eye—"I have needs. And you, priestess, will fulfill them for me. And your disciples will satisfy my men until they are done with them."

With that, he carried Jourdan Ambrosio to the altar by her throat, pointing out the cases of champagne she had ready for popping in the corner of the hall. "Drink and fuck, my brothers!" he yelled over her acolytes' screams and slammed her onto the remains of the sacrifice, pinning her there.

She slapped and punched at him, to no avail. He simply stared down into her face, hand still around her throat, cold blue eyes gazing at her like she was no more than a rabbit caught in a trap.

"For soon," he said low for her alone, "battle will come and Ragnarok will follow close behind. That is what you want, isn't it, priestess?" He leaned in and grinned. "Then let it be my honor to give you a taste of what it will be like when that time comes. . . ."

CHAPTER TEN

Erin waited until Stieg parked his car before she got out and headed into his building. She still had no shoes and her feet hurt. She was not a no-shoes kind of girl like many of her sister-Crows. And, hey, if they wanted to be all Southern California about it, that was up to them, but she'd like to avoid hepatitis if she could.

They got into the elevator without a word and went down the hall to his apartment. Once they were inside, Stieg did what he'd done the night before—turned on one light, turned on the TV, got himself a Norwegian beer—but this time he got two. He tossed one to her before he dropped onto the couch and began watching *American Greed*.

The man really liked *American Greed*.

Erin used the edge of the coffee table Stieg had his feet on to take the top off her beer. She took a long drink, decided she would never drink Norwegian beer again, and placed it on the table.

She slipped off her backpack and opened it, digging around for a few seconds before finding what she wanted. She held it in her hand and stepped closer to Stieg.

That's when he looked up at her. "What?" he asked when she just stared down at him.

Deciding conversation was the last thing they needed at the moment, Erin reached under her dress and removed her panties.

Stieg's eyes grew wide. "What the hell are you doing?"

She straddled his stretched-out legs and reached down to unzip his jeans. "Well, everyone is accusing me of taking advantage of you—because apparently that's what I do or something—and I figure I might as well live up to my horrible reputation among my own sisterhood. Lift your hips."

"Erin, wait. We just—"

Erin grinned. "I know. We just totally went Viking on a *church*. It was so Lindisfarne circa 793, right?"

She tore open the emergency condom she always kept in her backpack—because, as her mother told her when she turned sixteen, "A well-prepared girl is a disease-free girl"— and dug her hand into his boxer briefs, releasing his cock.

"Erin, wait—"

"Holy shit! Look at the size of that thing!"

"Hey!"

"Dude! That was a compliment," she informed him as she put the condom on.

"That's not the point!"

"And circumcised," she praised. "Yes!"

"Erin!"

She tore her gaze away from his cock so she could look him in the eyes. "What?"

"I'm not just a piece of meat, ya know."

"Oh, my God," she said with real affection. "You're so cute." She placed her knees on either side of his hips and dropped down on his now-hard cock, taking him inside her in one move.

They both let out groans and Stieg's hands immediately went to her waist, holding her there.

Eyes closed, he still wouldn't give up. "Wait, wait. We should . . . like . . . talk or something."

"About *what*?"

"Anything!" he shot back. "Absolutely anything."

Unbelievable! This woman was unbelievable! She was using him to get her after-going-Viking needs fulfilled. Whether pillaging a monastery, destroying a village, or raiding a kingdom, the Viking sex always came after. And the Crows were no different.

Erin was no different! She might have no blood connection to Ivar the Boneless but she was as Viking as anyone Stieg had known in this sometimes shitty world. And she was acting just like his ancient brethren by taking what she wanted. From him! A fellow Viking!

Did shieldmaidens do this to the warriors after all the villagers were dead?

No. No! It was ridiculous! Stieg deserved better than this! Dinner out. Maybe a movie. Perhaps a little sweet talk.

He wasn't a whore!

Some random booty call she'd picked up at a club.

He was Stieg Engstrom, Raven warrior for mighty Odin. Not some piece of ass!

He was going to tell her to stop right now.

Right this second.

Right this very second.

He really was.

Just watch him.

But then she kissed him. Kissed him and squeezed down on his dick.

The poor thing almost exploded.

Did she train for this sort of thing? Take a Pilates class that specialized in pelvic floor exercises or something? Because holy shit!

Erin's hips began to move while her pussy kept that grip on his dick. How was that even possible?

And all Stieg could do was sit there and let the woman fuck him because his ability to think and reason seemed to have gotten up off the couch and walked out the goddamn door, leaving him to be nothing but the receiving whore to the Viking warrior on top of him.

She kept kissing him. And the kiss was . . . astounding. He wasn't sure why. It wasn't like he hadn't been kissed before. By, to be quite blunt, way hotter women than Erin Amsel.

But his toes were curling in his steel-toe work boots and he was gripping her waist so hard he was concerned he'd tear flesh off.

She continued to rock against him. Her hands dug into his hair. Her mouth pressed tight against his . . .

He could only handle so much!

Erin shuddered against him and he knew she was coming. Could feel it in the way her pussy contracted. And knowing she was coming . . .

He followed right behind her, groaning and growling into her mouth, his hands releasing her waist so he could wrap his arms around her and pull her in tight while he powered into her from beneath.

It went on and on until he was sure he'd gone blind and deaf.

Then he was coming back. Breathing hard like he'd been in a marathon. Sweat pouring down his face. Limp and relaxed with Erin on top of him.

Until he was cold and alone.

Erin had pulled away. She was standing over him, putting her panties back on, grabbing her backpack, and pulling out her phone.

After a few seconds, she announced, "Got a car coming. See ya later." Then she was walking to his front door.

Stieg sat up, shocked. And pissed! "Where the fuck are you going?" he demanded.

She faced him. "Home."

"You're just leaving me sitting here? The condom still on."

"I got what I wanted. Cleanup's on you."

"That's not what I'm talking about."

"Then what are you talking about?" She gave a snotty little laugh. "Are you talking about, like . . . a relationship? Are you high?"

"I am not high. You just can't . . ."

"What? Walk away? Yeah. I can. And I am."

"Why?" He knew it wasn't because she hadn't had a great time. Her cheeks were still flushed, she was still a little out of breath, and she just seemed . . . satisfied. So what was the problem?

"Because I'd *break* you. That's why."

"That's bullshit."

"No, sweetie. That's me being honest. The bottom line is you're kind of a nice guy."

"Kind of?"

"A little rough around the edges. Definitely rude. But at your core, *nice*. And I am a *horrible* girlfriend. I'm sarcastic. I never take anything seriously. And I mock everything. I need a good sociopath or narcissist who I can tear down until he's nothing but a nub of his former self. While you need a nice girl like . . . Karen. She's so sweet. She'd make you dinner, be happy when you came home, not make it her life's work to torment you just for the fuck of it."

Erin's phone vibrated and she took a quick look. "Wow.

That was fast. My car's already here." She waved at him. "See you later!"

Then she was gone! Out his front door, down the hall, and into the elevator.

Through an open window, he heard her get into the car and heard the vehicle drive off.

Mouth open, his dick still out, condom still on, Stieg looked around the room, until he demanded of whatever gods were listening, *"What the fuck just happened?"*

CHAPTER ELEVEN

The car stopped in front of the driveway that led to the Bird House. The driver leaned down to look through the passenger window at the large sign outside the gates before glancing back at Erin. "You work here?"

"Yeah," she replied, reaching for the door handle.

"I'd hope so. Not sure a patient should look like they're coming in from an all-night bender."

Erin frowned, momentarily confused, then she remembered that what was the Bird House to the Clans was the Malibu base of world-renowned Giant Strides Rehabilitation Centers to the rest of the Unknowing.

"Yeah. I better sneak in the back. Can't let those booze-hounds and pill poppers see me looking like this, huh?"

"Good plan, sweetie."

Chuckling, Erin stepped out of the car and headed to the large gate that blocked the driveway. She hit the buzzer and waited. One of her sisters appeared on the screen. "Erin! Hey, girl."

"Hey. Open up, would ya?"

"Sure. And Kera's looking for you."

Erin rolled her eyes. "This isn't about Engstrom, is it?"

She was not in the mood to hear any more on that subject. She'd had a great night. Why ruin it?

"Don't think so, but you can ask her yourself."

The gate slowly opened and Erin walked in, stopping just on the other side to make sure no one followed her. The paparazzi were persistent assholes. Always trying to get in and snap pictures of their most famous residents. That was a dangerous game for the photogs to play, though. This particular parcel of land was not only protected by Erin's sisters, it was also protected by actual crows and ravens. More than one paparazzo over the years had had an eye pecked out or was knocked from a tree or suffered heavy blood loss because he got too close to the house. Without even being asked, the crows provided protection, and as the insanity that was fan-worship grew, Erin and her sisters were extremely grateful.

Once the gate was firmly closed behind her, Erin began the long walk up the driveway. By the time she reached the house, the sun was out, and several black town cars were waiting at the front to take a few of the actress-Crows to the sets of their TV shows, commercials, or movies. Some of the models were just getting home from long nights of partying.

As Erin neared her sisters, she listened to their conversations.

"Why do you insist on all that makeup when you know they're just going to redo it all when you get to the set?"

"You want me to look my best, don't you?"

"Not really."

"Did you read the trades? Now that Betty's awake, she's on a rampage. I heard there are producers going on sudden, long-term vacations in Eastern Europe just to avoid her."

"You've gotta be pretty scary as a human being if your enemies are running to *Russia* just to get away from you."

"I'm getting tons of modeling work, but all the jobs are for plus-size clothes."

"So?"

"I'm a size ten."

"Welcome to America. That *is* plus-sized, kid."

As Erin passed her sisters, they briefly stopped their conversations to greet her. Two of them said, "Kera's been looking for you."

Erin heard the same as she made her way inside and down the hall toward the kitchen. She grabbed a bowl, poured herself some cereal and milk, and after taking a spoon from the drawer, headed out the back.

If Kera was at the Bird House—rather than at her Viking boyfriend's house—she'd be outside meditating at that time of the morning. She had learned relaxation techniques while in the military and started off with meditation and then went into yoga.

Erin didn't actually see evidence that any of that relaxed Kera—a very uptight woman, in Erin's estimation—but it horrified her to think that without it, her sister-Crow would be even *more* uptight.

She found Kera—eyes closed, breathing even, in what Erin assumed was the "lotus pose" common in meditation—on a purple mat out on the big backyard lawn.

Having gotten yelled at more than once for interrupting Kera's meditation time, Erin sat down across from her sister-Crow and quietly ate her cereal. While waiting, she stared. She stared until Kera's eyes opened and she saw Erin sitting there . . . staring.

Kera let out a panicked, tiny squeal. "What the fuck are you doing, Amsel?"

Erin gave a small shrug and softly replied, "Just waiting for you to die . . ."

Kera's entire face contorted into a mix of panic, rage, and extreme concern. "*What?*"

"You missed the meeting."

Stieg finger-combed his wet hair off his face while staring at Vig Rundstöm at his front door. "I don't care."

"Josef's pissed," Rolf added, coming up behind Vig with Siggy.

"Care even less." Stieg walked away.

Vig followed. "It was important."

"I'm sure it was."

"It was about—"

"End of the world, blah blah blah. Yeah. I know."

Rolf closed the door. "Blah blah blah? Seriously?"

"Where is she?" Siggy asked.

Facing the big idiot, Stieg felt the urge to start hitting. "I can't believe you're asking me that right now," he growled.

"Why?"

"I don't want to talk about her!"

"But I want to see her."

"You see her nearly every day."

"No. I haven't."

Stieg stared at his friend. "What are you talking about?"

"The goat."

"Oh." Stieg went to his refrigerator, pulling out a gallon of orange juice. "She's still in the bedroom."

Siggy strode toward the bedroom and Vig asked Stieg, "You sleep with your goat?"

"She likes to be comfortable."

"Why are you barking at me? What's wrong with you?"

Before Stieg could answer Vig, there was a squeal from the bedroom.

"By Odin's beard," Rolf muttered, "what's he doing to that goat?"

Siggy walked out of the bedroom—or maybe it was more a skip—with Hilda in his arms, holding her like a baby. "She's so cute!"

"Oh," Rolf added, sitting at the kitchen bar. "Based on the high frequency of that sentence . . . that squeal *wasn't* from the goat."

"That's disturbing." Vig sat next to Rolf and looked at Stieg. "Anyway, you need to know what's going on."

Stieg slammed the juice carton on the counter, wiping his mouth with the back of his hand. "Besides our doom, Rundstöm . . . what else is there to tell me?"

Kera's eye twitched as Erin dropped her empty bowl and spoon on the grass and fell back against the ground, laughing hysterically. If nothing else, the woman knew how to entertain herself.

Deciding to ignore Erin's ridiculous behavior, Kera grabbed her phone and texted Jace, who was somewhere in the house.

When Erin finally managed to sit up and act like an adult, Kera forced a smile in the hopes of keeping Erin focused and less annoying during this conversation.

The redhead cringed. "What the hell was that?"

"What was what?"

"That thing you just did with your face."

"A smile?"

"Yeah. Don't do that anymore. It is not your friend." Always full of energy, Erin sort of bounced around while sitting, her fingers twitching at Kera, urging her on. "So . . . talk to me. What's going on? What do ya need? What do

you want?" she asked with rapid speed. Her mind already a
thousand miles away.

Kera had known this conversation wouldn't be easy, but
now she realized it would be even worse than she'd imagined. Because Erin was full of energy. Unfocused energy.

"We're waiting for Jace," Kera replied, keeping her voice
very controlled. "She's coming."

"Okay." Erin relaxed a bit, her gaze sweeping the extensive backyard of the Bird House. Then, "How 'bout I come
back?"

"How about you wait?"

Her head dropped back and she let out an annoyed sigh.
"I'm bored!"

"It's been less than thirty seconds!"

"So? What's your point?"

"Have you been tested for ADHD?"

"I   know . . . maybe . . . oh,   wait . . . yeah . . . well . . .
yeah! Okay!"

Kera opened her mouth to reply then changed her mind.
What would be the point?

After another minute or so of Erin's sounds of extreme
boredom—mostly sighing—Jace came around the corner,
her now-giant puppy, Lev, held in her arms.

"Look at that thing," Erin muttered. "Is it really necessary for her to still hold it when it's that size?"

"Considering all four legs work . . . no."

Originally, Chloe had wanted a meeting that would involve a lot more people. Erin's entire Strike Team; Betty,
Erin's one-time mentor; and Chloe. But Kera had a gut feeling that was not the way to come at Erin. Actually, she felt
like having more than one or two people was giving Erin
an audience. For this discussion, it was the last thing any of
them needed.

Jace placed her puppy on the ground, sending him off to

play with Kera's dog, Brodie Hawaii. She watched the two dogs for a moment before joining Kera and Erin. She sat down, cross-legged, and tried her best to give Erin a smile.

Didn't work. Erin saw right through it.

"Okay," Erin sighed out. "What's going on?"

Kera glanced at Jace, but her friend could barely look at either of them. Jace blamed herself for this, but, really, if anyone was to blame, it was Gullveig.

But Kera didn't have time to sit around, complaining about that bitch. "We were going to wait to tell everyone this, including you, but now that we hear the Vatican is involved—"

Erin chuckled. "Yeah."

"—and you didn't tell us."

The chuckling stopped and green eyes widened a bit. "Oh. Uh . . . well, the Vatican—"

"Shut up."

"Okay then."

"Now that we know about the Vatican despite you—"

"Wow," Erin muttered, "not lettin' that go."

"—we've decided to get everyone up to speed since it seems things are moving forward quicker than we thought."

"Okay . . . and?"

"We think we have a way to kill Gullveig."

"To actually *kill* her? Put her down for good? Not just send her somewhere else?"

"Yeah."

"Great. What will I need to do?" When Kera only stared at her, "I'm assuming you're having this conversation with me—and *only* me—because I'm the one who can do it. Whatever it is."

"It's a risk."

"Life is risk."

"Erin—"

"Jesus, Mary, and Joseph, Kera!" she exclaimed, hands thrown up. "Just tell me!"

"We need you to get the Fire Sword."

"What Fire Sword?"

"The—" Kera glanced at Jace again but her friend's head hung even lower. It was like she was trying to turn herself into a ball and roll away. "The flaming sword of the fire giant Surtr."

Erin thought a moment before asking, "Do you mean the sword protected by the *dragon*? The dragon who hates all humans? That dragon?"

Kera cleared her throat, now wishing that Chloe was there so she could do the explaining.

Why had Kera insisted on doing it? She didn't know how to handle Erin Amsel. She liked her. She was a close friend. But they didn't actually get along except in battle. Erin thought Kera was too uptight and Kera could barely tolerate Erin's ability to be a goddamn human Ping-Pong ball.

"Yeah," Kera finally said. "That's the one."

Erin glanced off, lips pursed, before she stated, "Of course it is."

Then Jace burst into hysterical tears . . . which seemed about right.

Stieg stared at his Raven brothers until Rolf leaned forward and asked, "Are you all right? You haven't said a word in ten minutes."

"I'm trying to decide," Stieg said carefully, "the level of my rage."

Rolf nodded. "That's a fair answer."

"Are they *trying* to kill her?" Stieg asked, still feeling surprisingly calm. "Because there are lots of people who want her dead."

"No. We actually need her to survive. Her death would ensure Ragnarok, so we're trying to avoid that."

"By sending her to the lowest pits of the World Tree to face the dragon Nidhogg and take the sword from him, which will undoubtedly piss that dragon off? Is that the plan?"

"When you put it like that . . ."

"What other way would you put it?"

His brothers glanced off, trying to find an acceptable answer, but Stieg knew there was no acceptable answer.

"She could say no," Siggy suggested, still holding Stieg's goat in his arms like a newborn.

"She won't."

"How do you know?"

"How do I know?" Stieg leaned across the counter so his friends would understand his words clearly. "*Because she's insane!*"

"Okay," Erin said, getting to her feet. "I'm gonna go."

Kera grabbed her arm and yanked her back down. "You're gonna go?" she asked, brown eyes boring into her.

Erin glanced at a sobbing Jace. "Yeah. She's . . . uh . . . crying. So I'm just gonna go." She tried to get up again, but Kera yanked her back.

"Because your friend is crying? Because she's allowing herself to show emotion?"

"Yes."

"You're pathetic."

"You're a bitch."

Then Erin was rolling around the yard with Kera, the two of them trying to punch each other and calling each other names a priest would be horrified by.

"Stop it!" Jace screeched, grabbing at them. "*Stop it now!*"

Jace yanked them apart, the three of them on their knees, panting. Erin glaring at Kera. Kera glaring at her. And Jace glaring at all of them.

Her tears were gone, but her eyes were tinged red. At one time, not even a few weeks ago, eyes that color would have signaled it was too late to pull her back from the brink of Berserker-ness, but lately, she'd found a way to manage it.

"I can't believe you two," she chastised, working to get control. "I can't believe you're acting like this."

Brodie Hawaii, Kera's pit bull, apparently agreed. She circled them, barking. And Lev crawled into Jace's lap, licking her face. He was definitely trying to calm her.

Erin opened her mouth to speak but Jace cut her off. "If you say that Kera started it, I'm going to beat you to death and let the world burn."

Since that was exactly what Erin was going to say, she pressed her lips together and remained silent.

Jace, breathing heavy, jerked her hand at Kera. "Your nose is bleeding."

Kera wiped her face with the back of her hand, eyes growing wide at the sight of blood on her knuckles. "You punched me in the nose?" she growled at Erin.

"It's such a wide target, I could barely miss."

They were reaching for each other again when Lev, still on Jace's lap, gave a low warning growl that startled them both.

They stared at the dog, then each other, before quickly turning completely away, afraid they'd start laughing and really send Jace over the edge.

When Erin felt confident she wouldn't laugh, she said, "Sorry, Kera."

"Yeah." Kera swallowed, her voice a tad higher as she struggled not to laugh at the overwhelming cuteness of Jace's funny-looking dog. "Me, too."

Jace kissed her dog on the head and sent him off to continue playing with Brodie. She laid her folded hands in her lap, let out a very long breath, and said softly, "I know you both have a very distinct way of dealing with intense emotions, and that it often involves hitting each other or calling each other fat ass."

"I've never called Erin a fat ass."

"No, but you have called her a tiny leprechaun you could step on."

Kera shrugged. "Yeah. I have said that."

"I'm suggesting we try a different way of dealing with this."

Erin opened her mouth to reply.

"No!" Jace barked, cutting Erin off before she could say a word. "Part of this different way is for you *not* to say the first thing that comes into your head, because although it will make you laugh, it will do nothing but send me into a crazed Berserker rage."

Erin shrugged. "Then that's probably a good plan."

Rolf watched Stieg pull on a sweatshirt and sneakers and head toward his front door.

"Where are you going?" Vig asked from the kitchen, where all of them were eating Stieg's cereal and milk, probably leaving nothing for him when they were done.

"Where do you think?" Stieg asked, stopping briefly to grab his keys and open the door. "To kidnap Erin."

Then he was gone, the door slamming shut behind him.

Rolf shoveled another mouthful of Raisin Bran into his mouth before mumbling, "Should we be concerned about that?"

"Probably," Vig replied, reaching for another box of Frosted Flakes.

CHAPTER TWELVE

After a shower to get the scent of Stieg Engstrom off her skin, Erin sat on the front steps of the Bird House, taking a minute to get her thoughts in order. It was at times like this—when she was kind of confused and unsure—that she said things that did nothing but piss everyone off.

Wanting to avoid that, especially when Jace and Kera were kind of at their emotional peaks, she'd come out here to sit and relax. That lasted a total of thirty seconds before she was already so bored she could cry. She was just getting up to go inside and find something to do when her phone rang.

Pulling it out of the back pocket of her black jeans, Erin paused a moment to stare at the front of the phone in confusion. She finally answered. "Ma?"

"Hi, baby. How are you? I had a dream."

Erin rolled her eyes and smiled at the same time. "Oh, no," she said flatly. "Not a dream."

"Don't mock. My dreams are very prophetic."

"No they're not."

"No they're not!" her father yelled in the background. "I told her not to call you!"

"Shut up, Hersch!"

Laughing, Erin sat back down on the step. "Ma, everything's fine," she lied.

"Don't lie to your mother. Why do you always insist on lying to your mother?"

"Because it usually works in the moment."

"Well, it's not going to work now. My dream was very telling. Wasn't it, Hersch?"

"No, it wasn't."

"What was your dream, Ma?"

"Well, I don't remember exactly."

"Oh, my God."

"But I woke up *very* concerned."

"Of course you did."

"Listen to you. Just like your father. Judging."

"Because," her father barked in the background, "when *my* daughter hears insanity, she's been taught to judge!"

And people wondered why Erin was the way she was. Yet how could she be anything else when she had wonderful, amazing, ridiculous parents like these?

"I just want to make sure you're okay. Is that too much for a mother to ask?"

"Ma, I'm fine."

"You don't sound fine."

"In what way do I not sound fine?"

"A mother knows."

"Oy."

"Don't *oy* me."

Erin didn't know what to say to her mother. She didn't want to lie to her, but it wasn't like she could be honest either. *Yeah, Ma, I have to go into the pits of the universe and wrestle a flaming sword from a hateful dragon and, if I manage not to get killed doing that, challenge a pissed-off goddess to a fight.*

That was not something a child could say to a mother

who cared. It had been hard enough when Erin had come back as Crow. It was something she couldn't tell her mother the truth about, so she'd come up with some bullshit excuse to explain *why* she would be spending the rest of her life in Los Angeles.

A place that, at one time, Erin had said she'd rather set herself on fire than ever move to. Of course, when she'd come to Los Angeles, it had only been because she'd been on the run. It had never occurred to her she'd get killed here and decide to stay.

Her sister-Crows had even been nice enough to find her a place with the Tri-State Crows, but by then Erin had already experienced a Christmas season in cut-off shorts and bikini tops. Going back to face a Northeast winter became something she never really wanted to deal with again.

So there she was. In Los Angeles. Loving every minute of it, but missing her parents. They were great. And hilarious. And just goddamn ridiculous. Everything Erin adored in life.

"I can see you're not going to tell me."

"There's nothing to tell," Erin replied.

And, in the background, her father yelled, "There's nothing to tell, woman!"

"Who asked you?"

"You did! All morning! You were going to call her before the sun was even up on that coast!"

"Oh, look at you, Hersch Amsel. The great traveler!"

While her parents bickered, as they loved to do, Erin watched Stieg's big black pickup truck park in front of the house.

He got out and walked around the enormous vehicle, looking delicious. Jeans hanging off narrow hips. A dark blue sweatshirt, with the sleeves cut off, hanging loose to his waist. Blue and white sneakers on his feet. His hair tousled and a little damp.

He took the steps two at a time until he was right in front of her.

Erin smiled up at him, ready to greet him, until he suddenly reached down, grabbed her waist, and tossed her over his shoulder.

"Hey! Engstrom! What the fuck are you doing?"

"Erin?" her mother snapped. "Erin, what's going on? Who is Engstrom? *What* is an Engstrom?"

"Uh . . ."

The front door to the Bird House opened and a sister-Crow peered out, eyes widening when she saw Stieg carrying Erin down the stairs. "Oh, shit." She turned toward the house. "We have a Code Odin, ladies! Code Odin! Kera, you better get up here!"

They quickly reached Stieg's truck, Erin's mother barking in Erin's ear, her father joining her in the background.

"Ma, I gotta go."

"Erin Amsel, don't you dare hang up this phone! What's happening? Whatever you do," her mother blathered on, "don't let them take you to a secondary location! Never let them take you to a secondary location!"

"Call the cops!" her father ordered.

"No! Don't," Erin ordered back.

Stieg shoved Erin inside his truck.

"I'm just being kidnapped by a Viking."

"You know, Erin Aliza Amsel, you are *not* funny."

Stieg walked around the truck, and that's when they attacked. Not her sisters. The birds. Swirling around Stieg, until he bellowed, "*That is enough!*"

The birds scattered, landing in the trees surrounding the house.

Erin shook her head, chuckling. "Ma, I gotta go."

"You sure you're all right?"

"I'm fine. I'll talk to you later."

"We love you, baby."

"I love you, too, Ma."

Erin disconnected the phone just as Stieg got into his truck. He hadn't turned off the motor, so he put it into DRIVE and pulled off.

Her sisters were just coming down the stairs toward them, yelling at Stieg to stop . . . but he just kept going.

Erin settled back into the seat.

"You're not going to complain?" he asked.

"Nope. I can tell."

"Tell what?"

"That you're madly in love with me."

"Oh, shut up."

The Crows stood on the driveway watching Stieg's truck barrel away.

"Shouldn't we go after them?" Leigh asked.

Chloe shook her head. "No. Stieg would never hurt her."

"Didn't he stab her in the kidney once?"

"No. She fell on his knife during a fight." Chloe shrugged. "It was a lucky shot. Tessa?" she said to her second in command.

Tessa whistled at the birds in the trees and several took off after Stieg's truck.

"If there's any real problem," Chloe said, already heading back inside, "the crows will let us know."

"Yeah, but"—Jace cringed a little—"are you sure we shouldn't be worried?"

Chloe stopped walking and faced her sisters. "About Erin? Or about *Stieg*?"

There was a pause, then they all replied in unison, "About Stieg."

As Stieg drove, he realized he had no idea where he was going. He just knew he had to get Erin away from all those who would harm her. He hadn't thought beyond that. It bothered him. It was something his father would do. Go on emotion only. Stieg was smarter than that. Mostly because his brain hadn't been completely pickled by liquor.

He glanced at Erin sitting beside him. She was being very quiet and very cooperative. It made him uneasy. Erin was rarely cooperative and *never* quiet.

Her phone vibrated in the back pocket of her jeans and she answered. He assumed it was one of her sister-Crows, wanting to make sure she was okay, but her body suddenly tensed.

"Right. I understand. Your address? Yeah. Got it." She disconnected the call and began to put an address into his truck's GPS.

"What are you doing?"

"We need to go here."

"Why?"

Erin leaned back in her seat and for once, looked deadly serious in a way he could never remember seeing her. She flatly replied, "Because I told you to."

And for once, Stieg didn't argue. He just followed the GPS's direction to the small house in Pasadena.

CHAPTER THIRTEEN

They pulled up to the small house and parked right in front. Erin stared at the door for a moment before telling Stieg, "Stay here. I'll be back in a few minutes."

She didn't wait for an answer, since he wasn't exactly a chatty fellow, and stepped out. She closed the door and started across the quiet suburban street toward the house. No. She really didn't want to do this, even though her curiosity was practically eating her alive. But what could be waiting for her here? Should she go in that house? Was she making a mistake? For once, Erin felt insecure. She rarely did. One had to have a high level of confidence when permanently marking someone's skin with ink. And it was that same confidence that led her through life in general. Always had. Still, maybe this was a mistake. Maybe she should—

Erin stopped in the middle of the street and turned. Stieg stood right behind her.

Frowning, she wondered if she'd actually told him to wait or not. She had a lot on her mind . . . so maybe not. "Wait in the car. I shouldn't be too long. Make sure your phone's on. I'll call you if there's a problem."

Without answering, he gazed down at her and she turned

back around and walked to the house. She pushed the small white gate open, walked down the path surrounded by a very neat lawn and garden. She went up the stairs to the porch and knocked on the front door.

When it opened, Jace's grandmother stared at Erin.

Jace called her grandmother Nëna and, since no one knew her actual name, the rest of the Crows called her that as well. Although Erin didn't call her anything because she disliked the woman so much. She'd managed to do to Erin what very few people had ever managed . . . scare the crap out of her.

She was a tiny woman, maybe five feet, if that. But her tiny size hid a tremendous amount of power. Mystical power. The kind that Erin had only seen in very high-level witches. But unlike those witches, Nëna had no loyalty to any god or gods. She had no loyalty to any power higher than herself. The only loyalty she *seemed* to have was to her family.

And Erin wasn't family. Not as far as Jace's grandmother was concerned.

"I told you to come alone," Nëna reminded her, her expression already annoyed. And Erin hadn't even set foot inside yet.

"I didn't—" She let out a breath and looked over her shoulder.

Yup. Stieg Engstrom stood behind her. Idiot.

"I told you to wait in the car."

"Yeah."

"Then why didn't you?"

"I never said I would."

Erin, realizing she had a very stubborn Viking standing behind her, faced the old woman again. "You said don't bring Jace or the other Crows. I didn't. He's not a Crow."

Shrewd blue eyes sized Stieg up. "He ain't much human, either."

"Depends on who you talk to. Now you going to let me in or what?"

Nëna waited another moment, like she was actually debating letting Erin into her home. But, finally, she stepped back, and gestured with a wave of her hand.

Stieg followed, stopping briefly to wipe his big feet on the welcome mat that read NO SOLICITATION. Yes. Very welcoming.

He nodded at Nëna as he walked into the house. "Ma'am. Nice to see you again."

"I know you?"

"Apparently not, but that's okay. I'm friends with your granddaughter."

Nëna didn't seem to care as she closed the front door and passed the pair, heading deeper into the house.

As they began to follow, Erin muttered to Stieg, "Suck up."

"It's called being polite," he softly replied. "You should try it some time."

Nëna led them into the living room filled with men who smoked cigars and talked to each other in a language Erin didn't understand but was sure Jace would. The men kept talking until Stieg walked in. Then they fell silent and stared at him, gazes distrusting and definitely dangerous.

Erin knew in that moment, every one of these men was armed. Not with guns *or* knives but both, and more than one of each.

Nëna said something to them in their language and motioned the men away with a wave of her hand.

Still staring at Stieg, silent warning in their blue eyes, they all left.

"My sons and grandsons don't think you can be trusted, Raven," Nëna scoffed. "You are a Raven, right?" At Stieg's nod, she added, "Little do they know"—she suddenly pointed at Erin—"*you're* the one who can't be trusted."

"*Me?*" Erin asked, incredulous. "Let us not forget, old woman, that any problem you have with me . . . *you* started it."

Stieg shook his head at Erin. "Is that your excuse for everything?"

"In this case it's absolutely true!"

Stieg didn't know how much longer he could keep Erin Amsel alive. Apparently there was no one in this universe that the woman wouldn't challenge. Including a very serene-looking old woman whom, from what Stieg had heard, even Lucifer feared.

But that didn't stop Erin from calling Jace's grandmother "old woman."

Unused to seeing Erin Amsel actually angry, Stieg decided he had to intervene earlier than usual, stepping between the two glaring women and saying, "Before this turns ugly, I suggest you tell us why you called us here, Mrs. Bashir."

"She didn't call you anywhere," Erin harshly reminded him. *Wow, she is* really *angry.* "I told you to wait in the fucking car."

"And I told you I ignored you. Get over it."

"You two done?" the old woman barked. "And don't call me Mrs. Bashir."

"But . . . isn't that your name?" Stieg asked.

"That's not the point."

"Old woman then?"

Stieg closed his eyes, frustrated, and reached over to cover Erin's face with his hand and pull her behind him, stupidly using his body as a shield.

"Since you say you're Jace's friend, you can call me Nëna like the others."

"Oy," Erin growled behind his hand.

"And you," Nëna said, leaning to the side to catch a glimpse of Erin, "why are you still here?"

Erin pulled Stieg's hand away from her face. "In what sense?"

Stieg faced her. "In what sense?"

"Do *you* know what she means?"

Stieg was going to answer "yes" until he realized that he actually didn't know what Jace's grandmother meant. She had invited Erin to her house, so that couldn't be what she meant. "In what sense?" he finally asked.

Nëna rolled her eyes. "The pair of you. Neither much brighter than the other."

Erin, fed up, walked off, heading back toward the front of the house. But she only got a few steps before she abruptly stopped.

He watched her try to move her legs, attempting to lift one, then the other, but Stieg knew that she *couldn't*. From feet to knees, she was frozen in place.

"Old woman," Erin snarled, her voice low, her body struggling to be free, "release me or—"

"Or what?" Nëna asked, circling Erin. "What will you do, Crow?"

Erin's hand shot out, spinning Nëna around before yanking her close and wrapping her right arm against the front of Nëna's neck and her left pushing against the back.

Stieg moved quickly, grabbing Erin's wrist and yanking her arm back. She could move freely now; Nëna's spell broken; but having been in fights with Erin before, Stieg knew he had to get her away from not only Nëna but himself.

"Never get between a Crow and her prey," his father used to say. Probably the only good advice the man had ever given him.

Still twisting Erin's arm, he tossed her across the room,

sending her flipping into a table filled with framed family pictures. Everything crashed to the floor, including Erin, and the sound of heavy footsteps running toward them had Stieg quickly kneeling beside Nëna as she choked and worked to get her breath back. He wasn't afraid to admit, he was kind of using her as a human shield—a move he knew was the right one when the woman's sons and grandsons and grand-nephews and whatever other male relatives she had stormed back into the room, weapons out and ready.

"Are you all right?" Stieg asked her, pretending not to see the men, knowing eye contact at that moment would just get him shot or stabbed.

Rubbing her throat, she glowered up at him but still took Stieg's outstretched hand. "Get me up, boy."

He helped Nëna stand and she slowly faced her kin. "Get out," she ordered.

"Yeah, but—" one of them began.

"Out!"

Their eyes quickly looking away from her, the men left without another word.

That was her power. Those were not men who, in their daily lives, knew fear.

But they feared *her*, which meant so should Stieg and Erin.

Erin struggled to her feet, and Stieg winced when he realized that he'd accidentally yanked her arm from its socket.

Erin and Nëna, both panting, stared hard at each other, communication passing between them without either speaking. Neither woman looked away. Neither woman backed down. Erin finally reached for her dislocated shoulder, trying to push it back into place with her free hand while her gaze stayed fixed on Nëna.

With neither woman budging, Stieg made the first move. "Need help with your shoulder?" he asked.

Erin's glare was brutal and even Nëna, eyes widening, gawked at him.

Still trying to put her shoulder back in place, Erin snarled, "Fuck you!"

"*I'm just trying to help!*" Stieg yelled back.

"*You can stick your help up your tight—*"

"That is enough!" Nëna barked. She motioned them forward. "In the back. Both of you. Now."

"I don't know why you're so mad at me," Stieg complained as he followed behind Erin. "You'd never have forgiven yourself if you'd hurt Jace's grandmother."

Erin stopped, faced him. "Do you really believe that?"

Before Stieg could answer, Nëna passed them both and replied, "Even the Virgin Mary don't believe that bullshit."

CHAPTER FOURTEEN

"You need to get that sword, girly."

Erin pushed Stieg away with her good hand—he was trying to help her fix her arm—and moved closer to Nëna, which wasn't very close because Stieg kept between them, ready to jump in at a second's notice.

Bastard.

"That's what I'm trying to do."

"You are running out of time."

"What do you care?" Erin snapped. "Why are you suddenly so goddamn concerned?"

She didn't let people make her angry. In fact, she could count on one hand the times she'd ever been this angry and one of those times was her actual death and another was when she'd gone a round with Kera because she was being such a difficult bitch about her new life as a Crow.

But now? Now Erin had to use *two* hands to count how many people had pissed her off.

Not only that . . . but her shoulder hurt like a bitch.

"I've got family," Nëna reminded her. "They're part of this world. Besides, you don't do this, and my granddaughter will blame herself for *your* mistake."

"Look, old woman," Erin said, stepping closer, Stieg right beside her, "don't put this all on me. I'm just along for the ride. You want someone to blame, you track down Gullveig and you blame her yourself. I'm just trying to save the world."

"Well, you're doing a piss-poor job of it."

Erin didn't even have a chance to snap the old bitch's neck before Stieg grabbed her around the waist and carried her a few feet away to the picnic table. He pulled out a chair and sat down, keeping Erin on his lap with his big, stupid arms.

"How do you even know what's going on?" Erin demanded, her fucked-up shoulder making a struggle with Stieg a losing proposition. "Is Jace telling you all this?"

"What you and my granddaughter still don't seem to understand is that *no one* has to tell me anything. I just know."

The back door of the house swung open and Erin waited for what she thought would be more of Nëna's sons and grandsons to come traipsing through. But it wasn't them at all. She watched the four men dressed casually in jeans, boots, and surfing-related T-shirts kiss the woman on the cheek or give her a quick hug before they leaned against a nearby brick wall and proceeded to eat fresh fruit or containers of fruit-filled yogurt.

Slowly, Erin looked over at Nëna and watched the woman give her a large grin.

"You old bitch," Erin snarled.

"What?" Stieg demanded. "What's going on?"

Erin looked at him. "You don't know who they are, do you?"

"More of Nëna's Albanian offspring?"

With her good hand, Erin gripped Stieg's forearm. "Now look," she ordered.

And he did.

The Viking in him wanted to scream and throw rocks before getting weapons and killing everyone in a thirty-five-mile radius. But the street kid . . . the street kid pretended not to be bothered. Pretended not to notice.

That's what you did when you saw horror. You pretended not to notice and you kept walking. Except he couldn't walk. He couldn't leave.

Stieg grabbed Erin's hand and pulled it off his arm.

"Now you see," she whispered.

"Yeah. But I didn't need to."

"What did you do to your friend, Crow?" one of them asked.

"She showed him what you are," Nëna guessed. "She showed him the truth. Where did a little bitch like you learn such a skill?"

"Mother Berisha," one of them chided. "Please. Let's not be rude. There's no point in being rude."

Stieg winced. This was getting so weird.

"Perhaps if we introduce ourselves," another suggested.

The handsome man smiled, but Stieg had seen his true face. He could never forget that.

"I'm Death," he said simply. "These are my brothers . . . War, Famine, and Pestilence. And yes, we're the Four Horsemen of the Apocalypse."

Stieg had never really thought that Jace's grandmother— or anyone for that matter—would be on such friendly terms with the Four Horsemen of the Apocalypse. Yet there they were. All four of them. Eating the woman's food. Leaning against the woman's brick wall. Relaxing in her home like this was a common thing. They'd clearly been there before.

Did she invite them over for coffee cake on Sundays? Who invited the Four Horsemen over for coffee cake?

He was suddenly really glad that Jace wasn't here. Something told him she would not be okay with any of this.

"So," Death went on, "sorry to interrupt, but where were we?"

"I'm trying to talk to the idiot now," Nëna complained, pointing to one of the chairs by the table. "But she's being a little—"

"Ahhh, Mother Berisha, no," Famine quickly intervened. "Let's keep this civil."

Pestilence, holding the apple he was eating in his mouth, dragged a chair over to Nëna's side. He waited for her to sit before he went back to lounging near his brothers and eating.

That's when Stieg realized what her finger pointing had meant. It meant *Get me a chair*.

Erin gawked at the Christian God's harbingers. "Seriously?"

"What?" Death asked. "We're known for our politeness. At least until we are forced to unleash hell on earth because you humans have no self-control. But until that time . . . we're polite."

"And charming," War tossed in as he put another spoonful of low-fat yogurt into his mouth.

"Yogurt?" Stieg finally had to ask. "Really?"

"What? I like yogurt."

"Now," Nëna said, leaning forward, her elbows resting on her crossed thin legs, one finger pointed at Erin, "I know how you can get at least part of the way to where you need to go."

"Does it involve your sacrifice? Because then I am so in."

War laughed around his yogurt while his brothers just chuckled.

"If my granddaughter didn't need you, I'd turn you inside out, Crow."

"Bring it," Erin quietly challenged, throwing out one arm because the other was still too damaged to move without excruciating pain.

Nothing worried Stieg more than Erin being quiet. The woman was rarely quiet. Erin was boisterous and rude to people she cared about. So a quiet Erin meant she was plotting . . . plotting something very bad.

Stieg tightened his grip on Erin, keeping her pinned to his lap, which meant he couldn't help fix her shoulder.

With a sigh, Death tossed the core of his fruit into a nearby trash can. "Before you two ladies decide to kill each other, perhaps I should point out what's going on right at this moment. At this moment . . . Gabriel is practicing his trumpet. Which I can assure you, no one is happy about."

"He's not very good," Pestilence admitted. "Personally, I've always pushed for Satchmo to blow the final trumpet at the beginning of End Times, but Gabriel overheard and got kind of pissed, then we got in a fight . . . it was not pretty."

Famine shrugged. "Well, you know he gets touchy about that sort of thing."

"It's not like I suggested just *anybody*. I suggested Louis Armstrong. Who is better than Louis Armstrong?"

Erin raised her working hand. "I am about to set *everything* in a ten-mile radius on fire . . . so could we all just get to the point here?"

The four brothers glanced at each other, then Death stepped close, leaning down until he was eye to eye with Erin. "Once Gullveig sets off Ragnarok, then the End of Times for everyone begins—and there will be no stopping it. Whether you have a god you believe in or not."

"I know."

He stood tall, gazing down at her. "And the only thing that may possibly stop her"—he pointed at Erin—"is you."

"I know that, too," she said simply. "And I don't know about the rest of you, but," Erin finally yelled out, "*I personally find that extremely horrifying!*"

Now Stieg knew why Erin had gone after Jace's grandmother like a pit bull after a steak. *Fear.*

Not general fear, but the fear of failure. She wouldn't just be failing her friends, she'd be failing the universe. That was a lot of stress to put on one person.

Even when that one person was Erin Amsel.

Death crouched in front of her. If you couldn't see his real face—and Stieg didn't allow himself to see the real faces of any of the Four Horsemen, it was too traumatic, even for a Viking—then he looked like a model from one of those outdoor catalogs for rich people. A good-looking surfer whose face hadn't been completely damaged by the sun yet.

"If we thought for a second that you didn't have a chance, War would be in his armor, Pestilence in his bubonic plague–covered robes, I'd be carrying my scythe around, and Famine would be nothing but skin and bones."

"It's not a good look on me," Famine tossed in.

"But we're not, because *you*, Erin Amsel, daughter of a long line of very irritating women, have a shot. One shot, but it's more than most. But it will only work if you take that shot. If you take that risk."

Erin frowned, appearing confused. "Of course I'll do it. I never said I wouldn't."

"Then what's the problem?"

Erin pointed at Nëna. "She is."

Nëna threw up her hands. "What did *I* do?"

"You exist!"

Death, without even looking at Jace's grandmother, raised two fingers on his right hand at her and warned, "Don't even think about it."

Cracking her knuckles, Nëna lowered her hands back into her lap. Stieg didn't even want to think about what spell she'd been planning to release.

War tossed his empty yogurt container and plastic spoon into the trash, walked over to Stieg and Erin's side, and took hold of Erin's arm. As Stieg began to stand in order to pull her away from him, the very large man barked, "Calm down, Northman. Just trying to help."

Stieg sat back in the chair, but his muscles tensed and

he had the overwhelming desire to start killing . . . everything.

"Breathe through it, Northman," War suggested, the smirk on his face making Stieg want to cut his head off and wear his intestines around his neck. "Me being so close," War went on as he gripped Erin's wrist with one hand and her shoulder with the other, "is bringing out your natural combat instincts. But what I find fascinating is"—his head tilted to the side, his gaze sizing up Erin—"that I don't seem to affect you at all."

Then he yanked her shoulder back into place.

Erin let out a roar and suddenly her blade was in her hand and she almost rammed it into his eye, but Stieg caught her before she made contact with the harbinger, pulling her hand back and twisting until the blade dropped.

"That hurt," Erin growled at him.

War stepped back, unfazed. "That should feel better soon with the way you Crows heal and all. And you're welcome."

Once War moved away, the desire to destroy all fled Stieg's body and he panted like he'd just been in a five-mile race.

"Are you all right?" Erin grumbled, rubbing her now-healing shoulder.

"How are *you* all right?"

She gave a one-shouldered shrug. "I told you . . . I don't let little things annoy me."

"We, the harbingers of the Apocalypse, are a little thing to you?" Pestilence asked.

Erin was silent a moment, glancing off before replying, "Pretty much."

"That is . . . impressive."

Death grinned. "She's perfect."

"You better explain how I'm going to get into the Nine Worlds and steal that stupid sword."

The Four Horsemen looked at Nëna and it pissed Erin off that she needed this woman's help, but she had no choice. Not anymore. The Four Horsemen wouldn't be coming to any Crow, much less her, unless they truly had no other option.

"Tell her, Mother Berisha," Death pushed when the old woman didn't reply. "You brought us here. You have to know it's never a good idea to waste *our* time."

Nëna rubbed her chin. "You'll need the Key," she told Erin.

"What key?"

"*The* Key. When Hel sends her Carrion up from Helheim, she ensures that at least one of them is the Key who can make sure her troops can return to her when their job is done."

"So this Key will take me to Helheim?" That would be good. From there Erin could pretty much amble on over to Corpse Shore.

"No. Hel isn't that stupid. But it'll get you closer than Asgard. Much closer. But you'll still have to make your way through several worlds before you reach Nidhogg's domain."

"And that dragon is *not* friendly," Pestilence stated.

"No dragons are friendly," Death reminded his brother. "But let's face it, we've got the worst one."

"Well, unlike the Nordics' Nidhogg, ours has seven heads and a crown on each head. Those crowns make him mighty haughty."

Famine waved that away. "That's Lucifer's fault. He's raised a very narcissistic child. It's a real shame."

"I don't think it's the crowns, personally," Pestilence debated. "I think it's all the horns. That many horns just makes a male—of any species—cocky. No pun intended," he joked.

His brothers laughed with him until Erin cut in, "I'm sorry, but can we get back to *me*? And the Key?"

Death lifted his hands, nodded. "Sorry. Sorry. Our bad."

Nëna started again. "You'll need to find the key among the Carrion."

"Because that's so easy," Erin drily shot back.

"You can't miss him. He'll wear Hel's rune on the palm of his hand. All the others have her rune burned into their necks or foreheads."

"And then what? Cut his hand off?"

Nëna blinked. "Yes. Once you have his hand—"

"Have you ever fought the Carrion?" Erin demanded of the old woman. "Ever stood face-to-face with them?"

Nëna sighed. "Can't say that I've had the pleasure—"

"I have. And the Carrion don't die easy. I also don't think the Key is going to start handing off body parts to help me out."

"You wanted a way in, Crow. That's the way."

Erin looked off. She felt so damn irritated. That's when Death moved in close, again crouching in front of her. Stieg went tense beneath her, having Death so near probably turning him into a suicidal mess.

"You need to understand something," Death said softly. "You *are* the only one who can do this. Sweet Jacinda may still be looking for another option, but she was right from the beginning—you are it. And if you don't do this, I promise you, Gabriel's horn will blow and we, my brothers and I, will unleash every minion of hell upon this world. We will tear it apart and leave nothing but the unrighteous behind. So, you decide. Do you do what you can? Or let every religion's end-of-the-world scenario play out to the devastation of those who—most likely—don't deserve it. Most likely."

As a "most likely," Erin couldn't let that happen. She wouldn't.

"All right," Erin said, again focusing on Jace's grandmother. "Tell me what I need to do."

CHAPTER FIFTEEN

He didn't take her back to the Bird House, but Stieg Engstrom didn't spirit her away to far-off northern shores, either. Instead, they stopped at a nearby In-N-Out burger place.

"I'm hungry," he informed her before getting out of his truck.

Erin didn't follow him inside the fast-food restaurant, but she found an empty table outside under a big red and yellow umbrella and sat down. Grabbing a few napkins out of the container, she took a small pencil out of her pocket and began to draw on the napkin. She didn't really think about what she was going to draw. She just let her hand do what it did best.

It was lunchtime, so the place was pretty busy, but Erin didn't mind. It gave her time to relax. Although her shoulder still hurt like a bitch, it was already healing. Besides, it wasn't the first time it had been yanked out of its socket. Hell, it hadn't been the first time Stieg was the one who'd yanked it.

An open cardboard container filled with food landed in front of her and Erin finally looked up. Stieg had his own open container. Actually, he had two of them. And chocolate shakes for each of them.

Erin focused on the food. "You got me two Double-Doubles and two fries? That doesn't seem excessive to you?"

"I figured you were hungry," he said simply.

"Well . . . thank you."

He shrugged and began to eat like a Viking. Other patrons turned around to watch until Stieg caught them—and growled.

Most everyone spun back around and, as he dropped his head to continue feeding, Stieg smiled. A real one. Erin didn't remember him ever smiling before. He mostly sneered or stared. Smiling was not his thing.

Except, apparently, when he was terrorizing others.

Of course, that just made Erin actually like the big idiot. She chuckled a little. Maybe Kera was right. There had to be something wrong with her.

Stieg, having finished off two Double-Double burgers, could enjoy the third more slowly. While he consumed the burger, he used his free hand to reach over and picked up the napkin, frowning at Erin's artwork. "Jace's grandmother does not have horns. Or a crown. Or seven heads."

"Are we sure?"

He studied the napkin a little longer. "It's nice, though. Disturbing, but nice."

"Thanks."

"I like how each of her faces is just another example of her hateful disdain."

"It's all I saw."

He pointed at her food. "Eat."

"I'm not hungry."

"You have to eat."

"Why?"

Stieg gazed at her a bit before he finally answered. "I don't know. Isn't that what people say? You know, when bad things happen?"

"I don't know. I've never been asked before to go to the fiery pits of Helheim."

"Helheim isn't fiery. It's just boring, with no chance for honor. It's the Christians who have to burn."

"But what if somebody is truly evil?"

"That's a concept my people didn't really worry about. If you betrayed your own men in battle or unjustly murdered someone, then you . . ." His voice tapered off and he quickly focused on something in the distance. But he didn't really see anything; he was just avoiding her.

"What?" she pushed.

"Uh . . . if you are deemed by the gods to be truly evil, your bloated corpse is devoured until Ragnarok by . . . uh . . ."

"By who?"

He finally looked at her, face cringing before he spoke. "Nidhogg."

"The dragon that has the sword I need to get?"

"Yeahhhh . . . I didn't really think this conversation through," he muttered.

Stieg watched Erin grab her container of fries and shovel them in her mouth.

"I'm sure it'll be fine," he told her.

"Liar."

"I thought you didn't let the little things bother you."

"I don't. But facing a dragon that feeds on the corpses of the dead . . . not really a little thing, is it?"

"War just fixed your arm while you chatted with Death. I'm sure you can handle this, too."

"That was different."

"How?"

"They clearly don't *want* the end of the world. They are too happy surfing and sleeping with people who have no idea that beneath their beautiful façades are nightmare scenarios."

"So? What's your point?"

"I'm comfortable around the Four Horsemen because I know what they want. I've looked them in the eyes. I've talked to them."

"You were able to size them up."

"Exactly. I don't know anything about this dragon. No one does. He's been living outside of Muspellheim—"

"Niflheim."

Erin scratched her forehead. "Honestly, dude, there are too many *heims* with you people, but fine. He's been living outside Niflheim for an age and even Odin won't go near him. Only Ratatosk talks to him. *Ratatosk*. How can I handle that when I don't know what I'm facing?"

"I don't know."

She frowned. "Shockingly . . . I appreciate your honesty. Doesn't help me, but I appreciate it."

Stieg ate another burger and ran through some ideas. "What about the gods?" he asked, wiping his hands on a paper napkin.

"What about them?"

"Maybe they can help. Provide knowledge."

"Do you really think Odin will help?"

"No. Of course not."

"Freyja?"

"Probably not."

"Idunn?"

"Not after you juggled her golden apples."

"They were just sitting there . . . what did she expect me to do?"

"*Not* juggle her golden apples?"

"Whatever?" Erin dismissed him with a hand wave and a grab at more fries. "Heimdall?"

"He'll never leave his post on Bifrost to come here and help humans."

"Frigg?"

"Not since you referred to her as one of Odin's whores and asked her if she was a stripper, too."

"I still don't see what the big deal is about that."

"She's his wife."

A few more fries, then, "Sif?"

"Not since the fistfight."

"Ull?"

"Not since the fistfight."

"Hoenir?"

"You and the god of silence? *You?*"

"All right. Fine. Forseti?"

"Not since you called him a lawyer and spit at him."

"He's the god of justice and reconciliation, which is kind of a lawyer, and I *did not* spit at him. I was coughing and I—."

They stared at each other a moment, until she finally admitted, "Fine. I spit at him."

She reached for more fries but she'd finished them, so Stieg pushed his fries over.

After eating a few more, Erin asked, "Well, who does that leave?"

"A lot. We Vikings have a *lot* of gods."

"Any of those gods willing to help us?"

"Well, it's not just you being you, which doesn't help—"

"Thank you."

"—but also you're a . . . well . . . a . . ."

"A Jew?"

"No! They don't care about that. But you are a Crow. And that they can't let go."

"*That* is what they have a problem with? The fact that I'm a Crow?"

"They're not fans of Crows. You've been known to kill their human representatives."

"Fights they started."

"And you're all descendants of . . . um . . ."

"Say it."

"Our slaves."

"There you go."

"I'm not saying that's okay," Stieg argued. "I'm just saying what their logic is."

"So because of some petty feelings they have over the Crows, they're going to let the world burn?"

"Probably. But they're *gods*. What do you expect? Petty is what they do."

Erin pushed the remainder of fries away and wiped her hands off with a napkin. "Well, there is one god you haven't mentioned. A god who might help."

"A god you haven't pissed off?"

"Actually . . . yeah. There is one."

"Who?"

Erin smiled and Stieg's shoulders slumped. "No."

"We don't have a choice."

"You could apologize to one of the others."

"Could. Won't. Besides, even when I do apologize, no one ever believes me."

"Gee, I wonder why."

"Come on," Erin coaxed, getting to her feet and picking up what was left of their food and containers to put in the trash. "Might as well get this over with."

"You better appreciate what I'm doing for you."

"Nope," she immediately replied, finally laughing again. "Don't appreciate it at all!"

CHAPTER SIXTEEN

With his thumb marking the spot in the book he was reading, Ski walked down the hall to the front door. He pulled it open and smiled at the woman standing there. "Well, hello."

Erin didn't reply. She was too busy staring up at the sky.

Curious, Ski stepped past the doorway and stood beside her, looking up. He growled in annoyance before yelling, "Bear Ingolfsson, you put that Raven down right—no! No! *Not like—*"

Stieg Engstrom landed facedown, and both Ski and Erin cringed at the sound of it. The crunching.

"Oh, God," Erin muttered, "I think he killed him."

But Ravens were made of tougher stuff. It was never easy to kill a Raven and Ski knew it. The Protectors had been trying for centuries to lay waste to the Raven Clan with very little success. They were not immortal, but Odin had given them incredibly hard heads and strong bones.

Even now, Engstrom was moving, using his arms to push his body up.

Bear landed behind him, pulling his white wings into his body as he did.

"What were you thinking?" Ski demanded. "Unleashing your wings during the day? Attacking a Raven unprovoked?"

"I was provoked!"

"How?"

"The way he looked at me was *filled* with provocation."

Ski didn't even have time to roll his eyes at that bit of ridiculousness because Stieg had pushed himself off the ground and, face bloody, was charging Bear.

Bear tried to grab the Raven around the waist but just as his arms reached out, Engstrom's entire body flipped up and over the much bigger man until he was behind Bear; Engstrom's arms wrapped around Bear's throat in a move that would kill most Protectors pretty quickly, but Bear had a neck so thick it was hard to find shirts that fit him properly.

Ski desperately tried to separate the pair, but they were snarling and growling at each other; Engstrom trying to kill Bear; Bear trying to toss Engstrom off so he could kill him.

"Stop it!" Ski ordered. "Both of you! Now!"

Then they all froze, none of them willing to move.

The Crow had climbed up Bear like she was climbing an old redwood and pressed the rune-covered blades hand-forged by Vig Rundstöm against the jugulars of Stieg and Bear. And while her hands were busy with her weapons, it was Erin's exceptionally strong thighs that kept her attached to an unwilling Bear. There would be no shaking her off.

Even worse, one slight move of that blade would bleed both men out in seconds. And they all knew it.

Also, this was Erin Amsel. Not Kera. Not Jace. Not even Chloe, who was more of a puncher. But Erin Amsel.

The woman had gutted Thor once, a move he still hadn't forgiven her for, even if it was at a Valkyrie party where he got drunk on mead and then got a little "handsy."

"Gentlemen," Erin practically purred, no anger in her voice at all. She was enjoying this. "Don't tempt me to put a stop to this the only way I know how. Let's all just calm down."

Neither man budged. Even Bear, who was beginning to turn an interesting shade of blue.

Erin looked first at Engstrom. "You know what I'll do to you," she said, immediately dismissing him and focusing instead on Bear. "And when you're dead," she warned, "I'll make sure to burn your books. Every. Last. One. Of. Them."

Always worried about the books the Protectors safeguarded with their very lives if necessary, Bear quickly lifted his hands off Engstrom's big arms. But the Raven still didn't back off . . . until Erin pushed her blade against his throat. Not enough to kill him, but enough to get her point across.

A thin line of blood trailed down his neck. Shocked, he unwrapped his arms from Bear and stepped away. He touched the spot where she'd cut him, his hurt and angry gaze locked on Erin's face as she climbed down from a coughing Bear.

"You . . . you . . ."

"What? You thought I was kidding?" Erin asked Stieg. "You two were acting like assholes." She turned away from the sputtering man and faced Ski. "I need a favor."

"Anything."

"I need to talk to Tyr. Can you summon him?"

"Oh, a summoning ceremony isn't necessary. He's in the backyard playing with Jace's dog."

"Your god just . . . hangs out here?"

"Yeah." Ski shrugged. "When he can."

Erin began to say something else, but seemed to change her mind, walking off with a shake of her head into the house.

Bear and the Raven began to follow, but Ski quickly stopped them. "I'll just say this once . . . Jace is in the library. If you two get into it when she's this concerned about her friend, you risk the books," he pointed out to Bear. "And you risk having her tear the skin from your hide and the wings from your back, Raven. Understand?"

With mutual Viking grunts of agreement, the three men entered the house and went to see what Erin Amsel could possibly want from the mighty god Tyr.

Erin walked through the Protectors' house, amused at the way they all seemed to sense her presence. They came out of rooms, down the big, marble stairs, heads peeking around doors. She felt like a fox walking into a henhouse and making all the herding dogs panic.

Erin stopped at the big library. It was the biggest library she'd ever seen in a private home and the largest room in the entire mansion. She was sure the Protectors had gutted a large portion of the wing so they had a lot of space for their precious books.

Erin appreciated the work they did. She'd always liked old books. She liked how they felt in her hands, the binding, the paper, the artistic quality of each one. But she didn't let the Protectors know that. It was much more fun to torture them, which was why she faced the big glass doors of the library and cracked her knuckles. That was all she did.

But apparently that was all she needed to do. Because she was suddenly surrounded. Several of the Protectors stood right in front of the library, ready to sacrifice their bodies to her flames if it meant saving their books.

Now that was devotion.

Laughing a little, she moved on, walking down the hallway until she found sliding glass doors that led her outside to the backyard.

That's where she found the Protectors' "mighty" god Tyr. On his back in the grass, Jace's funny-looking puppy standing by Tyr's big head, licking the god's laughing face.

It was not what Erin expected, but she had to admit, it made her feel much better about her choice of which god to talk to.

She'd started walking toward him when a hand clamped on her arm and pulled her back.

"And where do you think you're going, young lady?"

Young lady? Really? "To start some shit!" she replied eagerly. "Wanna come with me?"

Clucking his tongue against his teeth, Haldor wrapped his arm around Erin's waist and carried her back into the house. "You will not bother our god with your . . ." He struggled to find the right word, so Erin decided to help him. "My beauty?" she asked, grinning. "My charm? My effervescence? My . . . *je ne sais quoi*?"

"No," he replied, voice flat. "None of those things."

"What's happening?" Stieg asked as he came around the corner, his hand still pressed against the tiny wound she'd given him on his throat.

Good Lord. What a big Viking baby!

"I'm trying to prevent this demoness from irritating our mighty god Tyr," Haldor informed Stieg. "And what are you doing here, *non-thinker*?"

Erin bit the inside of her cheek to stop the laughter, but wow, did she love the way Haldor had spit that out . . . like it was the absolute *worst* insult he could think of.

"Is Tyr back there?" Stieg asked her.

"Yes," Erin replied. "And he is literally playing with Jace's dog. *Literally.*"

Using his free hand, Stieg pushed Haldor aside and used his body to force Erin back into the yard. She stumbled past the threshold.

Tyr looked up from the puppy now on his lap. "A Crow?" he asked, his voice making everything sort of . . . vibrate.

Erin briefly wondered if the scientists who monitored California for earthquakes were staring at their fancy controls and wondering if the "big one" was coming right at that moment.

"What's a Crow doing in the sacred space of our books?"

"Big reader of books, are ya, Tyr?"

"Be nice," Stieg warned, holding the sliding door shut with his hand while the Protectors on the other side tried to pry it open.

"I was nice."

"No. You were sarcastic and mocking. Try something different. And no juggling or fistfights."

Stieg was right. They needed Tyr. So she took a deep breath, let it out, and moved closer to the very moral and upstanding war god—a combination one simply did not hear about very often.

"I need information. And I think you're the only one who can help me."

Rubbing the puppy's ears, the god looked directly at Erin, and his eyes narrowed in recognition. "Oh, it's *you*."

She shrugged. "It's me."

"Skuld's vicious little fire starter."

"I prefer flame master."

"Of course you do."

Tyr placed Jace's puppy on his shoulder and stood. And the god kept standing. He wasn't even in his "true" god form. He was in his mostly human one. And yet he was about eight feet tall and so wide.

Like the Great Wall of China.

And that wall was now standing in front of and over her, staring coldly down into her face.

Except for his size, Tyr looked more like an ex-roadie for

Led Zeppelin or Alice Cooper. He had on a very worn T-shirt with the logo from the *Heavy Metal* movie, torn black jeans, and black steel-toed boots. He'd braided his gray and brown hair into one long plait that rested casually over his right shoulder and his face had one big scar from his cheek down across his mouth and under his chin. So deep his thick beard couldn't even cover it. The hair had refused to grow. He had runes tattooed on his neck and arms, and the right hand that had been torn off by the wolf Fenrir was replaced by a metal glove, also covered in runes.

The god couldn't *be* more Viking, even in his modern— for the seventies—clothes.

"So what do you want, little Crow? What do you want to ask the mighty Tyr?"

And humble! Just like most gods.

Erin sighed. She'd hoped for better from the lesser-known god. "I need your vast knowledge."

"There's a library full of vast knowledge right in there. Why bother me?"

"I'm not a big reader," she replied.

Tyr stared down at her. "Who admits that? In public, I mean?"

"Plus, I'm not allowed in your precious library. Your men are very bitchy about it, too."

"Maybe you shouldn't threaten them so."

"I'm a Crow." She grinned. "That's what we do."

The god rolled his brown eyes. "Fine, Crow. Tell me what you want to know and I'll judge whether you are worthy to know it."

"Fair enough. I need to know about—"

Arms around her stopped Erin's words; sobs against her neck had her cringing.

Erin reached her hands up—the most she could do with her arms pinned at her sides—and patted Jace.

The god's expression changed instantly. "My little Jace," he said, awkwardly patting Erin's sister-Crow on the back. "What has you so sad?"

"I'm killing her!"

Erin cringed. She had no idea how to handle this. She looked over her shoulder to see if Stieg could help, but he was still holding the sliding door shut, which didn't make sense since Jace had managed to get past him.

"What are you doing?" Erin asked Stieg.

"Giving you time to get your answers from Tyr. What does it look like I'm doing?"

"Holding a door shut for absolutely no reason."

"What?" Stieg turned his head and saw that all the Protectors were gone. "Uh-oh."

They landed on him in one big pile, Protectors pinning Stieg to the ground with their big feet—the same way owls pinned their prey. It was not pretty.

The only one who didn't attack Stieg was Ski Eriksen. He came around the side of the house—probably the same way Jace had come—and moved behind his woman. With gentle hands, he attempted to pull her off Erin, but Jace just held on tighter, which did nothing but make Erin feel even more uncomfortable.

And trapped. Erin felt seriously trapped.

That's when they appeared, attacking the Protectors with their talons, squawking in their faces, and shitting on their heads. The only ones they didn't assault were Erin, Jace, and Stieg.

And Jace's dog, of course. Because none of the Crows—human and bird—wanted to deal with a raging Brodie Hawaii. The dog protected the pup like he was her own.

Ski stumbled back and hid his eyes from groping talons ready to yank them right out of their sockets while several landed on the back of Tyr's neck and pecked at the god's head.

Jace finally released Erin and stepped back. Horrified, she pointed an accusing finger at Erin. "You call them off right now, Erin Amsel!"

"I didn't know I'd called them!" she argued.

"I don't care! Do something!"

Erin, unsure what to do, raised her arms and loudly stated, "That's enough! Back off!"

And the Crows did. But they didn't go far, flying up into nearby trees and perching on branches. Keeping a close eye on the humans they trusted and the humans they didn't.

"Sorry," Erin said to the Protectors, several of which must have been hit by birds with diarrhea, they were so covered.

Snarling and grumbling, those Protectors went back into the house. Most likely to bathe.

Ski first opened one eye, then another. When he realized he was no longer at risk, he adjusted the eyeglasses he wore, only to realize that one of the lenses had been shattered by a determined crow.

The Protector's gaze locked on Erin and, nodding her head toward Jace, she whispered, "She started it."

Stieg managed to jump between Erin and Jace before the taller Crow could tear into her sister.

"I warned her, Stieg!" Jace roared between clenched teeth. "*I warned her if she used that excuse again—*"

"I know. I know. She's ridiculous and shallow. But we need her, right? We do need her."

"Shallow?" Erin demanded behind him. "I'm not at all shallow. I am filled with love and caring and—"

Stieg reached behind him, wrapped his hand around Erin's face, and shoved her away.

Her annoying laughter as she flew back proved he'd made the right choice.

"Let me handle this, Jace. Okay?"

Managing to rein in her rage—somehow—Jace gave a curt nod. "See me before you leave."

"We promise."

Jace stormed back to the house, Ski following, his smirk making Stieg want to slap the living hell out of him. But he had bigger issues than his righteous hatred of the know-it-all Protector.

Once they were alone with the god, Stieg faced Erin.

She'd gotten to her feet and was wiping dirt off her tight ass. "That was rude," she complained.

"Quiet." He focused on Tyr. "We need to know about Nidhogg."

The god studied Stieg. "What is this 'we,' Raven?"

"Yeah," Erin began, "what is this—"

"*Quiet*." Stieg barked again.

"Rude!"

"I'm helping her," Stieg explained to the curious god. "By Odin's beard, I think we both can agree she clearly needs all the help she can get, don't we?"

Tyr glanced back at Erin, sighed, and nodded. "Yes. She really does."

Laughing, Erin threw up her hands. "Hey!"

"Quiet!" both males barked at her.

Erin fell silent, but not before muttering, "*Rude*."

Bear walked into the library with her dog, Lev, under his arm, and Jace knew immediately something was wrong.

"What?" she asked, standing up from the table covered in ancient books and documents she'd been scouring just a few minutes prior, desperately searching for any information that could save her friend from unavoidable death.

"I went out to check on our mighty Tyr, but he, Erin, and

the slow-witted idiot"—Jace rolled her eyes because she knew she had to sit through Raven-related insults after what had just happened—"were gone."

"Erin and Stieg are gone?" That was surprising because Stieg had promised he'd stop by before leaving. Stieg never broke his promises. To anyone, much less Jace.

"They're all gone. And Tyr was staying for dinner," Bear went on to explain. "Haldor's making his beef stew and Tyr always stays for Haldor's stew."

"Are you saying Tyr took Erin somewhere . . . away?"

Bear shrugged his big shoulders. "I guess. But he left the dog." He took Lev in both hands and held him out for Jace to get a good look at. Not to hand off to her, just so that she could see her dog and know he was safe. It was becoming harder and harder to pry sweet Lev away from the big man each night. Jace, however, was determined to get Bear his own dog. She simply had to find the right one.

Deciding she wouldn't worry about what Ski now called "the Lev issue" or about Erin and Stieg, she suggested, "I'm sure this will be fine. I'm sure Tyr merely took them somewhere to talk. To help them get that information they wanted from him. See, gentlemen?" she said to Ski's nearby brethren. "Erin is thinking ahead and planning on how she will handle all this. I'm . . . I'm sure it will all be fine."

"Except," Bear felt the need to add, "our mighty Tyr is now trapped alone with a Raven—he hates Ravens—and, of course, he's trapped with Erin. *Your* Erin."

"Ooh," Borgsten said, wincing.

"What ooh?" Jace demanded. "Why are you oohing?"

"Well, Erin is the one that got Fulla—the goddess of fertility, known to be really sweet and caring—to spit in her face."

"That was a . . . a . . . misunderstanding."

"But then Fulla put a bounty on her head with the Giant Killers."

"That's how they got those unfortunate burns," Haldor reminded them.

"And at the time she'd only been a Crow, for what?" Bear asked. "Six months?"

"Three," Ski admitted.

Jace sighed and pulled her cell phone from her back jeans pocket. "I better call Kera . . ."

CHAPTER SEVENTEEN

Erin turned once, her head all the way back, her mouth slightly open, gazing at the shelves that not only ran from floor to ceiling but at the top of the ceiling. Somehow the books stayed in place no matter where they were placed and ancient Protectors flitted here and there, miles above, grabbing books they needed for whatever reason. She'd never seen anything like it before. "Wow."

"Yeah," Stieg muttered. "What you said."

"Sit," Tyr ordered. He'd dropped into the large chair at the head of the big table and placed his feet on the worn wood. He slapped his hand against the top and yelled out, "Food! Drink!"

Servants rushed out with wine and platters of food, placing them down and scurrying off.

"Eat," he ordered.

Another servant placed a horn of mead in his hand and the god watched them while he sipped.

"You're not hungry?" he asked when Erin didn't dive in.

"You're not eating," she offered.

"It's stew night. Haldor's stew. But you should eat. You'll need your strength against Nidhogg."

"Well, we just had In-N-Out, so—" Erin stopped and gawked at Stieg as he sat down and dug into the feast. "Dude, you just ate!"

"I'm hungry again."

"Wow."

Tyr pointed his horn at Erin. "So you want to know about Nidhogg."

Erin took the chair closest to the god. "Yeah. I need to know how to deal with him."

"Deal with him? He's not a mere human, little Crow."

"So he's a god?"

"He's not that, either. Dragons have their own . . . pantheon. Their own world. Their own rules. Their own universes."

"So . . . Nidhogg is trapped here?"

"No. He can come and go as he pleases. Our Nine Worlds hold no sway over him one way or another."

"He chooses to—"

"Yes. He chooses to sit on Corpse Shore, eating the bloated corpses of the dead, listening to the crazed rantings of a squirrel telling him what the eagle at the top of *Yggdrasil* says about him until the day comes when he can wrap his body around this world and crush it during Ragnarok. That is the life he has chosen for himself."

"Why would . . . why would anyone choose that life?"

"You expect me to understand the logic of dragons? *I* barely understand the logic of you people, and humans are stupid. So very, very stupid."

"We're not the one starting Ragnarok. That would be one of *you* people."

Stieg suddenly coughed and muttered under his breath, "Juggling."

Erin and Tyr frowned at each other and she asked Stieg, "What?"

"Juggling."

"What about it?"

"That's how you get in trouble. Juggling. Fistfights. Pissing off the gods."

"In other words," Tyr said, smiling, "stop being a dick."

She giggled a little. "But I'm so good at it."

A very large, ancient Protector dropped to the ground, pulled his wings in, and stalked to the table. He was dressed in furs and leather, weapons hanging from his waist.

"Why did you allow them here, mighty Tyr?" He sneered at Stieg. "A worthless Raven"—he pointed at Erin—"and a demoness Crow? Near our precious books?"

"Who I invite to this table is my own business, Ingjard Ingolfsson."

Stieg and Erin passed quick glances. *Bear's ancestor.*

And it was like Erin couldn't help herself. She lifted her forefinger . . . and lit it on fire. Not her whole arm. Not her entire body. Both things she could easily do. But just one forefinger.

And it was enough. Like Bear Ingolfsson, Ingjard dove backward, wings out again, arms spread wide, attempting to use his own body as a shield. "The books!" he bellowed to his brothers. "*Protect the books!*"

As Stieg and Tyr shook their heads, Erin curled her forefinger back into a fist, the flame snuffed out, and she hunched over in her chair. "You're right," she laughed hysterically. "I am a dick!"

"What do you mean, Tyr took her?" Ski watched his brothers analyze Kera's question.

Finally Borgsten stated, "I don't see how we can make

that particular statement any clearer." He glanced at the others. "Do you, brothers?"

"No," they all replied.

Kera dug her hands into her hair and Jace glared at him.

"What?" Ski asked.

"You guys are not helping."

"But we're not making it worse," Borgsten asserted.

Jace stamped her foot. "Danski Eriksen!"

"Kera," he said, grabbing the War General's attention, "I'm sure Erin will be fine."

"But *why* would Tyr take her?"

"We don't know. But we do know that Erin and that Raven—"

"His name is Stieg," Jace petulantly reminded him.

"—came here wanting to see Tyr. To talk to him. Ask questions. They didn't tell us the questions."

"Why didn't they all stay here to ask their questions?" Kera wisely inquired.

Ski turned to his brother. "Bear? Would you like to take that one?"

"The Raven *provoked* me," Bear growled.

Kera dropped her head into her hands. "So," she said through her fingers, "you're saying the only one who can *possibly* save us from Ragnarok is off with a god . . . and Stieg Engstrom?"

Jace let out a breath. "Pretty much."

"Great." Kera lifted her head and snarled, "*Just great!*"

"If you can't help us with the dragon," Stieg asked, licking chicken juice off his fingers, "what can you do for us?"

"Why should I do anything for you or this Crow?" Tyr picked up a loaf of bread, then put it back. It seemed the god really wanted to save his appetite for Haldor's stew.

How good is this stew? Stieg wondered. Now he wanted to try it.

"Because," Stieg replied, working hard to sound sincere, "it's the right thing to do."

One brow raised, Erin looked at Stieg and he gave a small shrug. She quickly turned her head, her lips twisted as she tried not to laugh.

"Oh, please," Tyr said with an eye roll. "You can do better than that, Raven."

Erin leaned over and placed her hand on the god's knee. "Whatever you need, Tyr," she said suggestively, "Stieg can give it to you."

Stieg slammed his fist on the table, the sound reverberating throughout the hall, panicking the Protectors and sending them scurrying to protect their books.

"You're pimping me out?" Stieg bellowed, not caring who heard.

"Aren't you willing to make sacrifices for the good of humanity?" Erin asked before she had to duck. "Did you just throw a chicken leg at me?"

"Next it'll be the table and I won't miss!"

"Stop it! Both of you!" Tyr ordered. He motioned to his Protectors. "Out! All of you!"

"But Mighty Tyr—" Ingjard began.

"Out!"

Reluctantly the Protectors abandoned their books, heading out into the fresh, cold air of Asgard.

"There is something I want, Crow. Something only you and your sister-Crows can provide."

"Blow jobs?" Erin asked.

Stieg shook his head. "What is wrong with you?"

"So many things," she admitted.

"Blow jobs I can get anywhere. I'm a mighty Viking god and damn good looking."

"True."

"But there's something else you Crows can provide."

"And that is . . . ?"

"Access."

"To?"

"Your library."

Erin blinked in surprise. "Our library? You want access to *our* library? Ski Eriksen said our library was a 'sad shack of pop culture frivolity.' "

"Yes," the god admitted. "I know."

"Oh, my God," Erin said, sitting back in her chair. "You want access to our Stephen King books!"

"Shhhhh!" Tyr said, using his hands to tell her to keep her voice down. "Yes!" he admitted. "Yes! Your Stephen Kings. Your Nora Roberts. Your Dan Browns. I want access to them all!" He suddenly grabbed her hand. "Tell me you have Agatha Christie," he begged.

Erin glanced at Stieg but, again, he could do nothing but shrug.

"Uh . . . yeah. I think we do. I think Tessa reads those. They probably sit right next to our H.P. Lovecrafts and our *Game of Thrones* collection."

Tyr gasped. "I've heard of those."

"*Everyone* has heard of those."

"Allow me to stop by and use your reading room when the mood strikes and I will give you something no one else can. Something that will help you on your journey."

"Yeah. Okay."

"But our deal must be between us."

Erin smirked. "You mean you don't want your snobby literature-loving Protectors to know that you got a thing for evil clowns and murder among the British gentry?"

"Exactly."

"Uh . . . yeah. Sure. We can do that."

"And you swear on your sword to keep the secret until your funeral pyre?"

"I don't have a sword, but I swear on my Second Life your secret is safe with me and my fellow Crows, Tyr, god of war and justice."

They shook hands and Tyr stood.

"Protectors!" he called out and they poured back into the hall through every opening the bronze building had. He motioned to Bear's ancestor, who quickly flew down and landed beside his god.

Tyr leaned over and whispered something in Ingjard's ear. Stieg laid his hand on the table knife that rested beside his plate, giving a small nod to Erin to prepare herself in case Tyr had changed his mind.

Still sitting in her chair, Erin rested her right heel on the seat, her arm around her leg where she had her weapons tied to her calf.

Ingjard reared back from his god, eyes wide. "But mighty—"

"Do it, Ingjard Ingolfsson."

Ingjard bowed his head and unleashed his wings. Taking to the air with one push, he traveled up and up until he reached the top level of those insane bookshelves. He seemed to know right where to go and returned to his god's side in a matter of seconds.

Using his arm, Tyr swiped dishes and food onto the floor until there was a clean space in front of Erin.

Very—*extremely*—reluctantly, Ingjard placed the book on the table. It was ancient. Bound in leather with silver accents.

Tyr opened the book, turning the pages until he reached the one he wanted. "Take it," he ordered.

Ingjard immediately gasped. "Tyr! No!"

Tyr held up his hand to silence his Protector.

"A book page?" Erin asked, sneering slightly. "Seriously?"

"Look at it, Crow. Open your eyes to what I'm giving you."

With a bored sigh, Erin leaned over and studied the page. After a few seconds, she leaned back, gulping. "Uh . . ."

"I can't get you in," Tyr told her. "You'll have to do that on your own. But once there . . . this will help you."

Erin nodded. "Yes. It will do that."

"Then we have a deal?"

"A deal we have."

"Then take it."

"Tyr!" Ingjard shook his head. "I can't allow—"

The god looked at his minion, and his eyes turned from calm brown to actual fire, forcing Ingjard to back up, head bowed.

Another Protector dropped down beside them, hands up to placate the angry god. Stieg knew, without even asking . . . it was Eriksen's ancestor. Not just from the look of him, but the demeanor.

"Now, now," the new Protector soothed. "Everyone just calm down." He placed his hand on his cowering brother's shoulder. "You know how our Ingjard is about books, mighty Tyr. That's why he's a Protector. But he understands this is more important than a book."

Yep. Definitely an Eriksen. And as smooth as silk, just like the one Stieg was stuck with.

"Ingjard, help the Crow to carefully remove that page." Eriksen gently pushed.

Ingjard nodded, but before he could make a move, Erin whipped out one of the blades she had secured to her calf, twirling the weapon with her fingers. "No need, gentlemen. I got it." She stood and pressed the blade to the precious book.

"You mad cow!" Ingjard cried out before Eriksen had a

chance to put his hand over his brother's mouth and push him back.

With obvious glee, Erin dragged the tip of her blade down the line of the book from the top to the very end. She returned the blade to the holster and pulled the page out from the book. Then, to add insult to injury, she folded it into fours and slipped it into the back pocket of her jeans. "All right!" she said, clapping her hands together and smiling. "Are we done?"

Ingjard Ingolfsson dropped to his knees with a wail that echoed throughout all of Asgard.

Stieg quickly turned away. He wanted to laugh so badly but that would have every Protector in the room coming down on him like an avenging horde. They couldn't touch Erin, but they could destroy Stieg without a worry. So he kept his mouth shut.

And it was the *hardest* thing he'd ever had to do in his entire life.

CHAPTER EIGHTEEN

Ski carefully returned the book he'd removed from the library. Sure it was exactly where it belonged, he turned—and faced Bear.

"You took that book out of this room?" Bear demanded, his angry eyes narrowed to slits, lips pinched, jaw clenched.

"Bear—"

"You, of all people, know that our books should *never* leave this room. This sacred space couldn't be more secure, and yet you risk our precious, precious books because you want to read in the bathtub!"

"I did not take it anywhere near a bathtub. I had it in the kitchen—"

"Kitchen? *Around all those condiments and Haldor's stew?*" he bellowed.

"Brother, brother, calm yourself." Ski placed his hand on Bear's shoulder. "I know protecting our books is your sacred destiny, but this entire house was built for the care and love of these precious books. Now"—he stepped in closer—"what's really bothering you?"

"I don't know." Bear put his hand over his heart. "I just

feel that something horrible has happened to a book somewhere that has my ancestors crying out in horror and pure
pain."

Ski lowered his hand and stepped back. "*Seriously?*"

"Yes, seriously!"

"My god, brother. We need to get you a dog."

"I have a dog."

"That's not your dog. That's Jace's dog. Never forget that."

"She shares him with me!"

"Only because you give her no choice!"

Borgsten appeared in the library archway. "Ski?"

"What?"

"They're back."

"Thank, Tyr." He gestured at Bear. "Because I can't talk
to you anymore."

"Why not?" Bear asked, hurt. "I'm friendly!"

While Tyr headed into the kitchen to get at Haldor's
stew—it did smell good—Erin grabbed Stieg's arm and
pulled him toward the side of the house.

"What are we doing?" he asked as he let her pull him.
"What about Haldor's stew?"

"I can't believe you're still hungry, and we're making a
run for it."

"Why are we running?"

"Because I don't know about you, but I don't want to—"

"Ah-haaaaa!" Jace said, dropping in front of them from
the second floor. She pointed at Erin. "You're trying to make
a run for it," she accused.

"No, we weren't."

"You're such a bad liar, Erin Amsel."

"I don't understand. I've always thought I was an *excellent* liar."

"You went off with Tyr—"

"It's not like he asked us."

"—and I know you were at my grandmother's earlier."

"That's—"

"Don't lie to me!"

Erin turned to Stieg, ready to accuse him of opening his big mouth, but he quickly reminded her, "I've been with you. I haven't had time to say a word to her."

She knew he was right, so she pointed at the birds in the trees.

"Rats! Rats with black wings!" One of the crows squawked at her and Erin unleashed her wings to fly up there, but Jace caught her arm to stop her.

"Leave them alone"—she yanked her closer—"and tell me what's going on."

Erin pulled her wings back in, gently placed her hands on Jace's shoulders, leaned in so she could look in her eyes, and replied, "No."

Then she walked away from her friend, dragging a confused Stieg behind her.

Stieg looked back at his friend. Sputtering and shocked, Jace stood there watching them walk away.

"She's . . . uh . . . starting to yell at us in Russian . . . or something, I think."

"Just keep moving. We need to get to your truck."

"Why don't we tell her—"

"Trust me. Just keep moving."

"She's getting really angry. She's going to blow."

"Keep moving." Erin pushed him forward. "Get the truck started. Now. I'll deal with her."

*   *   *

By the time Stieg got into his truck and started it, Erin was pulling the passenger-side door open and dropping into the seat.

"Go."

Stieg leaned forward and looked past her out the window. "Did you put her in a sleeper hold?" he demanded, seeing poor Jace out cold on the grass.

"It was the only way to calm her down."

"You didn't calm her down, Erin. You knocked her out."

"Tomato, toma—"

"Erin!"

"Just go!"

"You did the same thing to her grandmother. Was that to calm her down, too?"

"No. That was to kill her, but you stopped me. Look." Erin gestured at Jace. "The Protectors are already out there to take care of her. We need to go before she wakes up and charges your truck with her head like a bull coming after a matador."

Stieg put his truck in drive and pulled away from the house. After they'd been driving for a few minutes, he finally asked, "How do you live with yourself?"

Rubbing her nose with the back of her hand, Erin admitted, "Really well, actually."

CHAPTER NINETEEN

Kera was filling Chloe, Tessa, and Betty in on what was going on—that the last she had heard, their sister-Crow had disappeared with a Raven and a god—when Erin abruptly walked into Chloe's office.

"Hi," she said, surprising them all.

"Are you okay?" Kera asked, watching Erin's gaze quickly sweep the room. "Ski told me—"

"Yeah, we need to talk."

"Okay." Kera motioned her into the room. "Talk."

"Not here." Erin walked out and Kera looked at the others.

Chloe immediately got to her feet and came around her desk. "Now I'm *fascinated*."

Erin led them down the back kitchen stairs until they reached the lowest levels of the house, where the first LA Crows had erected a large statue of Skuld and on more than one occasion had held blood sacrifices. Thankfully those days were over. If they weren't, Kera would have made it her goal in life to shut that shit down.

But other than to torture her just before her welcome party a few weeks ago, the Crows had told Kera they never used this area. It was "weird" and "creepy" and many simply didn't want to be "down there if there's a goddamn earth-quake."

Erin looked around the main room and nodded her head. "Okay, good. This will work."

"To talk?" Kera asked. She didn't understand why they couldn't just talk in Chloe's office.

"Well, that too."

"What is going on with you?" Tessa finally asked.

Erin faced them. "Okay, this is the deal. We need to find the Carrion."

"Find them? How do we know they're here?"

"They're here," she insisted. "And I need to track down the one with Hel's rune on his palm, cut it off—"

"His palm?" Tessa demanded.

"Most likely his whole hand. And this space . . . we need to set it up like a little den and allow Tyr to come here quietly so he can read our books."

When no one else asked, Kera did. "Why?"

"Because that's how I got him to give me the map."

"What map?"

"The map of the Nine Worlds."

"Is it magical?" Betty asked.

"It's something. When I looked at it, there was movement on the page. I didn't really have time to study it, though."

"But you made a deal with him for the map?"

"Yes."

Chloe frowned. "To use our house to . . . read in?"

"Privately read in. And access to our library."

"*Our* library? You mean our books?"

"Well . . . yeah. You know, our Stephen Kings. Our Nora Roberts. Our Dean Koontz . . . ezzzzz." Erin frowned. "Koontzeses? No. That doesn't sound right. Let's just stick with Dan Browns."

"Erin," Kera tried, "I need you to focus, sweetie."

"I'm sorry." A phrase Kera had heard Erin Amsel say only once before. To anyone. "I've got a lot on my mind right now and I sense things are speeding up exponentially."

"Look at you with the big words," Betty teased.

Erin smiled. "I have my moments."

Betty's connection with Erin was one of the reasons Kera kept the woman close. She was considered an "elder" Crow, a term that pissed Betty off to no end. "I'm not *that* old," she'd complain, but she'd been a Crow for many years. And a talented one, considering she'd lasted as long as she had.

More important, she knew how to cut through Erin's occasional bullshit like a samurai sword through a side of beef.

"So what else did you agree to?" Betty asked, one eyebrow raised.

"Nothing, surprisingly. The Four Horsemen just wanted to *give* me information."

Chloe's back straightened. "You talked to the Four Horsemen alone?"

"No. Stieg was there. And Jace's grandmother, but don't tell Jace that. Even though she seems to already know, pretend you don't know anything when she asks."

"Why not?"

"She'll just get crazy and we can't deal with that now. That's why I knocked her out at Ski's place."

Betty laughed. Loud.

But Kera was desperately trying to understand the logic of the one woman she'd tried to kill with her bare hands. Because Erin was *that* frustrating! "You knocked her out?"

"Sleeper hold. Do it just right and you can put her out for ten, maybe fifteen minutes."

"Or kill her!"

"Doubtful. She comes from very strong blood. Jace's grandmother didn't even nod off before Stieg pulled me away—"

"*Her grandmother?*" Kera bellowed.

"She—"

Kera pointed her finger at Erin. "Don't you *dare* say she started it!"

"Except that she did," Erin said under her breath.

"I don't understand what's wrong with you. Why were you even *at* her grandmother's?"

"She told me to come over and not to tell Jace. And until the Horsemen walked into her backyard, I had no idea the mean bitch had some weird, twisted relationship with them. That," Erin suddenly added, "was probably sexual, because the woman looks as old as Methuselah. She probably knew the Four Horsemen when they were still teens."

"Why," Tessa abruptly cut in, "is Stieg Engstrom involved in any of this?"

"I can't shake him," Erin admitted with an annoyed sigh. "You sleep with a guy once . . ."

Kera pressed her fingers to her temples. "Jace said that was made up."

"It was, to hide the fact there was a hit out on me—"

"*What?*"

"—but then I was almost burned alive by that religious cult—"

"*What religious cult?*"

"—and afterward, I was so worked up, and he was, you know, *there*, and kind of vulnerable so I just took advantage. Now I can't get him to go away. It's like my pussy is magic or something." She shook her head. "Erin's Magical Pussy Tour."

Betty and Chloe were laughing so hard, they had to lean against each other to keep upright. Tessa just seemed confused, and Kera could only say one thing. "You are clinically psychotic."

"There is that school of thought—*oh my god!*" Erin suddenly burst out, forcing Kera to step back from outright fear. "I left Engstrom upstairs!" Erin tore out of the room.

Kera's mouth opened as she watched her friend run. "I was a United States Marine," she finally said to a quiet Tessa. "The pay was shit, but I had respect, an important job, and I helped save America from our enemies. Now I'm reduced to doing this—and *oh, my God! Would you two stop laughing!*"

Erin ran into the kitchen just as she heard Stieg tell a room full of her sister-Crows that, "Yeah, I never thought she'd pimp me out to a god."

Accusing eyes focused on her and Erin froze in the doorway. "Okay . . . before anyone judges me—"

Pelted with donut holes left over from that morning's breakfast, Erin turned and covered her head.

"You pimped him out?" Leigh—her own teammate!—accused, her hand resting on Stieg's oversized shoulder while the big bastard ate—again!—a large bowl of cereal.

How much food did the man need? How had he survived on the streets if he needed that much food?

"Do you know what he's been through?" Maeve whispered, as if Stieg wasn't sitting less than five feet away from her and listening to everything.

"Well, since you guys keep telling me . . . yeah," she whispered back.

"Then how could you?"

"Why do you keep whispering? He's sitting right there!"

The sound of running feet had Erin turning, but she only had a chance to glimpse Jace's face before her friend tackled her to the ground.

* * *

Spooning more cereal into his mouth, Stieg looked around at the Crows, waiting for them to get in between Erin and Jace. But when no one moved . . .

Sighing, Stieg dropped the spoon back into his bowl, and walked over to a screaming Jace and a laughing Erin.

How the woman could laugh when all this was going on spoke to the very high level of insanity she must deal with on a daily basis. Most people would have crumpled by now, but not Erin.

Never Erin.

He grabbed Jace around the waist and lifted her off Erin. He was debating what to do with her when Eriksen rushed in. Late as always.

Damn Protectors. Stieg handed Jace off to the smaller man before helping Erin back to her feet.

"I have to say," Erin announced, "I am a little surprised and disappointed at the lack of loyalty in this room and I think—*don't you dare throw that donu—*"

The chocolate glazed donut hit Erin right in the forehead and when it fell away, it left a smear of dark chocolate behind.

Deciding it was best to get out of there before Erin incinerated the entire room, Stieg grabbed her around the waist and walked out. He went out the first door he came to, which took them into the big backyard. He set her down, already thinking what he hoped were soothing words that would make her feel better about the whole thing. What came out was, "What is *wrong* with you?"

He asked that question because, with that chocolate glaze still on her forehead, Erin was hysterically laughing. Arms around her waist, she bent over, tears dripping from her eyes.

"You're crazy," he finally told her, when she was laughing so hard she couldn't answer his first question. "You're ridiculous and you're crazy."

* * *

Kera and the others made it upstairs to find Erin and Stieg gone and their fellow sister-Crows crowded around the kitchen windows.

Kera stopped and watched, listening to the women whispering about whatever they were watching.

"She's oblivious, isn't she?"

"Oh, my God. He likes her so much."

"You think? It's so hard to tell with him. He always looks like he's working the customer service desk at the DMV."

"I always thought he looked like a postal worker who's about one write-up away from losing it completely."

"Personally, I think the last donut throw was a bit much . . . Annalisa."

Kera's fellow Strike Team member smirked before replying, "It slipped from my fingers."

"You wanted to see if you could make her snap," Alessandra accused Annalisa, which was probably true.

"And yet, I can never find anything that sets Erin off . . . except Kera." Annalisa jerked her thumb back at Kera and everyone glanced at her before turning back to watch Erin and Stieg through the window.

All except Maeve Gadhavi, who walked over to Kera and asked, "Do you have an ETA on when all this stopping-the-Apocalypse thing might be happening?"

It took a lot for Kera not to narrow her eyes at Maeve, but her sister-Crow was sensitive to all physical reactions to anything she said or did. Instead, Kera replied, "Actually, no. At this time, we do not have an ETA. Why?"

"I think I'm getting a cold. Possibly the flu."

"Uh-huh."

"My throat's scratchy."

"And you want me to delay the end of the world for you because your throat is scratchy?"

Maeve crossed her arms over her chest. "Why do I hear tone?"

"Because there's tone."

"I'm just trying to—"

"What? You're trying to what?"

"Well—"

"We don't have time, Maeve, for your illness. If you have a cold when we have to battle Gullveig and her minions, then you drag your skinny ass out of bed and you get on the line with the rest of us. If you have the flu. Rickets. Measles. Ebola. An advanced form of venereal disease." Kera was no longer speaking to just Maeve. She was talking to everyone in the room, pacing back and forth in front of the women who'd stopped watching Erin and Stieg and were now focused on her.

"If you have lost two legs but you still have arms, then you will *drag* yourself to the line," Kera went on. "Because I—and humanity—don't have time for anyone's issues. Have I made myself clear?"

"Uh . . . yeah?" Alessandra said quietly.

"*I can't hear you!*"

"Sir, yes, sir!" they all barked back. Probably because they saw it in a war movie, but Kera would take it.

"Good! Now where's Jace?"

"Here," Jace called out.

"I need to talk to you."

Her friend started to walk toward her, but so did her boyfriend.

Kera held up her hand, halting the Protector in his tracks. "I said I need to see *Jace*. Not Jace and Ski, just Jace. So why don't you stay here and relax, while we go talk. Have something to eat. It's a fucking kitchen—there must be food here."

"Uh . . ." The Protector blinked behind his adorably dorky glasses. "Sure. I'll get something to eat."

Kera nodded and motioned Jace to walk out of the kitchen ahead of her. She followed, leaving the others standing there staring. They walked down the hall and as they neared the front door, Kera grabbed Jace's arm and yanked her into the bathroom.

Kera slammed the door shut, then dropped to her knees in front of her friend and panted out, "I can't do this. I can't do this. I can't do this."

Jace watched in horror as Kera had a major meltdown. She'd kind of known it might be coming. They were expecting her to be War General for a situation that could easily lead to Ragnarok. That was a lot to ask of anyone, but especially a woman who'd only been an active Crow for such a short time.

"I'm going to get them all killed, Jace. They're all going to die and it's going to be my fault."

Jace went down on her knees in front of Kera. She was still a little taller than her friend, but it was better than towering over the woman when she was feeling so vulnerable.

Suddenly Jace felt like shit. She'd been in full avoidance mode the last few weeks, just like she used to do when she still lived with her husband and his congregation. Focusing on books. Playing with her dog. Getting into fights with Erin. But not helping.

Not helping her sister-Crows. Not helping Kera.

Her friends deserved better.

Jace dropped her hands on Kera's shoulders. "You can do this, Kera. I know you can."

"They're all going to die and it'll be because of me."

"No. Absolutely not."

"I'm going to get them all killed and destroy the world. Me. I'm going to do it all because I'm a fuckup."

"Stop it."

"I'm going to be the reason a big serpent crushes the world. I'm going to be the reason hell's unleashed. It'll all be my failure. Mine. No one else's. But you know what?" Kera babbled on. "I'll probably survive. I'm going to survive all of it so that I can live with my failure and the corpses of all those my weakness has destroyed!"

Knowing the rant was only going to get worse, Jace did the only thing she could think of at the moment—she twisted Kera's nipple. Hard.

"Ow! What the fuck, Jace!"

"I need you to listen to me. I've been watching you. We all have. You've been amazing. Even now . . . the way you handled Maeve? Brilliant. Otherwise, she can start spiraling out on you, thinking she's got every killer bee–transmitted tropical disease ever created. You've been amazing with the Silent, never letting them get the best of you. Freida and the Giant Killers respect you . . . and they don't respect anyone. I would also say that you've been handling Erin great, too, but no one can handle Erin. You just let her be and hope for the best. But that's okay. That's how everyone deals with her. You've been smart enough not to push her."

"But if I fail—"

"You can't think like that. We're all in this together. All of us. Every Crow. Every Clan. Gullveig brought this battle to us, and we won't back down. Vikings *never* back down."

Kera gave a small chuckle. "What? We're *all* Vikings now?"

"Damn right we are. True, most of the Clans might not think so. But I've always felt being Viking was less about bloodlines and more about fuckin' attitude."

"Then, sweetie, your grandmother's a Viking."

"I wouldn't actually argue with you about that. I don't think Odin would argue with you about that."

Both woman were laughing and Kera put her arms around Jace, hugging her tight.

"Thank you," Kera whispered against her ear.

"Any time. Because if there's one thing I know how to get through, it's panic attacks."

Erin stood still while Stieg used a napkin to wipe the chocolate glaze off her forehead.

Well . . . she thought she was standing still until he said, "Stop wiggling."

Erin grinned. "Does it make you hot?"

"No. It makes me think you need to be on Adderall. Have you been tested for ADHD?"

"I had an appointment booked with a specialist in Manhattan, but I went to a Mapplethorpe retrospective at a gallery downtown instead."

Stieg stepped back, frowning. "How old were you?"

"I don't know. Twelve. Maybe thirteen."

"A twelve-year-old should not be checking out a Mapplethorpe anything."

Erin gawked at the big Viking. "You know Mapplethorpe? *You?*"

"I got knowledge."

"Do you? Really?"

"This gallery owner used to pay me and Karen to work some of his art shows. I handled security and Karen cleaned up."

"Galleries need a lot of bar-like security, do they?"

"The gallery was in downtown LA, near Skid Row. My job was basically to keep the riffraff away from the Hollywood glitterati, which wasn't hard because the locals all knew me. Anyway, the owner was really nice and he liked to explain the work to me and Karen. I learned about Jackson Pollack and de Kooning and Dorothea Lange. It was all interesting but not really my thing."

Erin sat down on the metal picnic table, her ankles crossed, legs swinging. "Stieg Engstrom . . . what *is* your thing?"

He dropped the dirty napkin into a nearby trash can. "Financial management."

Erin laughed until she realized that he wasn't joking. "Wait . . . what?"

"Financial management. I'm good with numbers and making money. When you live on the streets, you have to become good at hustling or become a hustler. Neither me nor Karen wanted to make our money on our knees or our backs, so we found other ways to make money."

"Holy shit!" Erin laughed, absolutely delighted. "That's amazing! Do you and Karen work together?"

"She deals with all the clients and I handle the money and the investments because, according to Karen, I am"—he made air quotes with his fingers—" 'terrifying' and a 'drain on business.' "

"So that stack of money she handed you the first night I met her . . . ?"

"Oh, that was cash from a client. A rabbi who runs a synagogue in Santa Monica. We used to go to their soup kitchen all the time. They had a tomato bisque that was amazing. Anyway, the rabbi is a really good guy and he was one of our first clients. We help invest the synagogue's money and give them money to help keep the kitchen open for our fellow street kids."

"So Karen's *not* a stripper?"

"*I told you she wasn't a stripper!*"

"Yeah, but you didn't say, 'She's not a stripper, she's my

business partner in our financial management company!'"
Erin shook her head. "You are so weird." Erin turned and
watched Kera and Jace walk toward her. "Hey"—she pointed
at Stieg—"did you know he has a financial management
company?"

"Yeah," they both said together.

"And neither of you told me?"

"Well," Kera explained, "I figured you already knew
since, you know, you've been here longer than I have."

"You have a point."

Jace nodded. "And I knew you wouldn't care."

"You're right. I wouldn't have." Erin smiled at her two
sister-Crows. "So what's up?"

"We need to talk."

Erin let out a long sigh, head dropping back so she looked
up at the sky. "That sounds serious and boring and I want
no part."

"Don't worry," Kera promised. "We'll keep it short and
pithy. Perfect for your itty, bitty—"

"Titty commitee?" Erin asked with a wide grin.

"—attention span."

"Oh."

"What do you need from us, Erin?" Kera asked, cutting
right to the heart of the matter, which was definitely her way.

How she managed to tolerate Erin Amsel as well as she
did was a constant discussion among the Ravens. Many wondered if she could be nominated for sainthood despite the
fact that she was no longer considered a Catholic.

"What do I need?" Erin glanced at Stieg.

He gave her a shrug. How she proceeded from here on out
was up to her.

"What I need is . . ." Her voice faded out and she looked

directly at Jace. "I need you to stop looking for a way out for me."

"But—"

"You asked what I need. That's what I need. *And my God, no crying!*"

"I'm not crying!" Jace screamed back.

But she was. A little. She was desperately trying not to, though.

"Instead," Erin continued, still talking to Jace, "I need you to focus on how I'm supposed to use that Key. It should get me in."

"A way in to Helheim," Kera said.

"It won't get me to Helheim, but Jace, I need a spell or whatever to get in and get out. As far in as you and that Key can get me."

Jace sniffed, nodded, sniffed again. She stood straight, shoulders back. "Okay."

"And you need us to find the Carrion."

Erin shrugged at Kera. "That's all we can do at this point. My suggestion is we send out the Strike Teams to hunt them down. But do not engage. Getting the Key will take a little more than one of our raids. We'll need to be . . . subtle."

Kera frowned. "Do we know how to be subtle?"

"Not even a little, but we have no choice. We can't fight and actually *defeat* the Carrion on our own."

"But if the Ravens—"

"It won't matter. Not with the Carrion."

"She's right," Stieg agreed.

Kera scratched her neck. "But you do want us to hunt them down."

"We find 'em first," Erin said. "Then we decide what to do from there. And I think I have an idea of where to start."

"Good. What else?" Kera asked.

"You need to prepare."

"For what?"

"We can't do guerrilla tactics with Gullveig and her people, Kera. We need to issue a direct challenge and face them head-on with the other Clans."

"Are you sure?"

"Positive. Random attacks won't mean shit to her once she's at full power."

The color drained from Kera's face. "She's not at full power?"

"Not even close," Erin replied. "So we've got to move fast."

"She'll never accept a direct challenge from us then."

"The good news," Stieg cut in, "you know, if there is any, is that Gullveig's troops are warriors of Hel. Unlike Gullveig, they won't turn down a direct challenge."

"Why not?" Kera asked.

"They're Viking. No true Viking will ever turn down a direct challenge. Because, in the end, it's about honor, and if that means dying, you better die with a sword in your hand and your enemy's blood on your face."

"That should be a poem," Kera replied with great sarcasm.

"It may sound wacky to us, but he's right," Erin agreed, surprising Stieg.

He didn't think she'd ever said he was right before.

"So we call Hel's minions out for what purpose?" Jace asked.

"If I can get the sword . . . I'll meet you on the battlefield, and kill the bitch myself."

"And if you don't get the sword?" Kera asked.

"Then we all burn anyway."

CHAPTER TWENTY

Yardley King sat with her sister-Crows in the TV room. They watched reruns of a reality show—"reality" being relative—that involved women yelling at each other. The TV room was divided into who was a fan of each woman and who thought whom was a liar and who was a whore, etc., etc.

While the arguments droned on, Yardley stayed up to date on the world around her by focusing on her phone and social media. She knew what was coming. She had taken emergency time off in order to be here for her sisters whenever they might need her. But her "mega superstar schedule" as Betty called it, was so busy, she'd had to make one of her classic excuses in order to get out of a few contractual obligations.

This time her absence was due to "exhaustion," which meant the Internet was abuzz with headlines like MOVIE QUEEN GOES BACK TO REHAB! and ANOTHER NERVOUS BREAKDOWN FOR MEGASTAR? and Yardley's personal favorite, PREGNANT WITH LOVE CHILD OF MARRIED COSTAR!

Most major actresses would be losing their minds over such headlines . . . mostly because a lot of them were true or as close to the truth as these things could get. Yardley found them wonderful entertainment because none of the ones about her were ever true.

The day she'd freak out was the day they'd say something like MOVIE STAR LOSES HEAD DURING RAGNAROK BATTLE! *That* she would find an upsetting headline.

"Oh, my God! Oh, my God, you guys!" one of her sister-Crows cried out. "It's my commercial!"

Everyone in the room began cheering as the newbie actress jumped to her feet and took very dramatic bows and even threw in a curtsy.

Yardley dropped her phone so she could join in. She knew what it was like to see yourself on screen the first time and it rocked. She didn't blame her sister for being so proud.

Erin walked into the room and over to Yardley. She crouched behind the back of the couch, her arms resting on the cushions. "I need your help."

"Anything," Yardley replied. "What's up?"

"I need you to track down Jourdan Ambrosio. I figure you might . . ."

The entire room had gone quiet and Erin looked up, eyes widening when she saw all her sister-Crows gawking at her. "What? What did I say?"

"She doesn't know," one sister said.

"She hasn't heard," said another.

"I don't know what? I haven't heard what?"

Yardley pointed at her sister who held the remote. "Turn on the local news, Sammy."

Sammy quickly changed channels and Erin immediately stood up. It was late afternoon, so all the news stations were talking about the same thing.

"She's missing?" Erin practically snarled. "What the fuck do they mean she's missing?"

* * *

Chloe turned her office TV off and tossed the remote onto her desk. She faced the others—Erin, Kera, Yardley, and Betty. "Do you think she's dead?"

"Along with her entire entourage?" Erin asked. "I doubt it."

"Then where the fuck is she?"

"We find Jourdan Ambrosio," Erin said, dropping into one of the chairs, her feet up on the seat, "we find the Carrion. Or at least the bulk of them."

"The problem is," Betty explained, "rich hos like her have more than one place to call home. For all we know, Jourdan and the Carrion are hanging out on her island in the Pacific."

Erin smirked. "She outbid you for that island, didn't she?"

"*That bitch!*" Betty exploded. "That island was mine!"

"Ladies," Kera cut in, "can we focus?"

"Find out what properties she and her family own," Chloe ordered. "At least any local ones the Strike Teams can hit tonight."

"Should we involve the other Clans?" Kera asked.

"No," Chloe replied. "We need the Protectors working with Jace, and the other Clans are wingless, so . . ."

"I'm going to call some friends," Yardley volunteered. "See if they've heard anything or if they know a place the family doesn't own where Jourdan would hole up. She's got a lot of billionaire friends and those friends have a lot of property."

"Great, Yardley. Thanks."

With the smile that got her on several *Vogue* covers, Yardley walked out.

"And you'll stay here," Chloe announced to Erin.

"Yeah, we all know that's not happening."

"Erin—"

"Why would you even bother trying to argue this with me?"

"Because psychopaths who want the world to end are trying to kill you. You have a bounty on your head. And if you die now—"

"Let her go," Kera said, shocking everyone in the room.

"Are you serious?"

"If we leave her here, doing nothing, she'll tear this place apart. Plus, anyone who is truly out looking for her will know where to find her if we try to hide her. We have to assume anyone that invested in the end of the world knows all the safe houses any of the Clans have in Southern California, and we can't afford to send her too far away. But if she sticks with Stieg—who seems to have become sadly attached—"

"It's my charisma."

"Shut up. She should be just fine. And this way she won't be a sitting duck."

"Yes! A sitting duck," Erin said solemnly. "Rather than a mighty crow meant to fly majestic—"

"Erin, shut up," Kera said without even looking at her. "Just shut up."

Vig walked into the open front door of the Bird House. Closing the door, he found Stieg standing behind it. Vig stared at his friend and Raven brother. "What the hell are you doing?"

"Waiting."

"For what?"

"Erin. She's going to try and sneak out. To get past me. She probably thinks I'm out back, so she'll try and slip through here. This is where I'll nab her."

Vig crossed his arms over his chest. "What's going on with you two?"

"Nothing. Why?"

"Why? Because you're lying in wait for Erin Amsel. Piss

her off and she won't just kick your ass. She'll set you on fire.
I've watched her do it. It is not pretty."

"I know what I'm doing."

Vig tipped his head to the side. "Do you?"

Erin and several Crows came down the hall. As they
neared, the other Crows split off just as Stieg pulled the door
open again so that it blocked any view of him. Erin, a backpack swinging from one shoulder, didn't see; she was waving
at her sisters, laughing at something they said to her.

"Hey, Vig," she said as she neared.

"Erin."

"Kera's in the back."

"Okay. Thanks."

As she passed the door, she paused long enough to bang
her fist against it as hard as possible. "Let's go, stalker. We're
on a tight schedule." She strutted out of the house

Stieg eased out from behind the door, eyes sheepishly
downcast as he moved past Vig.

"Still think you know what you're doing, brother?" Vig
asked.

"Shut up."

CHAPTER TWENTY-ONE

Stieg went to put his key in his front door, but it opened from the other side and Karen stepped out.

"Oh. You're home." She pointed into the apartment. "I left papers for you to sign in your kitchen."

"Okay." He walked past her. If Erin didn't know better, she'd swear the man was mad at his friend. But he wasn't. As her mother would often say about Erin's quiet grandfather, "That's just his way."

"Hey, Karen."

"Hey, Erin. Everything okay?"

"With him?" she asked, gesturing at Stieg.

"No. With you. You look a little stressed."

"I do? I never look stressed."

"You don't seem the kind of person who lets the little things bother her."

"I'm not."

Erin started to walk into the apartment when Karen asked, "Hey, I called your shop and they were talking about an appointment eight months from now. And I thought maybe—"

"Actually . . ." Erin began, ready to put Stieg's friend off. She didn't really have time to work on anyone's tattoo. As far as her shop staff was concerned, she was on leave for the next month, and with the appointments she already had on the books, she wasn't surprised by the response Karen had received.

But Erin paused in the doorway, thought a moment. "Can you be there at nine tomorrow?" she asked.

Karen spun to face her, mouth wide in a grin. "Yes! Yes, I can!"

"Bring your art. I'll see you there!"

Karen squealed and hugged Erin, making her laugh. "You are the best!" Then she was gone, down the hall to her own place.

Still smiling, Erin turned to head into Stieg's apartment, but found his giant chest blocking the way.

"What are you doing?"

"Setting up an appointment with your friend to give her a tattoo."

Stieg reached over Erin—which was a lot easier to do than she'd have liked—and closed the door so Karen couldn't hear. "Do you have time for that?" he demanded. "You know, with Ragnarok and all."

"First off, I'm trying to *prevent* Ragnarok. If I fail, you guys will be on deck to stop it. Until then . . . it's all on me."

"Right, which is why I'm wondering why you're setting up tattoo appointments."

"Because I figured this will probably be my last tattoo."

"That's sad."

"You know what's funny? Your 'that's sad' face looks exactly like your 'this is the best news' ever face. In other words, your face does not change. It's like stone." She stepped around him, headed for the couch, and saw his goat peeking out from the bedroom door.

Spotting Erin, the goat bounded out, hopping into the

room on all four legs. She pushed against Erin's leg with her entire body until Erin petted her head and neck.

"You ready or what?" Erin asked.

Stieg threw up his arms. "I just got here."

"And I'm ready to go."

"Do we even have a location?" he asked, heading to his bedroom to change into his Raven gear.

"Yes. Yardley texted me an address."

"Well, that's something."

Erin began pacing around the room, the goat right by her side.

"Let's go, Engstrom!" she called out when she felt he'd taken long enough.

"I'm coming! Good Lord, woman!"

He walked out of the bedroom, just pulling his tank top on. Erin had a moment to catch those superb abs before they were covered completely. He unleashed his wings, moved them around a bit, then retracted them. Since the sun had already gone down, Crows and Ravens could unleash their wings without question or concern. Their gods would protect them from the sight of others and modern technology.

Erin looked away and tried to get control of her libido. Between that shaggy blond hair, those black jeans, black tank top, and black wings, she was having a really hard time focusing on anything else.

"You can't stand still," Stieg accused as he grabbed his keys and wallet off the kitchen counter.

"I can if I want to."

"I'm doubting it. Every time I see you, your ass is moving."

"It's a fabulous ass. The whole world should enjoy."

He sighed. "I have no idea how to respond to that." He stood in front of her, towering over her. The giant Viking.

They stared at each other until he demanded, "Where are we going?"

"Huh?"

"Erin," he growled. "For the love of Odin, focus."

"Oh. Oh! Yeah." She looked down at her phone. "Laguna Beach."

"Nice area."

"Where did you expect Ambrosio to live? The Valley?"

"The Valley has some nice—"

"Don't even."

"Fine. Let's just go."

He walked to the sliding glass doors that led to his balcony and stepped outside. After dropping her bag on the couch and petting Hilda on the head one more time, Erin followed, jumping up on the balcony railing.

Once Stieg stood beside her, she smiled at him, enjoying the way his eyes narrowed until he appeared completely paranoid.

"Why are you smiling at me?" he barked.

"You haven't noticed?"

"Noticed what?"

"That now we're a 'we,'" she gushed. "You're so into me, you don't even know what to— *Hey!*" she barked when he placed his hand against her back and shoved her off the railing.

Stieg stared at the absolutely *giant* mansion that belonged to Jourdan Ambrosio. He'd bet anything that Karen would kill to have her as a client. Not that he'd blame her.

The home alone must be worth twenty, maybe thirty million. Four floors, views of the Pacific, lots of glass and an Olympic-size pool almost as big as the one the Ravens had.

"It's super quiet," Erin noted from her spot on the limb above him.

"There could still be people inside."

"Think we should wait?"

He thought a moment, then shook his head. "Nah. Let's go."

They unleashed their wings and flew to the roof of the house, landing silently. They walked along the edge, looking for any sign of Ambrosio's entourage. When she didn't see anyone, they let their wings take them down to a third-floor balcony. The window was locked, but Stieg jerked it open without much effort.

"It seems like you've done this before," she whispered.

"A little B and E when I was younger," he whispered back. "The Ravens beat that out of me, though."

"Delightful."

They walked into a bedroom that had Erin noting, "That is a lot of . . . tacky."

"This entire floor must be the master bedroom. She's actually knocked out walls."

Erin held her hands up, elaborately gesturing to one of the walls across from the double king-size bed. "Who has a giant painting of themselves, naked, on their bedroom wall?"

"A follower of Gullveig?"

"I told *you*," she whispered dramatically. "I'm from Staten Island. I know tacky. I can *be* tacky. But this"—she again motioned to the painting—"is a whole 'nother level of tacky. An unholy level."

Stieg couldn't disagree with her. He couldn't imagine living in a place like this. It wasn't the decadence. He could handle decadent. Versailles was decadent, but this . . . would be like living in one of those big Vegas hotels forever.

They made their way through the bedroom until Erin stopped and turned into one of the side rooms.

He heard her squeak and quickly followed her inside. "What?" he asked, still whispering. Neither of them knew if people might be sleeping somewhere on another floor.

"This is her closet!" It was nearly the size of Ambrosio's bedroom.

Erin pointed. "Who needs that many shoes?"

Stieg didn't know. He had steel-toed boots for fighting and a couple pairs of running shoes for everything else. He didn't understand who would need more than that. Even women.

"Can we keep this moving?" he asked while Erin briefly went through the woman's underwear drawer.

"So much tacky lingerie," she muttered, walking past him. Searching for the stairs, she stopped again, pointing at the shag carpet. "What is *that*?"

Stieg leaned in to get a close look. "That is small dog shit."

She shook her head, mouth open. Appalled. "Rich people are nasty."

"Erin—"

"Nas-*tee*."

"Walk," he ordered her, knowing they could be there all night with her critiquing the useless woman's house. "Just walk."

They finally found the stairs and headed down to the second floor. It was much more normal. A long hallway with several rooms, each with its own bathroom. They split, Erin walking down one way and Stieg going the other.

He went into each room, doing a quick search to see if he could find anything that would tell him where Ambrosio and her ridiculous friends might be. The woman had no idea what she was meddling with. Gullveig would feel no loyalty to her. And the Carrion . . . ? But just by looking at this woman's tacky home told Stieg Ambrosio wasn't a very logical or even a very smart person.

He reached the last room and walked in just as the lights in the house shut off. He stopped, his fingers curling into fists. He glanced down at his feet, realizing he was standing on something strange.

Straw. Straw inside some rich bitch's home?

No. Not even if she had horses on the property. There would be only *one* reason why straw would be on the bedroom floor of someone like Ambrosio.

He spun toward the door, about to yell out to Erin, when they were on him, their bodies wrapped around him, their hands gripping his head.

And the nightmares began . . .

A Mara landed on Erin's back and slapped her hands against Erin's head. Three others crouched in the dark corners of the house to watch, their wide grins showing their small, sharp black fangs.

Erin sighed. "Are you done?"

The grins faded, their brows furrowing in matching confusion. The Mara were demons who used their victim's worst nightmares against them. They simply touched a person's forehead and a Mara could torture the victim for hours, until death brought sweet relief.

The problem with Erin was that she didn't really dream.

She reached behind her with one hand, grabbed the screeching Mara by the hair, and flipped her over her shoulder. Still holding onto her hair, Erin slammed her foot down on the Mara's head twice before one of the others attacked.

Erin batted the new one away with her free hand and kicked the one at her feet across the room to slam into another. She crouched down and pulled her blades from the holster tied to her ankle. Before she could even stand, she had to slam one of the weapons into the gut of another attacking Mara. The move didn't kill it, though, and the Mara continued trying to bite her with those tiny black fangs.

Erin took a very brief moment to watch the Mara opening and closing its mouth, trying to bite her face. It took her seconds to get the timing right and when she did, Erin shoved the other blade into the Mara's open maw, pushing until the tip came out the back of its skull. Then she twisted and moved the blade back and forth until she severed any muscles her weapon could possibly reach. The Mara dropped, blood pouring from its mouth.

A roar from down the hallway had Erin running toward the door. Several Mara tried to block her, but she shoved them aside.

As she ran, more Mara came out from rooms or slid through walls like smoke.

Erin ignored them, slapping arms away, dodging their grasping claws. A Mara jumped in front of her and Erin simply kept running. She slammed right into it, knocking it down, and ran until she slid to a stop by the last open door that led into the room where they had Stieg on his knees . . .

Stieg was standing in front of his mother, who was already ill from cancer but refused to back down to his father or the illness. Though he was only ten, Stieg was using his body to protect her. His father's entire arm pulled back, fist cocked.

The fist came down, connecting with Stieg's head.

Now Stieg was twelve, his body wrapped around his father's back, trying his best to fight a man so much bigger, doing his best to protect his mother, who was clearly dying. His father was drunk again, and logic didn't get through that thick skull when he was drunk.

His father yanked Stieg off, threw him into a wall, came

after him. Pummeling his only son with fists, kicking him. Stieg didn't feel it. Stieg didn't care anymore.

He just wanted out. He just wanted out. He just wanted—

Stieg heard the screech. A female screech, not the sound his father made. He blinked, panting, bending over, his hands against the expensive rug rich people had paid a fortune for.

"Get up, Raven!" ordered a voice he recognized. "Get up or I'll burn this goddamn house down with you in it!" *Erin Amsel*.

Thank Odin. Other than his Raven brothers, the only warrior he'd ever want by his side when facing the Mara was Erin.

Stieg pushed himself up, struggled to his feet. Another Mara came for him. He didn't let her hands get to his head. He grabbed her arms, snapping them midforearm with a twitch of his fingers.

More screeching. He didn't care. He let that sound wash over him. It reminded him he was no longer trapped in the San Fernando trailer his father had had the nerve to call a home.

Stieg unleashed his wings, using their power to batter the Mara away from him, tossing the she-demons around the room like toys.

He glanced at Erin. She was using her blades with an expertise he'd only seen among the Elder sister-Crows. All that gymnastic and ballet training combined with the skills given to her by Skuld made her entire body a weapon.

What really impressed Stieg was that even in the close-quarter fight, Erin still used basic logic. Her blade didn't cut throats. It cut the facial muscles that controlled the Mara's jaws. When she was done, their mouths hung open, black spit oozing down their chins.

A few put their claws on Erin's head, but she only laughed and tossed them off.

But still, the Mara tried until they suddenly stopped, all of them scurrying away. Some disappeared back into the walls, dragging their fallen companions with them.

Stieg and Erin stood in the middle of the room, staring at each other. Confused.

"Freeze!" Cops held guns on them, ready to open fire.

At least that's what Stieg thought until Erin asked, "Who the fuck gave you two idiots badges?"

The two Claws of Ran warriors grinned.

"The city of Laguna Beach," one replied.

"That is so sad."

The Claws lowered their guns. "And what are you two pretty birdies doing here?" the other asked.

"Trying to save the world," Erin shot back. "And you?"

"With that rich bitch and her friends disappearing, we've been assigned to watch the house."

"Good job," Stieg mocked.

"Well, we weren't looking to the skies to see if some scavengers were sneaking in to steal the woman's panties to sell online."

Stieg took a step toward the ocean-loving bastards, but Erin placed her hand against his chest, halting him.

"Most days," she told him, "I'd be more than happy for a bird-fish fight, but we don't have time for that."

"Erin Amsel the rational one? The world really is ending."

Erin grinned at the Claw. "Be nice, Flipper, or I'll burn your lips off."

"You better go," the other Claw pushed when distant sirens came closer. "You two idiots set off the silent alarm."

Stieg looked at the black blood that had seeped into the rug and splattered the walls. "What are you going to tell them?"

"Rich kids out of control. They made a run for it." Smirking, the Claw motioned to the window. "Better fly, birdies."

Erin grabbed Stieg's arm and walked to the window. She opened it and pushed him toward it.

"Shouldn't you go first?" he asked. "I'm pretty sure I'm supposed to be watching your back."

She opened her mouth to respond, but simply pointed.

Stieg decided not to push it and flew out the window.

CHAPTER TWENTY-TWO

Jace closed another book that had provided no help and leaned back in her chair, sighing loudly.

"You need to eat." Ski leaned against the open doorway, watching her. The door had been redesigned a couple weeks prior.

"Better security," the Protectors had said as they watched the workers to ensure they didn't, somehow, damage their precious books. The doors were glass and slid closed, hermetically sealing the room. Of course, as often as those doors were opened and closed, Jace doubted they protected much of anything, but she didn't bother to point that out. Not now.

Because right now it didn't matter.

These days, all the Clans seemed to be doing things to keep busy. The Protectors putting in new library doors. The Isa focusing on their black bear program in Yosemite Park. The Giant Killers still planning the yearly motorcycle charity run they hosted that really sounded like a white supremacist get-together, but the last time Erin said that to Freida, she ended up with a broken nose and two black eyes.

If they weren't working on getting Erin over the Bifrost

Bridge, they were doing other things as if life was going on as normal. Even if it wasn't.

"I'm not hungry," Jace told Ski.

He smiled—God! That beautiful smile—and said, "I'll make you something to eat." A man with a beautiful smile who never listened. He disappeared down the hall, her dog following him.

It seemed Lev's loyalties had changed.

"They go where the food is, but Lev's heart will always belong to you. He knows who saved him."

Wincing, Jace turned without standing up and there they were, crouching on the chairs throughout the library.

"You shouldn't be here," she said gently. "The Protectors won't like it."

"We're not staying."

Jace forced herself not to turn from the piercing blue eyes gazing at her. It was what her grandmother had taught her. How to handle them. *Never show fear. Be direct.*

So Jace was. "Are you here to stop me?"

"If we wanted to stop you, Jacie-girl, we would have sent the nuns. But the nuns sent us." He smiled. "Besides, we decided long ago that fighting Crows was . . . not in the world's best interest."

"You ladies cheat," another muttered.

"Now, now, Raphael."

"They do." Raphael looked at Jace. "I have to admit, I was disappointed when you joined."

"Your grandmother never chose," Michael reminded her.

Jace's nose twitched. "Her husband never killed her."

"Ah, yes. The false prophet. We have such plans for that soul. Once you ladies are done with him, of course."

"If you're not here to stop me then . . ."

"Khamael," Michael prompted.

Khamael walked over to Jace's table and carefully laid

a book on the wood. It was ancient and written in runes. "We're sure you can find some Neanderthal pagan to read this."

"Oh, we can," Haldor said from near the doors.

The Protectors had come into their library without making a sound. Ski's cat, Salka, hissed at the archangels from the top of one of the shelves.

"Nice cat," Raphael sneered.

Jace didn't want a fight, so she redirected the Protectors the only way she knew how. "I can't read this book."

"What?" Bear said, pushing past Khamael like he wasn't one of God's assassins. "What do you mean you can't read it?"

"I'm still learning about runes. I'm not fluent. And these are *ancient* runes. We need someone with more knowledge than I have."

The Protectors surrounded the table, all of them except Ski studying the book.

The archangels exited out the back sliding doors, Michael pausing long enough to wink at her before unleashing his wings and disappearing into the night.

Ski smirked. "Nicely handled," he said to Jace, his voice low. Not that it was necessary. His brothers were so lost in the book before them, they noticed nothing else.

Finally, it was Haldor who said, "We can't read this."

"None of you can?" Ski asked, surprised.

"These aren't just runes. When we try to focus, the runes move. That's not normal."

"So, highly mystical. We should call the Maids. They can help."

"Or . . ." Jace said, letting the one word hang there.

"Or?"

"No," Bear said. "Absolutely not."

"He'll be here in minutes. The Maids have to drive."

Ski shrugged at her logic. "She's right."

"Yes," Bear admitted, "and we hate her for that."

Erin grinned at the large Latin man covered in tattoos and he smiled back.

"Erin! Hey, girl!"

"Hey, Junior." She went up on her toes and leaned over the counter of the small outdoor taco stand, kissing the man on the cheek. It was a carry-out-only joint, a few outdoor tables and chairs scattered around for those who didn't want to take their food back home.

"How's it been going?" he asked.

"Great."

He gestured at Erin. "What's all that?"

Not sure what Junior was talking about, Erin looked down. Saw all the black blood from the Mara. "Uh . . . it's paint. Just came from a painting party."

"Have fun?"

"Had a blast."

"What do you need?"

"One meat lover's taco for me. And three for big boy here."

Junior stared at Stieg before replying, "Even I only eat two."

"Trust me."

"Okay."

"And two extra-large Cokes and chips."

"Got it."

The food arrived and Erin pulled money out of the back pocket of her jeans. She handed it over to Junior and walked away before he could give her any change.

"You're the best," he told her, laughing.

"I know!"

Stieg found an empty table and sat down. "I need more than three tacos," he warned her.

"You haven't even unwrapped the food yet." Erin sat across from him, tore open a bag of hot chips, and took the caps off a bowl of salsa and another of guacamole.

With an annoyed sigh, he opened the bag Erin had handed him and unwrapped the first taco. He stared at it. "Okay," he said after a long moment. "This might do."

"Told ya."

Junior's tacos weren't like generic tacos that tourists could find all over LA. He made the shells himself and they were wide and long. Then he filled each one up with three different kinds of marinated meat, lettuce, tomato, cheese, and sauce. Erin was sure Junior's food had caused more than one Los Angeles resident a heart attack immediately after eating.

A risk Erin was willing to take because they were so damn good.

They ate without speaking, both hungry after their battle.

Stieg was working through his last taco when Erin asked, "So . . . are you okay?"

He grunted around the food, nodding his head.

She laughed, working on the chips and salsa. "I don't mean about the food. I mean are *you* okay?"

He paused midchew, his gaze locked on her. "Am I wounded?" he asked around a mouthful of meat, cheese, and tomatoes.

"Not that I'm aware."

"Then why are you asking?"

"I don't know. I just . . . I . . ." She looked away. "Stop staring at me! It was just a question."

"A question you've never asked me before in the *history of the universe*."

"All right, all right! I'm sorry I asked."

He narrowed his eyes like he thought she was going to cut his throat, but kept eating.

Her phone buzzed and she glanced down at the text. "Finish up. We gotta go."

"Go where?"

"Protector house."

"Why?"

"I don't know."

"You're not going to ask?"

"No."

"Why not?"

Erin slammed her hands on the table. "Because I don't feel like it."

"You sure are getting snippy."

"Could you please finish inhaling your food so we can go?"

"Snippy."

Stieg was surprised when he found his Raven brothers at the Protector's house. It was not like they were welcome. Ever. At all.

But Rolf Landvik was already sitting in their library, appearing cool, calm, and bored out of his mind. Siggy, much to the horror of the Protectors, had his feet up on the table. And Vig stood brooding. Something the man was very good at.

Erin's Strike Team and Chloe were also there, still in their battle wear. An argument was well underway, but it wasn't with the Crows or even with the Ravens. Not even Chloe and Josef bothered to argue about their divorce these days, the pair seeming to have decided that ending Ragnarok was more important than whether Josef would get spousal support from Chloe's book royalties.

No, this particular fight was between the Protectors and Bear.

The back glass doors slid open automatically and Stieg paused so he could stare at them, wondering how they worked. But he didn't have time to figure it out because Erin came back grabbed his arm and pulled him into the room.

"Bear, give him the book," Ski ordered.

It was the first time Stieg ever remembered the man looking that angry. Most things rolled off his back. Stieg did recognize the expression on Bear's face, though. The man had made up his mind, and it seemed nothing would change it.

He held an old looking book to his chest, both his big arms wrapped around it to keep his brothers away. "I am not giving that barbarian this book. It's clearly precious."

"Bear, we're Vikings. We're *all* barbarians."

"I don't care—*and what is she doing here?*" Bear suddenly yelled, pointing at Erin.

Erin stopped. "I didn't do anything."

"Yet."

"Jace told me to come here."

"And I'm telling you to leave, fire starter."

Stieg was getting pissed. He stepped in front of Jace and dared, "Talk to her like that again, Ingolfsson, I'll start burning books myself."

"Or," Kera cut in, her hand against Vig's chest—probably the only thing keeping him from leaping over the table and yanking Bear's testicles off—"we can all calm the fuck down. *Right now!*" She let out a breath. "Now, Jace . . ."—Kera suddenly looked around—"Jace? Where's Jace?"

When all Kera received was shrugs, she stalked over to the table Rolf and Siggy were sitting at and slammed her fist against the wood three times. "*Jacinda Berisha! Get out from under that table right now!*"

Jace appeared. "I thought I dropped—"

"Stop lying," Kera ordered, stepping back so Jace could stand and not collide with her.

"I didn't mean to cause a fight," Jace explained. "I just thought we should all be together doing this."

"Ingolfsson's insane, so you shouldn't have invited him," Rolf teased.

"I am *not* insane. I just don't trust you."

Kera looked down at the floor, took a breath. "Okay, Bear . . . what could we do to make you feel more comfortable about letting Rolf look at the book?"

"Nothing."

Kera rubbed her forehead with her forefinger. "Bear," she warned, "I will use my talons and *rip* that goddamn book out of your hands . . . or you can work with me here."

"Well, it would help if Kaspersen would get his big feet off our table."

"Get your feet off the table, Siggy."

"And maybe the Ravens can go into the kitchen. Away from our precious library."

"Are we really listening to this idiot?" Vig asked.

"*Sacred space!*" Bear suddenly bellowed.

"Fine." Kera motioned to the other Ravens. "Gentlemen, could you please?"

"Unbelievable," Vig complained while Siggy got to his feet.

Bear pointed at Erin again. "And she needs to leave completely."

"But I really haven't done anything."

"Erin, please—" Kera turned toward her sister-Crow but stopped speaking and gestured at her. "What is this?"

"Mara blood."

"Again with them?"

Chloe pointed at Erin and Stieg. "They're not the only ones," she said, holding up her phone. "I've been getting texts all night from the other Strike Teams."

"Okay. We'll deal with that later. Erin, just go."

"Because *Bear* said I had to go?"

"Because Bear is holding the book that we need. Now go."

"Fine. Whatever." Erin spun around and stormed out, and Stieg immediately followed her.

Once Erin was outside, she unleashed her wings, but before she took off, she noticed Stieg. "What are you doing?"

"Following you."

"Why?"

"No idea. Maybe because you look so irritated."

"I *am* irritated. *I'm* the one risking everything and they're kicking me out because Bear said to kick me out. How is that cool?"

"Want me to beat him up? He bugs me, so I don't mind beating him up."

First Erin frowned; then she smiled. "You beating up Bear Ingolfsson is like me beating up Jace's puppy—cruel and unusual."

"Look, why don't you come back to my place? Your backpack is still there anyway. And something tells me, Erin, that if you go back to the Bird House the way you're feeling right now, you're just going to start some shit."

She snorted. "Yeah. I will." She glanced off. "Do you have ice cream?"

"No. But that little store next to my place is open late. We can always buy some."

"Chocolate?"

"Okay."

"All right then."

"See?"

"See what?"

"Startin' shit."

"I didn't—"

"What if I'd said no to the chocolate? What if I'd insisted on butter pecan? Or strawberry?"

"Ew."

"See? Startin' shit."

She laughed and waved him off. "Just go."

With the rest of his Raven brothers safely put away in the kitchen, Erin out of the house, and everyone calm, Rolf stared at Bear Ingolfsson and asked, "Can I see the book now?"

Grudgingly, as if he was handing his only child off to Lucifer himself, Bear placed the book on the table in front of Rolf. "Be careful," the Protector warned, making Rolf want to hit him.

Rolf didn't even open the book. He simply laid his hand on it and closed his eyes. He didn't read runes as much as they "spoke" to him. As much as they led him down the path to knowledge.

And these runes not only spoke to Rolf. They screamed.

"Write this down," he ordered. But even with his eyes closed, he sensed that no one was actually *doing* anything. "I'm waiting," he barked.

"I don't *do* secretarial work anymore," Maeve complained. Before her untimely death and subsequent Second Life, she'd done temp work. Now, of course, she ran her own very lucrative medical website specifically built for the hypochondriacs of the world who were sure they were dying any second.

But none of them had time for this.

"In about twenty minutes, I'm going to get a migraine

that could kill a small elephant. We need to get this done . . . *now.*"

Maeve's sigh was dramatic but he could hear movement as she sat down near him at the table and the clattering of computer keys as she began working on a laptop. "All right," she muttered, resigned. "Go."

Rolf began, the runes still screaming, and he quickly realized that giving himself twenty minutes before one of his rune-related migraines took over might have been a little too generous.

CHAPTER TWENTY-THREE

Erin took a quick shower while Stieg took his goat for a walk. Because that's what modern-day Vikings do apparently. Walk their goats.

By the time Stieg got back, Erin was on his couch, wearing one of his ridiculously big tank tops and watching one of her favorite movies on cable.

Stieg stood behind the couch, staring at the TV until he asked, "What *is* this?"

"The greatest movie ever made."

"*Citizen Kane*?" She looked at him over her shoulder and he added, "I like that movie."

"No. This is not *Citizen Kane*. This is *Beyond the Valley of the Dolls*."

"You're not serious."

"This movie has everything. Sex, drugs, rock and roll, bad acting. I mean *really* bad acting. It's brilliant."

"I find your taste disturbing."

"Yeah. You and everybody else. But you people just don't understand."

"Understand what?"

"True art."

Stieg rolled his eyes and walked to the bathroom. Erin had turned back to the TV when Stieg's dirty shirt covered her head.

She squealed and yanked it off. "Not cool, dude! I just washed that damn Mara blood out of my hair!"

Scrunching up her nose, she tossed the shirt to the floor and went back to her show. She could hear the shower go on in the bathroom while Hilda got on the couch with her. Erin reached over and petted the animal until a pair of filthy jeans hit her in the head. Quickly followed by the man's nasty drawers!

"I'm gonna kill him," she snapped, throwing his dirty clothes aside. She jumped off the couch in time to see a naked Stieg slam the bathroom door in her face.

She marched over and tried to knob. He'd locked it, so she banged on it. "Open this door, mister."

When she didn't get an answer, she looked over at the couch. Hilda's chin rested on the back as she watched the goofiness before her.

Erin pointed at the door. "Do it, Hilda."

Happily, Hilda leaped off the couch, charged across the room, and rammed her head into the bathroom door.

"Hey!" Stieg barked from the other side.

"I'll let her take it down!" Erin warned.

Stieg snatched the door open. "Keep my goat out of your tantrums— Hey! Cut it out!"

Erin had launched herself at Stieg, wrapping her legs around his chest and her arms around his head.

"What are you doing?"

"Wrestling you to the ground." She heard Stieg snort and then she was upside down, held only by her ankle. "Put me down!"

He didn't. He just walked over to his shower and got in with her in tow.

"Dammit, Engstrom! I just took a shower!"

"Not with me, you didn't." He flipped her up, yanking the tank top off her body and pushing her against the far shower wall. He pinned her there, his mouth landing on hers, his tongue pushing its way inside. Invading her mouth while his hands invaded her body.

Big hands palmed her breasts before moving lower, fingers sliding inside her pussy.

He didn't stay too long anywhere. He was just teasing her. Torturing her. Erin's laughing curses and promises of cruel retribution turned into groans and gasps.

Finally, while he sucked on her nipples and his fingers thrust inside her, she felt an orgasm tearing up her spine and . . .

Shocked, Erin opened her eyes and stared up at the Viking. "What the hell are you doing?" she demanded. She'd been so close. She was still so close. Just a little more . . .

Stieg held out a bar of soap. "Wash me first."

Despite her painfully hard nipples and empty pussy, Erin still managed to laugh. "Are you kidding?"

He stepped close, the heat of his body competing with the heat of the water from the showerhead. "You want me inside you? Fucking you? Then wash me first." When her lip curled and she snarled, he added, "You wouldn't want me to fuck you while still covered in Mara blood, now would you?"

She hated him. She hated him. She hated him!

Because she wanted him. Had to have him!

Erin snatched the bar of soap from him and began scrubbing him to get the Mara blood off his skin. Stieg picked up the shampoo and took care of his hair.

As she moved down his body, she saw how hard he was. So as she crouched in front of him, she made sure to nudge his cock with her nose.

Stieg froze for a moment, but then went back to washing his hair, pretending not to notice.

But they both knew he'd noticed.

Erin washed his legs since Mara blood had managed to get under his jeans—she didn't know how, and she didn't want to know how—and as she did, she made sure to constantly bump into that thing.

It wasn't hard to do. It was like a goddamn elephant trunk in her way. She wondered if he could pick up things with it.

When she knew he was clean, she started to stand back up, but stopped to suck the head of his cock into her mouth.

Stieg was just washing the conditioner out of his hair and he almost lost his footing, his loud, surprised groan filling the room.

Erin circled the head with her tongue, sucked again, then deep-throated the entire thing.

Stieg went to grab the back of her head, and that's when Erin pulled away and stood.

She daintily wiped the corners of her mouth with her index finger before lowering her head and lifting her eyes to gaze up at Stieg.

"You dirty little—"

"Ah-ah-ah," she cut in, waving her index finger in his face. "If you want to be inside me, fucking me," she taunted, "then be nice to me."

Stieg took in a breath, his hands pushing his wet hair off his face, and Erin knew at that moment, she might have played the game a little too hard, you know, with a Viking.

She made a run for it.

But he was right behind her, his arm snaking around her waist and locking her against his body before she even made it out of the bathroom.

"Uh-oh," she muttered when she knew she was caught.

Stieg held onto Erin like his life depended on it. He felt like it did. "Evil little tease," he growled as he carried her across the room.

"Let's discuss this like adults," she offered.

"Shut up."

He stopped in the kitchen and dumped the shopping bag of items he'd gotten from Mr. Matucka's store onto the counter. He'd put the ice cream away in the freezer before Erin hit the shower, but the rest was still in the bag.

Stieg grabbed the box of condoms he'd purchased because he couldn't remember how many he had left in his bedroom end table.

He started to carry Erin to the bathroom, but that seemed so far away. Stieg spotted the couch and walked the few steps over to it.

Hilda was sitting on it and he gave her a short snarl that had the goat high-tailing it into the bathroom. She even shut the door with a kick of her back legs.

"You are even freaking out the goat!" Erin said, squirming in his arms. But that squirming was not helping her. It was just making him hotter and harder.

He bent her over the back of the couch and pushed her legs apart with his knee.

"Dude!" Erin gasped, still trying to get away. "I'm not some peasant girl you just found hiding in the stables of the family farm!"

Deciding she talked too much, Stieg slapped her ass. Kinda hard, too.

Erin froze in midcomplaint. "Did you . . . did you just slap my ass?"

In answer, he slapped the other cheek.

"Stieg Engstrom!"

He had the condom on and before she could wiggle away, Stieg gripped her thighs and pulled her back while he thrust forward.

"You asshole! When I get free, I'm going to—oh, God! That feels good." She was right. It did feel good. It felt amazing.

Even better, Stieg didn't need to worry about how much Erin Amsel could handle. The woman could handle anything he was ready to give her. He thrust in hard and she pushed back against him, her hands pressed against the couch cushions, giving her a little bit of leverage since her feet didn't even touch the floor. Her pussy gripped him like a vise and, even better, she still taunted him.

With a toss of her wet red hair, she looked over her shoulder. "Show me how hard you can fuck me, Stieg. Show me. Fuck me!"

So he did. He fucked her as hard as he wanted and Erin did nothing but beg for more.

With each hard thrust, she groaned or growled. Sometimes she just said "yes" over and over.

While she balanced on one hand, she used the other to grip her own breast, her fingers toying with her nipple. She was so hot and wet, he couldn't believe how turned on she was.

How turned on he was!

He couldn't even think straight. He just knew one thing and one thing only. He had to get her off before he got off.

It was imperative.

Stieg stopped thrusting, holding her ass tight against his crotch.

"Why did you stop?" she demanded. "Don't fucking stop."

He reached around and slid two fingers down until he found her clit. He circled it with the tips, focused on nothing but Erin's reaction.

At first, she squirmed, wanting him to keep fucking her. But then her eyes closed, her head dropped, and her entire body tensed.

Stieg gripped her clit between his two fingers and stroked it until Erin began to shake, her moans becoming louder, the top of her head resting on the couch cushion.

Her toes curled and she gasped and growled into the couch as she came, flooding his fingers and hand with her wetness.

When she finally reached back to move his hand away, unable to take anymore, he gripped her upper thighs again and began fucking her hard. Harder than he'd ever fucked anyone before.

He couldn't help himself. He wanted to bury himself as deep inside her as he could. Wanted to make her his own. He knew it as soon as he came, his entire body lost to the release.

When he was done, his body drained dry, he lifted a limp Erin Amsel with an arm around her waist and, with his cock still inside her, walked her to his bedroom.

They dropped on the bed, still fused together, neither ready to move, and sort of passed out that way. Both too exhausted to bother un-attaching.

CHAPTER TWENTY-FOUR

"Ice cream?"

Erin opened her eyes and saw that Stieg was holding out a bowl of chocolate ice cream for her. Yawning and scratching her head, she sat up and took the bowl from him.

It was still dark outside, but Stieg had the bedroom TV on.

"What is it with you and *American Greed*?"

"That's how you learn what not to do if you don't want to go to prison or make bad investments. I don't want to do either, so I watch and I learn."

"That's probably a good plan. Ravens in prison can't be a good thing."

"Not when I can just fly away. But then I'd be hunted, which doesn't sound entertaining at all."

Erin ate her ice cream and watched the show with Stieg. When she finished eating, she put the bowl aside and leaned her head against his arm. "Why are you helping me?"

"Because I'm pretty certain I'm the only one who can put up with you."

"I'd be insulted if you didn't have a point." She yawned again and stretched, leaning back against the bed. When she was done, she saw that Stieg was staring down at her, a little bit of leftover chocolate ice cream on his chin. She reached up and wiped at it with her finger, then held it in front of Stieg.

Smirking, he sucked her finger into his mouth and Erin immediately felt her nipples get hard and her pussy get warm, then wet.

The man did have some technique.

He swirled his tongue around her finger one more time before pulling back. "You never ask me," he suddenly announced, placing his empty bowl on the opposite end table.

"Ask you what?"

"About my past."

"I've asked some questions."

"Not really and when you do, it's mostly mocking."

"That's true." She dragged her finger down his chest. "I never thought you wanted any questions about your past. You don't exactly present yourself as a chatty person."

"Does my past make you uncomfortable?"

"No."

"Not at all?"

"No. Do you want it to?"

"Not really. Just surprised. You seem so curious about everything else."

"I never said I wasn't curious about you. But I don't pry into people's real problems."

Stieg raised an eyebrow and Erin explained, "I'll give Maeve shit until the end of time about her 'illnesses,' but what I won't do is ever ask her about her mother. Whatever her issues are, I know they stem from that woman and she does *not* want to talk about it. If she suddenly did, though, I'd listen, but at the end of the day, we all have our private issues, and they're none of my business unless you want them to be."

"So you do have boundaries. Lines you won't cross."

"Of course I do. I'm not—no matter what Idunn says—a monster."

"She really hates you."

"I know. But they're *golden* apples all together in a basket. How does she not expect me to play with them?"

Stieg curled several strands of her hair around his finger. "I don't want you to go," he suddenly admitted.

"You mean right now? Because I wasn't planning to." When he just stared at her, she said, "Oh. You mean . . . *go*." She shrugged. "It's not like I have a choice."

"You could run." He gave a short snort. "But Crows don't run."

"It's not even that. I tried running once. It did not end well. But every extra day I've had as a Crow . . . a blessing. So if that means sacrificing myself to prevent the end of everything, I'll do it. But you'll have to promise to remember me fondly and make sure that no other woman you're ever with again measures up to the wonder that is me."

Stieg moved in closer, snuggling down beside her. "You better get to work if you want all that."

Erin laughed. "I'm the one risking life and limb and you want *me* to get to work? You're such a dude." She snapped her fingers and pointed down. "*You* get to work." She put her hands behind her head. "And I'll just lie back and enjoy."

And that was it. That's how Erin Amsel grabbed his heart. His angry, vicious, doomed heart. The heart he thought he'd encased in concrete. Never to be hurt again by anyone! That was the plan.

But how could he not fall for a woman who'd accepted a suicide mission like she was being forced to take on a daily carpool of obnoxious children? Who gave as good as she got in bed and out? Who never went down without a fight? Who pissed off gods for her own twisted entertainment?

He couldn't. Stieg knew that now. He couldn't resist this woman.

This foolish, ridiculous, pain-in-the-ass woman.

Even though he was certain he'd lose her forever in the next few days.

But that was the price they all paid. The risk they all took.

So, for now, he'd enjoy her while he had her.

He wrapped his mouth around her breast, his tongue circling her nipple, and Erin's body instantly responded. She settled down on the bed, her hips squirming a little bit.

Stieg took his time. He was in no rush, even if Erin was. Her hand started to move down to her pussy, ready to jack herself off since he hadn't touched her there yet, but Stieg grabbed her, pinning both hands against the bed as he moved from one breast to the other.

She struggled against his grip, her hips squirming more, her legs becoming restless. He didn't let any of that bother him, though. He was on his own timetable. Much to Erin's annoyance.

He finally slid down, his tongue leading the way, until he reached her pussy. He saw the hands he'd just released ball into fists. She didn't want to do anything that would make him stop, but she was running out of patience.

Once settled between her legs, he leaned in, but before touching anything with his mouth, he blew on her clit. Erin's toes curled as she raised her knees on either side of him.

He pushed her legs wide apart, leaned in again . . . and blew.

"*Stieg*," she growled in warning.

He lifted his head, one eyebrow raised. "What?"

She gritted her teeth before snarling out, "Nothing."

"Yeah," he taunted back, "That's what I thought."

He went back to blowing. Then, he licked her clit. But little licks that he knew were doing nothing but torturing her.

Sometimes he used his nose to circle but still . . . not enough to get her over the edge. He knew it. She knew it.

Finally, she lifted her head a bit, her face covered in a sheen of sweat, and glared at him. Silently demanding to know when he was going to get to it.

"You know what I want to hear," he teased.

"Oh, come *on*," she bit out between those still-clenched teeth.

"Say it . . . or I'll keep this up until dawn. Say it."

She fell back on the bed, refusing. And he kept toying with her until her entire body was sweating and she was trembling on the edge of release with no hope in sight.

When this was all over, she might actually kill him.

Finally, she lifted her head again and barked, "Please."

"Now that wasn't so hard, was it?"

Her eyes widened in rage, but he simply ignored that and went back "to work." He sucked her clit into his mouth and sank two fingers deep inside her.

Erin's hands reached up, gripping the headboard, her hips rising off the bed as he sucked hard and stroked deep.

It took seconds before he pulled her over the edge, but he wasn't done. He kept going, not letting her wiggle away when she tried. He held onto her waist with his arm as he continued to suck and fuck her pussy with his mouth and fingers.

Erin let out a sharp, short scream when she came again, her entire body rigid as she thrashed beneath him.

She finally pushed him off, using her legs and hands. But he didn't let her scramble off the bed. He grabbed her ankle and dragged her back. By the time he had her on his lap, he had a condom on and was buried deep inside her.

"Bastard," she snapped at him before she kissed him hard on the mouth, her hips pressed against him.

Stieg kept her on top as he stretched out beneath her. He gripped her waist with both hands and made her ride his dick.

Erin slapped her hands against his chest, her knees resting on either side of him. "I'm so going to make you pay for this later," she warned. "I'm going to make you pay so hard."

Stieg, nearly ready to come just watching her get off on what he was doing, was about to explode. But after hearing her warning, he held back long enough to reach down with one hand and grip her clit again between his fingers.

She grabbed his wrist, trying to stop him. "Stieg. Not again."

"One more time," he pushed. "Just for me. Only for me."

Erin's head fell back, her mouth open, her body shuddering on top of his. She came again and this time Stieg came with her.

When Erin landed hard on his chest, Stieg's arms too weak to do anything except flop uselessly at his sides, she reached up and grabbed a hank of his hair, pulling hard.

"Ow!"

"Bastard!"

"Cock tease."

Then he hugged her close . . . and she let him.

CHAPTER TWENTY-FIVE

Erin woke up smothered. More than three hundred pounds of Viking muscle sprawled across her.

"Great," she muttered. "He's a cuddler."

She tried easing out from under him but he wouldn't budge. She tried gently pushing his shoulder. That, too, was ineffective.

She finally gave flailing a try and, growling, Stieg rolled off her, but kept right on sleeping.

Erin scrambled off the bed before he could roll back and found another black tank top to put on. She padded out into the living room, closing the bedroom door behind her, and went to the coffeemaker to get the coffee started.

She frowned when she heard a soft knock at the front door. After a pause, she answered it and found Karen standing there, grinning at her. Especially when she saw what Erin was wearing.

"Good night?" Karen asked.

"He's sleeping."

"I bet he is."

Erin laughed at Karen's tone.

"Want to go to your shop together?" Karen offered.

"Yeah, sure. Give me a little time to wake up."

Erin closed the door in a giggling Karen's face and went back to the kitchen. She poured herself a cup of coffee and went out on the balcony. She rested her arms against the railing and stared out over the ocean while the sun came up behind her back.

She heard Hilda the goat come out on the balcony but the affectionate animal didn't press up against Erin's leg as she liked to do.

Erin turned her head and gazed up into the one blue eye watching her close.

Odin, the Allfather, had Hilda in his arms, petting the goat's coat with enormous, but gentle hands. "Crow," he greeted, smirking at her from beneath his eye patch.

Erin stared at him a moment before asking, "You're not going to do anything weird with that goat, are you? Pervert."

Chloe and Kera stood next to each other. Legs braced apart. Arms crossed over their chests. Staring out Chloe's office window.

"How's Rolf?" Chloe asked.

"Still vomiting and sleeping off that migraine on the Protectors' couch. They're not happy. But the Maids are going over this morning. They can give him something to help."

"Erin?"

"At Stieg's. I suggest we let her hang out there today. After their run-in with the Mara last night, I'm not sure I want her going through that again."

"I guess. Speaking of which . . . I guess Erin was right all along. About that girl."

"We found more Mara at six of her eight houses. They'd made themselves quite at home."

"But no Carrion."

"No Carrion. Yardley thinks she may have a line on a place where we can find Ambrosio. Yardley is just waiting for her contact to get back to her. He's in Thailand on a film site right now."

"Big movie star?" Chloe asked.

"Hair stylist."

"Seriously?"

"Apparently that's how these things work. If the info comes through, I suggest we go over there tonight. It may be a long shot. I'm sure Gullveig has other priestesses but Erin seems so certain. And if she's right and we bring the Ravens—maybe we can get the Key."

"What about Erin?"

"Keep her with Stieg. Once we have the Key, the Maids will be ready to do their thing."

"She won't be happy she's not involved."

Kera briefly closed her eyes. "She's already too involved."

"Don't give up on her yet. Many of the Clans think she's too mean to die. You know . . . like Betty."

"So do you have any words of wisdom, O Great Odin?"

"Nope."

"Helpful as always," Erin replied, toasting him with her coffee cup before taking another sip.

"We do not spoon-feed our people."

"We're not asking for spoon-feeding. We're asking for a little . . . assistance from our gods. We've already had help from Old Testament and New."

"How Christian of them." Odin snorted. "Get it? How *Christian* of them? Get it?"

"Nothing I hate more than someone who spells out a joke."

He sighed, loudly. And rather dramatically. Like he was doing her the biggest favor in the universe just speaking to her. "I will tell you this, tiny little female—"

"I'm not that small."

"—if you make it past Bifrost Bridge, then I strongly suggest that you never reveal what you are unless you have absolutely no choice."

"Why? Because I'm human?"

"No. Because you're a Crow. "

"That whole slave thing again?"

"It's not that simple. Not for those who live in the other Worlds. Crows have a reputation. Worse than any other human Clan."

"Really?"

"They aren't fans of my Ravens, and the Giant Killers aren't allowed back into Jotunheim, but all Nine Worlds hate you people more."

"Good to know. Anything else?"

"No."

Erin, frustrated, slammed her coffee cup down on the rail. "I don't understand."

"I'm sure you don't understand lots of things."

"You come here and you tell me nothing. You are of no use to me. So why bother me?"

"I'm Odin. You should feel blessed by my mere presence."

"Bitch, I don't have time for your *presence*. If you want to help me, then help me. Give me something. A magical necklace or a mystical tattoo or anything that will help me get through this. Instead, you bring your fat ass here, pet Stieg's goat, and give me cryptic shit that is unhelpful."

Erin didn't even see Odin move. But Hilda was running back into the apartment and his hand was around her throat, holding her over the railing, her bare feet dangling in midair.

"*You dare talk to me like that, worthless slave!*" he bellowed, black clouds appearing, the sound of thunder rolling overhead. "*You live because I allow it! You exist because of me!*"

She grasped his hand, feet kicking out, and she tried to speak.

His smile cruel, Odin pulled her a little closer. "What was that, slave? I couldn't hear you."

That's when Erin shoved two fingers into the only eye he had left.

Roaring, Odin dropped her, and Erin grabbed for the railing. But the metal was still wet from the early-morning ocean fog that hadn't burned off yet in the LA sun, and her hands slipped right off.

Then her wrist was caught and held and Stieg yanked her up.

"I can't even sleep in with you around," Stieg complained, placing her back on the balcony.

Together, they walked into the living room where Odin had a hand over his wounded eye. Erin thought he was raging, but he was too busy laughing. Hysterically.

"Mad bitch!" he cheered. "You were meant to be a Crow."

Odin lowered his hand. He could still see, but blood slid down his face, his blue eye now red. Yet he smiled at Erin and Stieg. Because he was Viking and they seemed to weirdly enjoy when women slapped them around a little.

"I bet she's a wild fuck in bed, boy."

"Why are you here, Odin?" Stieg asked, stepping in front of Erin.

She wasn't even sure he knew he'd done it.

Odin didn't answer, just wiped the blood from under his eye and studied his fingers. Without warning, he suddenly flicked the blood, splattering them both.

"Ewww!"

"Shit, Odin!" Stieg yelped. "Was that really necessary? We just got Mara blood off us last night."

"Think of it as a blessing," the god replied, still laughing.

Erin rolled her eyes. "Do you make your stripper-girlfriends say that, too, when you come in their faces?"

Odin nodded. "Yes." Then he was gone.

Stieg faced her. "'When you come in their faces'?" he repeated back to her.

Erin shrugged. "What? Too far?"

"Is there anything you do that isn't too far?"

"According to my mother . . . no."

Karen sat in the chair similar to one you'd find in a barbershop.

The place wasn't big. There were stations for six, maybe seven artists. And there was no flash art on the walls. Images some half-drunk dude-bros could pick from on a Saturday night when one dared another to get a piece that, eventually, he'd have to get lasered off before his big wedding.

She liked Erin's shop, though. It was small but cozy. And there were a few casual pics of Erin with her clients. Even Yardley King! How cool! She was going to the same tattoo artist who gave Yardley King one of her tattoos. Karen couldn't wait to tell her friends. They'd definitely be impressed.

Swigging from a plastic container of orange juice, Erin came out of the back and over to her station. "Okay." She put the cap back on the container and dropped it on the counter. "What are you looking for?"

Karen handed over the drawing she'd made for herself years ago. This wasn't her first tattoo, but it would be her first *real* tattoo. She didn't count the broken heart on her ankle that another street kid had given her with a needle and thread. She was just grateful that she somehow managed not to get Hep C from doing something so stupid. But she'd only been sixteen and freshly dumped.

It was just what one did back in the day.

After her first tattoo, she'd waited until she could afford the best work available. She was still looking when she found Erin Amsel sitting on her best friend's couch.

Erin took the paper from Karen and glanced at it.

"You can't draw," Erin stated.

"Uh . . . no. That's not really my—"

"Are you married to this?"

"No, I just want something sim—"

"Okay, good." She crumpled Karen's drawing and tossed it into a nearby garbage pail. "Where do you want it?"

"Uh . . . well, someplace I can hide from clients, of course. Maybe on my bicep or—"

"Take off your shirt."

Karen watched another artist walk by with a donut and coffee, muttering a greeting to Erin. "Um . . . pardon?"

"Take off your shirt. And your bra."

"And why would I do that?"

"I'm going to put your piece here." Erin gestured to her side above her hip.

"Do I, uh, get a say in any of this?"

"After showing me that drawing . . . no." She handed Karen a towel to cover her chest. "Let's go, stripper. I'm going to get set up. Bathroom is over there." Erin walked off.

As soon as she disappeared into the back again, the receptionist rushed over. "We all know she's crazy," she whispered, "but you really couldn't be in better hands. I promise, you will be so happy with what she gives you." She smiled, then added, "But she is crazy."

Karen watched the receptionist scurry back to her desk.

Erin returned, carrying a box of black nitrile examination gloves and several items sealed in plastic bags. She laid them on a metal instrument tray with wheels. "Why are you not half naked?"

"Uh . . . right. Right." Karen quickly moved to the bathroom, which she was happy to see was ultra-clean with a note reminding all staff to wash their hands after bathroom use. She closed and locked the door, then pulled out her cell phone and made a quick call.

"Yeah?"

"Okay, I know you're fucking her," she said to Stieg, "but on a scale of one to that girl we met on Western Ave that time who believed she could fly because she believed she was Jesus Christ *and* Cleopatra reborn . . . how crazy is your girlfriend?"

"She's not my girlfriend," was Stieg's immediate reply.

"My eyes are rolling all the way to the back of my head. Just get to the point."

"I don't know. I know some really crazy bitches. Erin's not the craziest."

"That is not making me feel better."

"I will say I've only heard good things about her tattoo stuff. Even Vig's girlfriend Kera let Erin put a tatt on her. She loves it. Erin worked freehand and picked the image for her. Oh, and Jace's too."

"She showed me that one. The chained bird, right?"

"Yeah."

"Well, if Jace trusts her . . ."

"Feel better?"

"Maybe. I guess. Kinda."

"Or you can just not let her tattoo you."

"Yardley King gets tattooed by her, dude. *Yardley King.*"

"So? I *know* Yardley King."

"Yeah, right," Karen laughed before disconnecting the call.

Erin ran green soap across the tattoo again before wiping it down with a paper towel and rolling her chair back to study what she'd done so far. Happy, she went back to work. She couldn't believe how fast she was going.

Karen's skin was perfect, absorbing the ink beautifully. And she had a high tolerance for pain. She didn't make a sound, move around, or complain.

Perfect.

Erin was so into the work, so lost in the design and what her hands were doing, that she was enjoying every second of this. She'd already done the outline and now she was filling in, using only blacks, grays, and a touch of white for highlights. She decided to avoid any color in this piece. It just didn't feel right.

Halfway through filling it in, she wiped the tatt down again and pushed her chair back, moving her head from side to side, trying to stretch out her tense neck muscles. "Wanna take a break?" she asked Karen.

"Yeah. Sure."

Erin helped her adjust the towel she was using to cover her chest, handed her a bottle of water, and they walked out the back door to the alley. They stood on either side of the door behind a protective panel screen, drinking their water and watching two stray cats fight.

"Twenty bucks says that gray takes out the red one," Erin offered.

"They're not fighting. That's their mating dance. Before you know it, they'll be doing it."

"Ew."

Karen moved a bit and winced.

"How ya holdin' up?" Erin asked.

"Fine. It's sore, but fine. Are you going to be able to finish today?"

"Yeah."

"You sound so . . . positive."

"Because I am."

Karen took another sip of water before asking, "How did you get into tattooing anyway?"

"My best friend in high school . . ."

"Yeah?"

"I broke her leg."

"On purpose?"

"Yes and no."

"I don't know what that means?"

"We were playing field hockey in gym class—"

"Ooooh. Field hockey. Someone's parents had money."

"You done?"

"Yeah."

"And we were split into two teams. And this girl on the other team who I hated anyway pissed me off and I went to nail her with my stick, but she moved and I ended up nailing my friend. When my friend got the cast on, she asked me to put a design on it, which I did—"

"Since you broke her leg and all."

"Exactly. Anyway, she had an older boyfriend who wanted to get a tattoo and since he had the beer, we went with him to the shop."

"Many of my decisions back in the day were based on where to find the beer . . ."

"The shop owner and artist wouldn't give the boyfriend a tattoo because he was already drunk—"

"Hope you drove home."

"—but she did like what I'd done on the cast. She offered me an apprenticeship position. First on weekends, then around my classes at art school."

"How did your parents feel about that?"

"Hated it. They didn't have a problem with me being an artist . . . but tattoos? *That* they weren't okay with. They had this vision of me being at the head of the artists' version of the Algonquin roundtable. Gallery shows on weekends. Impressing their friends with articles about me in *Artforum*."

"Instead you end up in *Ink*."

"I've had three covers on *Ink*."

"The *Rolling Stone* article must have helped."

She grinned. "It did." Erin finished her water and motioned toward the door. "You ready to go back in?"

"Sure. I'm so excited to see! Can I peek?"

"No."

Erin opened the door. "I have to say, you are a great sitter."

"I have a very high tolerance for pain."

"I bet you get a lot of guys with that line."

"I think we've found Ambrosio," Yardley announced as she ran out into the backyard, her phone in her hand, a wide smile on her face.

Kera loved that no matter how big Yardley was as a movie star, to her it was all about her sister-Crows. Nothing else took precedence. But when she could use her Hollywood connections to help them, she seemed especially proud.

"Where?" Chloe asked.

"A resort in Palm Springs."

Jace looked up from the pages that Maeve had typed out from Rolf's dictation. The runes were spells, explaining exactly how to get Erin into the heart of the Nine Worlds. They would use the Maids for the spell casting and the Carrion's Key for transport.

"Palm Springs?" Jace asked. "Are you sure?"

"Yeah. Why?"

"Ski and his brothers found evidence of a sacrifice at some resort in Palm Springs. Back just before we shoved Gullveig out. They fought the Mara there."

That was enough for Kera. She raised her arm and made a circle in the air with a forefinger. "All right, Marines! Let's move out!" When no one moved, she nodded. "Sorry. Sorry."

Leigh stepped close. "Another PTSD flashback, sweetie?"

"Stop asking me that. Let's just go. Please. I want to be airborne by the time the sun goes down."

"What about Erin?" Chloe called out in case any of them knew where she was.

"She's at her shop giving some friend of Stieg's a tattoo."

"Call her in?" Annalisa asked.

"No," Kera said. "Let's do this first. Jace, contact the Maids. Tell them we're nearly ready. You work with them. Tessa, get in touch with the Ravens. Tell them to get a crew together and get ready to move out. Also call Ski and see if this is the same place he hit before. I want details."

Kera's sister-Crows headed out as Chloe stepped beside her. "Are you sure about Erin? Leaving her behind?"

"She'll be safer here. No point in pushing our luck. Besides, if something happens to us tonight, the other Clans will still have her."

"Okay. Open your eyes."

Karen did, and then she gawked, stunned speechless, which was new for her since rarely did anything make her speechless.

"Well?" Erin pushed when Karen didn't say anything. "You like it or are you gonna have Stieg kick my ass?"

Karen had originally drawn a simple flower design, assuming that Erin would give it a little punch and make it cool. What she hadn't expected was the tribal flower piece in black and gray that went down her side, from just above her breast to the top of her hip bone. It was unbelievably detailed and gorgeous, and it didn't just say "pretty girl tattoo" to Karen. It said "survivor." She didn't know how Erin got that in there without anything obvious, but that's how Karen read it.

Standing in front of the full-length mirror, the white towel still held up in front of her tits, Karen turned and wrapped her arms around Erin, hugging her close.

"Uh . . . hon?" Erin cleared her throat. "You dropped that towel."

"I don't care," Karen said, crying into Erin's hair.

"Yeah, but I'm not sure I'm comfortable with your bare tits against me."

"Suck it up, whore."

Erin laughed, finally wrapping her arms around Karen and hugging her back. "You're welcome."

CHAPTER TWENTY-SIX

Six Crow Strike Teams, three Raven teams, and Ski's team, including Bear and Gundo, landed silently in Palm Springs. They surrounded the mansion used by the finest clientele of the resort, three of the Crow teams taking the roof, the rest going in from the ground floor.

Kera took the lead, pulling her blades out and keeping low, she sprinted toward the back of the mansion. She eased up, peering into the windows. Hearing a whistle, Kera looked over her shoulder. Leigh motioned to her and Kera ran to her side.

This window faced the well-lit ballroom. Bodies littered the floor and blood streaked the walls.

"It's a breach," she ordered, running past the teams and kicking in the door. She ran into the mansion hallway, Vig right by her side, the others bringing up the rear. They split off when they hit the door to the ballroom. Vig and his Raven brothers headed upstairs. The teams on the roof would keep lookout until they heard another order.

Kera and her sisters entered the ballroom and immediately stopped, their hands covering their noses and mouths.

"God," Maeve gasped, "that's a revolting smell."

"Well . . ." Annalisa added, looking at all the bodies ly-ing around, "now we know what it was really like *after* the raping and pillaging."

"Is everyone dead?" Kera asked, moving past the bodies, some of which were already decaying.

"It looks like—"

"Kera!" Vig bellowed from a floor above.

Glad to be away from the ballroom, Kera took off run-ning, her sisters with her. They charged up the stairs, for-going the elevator, taking two steps at a time. They found Vig and the Ravens on the third floor in the master bedroom. The Vikings separated and Kera moved forward.

Jourdan Ambrosio had curled herself into a corner—her face and body bruised, patches on her scalp where her weave had been pulled out, and old makeup still caked under her eyes, a thick gold necklace the only item she still wore.

Well . . . the necklace and the six-inch boots.

Kera motioned the Ravens back with both hands so An-nalisa could come forward. But the forensic psychologist whispered something to Tessa and it was Tessa, the regis-tered nurse who'd spent most of her First Life career in tough ERs, who now crouched a few feet away from Ambrosio and spoke softly to her, gently trying to coax her into assisting them before they got her the help she so desperately needed.

Tessa was good, but after about thirty minutes, Kera could feel her own patience running out and she hated her-self for it. She was better than this, wasn't she? Much better than this.

Or she was slowly becoming her mother, which was too horrifying a scenario to even contemplate.

As she forced herself to continue to wait, Annalisa moved to her side. Keeping her back to Ambrosio, she whispered, "That feeling you have at the moment is annoyance."

"I'm not that big a bitch, am I?" Kera whispered back. "Please tell me I'm not."

"Your annoyance, sweetie, is because the little cunt is lying."

Kera's gaze snapped to Annalisa's. "No way."

"I know my own kind, Kera. She's a sociopath. Whatever may have happened to her . . . she's *so* over it. They can endure anything if it gets them what they want, which is usually other people's suffering."

"What time is it?" Ambrosio asked softly.

"Time?" Tessa leaned back, searching the room with her eyes until she found a digital clock on a side table beside dead flowers. "Uh . . . it's nearly ten."

"Thank God," the woman snipped, her voice no longer soft. She stood. Naked and comfortable in that nakedness. "I didn't know how much longer I could keep that bullshit up."

That's when Kera knew that Annalisa had been right. Ambrosio's bruises were real, but her suffering had not been like that of the women and men whose bodies littered the ballroom.

Ambrosio smirked at Kera. "Your girl should be dead by now."

Stieg suddenly turned and ran, charging out of the room.

Tessa exhaled. "Erin."

Erin and Karen ended up staying at the shop until closing. In that time, Karen had taken one of the girl-sized tees and cut off the sleeves and most of the bottom so that it barely covered her breasts. Then she sat around letting her tattoo hang out. Erin kept telling her she needed to cover it up for at least an hour, but she wanted to show it off.

Finally, Erin convinced her to put a bandage over it, but

she could already tell that this would not be Karen's last tat. She just didn't know if she'd be the one giving Karen her future pieces. Just in case there were any problems with her skin's reaction to the ink, Erin told her, "If I'm not around, any of my other artists here can help you out."

"Okay. But why wouldn't you be around?"

"I'm busy," she lied. "All the movie stars and everything."

Thankfully Karen accepted that excuse, and they eventually headed out, Erin's team closing the shop for her.

As they began the several blocks' journey to Karen's car, Karen's energy level was pretty high. She was kind of bouncing all over the place, feeling really good about everything. Erin wasn't sure all that energy would last, though, once Karen got home and went to wash her tattoo the first time. It would be sore for the next forty-eight hours at least, but nothing quite like the first time she put water on it.

"Why do you keep telling me that?" Erin finally asked Karen, coming to a stop on the sidewalk.

"Telling you what?"

"You've said at least six times today that you and Stieg never hooked up."

Karen faced her. "Because I don't want you to think I'm in the way of you two getting together."

"I know you're not in the way."

"No. You know I'm not in the way of you two fucking. But I'm talking about a relationship."

Erin laughed. "Me and Stieg Engstrom? Are you high?"

"He likes you."

"He likes pussy. He's a *guy*."

Erin started walking again and Karen quickly caught up to her, arguing her point.

As they moved down the street, they passed three large men. They sized up a non-bra-wearing Karen and one called out, "Hey, *mamacita*!"

Karen missed it completely, busy as she was trying to convince Erin to make Stieg a part of her daily diet. Like Cheerios.

But Erin kept a close eye on the three men as they passed, wondering if they were more gang members hoping to make money on her head. She really hoped she wouldn't have to put poor Karen in the middle of a fight with gangbangers. Erin wasn't sure Stieg would ever forgive her for that level of fuckup.

As they continued on for a bit, Karen abruptly stopped talking. And stopped walking. Then Erin noticed that the three men behind them had suddenly disappeared.

"Uh . . . Erin?" Karen said, her voice soft.

Erin didn't even turn around. She didn't have to. She sensed them. Moving in.

She reached out and took Karen's arm. "I need you to run."

"I'll be honest with you . . . I'm a runner. I'm more than happy to run when danger's near. But I don't think that's an option at the moment."

Still holding Karen's arm, Erin looked one way, then the other. The Carrion were moving in from both sides of the sidewalk and down at the corner. When she returned her gaze to where the three men had been standing earlier, she saw that they'd been replaced.

Two of the Carrion walked a bit closer, one wrapping his arm around the other's shoulders, leaning on him.

"Heard you were looking for my friend here."

The "friend" lifted his hand to wave and she saw Hel's rune burned into his decaying flesh.

"So . . . here we are, slave. Come and get us."

Erin zipped through her options. She could fly. She could even carry Karen with her, but the Carrion could also fly. She could fly without Karen in the hopes of leading them

away from her, but the way a few of the Carrion were looking at Stieg's wingless friend . . .

No. Erin couldn't leave her.

Erin heard a squawk and she shifted her gaze to the top
of the building she stood in front of. The nosey crows were
there, watching her. Three took off and she knew they were
going for help, but that would take time. Erin needed help
now.

She motioned to the Carrion and the bird squawked at her
again. *Really*? They were giving her shit about calling them
rats with wings? Seriously? *Now?*

Gritting her teeth, Erin nodded at the Carrion again.

"What the fuck are you doing?" Karen demanded, her
muscles vibrating against Erin's hand.

The birds lifted off and Erin did the only thing she could
think of.

Keeping her grip on Karen's arm, she took hold of the
back of Karen's jeans, lifted her off the ground and chucked
the bigger woman across the hood of a car parked at the
curb.

Karen squealed as she flew, but when she landed, she
rolled over, quickly got to her feet, and took off running.

Grateful the girl had some natural survival skills, Erin
followed, relieved when she saw the birds descend on the
Carrion like a vicious horde. She jumped over the car and
went after Karen. Together they ran into an alley until they
reached an apartment building that was being renovated.
That meant it had a lot of rooms but no tenants.

Erin dodged through the construction equipment, and
Karen managed to keep up with her. Reaching one of the
doors that had been chained shut, Erin lifted her leg and
kicked once. The chain broke and the door slammed open.

"Go." She pushed Karen ahead of her and down the hall.

Thankfully the interior was still intact so she searched for a good apartment to use.

"Karen, you are going to see some things. I just need you to roll with it. Understand?"

"No. But you don't survive six years on the streets if you don't know how to roll with bizarre shit."

"Good enough."

Erin stopped in front of an apartment. She went to kick the door open, but Karen tried the doorknob first and it was unlocked.

Raising her eyebrows, Karen walked in and Erin followed. Just what she needed. Stieg Junior.

She heard the battle cries of the Carrion and knew they were coming. She closed the door, stepped back, and quickly pulled her blades from the holster around her ankle.

"You walk around with knives?"

"LA's a rough town."

"No kidding. Who are those guys anyway? They look . . . dead."

"They are dead. Dead-ish."

"Is it the zombie apocalypse?"

Erin glanced away from the door so she could give Karen her best *Are you fucking kidding* me look.

"I'll take that as a no," Karen mumbled.

"When they come after me, go out the window. Just run. Don't stop."

"Leave you?"

"Sweetie, you have to. Please. For—"

The door exploded in and Karen screamed, using her arm to block the wood skittering across the room.

Erin moved, jumping forward and slamming one blade into the eye of a Carrion and the other blade into a nearby Carrion's throat. From the corner of her eye, she saw Karen make a mad dash for the window, but as soon as she reached it, Carrion standing on the outside punched their fists through the glass, reaching for her.

She jumped back and several Carrion grabbed her, dragging her back into a dark corner.

A hand fell on Erin's wrist and her muscles retracted as her skin burned. The touch of the Carrion could turn a human into dust, if allowed to linger for a long enough time.

Erin didn't wait for that. She used her other blade to cut off the hand holding her, then shook off the still gripping fingers.

She tried to move toward Karen but, again, more Carrion came between her and her friend. Now there were more men on Karen because the former street kid was putting up such a fight, but she wouldn't be able to hold out for long.

Then again, Erin wouldn't be able to hold out much longer, either.

She heard Karen scream. One of the Carrion had her around the throat, lifting her off the ground.

"Let her go!" Erin bellowed, cutting the throat of another Carrion. She knew she wasn't killing any of them. It took a lot more to kill them. But she was hoping to buy enough time to let Karen get away.

The Carrion yanked Karen to the floor and she disappeared underneath all their big bodies.

"*Karen!*" Erin started to push her way through the Carrion, trying to grab her friend, but the entire group froze at the same time when they heard it.

As one, they all took a step back. Then they heard it again.

She knew that sound. She ought to from watching so much *Animal Planet* and *National Geographic*. It was . . . it was a . . .

A leopard?

The big black cat she knew was Karen tore her way through the Carrion and tackled one of the men standing beside Erin, taking him to the ground. Karen dug her fangs into the Carrion's neck and even though he tried to push her off, she held on until she'd completely removed his throat—leaving the Carrion dead.

Not dead-ish, but actually dead.

And with that throat in her mouth, Karen charged across the room to the broken window and spit the flesh out. She followed up with several long and loud roars. But she didn't run.

Why didn't she run? "Karen! Go!"

"Kill it!" the lead Carrion bellowed. "*Kill them both!*"

A fist hit Erin hard, sending her flipping and rolling across the floor. As blood splattered, she was sure her nose was broken. Thick boots kicked her in the side, the back.

Erin switched her blades to her left hand and unleashed flame from her right, hitting the Carrion in the face. He growled, stumbling away, but another moved up to take his place. Erin flipped over and slammed her blades into his Achilles. He dropped, screaming.

At least they felt pain. That helped.

She got to her feet, but another hand wrapped around her throat, lifted her up. Unlike with Odin, though, the hand on her flesh instantly began to burn. To sear.

Erin stabbed at the hand gripping her, trying for the eyes. But even as she fought, she heard stomping moving down the hall.

Her sister-Crows were quieter, and the Ravens and Protectors made no sound at all. Still, she never expected to see the weak walls of the apartment torn apart as three grizzly bears burst into the room, her attacker immediately dropping her in panic.

Because there were grizzly bears. In a soon-to-be-demolished West LA apartment building.

What the fuck was happening?

The bears roared and charged, going after the Carrion attacking Karen, dragging them away from her before slapping them around the room like toys. Other Carrion tried to use their hands to harm the bears the way they'd hurt Erin, but the power didn't work.

It was the strangest thing Erin had ever seen.

Fortunately, though, the presence of the bears distracted the Carrion from her as they began to pull out their flint-edged weapons. Weapons they'd kept hidden. They knew that Erin—a Crow—would use them the first chance she got. As they were the only weapons she knew of that could actually kill a Carrion.

Erin dove at a Carrion, landing on his back and reaching over his shoulder to grab hold of the long-handled axe he held. They struggled over it, but he refused to hand it over. She slapped one hand over his eyes and unleashed fire. He screamed and she yanked.

With weapon in hand, she jumped down, hefted the axe and swung, taking the screaming Carrion's head off. She stepped over his body and began hacking wildly, moving closer to her goal.

A few bear claws lashed out at her, one dragging across the skin of her bicep, leaving deep gashes, but she kept moving. She had no choice.

The Carrion seemed to have had enough. They began fleeing toward the exits—the doorway, the windows, the large holes in the walls. But as they escaped, she saw her target going with them.

The problem was the bears that stood between her and what she absolutely had to get. She knew it was her one and only chance.

"*MOVE!*" Erin bellowed at the top of her lungs, which she then followed up with a blast of flame at the space on the floor between the bears.

As any mammal would do, the bears jumped away from the fire and Erin hefted the axe and threw it with everything she had. It hit the Carrion right in the spine, laying him out.

As he was the Key, the Carrion came back for him. The lead fighter grabbed his compatriot by the head to drag him away. Erin slapped her palms together, released the power of her flame between them, then unleashed the large ball of flame at the Carrion's face.

With a roar he stumbled back, arms flailing, and then he was abruptly dragged back by Vig Rundstöm.

Crows came in through the windows, Ravens and Danski Eriksen rushed through the front doorway. The bears panicked, roaring at all the new people.

"Everyone calm down!" Erin yelled, trying to keep her sisters and the Ravens from attacking. By now the Carrion had made a run for it, leaving a few of their weapons behind, which the Clans would add to their battle arsenal. Erin reached down and grabbed the foot of the dead Carrion and pulled him close. Placing her foot against his ass, she gripped the axe handle and pried the blade from his back.

She moved around to his side, put her foot against his arm, raised the axe above her head, and brought it down, severing his hand from his wrist. Grinning, she crouched down and lifted the hand.

But when she went to stand, she found three giant bear heads glaring down at her.

Then they roared.

CHAPTER TWENTY-SEVEN

Stieg yanked away the Carrion sword that Vig held and was moving toward the first bear to cut him down where he stood roaring at Erin, when a black panther jumped between him and the bears and Erin. Freezing, his arm raised to strike, Stieg asked, "Karen? What are you doing here?"

"Wait," Erin said. "You knew about this? And you never told me? Dude, that's so uncool!"

Stieg lowered his arm. "Is that *really* your big concern right now?"

Erin grinned. "Yeah."

The panther began making noises. Yips and snarls and tiny purrs until Stieg pointed out, "I don't know what the fuck you're saying to me, Karen."

The panther blinked, took a step back, and suddenly she was Karen again. Tall, beautiful, and extremely naked Karen.

"Dude!" Stieg glanced back at his now crowding Raven brothers, most of them trying to get a good, long look at his friend. "Put on some clothes!"

"Oh, my God, *dude*," she shot back. "You have wings. Get over it. And don't hurt the bears. They're with me."

"Since when?"

She rested her hand on the big hump between one of the bear's shoulders, a bear that had to be at least a thousand pounds and probably nine to ten feet tall if it went up on its hind legs. "Since they just saved our asses."

Stieg blinked and the three bears became three men. They were no longer ten feet or a thousand pounds, but Stieg still wouldn't turn his back on them.

"Thanks, guys," Karen said.

"We shouldn't leave you here, *mamacita*," one said, his untrusting gaze looking over Stieg and his brothers before glancing back at the Crows still standing by the windows. "Freaks," he sneered.

Erin laughed from her spot on the floor. "Wow. Throwing stones from that glass bear cave, aren't ya, Gentle Ben?"

Karen winced and her gaze implored Stieg.

"You better go," he pushed the shifters. "Before we let the girls kick your ass."

"That's you helping?" Karen asked.

"Yes."

The bears looked at Karen again.

"You sure?" one asked.

"I'll be fine. Thank you. Really."

The bear gave a tough, street boy nod before heading toward the hallway, but for some unknown reason, Erin jumped up, still holding that Carrion hand and planted herself between the shifters and the exit.

"Wait. You can't go."

"Want us to kill 'em?" Vig asked.

Erin looked at Stieg's Raven brother over her shoulder. "*No.*"

"Just asking."

With a frustrated sigh, she faced the suspicious male shifters again. But Stieg knew things were about to get weird when she forced a big smile. "How would you gentlemen like to help save the world?"

"No," the lead shifter immediately replied.

"What do you mean no?"

"We mean no. If you guys fuck up the world, it's your problem. And everyone knows you fucked up the world. But we're not about to help you out of that shit. We weren't even helping you now." He gestured to Karen with a jerk of his thumb. "We were helping her. She called. We came. That's what shifters do for each other. No matter the breed or the species. Shame you Nordic fucks can't say the same thing."

Erin's arms shot out, which was good. She stopped Stieg and Vig from throttling the big idiot.

"So . . . if you ladies and gentlemen—"

"And freaks," another shifter tossed in.

"—and freaks would excuse us—"

"How about cash?" Erin suddenly asked the shifter.

"Cash?"

"You may be able to turn into a bear, but you're still human. And cash trumps everything."

"Why do you want to pay them?" Vig asked.

"Because the Carrion couldn't hurt them. Not like they can us."

"Magic doesn't harm us the way it does you," Karen explained. "We're considered part of the animal kingdom by higher powers. That's why witches' pets can walk in and out of their circles without any problems. Those dead things, though, can hack us to death with their weapons."

"Well, are there more of you?" Kera asked.

"Yeah," Erin agreed. "Is there like a herd of bear we can hire?"

Karen winced again as the shifters growled.

"We don't roam in herds," the shifter growled. "We're not prey animals."

"Okay. Fine. But think about it. We'll pay you well and you'll have the benefit of saying you helped save the world."

"The world you fucked up."

"Are we going to go there again?"

"Here." Alessandra leaned in and handed one of her business cards to the shifters. Why she carried business cards around with her, Stieg didn't know. Maybe he didn't want to know. "Take this. Call me."

She grinned and leaned back as Maeve reminded her, "You have a boyfriend."

"In Germany."

"And how come the shifters get enhanced immune systems?" Maeve demanded. "We're warriors of gods. We should have enhanced immune systems."

"*You do have an enhanced immune system!*" Erin practically screamed. Maeve was one of the few people Stieg knew could piss her the hell off.

"But I'm—"

"Noooo!" Erin cut her sister-Crow off. "I can't deal with your level of crazy right now! So just shut it."

"But—"

"Shut. It." Erin looked back at the shifters. "Cash. And saving the world. Think about it." She moved and the three shifters walked out.

Once they were gone, she held up the Carrion's hand, her grin wide. "Got it!" she cheered, waving that stupid hand around.

And that's when the muscles on Stieg's neck got tight.

Erin waited for Stieg to congratulate her or something. She had not only gotten the Key, she'd also protected his best friend until Karen's fellow shifters showed up. She expected some major kudos for that.

Instead, Stieg looked at Karen and barked, "Are you just going to stand there naked? Like that's normal."

Karen crossed her arms under her chest, standing tall and proud in her gorgeous nakedness and replied. "You've got wings and you're coming after me?"

At that point, they both started yelling at each other. Erin wasn't in the mood to hear any of it. She walked over to Kera and the others and held up the hand. "Look! I got it!"

Her sister-Crows just stared at her and Erin became annoyed. "Are you treacherous bitches telling me that no one gives a shit how I kicked major ass?" She gestured to her bleeding arm. "I got swiped by a bear, and I am still all *no bigs*. None of you seem that impressed."

That's when Maeve, of all people, suddenly threw herself at Erin, hugging her tight.

"What's happening?" Erin asked the others. "Why is she hugging me?"

"You got the Key," Annalisa reminded her. "That means you're going."

"I thought that was the point."

"We're worried about you, whore. Deal with it."

"Oh. Well . . . I'm worried about me, too. Yet I've still managed to be super impressed with my mad skills."

Kera snorted. "You're always impressed with your mad skills."

"Because that's how awesome I am. You don't have to be jealous."

"Jealous?"

"Because we both know that if I'd joined the Marines or whatever, I'd be, like a colonel or admiral dictator or whatever your fancy titles are. But lucky for you . . . I focused my talents elsewhere."

Kera shook her head. "I can't even." The phone in the

back pocket of her jeans buzzed and she checked it. "The Maids are ready for us."

"Cool. Let's get this done."

With tears in her eyes, Maeve finally pulled away from Erin and patted her cheeks. "My brave little soldier."

Erin started to reply to that level of insanity, but Kera slapped her hand over Erin's mouth and pushed her away from Maeve. "We don't have time for you to be yourself. Let's just go." Kera began to lead her to the doorway, but Erin pulled away and went to Karen's side. The woman had managed to get most of her clothes back on.

"You two taking her home?" Erin asked Rolf and Siggy, who were standing nearby.

The men nodded and Erin smiled. "Good." Leaning in, she said to Karen, "No wonder his goat's afraid of you."

"Every time I smell her, I get so damn hungry."

Erin laughed. "And to think, I just thought you were some greedy stripper."

"Aren't we all?" Karen asked. "Especially these two," she added, motioning to Siggy and Rolf.

"So you've known all this time about Stieg?"

"Ever since he was fifteen and sneezed. His wings came out."

"Such a goofus."

"And he's known what I was. The man knows how to keep a secret. He didn't tell me shit about you, either. I just assumed you were a really short Valkyrie or something. But a Crow . . . eeks. He's always kept me away from you guys. I thought." Karen took Erin's hands with her own, held them. "Look, I have no clue what's going on, but . . . good luck."

"Thanks."

"And thanks for my amazing tattoo."

"I sense a lot of crop tops in your future."

"Gotta bare it while you still have it." Karen hugged Erin, and for once, Erin didn't mind.

"I never paid you," Karen whispered.

"Take care of Stieg. We'll call it even." Erin pulled away. "See ya, stripper."

"Bye, ho."

Erin walked toward the exit, but Karen's voice stopped her. "Like I said, I don't know what's going on, but I've got some contacts, can call in some favors. I'll see if I can round up some of my fellow people."

"Don't you mean wildlife?"

Karen laughed and Erin walked out into the hallway, where she stopped and said to the Viking looming over her shoulder, "And stop looking at me like I'm already dead. It's irritating me."

"Everything irritates you," Stieg growled.

"No. That would be you." Erin looked at Stieg and smiled. "Now come on. Let's go send me to the very pits of Helheim! It'll be fun!"

"Just stop talking."

CHAPTER TWENTY-EIGHT

By the time they all arrived back at the Bird House, the Maids were waiting for them.

Inka not only had the rune-language spell book given to them by the archangels and Rolf's decipherings of those runes, she also had a spell that would help Erin make the giant's sword manageable and a return spell that would quickly get her out of Nidhogg's world and back to her own . . .

If she made it that far.

Inka never said that, out loud, but it hung in the air above them. Even as she taught Erin the spells, even as she helped with the even-quicker healing of Erin's broken nose.

And Stieg knew it. They all knew it; just no one was saying it. Not even Erin.

So to stop himself from grabbing her and running off to some far-off place to keep her safe, he followed Erin around the house. He listened to what she listened to, learned what she learned, and tried to pretend that he didn't know he'd never see her again in this lifetime.

* * *

Runes were burned into the grass, creating a circle. The Holde's Maids surrounded the new addition to the Crow's yard. Animal sacrifices were made—much to the disgust of the vegan Crows—and gods called upon.

And while the Maids readied the circle that would take Erin to new worlds, she showered, put on her battle clothes, and strapped weapons to her legs and a thin Gucci belt around her waist—a Yardley gift from her vast collection of designer accessories.

Combing her wet hair off her face, Erin walked out of the bathroom and down the hall to her bedroom. She wasn't surprised to find Stieg sitting on her bed, waiting for her.

He looked more pissed off than usual. "This still seems like a bad idea," he complained after she closed the door.

"No one has said it's a good idea. All anyone says is that it's the *only* idea."

"You shouldn't go alone."

"I'm not dragging one of my sister-Crows down to Corpse Shore with me, and no one else will volunteer."

He looked up, his blond hair typically a little wild and almost hiding his gray eyes.

Did the man even have a comb? She couldn't remember seeing one in his apartment.

"I'd volunteer."

Erin had had a feeling this was coming. She placed her comb on top of her chest of drawers and stood in front of him. She pushed her hands into his hair and finger-combed the strands off his face. "Besides the Crows, who are the best fighters in the Clans?"

"Honestly?"

"Yeah."

"Vig, Rolf, Siggy, Kafli, Old Finni. Most of the Protectors when they bother to fight. The Giant Killers when they don't lose their hammers."

"And who are the meanest?"

"You."

"And with me gone?"

Stieg let out a long sigh. He was smart enough to know that would be coming. "Me."

"You have to stay. They need you. It's time for mean."

"Yeah. You're right."

She cupped his jaw in both hands and lifted his head. "But don't give up on me yet."

"I promise not to do that."

They stared at each other for a long time, but a knock at the door had her pulling away.

"Yeah?" she called out.

Kera leaned in. "It's time."

The Maids chanted and danced, animal blood smeared on their faces, hands, and across their blue robes.

Stieg stood back with his Raven brothers, watching the ritual. Erin stood in the center of it all, the Carrion's hand— the Key—held in her fist. Her eyes closed, her body tense, waiting for it all to be over.

Or, he guessed, for everything to begin.

"You all right?" Vig asked, keeping his voice low, although it didn't really matter. The Vikings were not big on *quiet* rituals and ceremonies. The Maids were basically screeching at this point.

Stieg never lied to Vig, so he replied, "No. I feel like I'll never see her again."

"You don't know that. If anyone's crazy enough to pull this off . . . it's Erin Amsel."

"Yeah. I guess."

Stieg glanced over his shoulder, keeping an eye out for any trouble, like the Mara or more Carrion making an appearance, trying to stop the ritual and kill Erin outright. But he saw nothing like that.

Yet what he did see worried him just as much. "What the fuck is Odin doing here?" he asked his brothers.

As one, they all looked and the god waved lightly. It appeared as if he was just watching. But why? Odin refused to involve himself in the affairs of the world, and Stieg was sure the god had seen enough Maids' rituals over the centuries to last him forever. Why was this one worthy of the great Odin's attention?

What most people didn't understand was that Odin didn't choose warriors for his human Clan who worshipped him without question, who trusted him implicitly. Only a fool would trust Odin, of all gods, implicitly.

So his presence simply made them nervous.

It also made Stieg nervous that no one else seemed to see him. He was only showing himself to the Ravens. To those loyal to him.

"What's he up to?" Stieg demanded, beginning to panic. "He's up to something."

"Calm down," Josef, their leader, told him. "He could be *trying* to freak you out so you'll do something stupid. You know how he is. Just ignore him."

"I can't ignore him."

"*Pretend* to ignore him then."

Stieg tried. But then Odin was moving, stepping past the Ravens, and then the Crows. Stieg briefly thought the god was going into the circle to do something stupid or cruel to Erin because he was pissed at her for fucking with the only eye he had left.

Until Odin abruptly veered away from the Maids and the circle and made his way over to . . .

"Vig . . . ?"

Vig looked at what had Stieg's attention. "Uh-oh."

Odin had crouched down and was whispering in Brodie Hawaii's ear. Ears that were straight up, dangerously alert. The dog's tail was wagging wildly and her body entirely too tense.

She shot off, Odin grinning.

A grinning Odin was never good.

Stieg watched Brodie dash around and through the Crows. Kera was focused entirely on Erin and the ritual, so she was oblivious to what her dog was doing.

"Kera!" Vig called out. "Brodie!" He pointed.

The dog dashed past the oblivious Maids, into the circle, and right at Erin. The hundred-pound pit bull leaped a few inches off the ground and snatched the Key right out of Erin's fist.

"Brodie, no!" Kera yelled, immediately chasing after her dog. The Crows joined in, trying to help.

Erin, however, didn't join in. She stayed, knowing it could be her only chance to get into the Nine Worlds, with or without the Key. But she did yell. A lot. "*Get that fucking dog! Bring back that hand!*"

But Brodie wasn't giving it up. Instead she led the group of deadly warriors on a ridiculous chase all over the backyard. It wasn't like she was even running. It was more like she was prancing. All four paws off the ground. She was just so happy!

The energy around the circle picked up and the Maids' screeching became much louder as their ritual began taking hold. Working. Stieg knew they were running out of time.

Brodie was heading right for him, probably because she loved to tackle him. This time, though, he didn't let her take him down. He grabbed hold of the Key in her mouth and yanked. Brodie yanked back. She refused to let go and began dragging Stieg.

"Drop it, Brodie!" Stieg ordered, pulling as hard as he

could, hoping to throw the hand to Erin before she disappeared. "*Drop it now!*" he bellowed, as loudly as he could.

Brodie released the hand at the same moment that Stieg pulled with all his strength. When she let go, he was relieved but also surprised—and definitely unprepared. He tripped backward over his own feet and stumbled. Past the Maids, past the protective runes of the circle, and right into the arms of Erin Amsel.

He hit her hard and together they went down. They didn't hit the ground, though.

And it seemed like they would never stop falling . . .

Mouth open, Kera stood outside the circle and stared at where her sister-Crow and Vig's Raven brother had disappeared. "Oh, Brodie," she gasped. "Oh, God, what did you do?"

"It wasn't Brodie," Vig told her, stepping between her and the dog.

"Stop trying to protect her."

"I'm not. It wasn't Brodie. It was *him*."

Kera saw the god leaning against their house. Just standing there! "*Motherfucker!*" she yelled, running over to him as the others moved quickly out of her way. "*What have you done?*"

"Helping," Odin replied. "Just like the little bitch asked."

Kera went to swing at him, but Vig caught her around the waist and pulled her back. The other Crows crowded in behind them.

"That was fucked up, Odin," Chloe angrily chastised.

"And here I was, trying to help you ladies. And, of course, humanity. I'm all about humanity."

"You—"

"She has the Key, doesn't she? She has one of my precious

Ravens. She's better off than she was a couple hours ago." He rubbed his hands together. "Well . . . I have to go. Got a hot date and I better get all my hot dates in while I still can," he joked. He walked into the Crows, pushing past them, ignoring the vicious stares and accompanying hisses.

"Oh, by the way," he said, again facing them. "Have you noticed it? In the air?"

"Noticed what?" Chloe asked.

Kera was still unable to say anything to the god without cursing and demanding his death. He'd used her dog. Her dog!

Odin smiled at Chloe's question, head dipping down . . . then he was gone.

"What did *that* mean?" Leigh asked.

Vig released Kera and paced away. He and his Raven brothers exchanged glances.

"What?" Kera demanded. "What is it?"

"She's back," Annalisa guessed. "And if she isn't, she's coming."

Kera turned to Vig and he silently nodded his agreement.

"Nothing changes," Kera said. "We move forward."

Chloe frowned. "But—"

"We move forward." Kera gestured to Annalisa with a crook of her finger and walked off.

When Annalisa joined her, Kera said, "I need you to take care of something for me. It might be too late, and a waste of time, but do it anyway."

The forensic psychologist smiled. "Just tell me what you need . . ."

Jourdan laughed at some joke the owner of the Palm Springs resort told her as he counted up the bodies and added up the cost for this little "event" and the subsequent "extensive cleaning" that would be necessary. The beauty of this establishment was that it was owned and run by men who understood power. For the right price, they could handle anything one needed done. They'd helped her manage *this*. *This* being the bodies left by the Carrion.

She didn't even know who they were going after. Didn't know who the "girl" was that she'd told those "warriors" about, because none of it mattered. Nor did it matter that all the leeches who'd glommed onto her over the years were decaying in the first-floor ballroom. It also didn't matter that her body was sore and abused.

None of it mattered because in the end, Gullveig would reward Jourdan well. She'd promised.

Pushing her hair off her face and mentally preparing for her next performance, Jourdan walked out the doorway and down the hall to a quiet bedroom. Once everything was set, she'd make the call to the police and then she'd go back to her amazing, glamorous life, only now with even more headlines in the papers.

She reached the bedroom off the hall, and that's when she stopped and slowly faced the woman standing behind her. A Crow.

She'd researched these Crows. They had a moral compass, as her mother would say. Especially with that new War General of theirs. Since Jourdan was unarmed and a fellow woman, she knew she was safe. These women would never hurt her.

She searched her brain, trying to remember this one's name. *Ahhh, yes.* The one the Crow leader had called Annalisa.

"What do you want, Annalisa?"

Best to make her think of Jourdan as more than just an enemy. That's why always remembering names was so important.

"I know you," Annalisa replied. "I was you. Long time ago."

"So?" Jourdan asked. "What do you want me to do about it?"

"Die."

A blade flashed and Jourdan saw her blood splatter on the white wall beside her. She dropped to her knees and wrapped her hands around her throat, trying to stop the flow. She needed to call to her goddess. She would protect her. "Gull—" she got out, but the evil bitch grabbed her tongue.

"No, no. Sorry, sweetie. Not an option for you."

The blade flashed again and the Crow held Jourdan's tongue in front of her eyes.

Annalisa smiled and Jourdan realized the Crow hadn't been lying. She was like her.

"Your glamorous days are over, bitch." The Crow walked off, tossing Jourdan's tongue out a window as she passed it.

Jourdan fell forward, too weak to keep the pressure on her neck . . .

CHAPTER TWENTY-NINE

Hands beat against Stieg's arms and neck and didn't stop, forcing him to lift up and away from the body beneath him.

He found a panting, nearly blue Erin Amsel buried underneath him, the Carrion hand caught between them. "Ew!" He rolled away from her.

Erin pushed herself up on her elbows. "Really?" she barked, still trying to catch her breath. "The *hand* is freaking you out?"

"Once I cut things off, I don't play with them."

"What the hell happened?" she asked, sitting up and looking around.

"Odin."

"What?"

"Odin sent Brodie to grab that hand." Disgusted, Stieg used two fingers to take the hand sitting in her lap and toss it to the side.

"He . . ." Erin glanced off, and then she began to laugh. "That bastard."

"What?"

"When we were on your balcony, I asked him if he was going to help."

"Well, that was dumb."

"Yes. I'm aware of that now. I forgot who I was dealing with."

Stieg sat up, his arms resting on his knees, and looked around. It was cold. Freezing cold. And he was in a tank top and jeans. Erin wasn't much better off. "Where do you think we are?"

"No idea." She stood, wiping dirt off her jeans.

"Where's the map?"

"What map?"

Stieg closed his eyes. "Please tell me you brought the map."

Erin stared at him for an impossibly long time, head tilted, eyes narrowed in confusion. Then she blinked a few times and exclaimed, "Oh! The map!" She chuckled and reached into her back pocket. "Totally forgot about that."

"I really wished you'd gone to get that ADHD test."

"Yeah." She crouched down next to him, spreading the map out in front of them. "But then again . . . me on medication? Is that *anyone's* idea of a good thing?"

They studied the map.

"Okay," Erin said, glancing up at a distant, snow-covered mountain top. "Based on that mountain, I'm going to guess that we are—"

"Shit."

"—right about—"

"Shit."

"What's wrong with you?"

Stieg grabbed Erin's arm and yanked her back, pulling her around a nearby tree.

"Shit, shit, shit, shit—"

"Calm down," Erin said softly.

"I hate you."

"Calm. Down. Think of Texas."

"Texas? The line is 'think of England.'"

"Why would I think of England?"

"Why would you think of Texas?"

A snout came around the corner. A giant, *giant* snout. Quickly followed by an entire dog.

A giant, *giant* dog.

Wet, cold nostrils bigger than Stieg, sniffed, searching them out.

Deciding he wasn't going to die as doggie kibble—at least not without a fight—Stieg began to move forward, but Erin used her forearm against his chest to push him back and hold him there.

He could have pushed her off, but she shook her head, mouthing, *Wait.*

"Old Boy!" a harsh voice rang out. "Old Boy, come!"

The dog woofed and Stieg ended up grabbing Erin before the dog's puff of air sent them flying. He managed to keep them grounded, and the dog ran off to its owner.

The earth beneath their feet shook as the giant stomped by, a giant deer slung over his shoulder, his dog running around his legs and barking.

"You do know," Stieg felt the need to point out, "we're not in a forest . . . we're just in the *grass*."

Erin glanced up. "Shit." Her eyes widened and she ran. "Shit!"

Stieg blew out a breath. "This can't be good . . ."

Erin ran to where they'd been standing before that humongous dog appeared. She picked up the map, quickly folded it, and slid it into her back pocket. She was grateful for that, at least.

"We have a problem," she told Stieg when he caught up to her.

"What problem?"

"We need that Carrion hand to get back home with the sword that will save the world."

"Yeah? So?"

"It's gone."

"What? Are you sure?"

She pointed at a spot in the dirt. "Yes. That's where it was when that dog showed—" She stopped talking, her breath catching. That wasn't just a natural depression in the dirt. That depression had been placed there. By a dog paw. Her eyes focused past Stieg.

"What?"

"Shit!" Erin took off running, jumping up a few times in order to get a visual of where she was and her target. "I swear," she told Stieg once he caught up to her, "I am never getting a dog!"

They ran after the dog and its owner, thankfully hidden in the grass that to them seemed more like a forest.

And the reason the grass was like that was because they were in Jotunheim. Land of the giants.

It had never occurred to Erin that this would be where that stupid Carrion hand would take her, but it seemed that Hel was even more paranoid than her father was rumored to be. She wanted to make sure that if someone other than her Carrion used the hand to get into the Nine Worlds, whoever it was would end up being either stomped or eaten. Because the giants in Jotunheim were known for their taste in human flesh.

So running after one of those giants? Definitely not one of Erin's best ideas, but it wasn't like she had any choice. She needed that stupid hand back!

The giant made his way to a camp at the edge of an actual forest. The trees. Good God, the trees. The redwoods looked like toothpicks in comparison.

The giant tossed down the dead deer, which turned out to be still sort of alive. It kicked and tried to get back up. The giant grabbed it by its antlers, put his foot against the animal's back to hold it in place, and gave a sharp twist, killing it instantly.

Stieg and Erin looked at each other, then as quietly as possible, backed up nearly a mile.

"We are so fucked," Stieg announced.

Unfortunately, Erin couldn't argue with that. "We need to figure out how to get in there and get that hand."

"How do we know the dog even has it?"

"I saw it stuck between the pads of its paw."

Stieg held his hands out, like he was pleading. "How are we going to get it out of *there*?"

"Wait till they're sleeping?" When he threw his hands up, "I know, I know. Not my best plan."

"A really shitty plan!"

"I can't think of anything else. And we have to at least *pretend* we're going home."

"Not if that giant catches us. He will eat us."

"I know. I know." Erin began to pace. "Maybe," she suggested, "we can find someone else to send us home."

"Like who?"

"Light elves. Snorri Sturluson says they're as beautiful as the sun. They can't be too bad."

"It's like you've never been to Hollywood."

"Good point."

"All right." Stieg threw back his shoulders, cracked his neck . . . like he was psyching himself up. "We can do this."

"Can we?"

"Okay. If we're going to even *attempt* to make it through this, we can question plans, but we can't always be negative. We're both being negative."

Erin reached out, took his hand. "I'm sorry."

"For what?"

"That you're here. I was the only one supposed to be sac-rificing myself for the common good. Fucking with Odin got you here."

"Odin deserved it." Stieg sighed. "Sadly, he always de-serves it."

"Well . . . I'm sorry, which is strange. I'm never sorry. Or rarely so."

Stieg stared down at her for so long she began to wonder why. "What?"

"We're gonna do this."

"Wait until they fall asleep and—"

"Get back our hand."

Erin giggled.

"What?" he asked.

"It's just funny when you say it like that."

They had to wait until sundown, which sucked because it meant that it became even colder. They were actually lucky that they were Raven and Crow, because a normal human wouldn't last two minutes in this world.

Together, Stieg and Erin inched closer to the campsite, watching as the giant sat in front of a pit fire, sucking the marrow from the deer's leg bone. He tossed a full thigh to the dog, and it trotted around with the meat in its mouth for a minute or two before settling down and eating.

After that there was some burping, some drinking, a little farting, and then traveling into the trees to take care of per-sonal business. Sadly, none of that was from the dog.

Erin had to run off so she could gag some distance away. Stieg had to follow. Not because he was worried about her; he just needed to gag, too.

The giant then sharpened his swords and knives, made a few arrows for his bow, and cleaned the spikes on the head of his mace. Finally, he pulled out his bedroll and settled down for the night. The dog went to sleep by his feet.

Erin and Stieg moved closer, keeping silent, desperately trying to ignore the brutal wind blowing past them.

Erin motioned for Stieg to hold his position while she made the final steps to the dog. She eased around it until she reached the feet. She got close, reaching up to grab the Carrion's hand from between its pads just as the dog started dreaming. Its paws suddenly twitched, sending her flipping end over end.

Stieg cringed, but didn't go after her. They needed to get that stupid Key. He ran to the dog's paws and did see the hand tucked tight between the pads. It was so high up, though, he was surprised Erin had tried to reach for it. He couldn't reach it and he was way taller than her.

Shrugging, Stieg unleashed his wings, intending to fly up to get the hand. Yet in the silence of the surrounding land, the unleashing of his wings cracked through the air like a whip and the dog woke up, scrambling to its paws and facing Stieg.

"Fuck," he muttered seconds before big fangs tried to snatch him out of the air. He turned and flew off, the dog right on his ass.

Erin finally landed facedown in the dirt. When she got back to her feet, she watched in horror as Stieg shot by and then that goddamn dog charged toward her. She dropped to the ground, hands on her head, and the dog ran right over her. Thankfully, its paws missed her completely. Erin jumped up and watched Stieg zigging and zagging, trying to shake the beast loose, but the dog kept chasing, snapping at him with those massive jaws.

"Shit, shit, shit." Erin looked around, trying to find something—*anything*—to distract or stop the dog.

That's when she saw it. Sitting on the lowest branch, watching the antics; thoroughly enjoying itself.

Erin whistled at it and black eyes focused on her, head turning one way, then another. She motioned to it with both hands. "Please, please, *please*," she begged.

But the black crow simply stared at her, unmoved by its tiny human namesake. Wondering what could get the bird on her side, Erin heard sniffing and looked up to see that the giant was now awake and glaring at her.

"Human," he said, before reaching down for her. "Ow! Little bitch," he snarled when Erin stabbed one of his fingers with her blade.

Now she was running, but she went right at the giant, running between his legs and around his right foot. She stopped there and quickly studied the giant's fur boots. She found a seam and tore it open, then shoved her blade into where the Achilles should be on his ankle.

The scream that followed told her she'd guessed right.

The giant dropped to one knee and Erin stumbled back, the flood of blood nearly knocking her down.

Unfortunately, what was a flood to her was simply a healthy amount to the giant. He wouldn't die from it.

Still on one knee, he turned, his fist raised. Erin ran backward, watching the fist coming toward her. But before it reached her, black wings swooped past, a painfully loud squawk startled the giant, and he dropped back as the bird flew at his head, right for his eyes.

He got to his one good leg and hopped back, swatting at the bird with his hand. He hit it, sending it crashing into a tree.

Erin's hands covered her mouth. She'd never meant to get the bird hurt. Even worse, she was afraid it was dead as she watched it slide down the tree trunk to the ground. Pointing her bloody blade, Erin screamed out, "You motherfucker!"

The giant focused on her and began to snarl, but he stopped when they heard it. Another squawk. Then another. Then they were on him. A murder of crows, attacking the giant's head, swarming him, pecking at him, beating at him with their wings.

The giant went down, trying his best to fight the crows off.

Erin screeched in panic when talons took hold of her shoulder and lifted her up, carrying her away. When she realized it was a crow trying to get her to safety, she called out, "No! Take me back!"

It didn't. But it did drop her about two miles away, right on the snout of that damn dog.

Erin landed on both feet, her arms windmilling back as she fought to maintain her balance. The dog was on its back, paws up in the air—and Stieg had hold of the hand.

"What's happening?" she asked.

Stieg shrugged. "It's a puppy."

"What?"

"It's a puppy. Like Lev. I just . . ." He shrugged again, clearly uncomfortable.

"You just what?"

"I . . . uh . . . flew under him, rubbed his chest, and like Lev, he stopped, dropped, and rolled over."

"So you could rub his belly?"

"It got me the Key, didn't it?"

Erin laughed. "That's the best!"

"Shut up," he barked at her, which got him a squawk that nearly had him making a panicked run for it.

Not that she blamed him. A crow squawk in Jotunheim was as close to a sonic boom as she ever cared to hear. "Don't freak out," she ordered him, before his natural human instincts took over. "It's one of us."

"That's a giant crow."

"A giant crow to us. A tiny black bird with spindly legs to them."

The crow flew them over the giant's campsite as the other crows returned to the trees, keeping a close eye on their enemy. The giant was trying to pick himself up off the ground. His face was torn and he had a hand over one eye. Stieg didn't think the birds had pulled it out, but he did think that they'd tried.

The crow landed at the campsite for some reason and Erin slid off its back.

"What are you doing?"

"Just stay there." She ran over to the giant's fur bedroll, and using her blade, she cut parts of the fur into big pieces and yanked out a couple of strands off a nearby rope. When done, she ran back to the crow and lifted herself onto the bird's back with her wings.

"You know, we can fly ourselves," he reminded her.

"She can fly faster and farther than either of us. Besides, you made a friend."

Stieg looked over his shoulder and saw the puppy running after them. "Now I feel bad."

"Why? You didn't hurt him."

"They get so attached. He'll miss me when I'm gone."

"Oy," Erin muttered before handing him a large fur. "Just put this on so you don't freeze to death."

A very good idea since the crow took them high up into the Jotunheim mountains, where even being a warrior of the gods couldn't protect them from the deadly cold.

CHAPTER THIRTY

Perched in a tree, Stieg held the map open while Erin's right hand, raised and covered in flames, gave them a bit of light. "We're here," he said, pointing at a spot on the map. "We need to get here."

Erin shook her head. "No. Here."

"If we want to get there, we have to get *here* first."

"I'm confused. Why go through Dark Elf territory? They hate humans."

"They all hate humans to some degree. But underneath Svartalfheim is Nidavellir, land of dwarves. If we want to get to Corpse Shore, we have to go into Svartalfheim and down to Nidavellir."

"That's very complicated."

"You're dealing with Vikings. What did you expect?" Stieg again studied the map. "It looks like there are land connections between each of these worlds. We can fly—"

"No." Erin shook her head. "We can't fly."

"Are you high?"

"Odin warned me. Crows and Ravens are not appreciated this far into the Nine Worlds."

"Sure he wasn't fucking with you?"

"Didn't feel like it. At all. So we'll need to find another mode of transportation."

He glanced at the crow perched on the end of the branch. "Any chance our friend here can travel between worlds?"

"With our luck?"

"Yeah. That's what I was thinking. And how much time do we have here?"

"Two days here for every one back home."

"And based on what Odin said to me back at the Bird House . . ."

"We have three days tops," Erin guessed. "So six days to get from here to Nidhogg. That is not a lot of time."

"No. But there must be other forms of transportation. Horses, maybe."

"Think anyone has a Ferrari in Alfheim?"

"Probably not."

"If nothing else . . . we need to get out of Jotunheim. It's freezing here."

"It's not that bad."

"You're blue."

"Stop being so negative. Wow," he said, gesturing to a branch above them. "Look at the size of that snake." He frowned. "It moves funny, though."

Erin glanced over, tightening the fur around her shoulders. She sighed. "That's because it's not a snake. It's an inch worm."

As if to prove that point, the crow snatched the worm off the branch and gobbled it down, making sounds Erin hoped to never hear again.

Stieg nodded. "Okay. You're right. We need to get out of fucking Jotunheim."

The crow took them as far as it was willing to go, setting them down about midway up a mountainside on a set of rickety-looking stairs that went up and up, circling the entire mountain until it reached the top.

"This is not going to be fun!" Erin yelled over the howling wind.

"I know! Think you can make it?"

"What does that mean?"

"That you look weak and pathetic. Need me to carry you?"

That middle finger slammed into his nose, then he watched Erin stomp up those stairs until the power of the mighty Jotunheim wind nearly knocked her off.

Stieg raced up to meet her, placing himself next to her so she couldn't flip over the railing and plummet off the mountain, but also keeping her within easy reach if the wind changed course and she went the other way.

They marched up those endless stairs for hours, although it felt like days. And Stieg realized pretty quickly that even unleashing their wings was not an option. They might be torn off if they tried to fly. At the very least, they'd be pushed back into Jotunheim.

So they trudged on, pressed together, heads down. Neither speaking,

It was hell.

Yet he was impressed that Erin never complained. She never stopped. She pushed on. As determined as she ever was.

Finally, they reached the peak but . . . there was nothing. No bridge. No new set of stairs for them to take. Nothing that would lead them out of Jotunheim.

"*Fuck!*" Erin screamed into the wind. "We're gonna die up here!"

"Probably."

Erin faced him. "Didn't you say we should be positive?"

"No, I said we shouldn't be negative, but let's face it. The only reason we're still alive is because we've been blessed by gods. Otherwise, we would have been dead two minutes in. It's still impressive, though."

"How?"

"Everybody else thought you'd be dead by now. Ravens and the Killers had a pool going. The longest time was three hours and I don't think anyone actually picked that."

Erin opened her mouth . . . closed it . . . opened it again . . . pointed a finger at him . . . stomped her feet . . . before spinning away from him.

Stieg tapped her on the shoulder.

"*What?*"

"That icky hand."

"What about it?"

Stieg grabbed the rope strand Erin had used to secure the Carrion's hand to a loop on her jeans. It had bounced against the back of her leg every time she took a step. He held the hand up close to her face so she could see it. "The rune . . . it's glowing."

Erin grabbed it and turned in a circle, holding the hand palm up. When it glowed at its brightest, she reached her arm out into the empty air in front of her. Stieg grabbed her by the waist so that she didn't fall to her death. She pressed forward and her hand suddenly disappeared.

A doorway. Into the next world.

Erin leaned back and looked up at him.

Stieg shrugged. "Let's go for it."

They took as many steps back as they could on the extremely tiny mountaintop. Not knowing how wide the doorway was, he waited for Erin to start her run, then went after her. She leaped and he had a second to see her disappear before he followed right behind her.

* * *

Erin was falling, spinning until she hit the ground hard; then she was tumbling, down, down, her body rolling, bouncing, slamming, unable to stop herself. Unable to think.

She hit something vertical, bounced high but when she landed, it wasn't hard ground. It was water.

She didn't know how far down she was; she just knew she couldn't figure out which way was up and which way was down. She still felt like she was rolling down, down . . .

Something brushed against her shoulder, spinning her again. It wasn't a giant fish. It was a giant Viking. Blood flowed from the back of his head and he dropped like a stone. Eyes closed, arms and legs loose.

Focusing on Stieg only, Erin chased after him, swimming deeper until she caught his hand. She turned and, moving her grip so she held his forearm, she swam back up, aiming toward the sunlight pouring down.

Erin broke the surface and slid one arm around Stieg's neck, using the other to swim to shore. She dragged him out of the water and, panting, dropped beside him on the ground.

Knowing she needed to help him, Erin attempted to turn over. A hand on her shoulder pushed her back.

"Shh."

"Stieg—"

"We'll take care of him." Fingers pushed the hair off Erin's face.

Blinking wide, making sure she saw what she thought she saw, she smiled. "You are as beautiful as the sun."

Then she passed out.

CHAPTER THIRTY-ONE

Kera met with the leaders of the Clans in the only place they could finally agree on. A synagogue in Beverly Hills.

Rabbi Tavvi Mankiewicz met her at the entrance. "Ms. Watson."

"Rabbi."

"Please," he said with a smile, "come in."

Kera walked inside. She'd never been in a synagogue before. It was cool. She'd have to come back when the world wasn't hanging in the balance.

"Right this way." The rabbi started walking and Kera fell into step beside him. "You do know the rules, yes?"

"Rules?"

He smiled although she could tell he was annoyed she hadn't been given the information. "No yelling. No threats. No cursing."

"Who would do that in a synagogue?"

"I haven't finished. No slapping. No punching. No kicking. No throwing things. Especially any ancient holy text."

"Oh, my."

"No weapons."

Kera stopped, stared at the rabbi with her mouth open. "Pardon?"

"That means no knives, no swords, no maces, no giant *hammers*."

She briefly closed her eyes, disgusted. "Of course, Rabbi."

"Do we understand each other, Ms. Watson?"

"Absolutely. We are just here to talk."

"Sadly I've heard that before. As has my father and my father's father." They began to walk again. "But for the sake of our world . . . I will allow this meeting."

"Thank you, Rabbi. I'll make sure complete control is kept."

He glanced at her from the corner of his eye, smirked. "I get the feeling you will."

They went down a set of stairs to a conference room, where the others were already sitting at the table.

"If you need anything . . ."

"Thank you, Rabbi. We're fine."

He nodded and walked out, closing the door.

Kera swung her backpack off her shoulder and dropped it onto the table. "Ladies and gentlemen . . . and Brent."

"It's *Brandt*."

"Whatever. I made a promise to the Rabbi. We will all be nice and friendly to each other, even if it kills us. And if it does kill us, we'll die outside. Understand?"

It took a while, but they all eventually nodded their agreement.

"Here is where we are. Erin has gone into the Nine Worlds; we, of course, have no contact with her—"

"So she could already be dead," Brandt Lindgren said flatly without an ounce of emotion. Typical for the leader of the Silent.

"*Chloe*," Kera said before her leader could get over the table and wrap herself around Lindgren like a cobra. "You promised."

Growling a little, Chloe sat back down.

"It's true." Kera looked directly at Lindgren. "Erin could be dead, but we're going to move forward under the delusion that she's still alive, okay? *Great*," she snapped before he could say anything else.

"So what's the next step?" Ormi asked.

"Odin has suggested that Gullveig is already back or on her way. I believe we might have run out of time. But we've . . . *managed* her high priestess, which might slow her down a bit."

"We also don't think she'll be back at full power yet," Inka added.

"Which means what for us?"

"The Carrion," Kera answered. "We need to lure her out before she's at full power."

"Lure her out? How?"

Kera glanced at the Holde's Maid and she nodded her encouragement. "We challenge the Carrion."

"To *what*?" Rada asked with a stunned laugh. "A street fight?"

"Yes. A proper Viking challenge. In three days' time we meet them for battle."

Rada looked at the others before refocusing on Kera. "Have you lost your mind?"

"What's wrong, Jaws?" Freida asked, cackling. "Are you afraid of the Carrion?"

"No. I'm just not stupid."

"We all know it won't be an easy battle, Rada," Ormi pointed out.

"No," Kera agreed, "but I think it'll be the only way we'll be able to get Gullveig out in the open before she's at full power."

"For what purpose?" Rada pushed.

"The hope is that Erin will be back with the sword by then and we'll be able to strike."

"And if the Crow doesn't make it back from Corpse Shore with the sword?" Lindgren demanded. "Then what?"

"We could give Gullveig *you,* Brandt," Inka offered, "and hope that your giant, slightly sloping head appeases her appetite."

Josef snorted a laugh, Lindgren's glare not bothering him in the least.

"Look," Kera explained, "we're going to have one chance at this. We either kill her with that sword or we shove her back out of this world again and pray—to whatever god is listening—that Hel is bored with her and won't even bother helping her a second time."

Lindgren glanced around the room before asking, "And if we don't manage to do any of that?"

"Then Ragnarok begins," Inka explained, "and it starts a chain reaction that won't end until nothing of this world is left."

Kera shrugged. "And you think a challenge will work to get her out of wherever she might be hiding?"

"I think it will definitely get out the Carrion. Erin did just kill their Key. But Gullveig hates us, so yeah. I think she'll grab at the chance to watch the Carrion stomp all of us into dust."

She could tell from everyone's expression that they believed that, too, so Kera moved on. "Now, I've spoken to Clan leaders in the rest of the States, Latin America, Europe, Africa, and Asia. They're all preparing for the worst, but those closest will be traveling in the next three days, so they'll be here for the battle. Whether Erin makes it back or not."

"Or she makes it back and this sword idea doesn't work anyway," Lindgren tossed in.

"Yes, Mr. Positivity, that, too. But in the end it's all on us. When the fight starts, we're all in."

"We can't," Sefa Hakonardottir suddenly announced, her eyes barely looking at any of them. "When the battle happens, the Valkyries will be there. But only to help those who fall get to Valhalla. Freyja's orders."

"Does she understand—"

"She understands, Kera. It just doesn't matter."

"Fine," Kera said, unwilling to focus on what didn't help. "We move forward. At this point, it's all about the timing." That was officially her mantra now. It had to be; she had no choice.

Kera reached into her backpack and pulled out her clipboard and pen, to the groans of everyone at the table—which she ignored—"Let's get down to it, shall we?"

Gullveig stared at her onetime priestess. They'd cut out her tongue, something Gullveig considered extremely tacky. Were there no boundaries these humans would not cross?

She paced back and forth in front of the body, at least grateful that she'd finally rid herself of those ridiculous robes that Hel had insisted she'd dress in while in Helheim. She was back in clothes that fit her style. A Dior dress, Gucci shoes, Prada purse, and Harry Winston jewelry. She had no idea why anyone would dress any other way.

Gullveig looked at a those assembled in front of her. "And you say they have . . . ?"

"The Key," one of the Carrion explained.

"Why would they need that?"

"It seems they wanted to send someone into the Nine Worlds. We just don't know for what."

"To get something that they think will destroy me, of course."

"And is there something that can do that?"

"I doubt it, but why risk it?"

"Perhaps we should get you back to Helheim."

"Oh, no, no, no." Gullveig smiled. "Not when things are just getting interesting."

Vig grabbed several Norwegian beers from his fridge and walked out to his porch. He handed the bottles to Jace, Eriksen, and Kera before sitting down in a chair. Brodie Hawaii moved over to lie next to his feet.

Jace, sitting on the porch stairs with Eriksen behind her rubbing her shoulders, softly asked, "Does anyone else feel—"

"Panicked?"

"Terrified?"

"A little hungry?"

They turned to Vig.

"I can't be the only one who's hungry."

"Actually, I was going to say *nauseous*." Jace studied the label on her beer. "I've sent my best friend to her death. We're planning to directly challenge the Carrion. And the world's probably going to end."

"You didn't send Erin to her death," Kera replied. "I did. It's been my decision to move forward. If this ends badly . . . it's all on me."

Jace looked over her shoulder to debate the point, but Vig held up one finger to silently ask her to wait. A few seconds later, Kera got up and went back into the house, Brodie Hawaii following behind her.

"She went to throw up," Vig explained to the couple's apparent confusion. "But don't worry. She vomits, then she's ready for anything."

Eriksen pointed at where the dog had been lying down. "And Brodie went with her because . . . ?"

"Hold her hair back." When the couple only stared, "That

was a joke, but I have been told by my brothers that I'm not good with those."

"But you tried," Jace sweetly cheered. "And that's what counts."

A few minutes later, a paler Kera walked out of the house. "Sorry about that."

Vig reached out and caught her arm, tugging her over until she sat on his lap. "It's going to be fine," he told her, stroking her hair. "It's all moving forward just like it needs to. The rest is up to Erin."

"And Stieg Engstrom," Eriksen added. "Of all the Ravens, Stieg Engstrom is in the Nine Worlds . . ." He winced. "Now I feel nauseous."

CHAPTER THIRTY-TWO

Stieg woke up swinging, cold-cocking the man who had been standing over him. Dropping his feet on the floor, he looked around. The walls were stone and he knew he was in a castle. He looked down at the man he'd hit and quickly realized he wasn't a man at all but a light elf.

Stieg also noticed that there was no Erin. He didn't like that they'd been separated.

Standing, he took a moment to make sure he could move without passing out. He felt strong, his fingers briefly touching the spot near the top of his head that had been sewn up. He'd gotten that wound after he'd gone through the door and hit the ground. He'd guess a jagged rock had done the job. But he was already healing, and he was now more worried about Erin.

Stieg reached down and grabbed the elf.

Catlike eyes snapped open and the elf began to fight, but Stieg quickly yanked him up and wrapped his arm around the elf's throat. He held the elf in front of him like a shield with enough pressure to ensure his hostage knew that with one move he could snap his neck like so much kindling.

The elf raised his hands in supplication and Stieg began

walking, forcing the elf to go with him. Stieg didn't speak. He had nothing to say. Besides, words tended to ease others and that was the last thing he wanted. At least until he found Erin.

He made the elf open the thick wooden door and they entered the torch-lit hallway. Stieg stopped and checked each room, but he was growing more frustrated with every second he couldn't find her. Seeing a small elf child standing at the end of the hall, her hair in multiple braids, her narrow eyes curious, he was forced to stop.

"You're looking for her, aren't you?" the child asked.

Stieg nodded.

"This way." She led him into a circular corridor.

Over the railing, he could look straight down. Surprised, he realized they were in a tower. He'd always heard that the light elves created their homes out of trees and rocks. A stone castle didn't seem their style, as Rolf would say.

The girl led him into another hallway and to the first door. She pushed it open and Stieg walked in, his hostage still leading the way.

A She-elf gasped in surprise and quickly stepped back from Erin's prone form. The Crow was stretched out on a stone slab. Stieg moved closer, concerned she wasn't awake yet. Still holding his elf hostage, he bumped his ass against her hand.

Erin woke up. Swinging. Her fist slammed into the elf's face and he went down like the *Titanic*, crumpling in Stieg's arms.

Stieg dropped him then, since he had no intention of carrying him.

Erin swung her legs over the edge of the slab and shook out her fist. "It's you. Thank God." She gazed at him for several seconds, her eyes trying to tell him something. "You all right?"

Stieg nodded but didn't verbally answer. That seemed to be what Erin was hoping for. He could tell by the small curl of her lips.

When she jumped off the slab, Stieg was ready to catch her if she couldn't keep herself up, but she landed steady on her feet.

Glancing around, she softly cursed, and asked the She-elf, "My weapons?"

The elf's head cocked to the side, one brow raised.

"Fine." Erin looked at Stieg. "Let's just get out of here." She grabbed his hand and led him to the door.

The She-elf held the child close to her body, the pair watching them, but saying nothing.

Out in the hallway, Erin took a quick scan of her surroundings before spotting the stairs and heading that way. Down they went. Several floors until they reached the bottom.

Another quick scan and Erin started off again, still holding onto Stieg.

"My friends!" a female voice cheered.

Erin looked directly at Stieg and, again, he felt the warning in her eyes. He gave a small, brisk nod, and she turned to face whatever was behind them.

The She-elf glowed like the goddamn sun and Erin wished she would turn it off. It was making her eyes hurt.

Warmly, her smile bright and open, the She-elf said, "I am so glad you are both all right. We were very worried when my soldiers brought you back here." She moved closer, an entourage of elf men and women behind her. She wore a simple gold crown that resembled the twisted branches of an ancient tree and her gold and white gown reminded Erin of medieval tapestries. "My name is Princess Uathach and I am ruler here. And please know that you are both welcome, my new friends."

Erin attempted to size the princess up quickly, but she was short on time. She didn't have the luxury to find out too much about her. "Princess?" Erin looked down at what she wore. "I can't . . . I mean . . . look at me!" She scrunched up her nose. "I can't meet a princess looking like *this*."

"Oh, my dearest girl." The princess took Erin's hand in both of hers. Warm hands. Warm smile. "Don't worry about that. It's not like you came here for a proper presentation . . . um . . . ?"

"Erin. I'm Erin. This is my companion Stieg. Say hello, Stieg."

Stieg grunted, his apparently slow-witted focus examining everything around him but the princess. He was perfect, catching on quicker than she'd thought he would.

"I can't tell you how much it means to me that you saved him," Erin went on. "I was simply too weak to do anything at the time."

"It was our pleasure." The princess put her arm around Erin's shoulders and led her away from what Erin had assumed was an exit, moving her deeper into the castle. "I have to say, we so rarely get . . ."

"Outsiders?"

"Humans. Not like we used to. Especially ones like yourselves." She gave Erin a hug. "A Valkyrie. We haven't had a Valkyrie here in a century. Perhaps more."

Uh-oh. A Valkyrie?

They thought Erin Amsel of German-Jewish descent was a Valkyrie? Wow, she'd never wished Betty had been around more in her life. Her mentor would be loving every second of this.

Since they seemed so excited by the prospect, Erin ran

with it; Odin's words about the lack of love for Crows in the other Worlds still playing in her head. It was a risk, but probably a better one than revealing her true source of power.

And Erin did enjoy game playing, so it wasn't like she had a moral issue with any of it.

The princess led them into a giant hall. Several pit fires heated the room, and lit torches on the walls made it bright. Yet none of it seemed to fit the princess and her woodland motif. Her jewelry. Her hair. Her crown. She should be deep in some woods somewhere, not trapped behind black stone.

"Please, you and your companion sit with me. I know you both must be *starving*."

"I could eat. And I know Stieg could eat. He never *stops* eating."

The princess laughed, a soft, lilting sound. "Of course. I know how Giant Killers do love their food."

Erin barely managed to stop herself from hysterically laughing, rolling around on the floor, legs kicking . . . for *hours*. She couldn't even *look* at Stieg, but she wished she could. God! Did she wish she could!

There were all sorts of insults that each Clan couldn't handle. Protectors hated when they were confused with Ravens. Holde's Maids got real nasty when they were confused with the Isa. Crows got homicidal when they were referred to as slaves. And nothing, absolutely *nothing* set Ravens off more than when people assumed they were Giant Killers. Big, dumb Thor lovers.

The mix-ups didn't exactly set off any race wars, but they had been known to lead to quite a few historical massacres.

Thankfully, Stieg wasn't exactly like his brethren. A Raven happily raised among Ravens would immediately lash out at the insult of being called a Giant Killer. But Stieg had spent years on the streets. And, from what Erin could tell, he'd learned fast and early when to let things slide. When to ignore. When to play along. That skill had definitely kept him alive out there on some of the cruelest streets in the States and it was definitely going to help now.

They were seated at the long table at the head of the hall, where two chairs were slightly raised above all the others. The princess took one of those chairs and a male who looked almost exactly like her took the other.

"Erin, this is my brother, Prince Uinseann. Uinseann, this is the Valkyrie I was telling you about."

"How exciting!" He leaned forward to peer around his sister. "I hope you have been treated exceptionally well, Lady Erin."

"Very well, thank you."

She glanced at Stieg and his eyes said it all. Lady Erin? *Really?*

The food just kept coming. Giant platters of meats and vegetables. Nothing too weird, which Stieg appreciated. He wasn't a picky eater but he also didn't like anything he couldn't name. A lot of game meats but animals he was acquainted with, which helped. Of course, he didn't just dive into the food. He waited to make sure the elves ate first. And heartily. Once he felt comfortable that his food wasn't poisoned, he dove in.

Surprisingly, Erin didn't hesitate. She ate as soon as the food was in front of her. Drank as soon as they poured the wine. Although she only allowed herself two chalices of the wine before switching to water.

"How come I can understand you?" Erin asked the princess, who appeared truly fascinated with the "Valkyrie." *Heh*.

If the Valkyries knew what was going on, they would lose their collective minds. A Crow pretending to be a Valkyrie? Few things could be a bigger affront to them.

"We speak in our language and you speak in yours and the light does the rest."

Erin took a bite of chicken before admitting, "That makes no sense to me."

"Of course not. You're only human."

"Should I take that as an insult?"

"No, no. Not at all. It's just the way of things. Being a human, even one blessed by the great Freyja, limits you in ways that the elves can never imagine. But it's nothing we hold against you."

"Good to know." Erin went back to her food, a smile on her face, but Stieg wasn't fooled. She would file the insult away in that brain of hers, not to be dwelt upon, but never to be forgotten, either.

When dinner was done, musicians made an appearance and there was dancing, more wine, and sweet treats.

Stieg stood against a wall that gave him a clear view of all entrances and a good view of the guards. They didn't make a terrifying presence, but it was their tendency to disappear in the shadows that concerned him.

The only outsiders at the moment were Erin, a "Valkyrie," and Stieg a—*dry heave*—"Giant Killer." Could they do damage? Absolutely. But only so much. So why the worry?

Then again, the truth was they *weren't* a Valkyrie and a Killer. They were a Crow and a Raven. They could do a lot more than *so much*.

Knowing that—and feeling confident in it—Stieg watched, listened, and learned.

"So," the princess finally asked after several hours, "what brings you both here to our lands?"

"A quest, my lady," Erin said, making sure she sounded as deferential as possible.

"A quest! How exciting. A quest for what?"

Measuring her words carefully, Erin replied, "We need to get to Helheim."

"Land of the Dead? Why would anyone *need* to go there?" The princess's smile was almost cruel. Almost. "Hel is no fan of humans, sweet Erin."

"I am aware of that. But we have no choice. The human world is at risk; she may be our only chance."

"Well . . . that is terrifying if it's true. I hope you have some other options."

"Not at the moment. Sadly, I have no choice. I made a pledge."

"Of course." The princess smiled again. "Still, I do hope you and your companion can stay the night. Get some rest."

Erin returned her smile with one of her own. "That would be wonderful."

"Excellent!" The princess clapped her hands together. "Musicians! Something we can dance to!"

The music changed and one of the males bowed to the She-elf. She took his hand and they joined the others.

Erin watched them, making sure to keep smiling, gently turning down the few elf males who came to ask her to dance. And as the pleasant evening slowly wound down, Erin knew one thing as well as she knew her own name.

She and Stieg were prisoners.

CHAPTER THIRTY-THREE

They were led up several flights of stairs, the princess chatting away as they walked. On the fourth floor, they were led down a long hall to bedrooms.

"Here you go. You'll be able to get a good night's sleep here, I think."

Erin walked in first, nodding as a servant lit torches so she could see everything clearly. "Perfect."

"Oh, excellent! Then rest well, my friends."

"Thank you, Princess. For everything."

The princess, her entourage, the servant, and her guards quietly left; the elves never made a sound. Once the door closed behind them, Stieg watched that smile slowly fade from Erin's face until he saw nothing but the hard Crow who once stabbed him in the leg because he got between her and a demon she was trying to kill.

Her eyes were like sharp glass as she moved to the bed, sitting on it, her legs hanging over the edge.

He opened his mouth to speak, but Erin put her finger to her lips, silencing him. She motioned him over with her hand and he sat beside her. Before he could do or say anything, she jumped to her feet, walked to the door, and pressed her ear against it. A few seconds later, her nose scrunched up in annoyance.

Guards stood outside the door. Not that Stieg was surprised.

She stalked to the other side of the room and studied the stained glass window. She pushed something in the corner and the window opened.

Stieg watched her crawl outside and followed her, leaning out the window to see what Erin was up to. She stood on the ledge, staring down. He looked down, too, seeing nothing but more soldiers and guards. And archers. Archers who could knock them out of the sky if they tried to fly.

Erin looked up and before he knew it, the woman was climbing up the side of the building. Why? Because she was insane. And yet he followed.

He expected her to go straight to the top, especially since he didn't see any soldiers hanging over the roof, but she stopped at the top floor window and gazed in. He wondered what she could see. It wasn't as if it was clear glass. It was beveled. She pried the window open and disappeared inside.

Stieg sighed, wondering what the crazy Crow was up to now, but he followed anyway.

No wonder the odds on Erin Amsel making it back were 100 to 1 in favor of her being dead in the first five minutes.

She rolled through the window and immediately got to her feet.

The black-and-gold-haired elf inside glanced up from his work, but showed no sign of fear or even surprise. "What do you want?"

Erin pointed. "My weapons, to start."

Silken black robes swirled around the extremely tall elf as he seemed to glide across the room until he reached the long wood table where her weapons were laid out.

The elf lifted one of her blades, handmade by Vig Rundström. "This," he said, holding the blade by its tip, "is not a Valkyrie weapon. Nor are the runes that you and your companion have burned on your flesh representative of the gods of the Valkyries or Giant Killers. I noticed them when I was dealing with your wounds. Princess Uathach has asked me to translate them."

"Why can't she translate runes herself?"

"The Aesir never allowed elves to learn their language. They felt it would be giving them too much power. Instead, we have our own rune language. The few of us who can translate the Aesir runes are usually witches because strong blood-magics are required."

Erin briefly debated lying, but she knew there was no purpose. Not with this one. "Did you translate the runes for her?"

"If I had, you'd have been dead hours ago. The runes on these weapons and the runes on your bodies spell out exactly what you are and those you both worship. Very foolish."

"We don't normally shy away from conflict."

"Except now. Not that I blame you. The princess has a rather unhealthy lust for gameplay. And her games are not to everyone's tastes. I'm sure they won't be to yours."

"Are they to yours?"

The elf carefully placed the blade back on the table, taking a moment to align it with the others. His care was obsessive.

Obsessives were the most fun.

"Used to be. Long time ago. Most of us age and change. She does not." With the blades perfectly lined up, he gestured to the walls around them. "Does this seem like the kind of place for elves like the princess?"

Erin smirked. "No. It doesn't."

"That's because a few centuries ago, this was dark elf territory. You are in what was once Svartalfheim."

"I thought we were in Alfheim."

"No, no. The entrance into Alfheim from Jotunheim was closed off long ago by the elves. They feared the giants coming in and stomping them to death. We're immortal, but not *that* immortal."

"You don't seem to fit here, either," Erin noted.

"Unlike the princess, I fit nowhere. My mother was of Svartalfheim, my father of Alfheim, which means I have no true home."

"I get that. My mother's Jewish, my father's Catholic, but both are more agnostic, which made my bat mitzvah slash confirmation quite the event with the rest of my über-religious families." She shrugged. "Cops were called before the night was out."

The elf smiled and she saw fangs. Neither the princess nor her entourage had fangs.

"What would make a human such as you and your friend"—he nodded toward a still-silent Stieg—"attempt a trek through this territory?"

"I'm on a quest and I'm running out of time."

"A quest for what?"

Hedging, Erin replied, "I need to stop the goddess Gullveig from starting Ragnarok."

He snorted. "Gullveig? I remember her. She is . . . a problem for you and your precious Aesir gods. She loathes all of them for what they did to her."

"I know. That's why I don't have time to sit around here, playing games with your princess."

The elf turned away, moving to another table. "She's not *my* princess. No one is my anything."

"We can't stay here," Erin calmly insisted.

He faced her again. "You act like you have a choice. She's not going to let you go. You and your oversized friend are her entertainment. She plans to use you for as long as she can."

"And when we're no longer entertaining?"

"How do you people put it? Ah, yes . . . she'll throw you to the wolves. Literally. The forest is filled with wolves."

Erin looked at Stieg and he nodded, agreeing with her. They'd gotten really good at communicating with each other without saying a word.

She walked over to the elf, leaned against his table. "What's your name?"

"Dualtach the Witch."

"Well, Dualtach the Witch, tell me what we can do in a short amount of time to become *less* entertaining."

The elf gazed down at Erin, his eyes searching every part of her face. She didn't turn away; she waited. Patiently.

He eventually moved to another window and stared out into the darkness. She couldn't tell if he was contemplating her request or if he saw something. Or more important, if he *saw* something. The mystical shit.

Whatever it was, he finally told her, "Take your weapons, hide them on your person, and go back to your room. And if I were you, I'd go very quickly."

Erin didn't know how to read that, but she grabbed her weapons and put them on under her clothes. The only two things she couldn't find . . . "I need the hand and the map."

"Be careful," he said, still staring out the window and ignoring her request, "on your way back. The walls have eyes here."

Stieg touched her arm and gestured to the window they'd used to get in. Realizing she didn't have any other choice, Erin went.

Before she could climb out, the witch said to her, "You

are very calm for a human. I strongly suggest you keep that up. The less you give the princess, the more . . . spontaneous she will be. It could work in your favor."

Erin nodded at his recommendation, and climbed out the window first. Stieg followed and down they went to the bedroom they'd been given.

Once back in their room, they sat down on the bed, side by side, their thighs touching. After several minutes of silence, they looked at each other. Looked away. Looked at each other. Looked away. Looked . . .

Stieg abruptly stood and went to the head of the bed. He placed his hand against the wall and moving slowly, he walked from the bed all the way down the length of the room, perpendicular to the wall, his hand dragging along the stone. When he reached the end, he began to do the same to the next wall—the wall that faced the bed they were to share. He suddenly stopped, his head twitching the slightest bit. Balling up his fist, he rammed it into the wall.

Erin watched, fascinated, as he pummeled the stone into submission with both hands, putting a sizable hole into it. He shook out his battered fists before digging his right hand into the hole.

When he looked back at Erin—she knew.

She charged over to Stieg's side, waiting until he'd managed to get the elf male watching them halfway out of the hole. She grabbed the elf by his finery and together they dragged him out and slammed him to the ground.

When the elf witch had warned them that *the walls have eyes*, Stieg had thought he meant the other elves would rat them out if they found them roaming the halls. But as he and Erin had sat on the bed, silently trying to figure out what to do next, they'd sensed—as only humans with the instincts of birds can—that they were no longer alone. That they were being watched.

For entertainment. Just as Dualtach had said. And what's the best entertainment for adults? A human sex show.

The thought clearly irritated Erin, considering the way she was *stomping* the elf into the cold stone floor. She was a little thing, but those legs of hers—after years of gymnastics and ballet training—were mighty.

She kicked the elf in the head a few times until she was sure he was unconscious. Then she looked up at Stieg . . . and smiled.

They grabbed the elf again and lifted him to his feet, dragging him across the floor until they reached what was quickly becoming their favorite window. With a hearty grunt, they flipped him up and over and *out* the open window.

Unfortunately for the elf, he woke up in time to realize what was happening, his screams echoing off the walls as he fell and fell . . . until the screaming was brutally cut short.

Erin cringed a bit. "That had to hurt."

In the distance, they could hear the calls of the guards and screams of horror from the royals.

Stieg and Erin sat down to wait.

It took almost ten minutes before the bedroom door slammed open and the guards flowed in, followed by a seething princess. She wore a very thin nightshirt that hid nothing—she might as well have been naked—and her several feet of blondish-brown hair appeared artfully tousled.

Erin leaned over and whispered, "Bet she was hooking up with her brother."

Disgusted, Stieg pushed her face away. The woman had been binge-watching too many cable shows.

The princess stalked up to them. "Can't you two just

do what you would normally do anyway? Like good little pets. Must you make things so difficult? Just"—she waved at them—"perform!"

Stieg exchanged a glance with Erin. Her smile was so intense, he actually saw her dimples.

Then, without warning, Erin backhanded the princess into the pit fire, nearly setting the She-elf on fire.

The guards were on them in seconds, dragging Stieg to his knees, putting a thick chain around his throat and metal cuffs on his wrists. They did the same to Erin but didn't make her get on her knees.

The princess was helped up by her guards, who patted her down to put out the smattering of flames.

Pushing the guards off, she moved to stand before the prisoners and leaned in close to Erin, her voice no longer soft and alluring as it had been, but hard as glass. "Don't worry, human. I have a game that you can't help but play."

CHAPTER THIRTY-FOUR

Erin wanted nothing more than to unleash her wings and kill everyone, but she knew it wasn't the right time yet. She was going on instinct here and more than once, her instincts had been wrong. Like when she didn't think Tommy Boy would kill her if she moved to Los Angeles. She'd been wrong about that.

She could be wrong now.

But ever since becoming a Crow, she'd forced herself to start trusting her instincts again. So she'd wait until the time seemed right and hope that the plan didn't get her and Stieg killed.

The guards took them deep into the bowels of the castle. Thankfully, the hallways were well lit. She wasn't in the mood for the dark lighting of a fantasy movie where everyone died.

The problem was that the light showed the remnants of others who'd been there before. Some were just mounted heads. There were even a few sets of wings. Ravens, Crows, and even Protectors.

The group turned a corner and stopped in front of a long

row of cells. They appeared empty. Although the light didn't reach all the way into the back of each cell. One of the guards opened a cell and shoved Erin inside. She assumed Stieg would be thrown into the next cell but that didn't happen.

Instead the princess growled, "I really want you to meet your new neighbor."

She came from the shadows of the other cell, throwing herself against the bars. A Svartalfheim She-elf who'd been turned into a psychotic wild animal. Scars covered her dark elf skin and bald patches showed on her scalp where someone had ripped the hair out. Old and fresh blood was everywhere. On her. On her cell.

The She-elf raged and screamed, completely incoherent.

All Erin could do was stand there and watch. She was grateful for the bars between them since her hands weren't free. She still had her weapons—the guards hadn't bothered to recheck—but she couldn't reach any of them so it didn't really matter. And what was that smell? Was that the remains of those killed before her or just the general funk one finds in dungeons and New Jersey prisons? How long would she have to deal with that smell? How long would she be trapped in this jail with the crazy elf?

"Hey!" the princess yelled, startling Erin.

"What?"

"What are you doing?"

"Standing here. What *should* I be doing?"

"Recoiling in fear?"

"Oh. Right." Erin looked at the crazed She-elf still trying to reach her through the bars and let out a less-than-enthused "Aaah." She turned back to the princess. "Like that, you mean?"

"Worthless human!" She pointed a finger at Erin. "When you're in the pit, you better give a much better performance."

Erin smirked. "Oh. I promise."

With a flip of her hair, the princess stormed off, taking her entourage and Stieg with her.

"Wait!" Erin called out, moving closer to the front bars. "Where the fuck are you going with him?"

The princess said nothing, just kept moving.

But her brother stopped and gazed down at Erin. "Now I see fear," he murmured before leaving, the sound of the mad She-elf's screams the only thing keeping her company.

Stieg was pulled into the princess's room and forced into a corner, again on his knees.

Her brother lingered behind as the guards exited. "I don't think you should be alone with him."

Princess Uathach dismissed the notion with a wave of her hand, removing what remained of her burned nightdress and tossing the material on the fire. "He'll be fine as long as he knows we have the woman. He wouldn't risk her life . . . now would you, human pet?"

Stieg said nothing, just stared straight ahead.

"Besides," she went on, "he needs to get used to his new life." She giggled and stroked her brother's cheek.

Stieg couldn't help it—he sneered a little, assuming Erin had been right.

The brother caught Stieg in the act and quickly snapped, "Oh, come on! She's my sister! What is *wrong* with you humans?"

Finally, after several *hours*, the She-elf calmed down and literally crawled back into the shadows. Occasionally a guard came by, looking in on Erin, and they'd even brought her out once when she'd flatly refused to use the bucket they had for her in the corner of her cell. That wasn't going to happen and what she threatened them with—because no matter the species, males were males—had them moving fast enough to find a private place for her within the castle. Other than that, they left her alone.

Then, in the early morning, Dualtach the Witch appeared before her bars. She didn't believe for a second he'd come to release her. The elf was a survivor. She sensed in him the same thing she'd sensed in Stieg when she'd first met him— their lives had been much harder than what they now were surrounded by. So Dualtach wasn't about to do anything that could put his life at risk. Not for her.

Then . . . what did he want?

He glanced over at the cell where the She-elf panted in the darkness. "She doesn't sleep, you know. Barely eats. She's kept alive by rage and hatred. Her mind trapped there."

Erin let out a bored sigh. "Too bad."

"Her madness isn't natural, though."

Slowly, Erin turned her head to look at him. "What?"

"It isn't natural. It was forced upon her. By me. Could be removed just as easily."

"With blood magic?"

"Not everything requires blood. I wouldn't worry about that, if I were you." He walked away, "Soon you'll have more than enough for entire ceremonies."

She watched the witch disappear around a corner, her mind turning, until the She-elf again threw herself against the bars, reaching out for Erin, screeching, and desperately trying to catch her so she could tear her apart.

With the thick metal cuffs still on his wrists, his hands bound behind his back, Stieg rested on his knees in front of Prince Uinseann's throne. A leather collar was around his neck and the prince held the leash. His sister didn't want the bother since Stieg hadn't been "trained" yet.

He didn't think about any of that, though. He focused on seeing Erin again.

It had been nearly eighteen hours, the sun had gone down at least an hour ago, and they had returned to the hall. The tables, however, had been pulled back and part of the floor removed to reveal an actual pit. Not a deep one, thankfully, but the kind of pit used for dogfights back home. The kind of thing he'd gone to once in his younger days and vowed never to return to again. He'd been too disgusted and freaked out. Only this particular pit had a round metal cage over it that had been locked into the floor. There'd be no easy way out of it for Erin.

The royal audience was brought in first, cheering and ready for the imagined blood they were already banking on.

The princess waved at friends and called out to people like she was at some fun-filled brunch thing with girl-friends.

The prince occasionally yanked on the leash—in his mind, reminding Stieg who was in charge. In Stieg's mind, though, it was just giving him more reason to hate everyone in this room.

Finally, the guards brought in Erin, uncuffing her before shoving her into the cage with a kick to the stomach. She stumbled back and fell on her ass, making the crowd laugh loudly. Happily.

Wincing, she got to her feet, her hand rubbing her stomach while she looked through the crisscrossed bars until her gaze found his. Her eyes widened at the sight of him and he expected her to laugh at the picture he made. But she didn't. Instead, her eyes narrowed on the princess and he saw pure hatred. An expression usually reserved for worshippers who spilled innocent blood to call on their powerful demons.

Erin lowered her hands to her sides, her fingers curling into fists.

"Ooooh," the princess purred. "Your friend is angry at me, pet."

"Can we teach him to speak?" the prince asked about Stieg.

"To be honest I'm not sure I want to. I had a chatty one once. It got a little tiring. All that begging."

"Good point."

Guards brought in the She-elf from the cell next to Erin's. She had on a muzzle to protect the guards from her bite and a long leash attached to a collar like Stieg's that allowed them to drag the hysterical female through the frenzied crowd.

They wanted blood and knew the mad She-elf would give it to them.

Stieg eased his fingers around the thick chain between the cuffs. The cuffs were dwarf made. As a Raven, he'd retrieved enough enchanted dwarf-made items to know the difference. That meant the cuffs would not be coming off without a key or the help of an actual dwarf. But the chain . . . it was *not* dwarf-made.

Stieg lowered his head and watched in horror as the She-elf was shoved into the cage with Erin. Still leashed, she immediately went for Erin, and it was only the guards holding her back that kept Erin safe. But everyone in this hall knew that wouldn't last long.

Yet Stieg forced himself to do something he'd never really thought he could. He placed his fingers on the chain and waited until Erin Amsel gave him the signal.

Erin waited on the other side of the cage, her back against the bars, watching as the guards pulled the She-elf close so they could remove the leash at the princess's command.

She'd really only have one chance to make this work, but until that one chance came, she'd have to somehow keep this female from killing her. She just wasn't sure how she was going to do that. You know . . . other than running away. But guards with spears encircled the pit, and she knew they were there to push the females toward each other should one try to run.

Damn. All her best ideas . . .

Dualtach the Witch eased his way into the hall, staying in the back. Again, he wouldn't help Erin, but he wouldn't help the princess, either. He was just there to enjoy the party like the other attendees.

Erin knew she needed to focus if her plan was to work. Something she knew she could do, when it was important. Betty had taught her during her early battle training that one of the best ways for Crows to stay focused during a fight was to center on something that pissed them off. For Kera that was usually the injustice of things. For Chloe, it was people's stupidity, which caused her to miss another book deadline her editor did not want to fucking hear about. And for Jace, it could be anything. The tiniest thing set that woman off like a hand grenade.

But Erin didn't allow herself to get pissed too often.

She didn't let rage "sing through her veins" the way it supposedly sang through Betty's . . . until Erin saw Stieg Engstrom, descendent of mighty Vikings and warrior of Odin himself, chained up like a dog. Even worse, she knew he'd allowed it for her. He wasn't going to leave without her. He'd let these bastards treat him like a goddamn pet. In the hopes that she actually had a plan.

That was the anger she focused on.

Princess Uathach stood, raising her hands to silence the room. Stieg looked back at her, but her brother yanked that leash again to stop him. Apparently he didn't want *the pet* to eye his sister.

Stieg hoped that whatever Erin came up with included killing this guy. Because he really hated the elf.

"Friends, I am so happy you've all come this evening. It's been a long time since we've had such grand entertainment. Tonight, we will again witness a wonderful, but I'm sure tragically short"—the audience laughed and cheered—"battle between our reigning champion, the dear sweet Princess Seanait, and one of Odin's whores, a Valkyrie!"

Stieg was surprised that the princess still believed Erin was a Valkyrie. The witch they'd met apparently had kept his mouth shut. What shocked Stieg most was that the screaming banshee elf trying to get to Erin in that pit was a fellow princess. Even if she was a dark elf, she was still royalty. Yet Uathach and her brother had turned her into this mad thing for their amusement.

And if they treated their own like that . . .

Christ, we're screwed.

Erin took in and let out several breaths, her back pressed hard against the cage, her arms spread out and holding onto the bars. She crouched down, as ready as she was ever going to be and watched as one of the princess's guards pulled the mad She-elf close to him.

Another guard took hold of the back of her muzzle while the first guard placed his hand on the metal clasp that secured the leash. Like the guys who had to turn the key at the same time to open doors around a nuclear bomb, the two guards nodded at each and, at the very same moment, released the She-elf from her bondage.

Moving faster than anything she'd ever seen, the She-elf charged toward Erin, but before reaching her, she dashed to the right and up the cage. She *ran* up the side of the cage. Something Erin couldn't do without help from her wings.

Erin tried to keep the female in her line of sight but she moved so fast . . .

Her hair gripped from above, Erin was yanked away from the bars and thrown across the pit to the roar of the crowd.

She slammed face-first into the opposite bars, her right cheekbone breaking on impact.

Landing on her back, she looked up in time to see the She-elf jumping down on her. Erin rolled away and tried to get back to her feet but a kick sent her spinning across the pit again.

Well, this wasn't working out as she'd hoped. Nope. Not at all.

Fuck.

Stieg watched in horror as the She-elf tossed Erin around the pit the way Brodie Hawaii tossed around loose bones she dug up in the Crow's backyard. And while he watched every muscle in his body told him to go to Erin. To help her. But that would put him in the cage with her. All the elves would have to do was close them in and wait for them to starve to death.

If he started a fight outside the cage that would still leave Erin trapped inside. All the guards would have to do was stick her with a spear.

So he gritted his teeth and did the impossible. He waited.

Erin hit the roof of the cage before dropping back to the ground. The She-elf was still playing with her.

With the crowd roaring, she walked over to Erin as the Crow desperately tried to get back to her feet. Stieg watched Erin struggle, his entire body getting tight as panic began to sweep through him.

Wild-eyed, the She-elf reached down, grabbed Erin by the shoulders and lifted her up in the air. Erin flailed in the air for several seconds, but Stieg remembered a time he'd made the same move on Erin once. He hadn't planned to snap her back against his knee like the She-elf was clearly intending to do—although he'd thought about it at the time—instead he'd only attempted to throw Erin in the Bird House pool. But before he could toss her away, she'd—

With the She-elf holding Erin over her head by gripping her shirt, she lifted her knee up and began to pull Erin down. That's when Erin used her gymnastics training to flip forward, every muscle working to yank her away from the She-elf.

The crazed elf stumbled and fell to the side. Erin kicked her onto her back and did another front flip, both of her feet slamming into the She-elf's chest.

The crowd roared in approval, drowning out the She-elf's screams of pain as they realized the "Valkyrie" would be giving them a bit of a show.

The She-elf pushed Erin off her chest, but before she could get back up, Erin kicked her in the side, sending her flipping across the pit floor.

Erin went after her, quickly and expertly grabbing the female from behind. She squatted down behind her and used that damn sleeper hold on the She-elf as if it would be as effective as it was on a human.

But Stieg noticed that Erin had only one arm around the elf's throat. She'd used her free hand to grip her opponent's wrist.

And that's when he understood exactly what his tricky little Crow was doing.

Erin held onto the She-elf's wrist for as long as she could, then she was flying again. Rolling across that damn pit and slamming into those damn bars when she reached the other side.

Before she could get up, the She-elf was on her, pinning her to the ground with her legs and her weight. She leaned over her. And for one terrifying moment, Erin thought the female was about to kiss her. Although it would not be her first kiss from a woman, she would actually prefer such a thing with a female who'd actually bathed in the last ten thousand years.

As full-on panic began to set in, the She-elf got impossibly close and asked in a hideous whisper, "You're not a Valkyrie. What are you?"

Erin stared straight into those yellow-gray eyes and replied, "I'm a Crow."

The She-elf leaned back, her insane laughter ringing throughout the hall, drowning out the entire crowd cheering for Erin's death. Then she was back. Too close again, unfortunately, as if she was on the verge of the most life-altering orgasm, "Ohhhh, this is going to be so. Much. *Fucking*. Funnnnnnn."

Oh, shit.

What had she done?

The princess leaned forward. "What . . . what is happening?"

"Nothing," her brother answered. "She's insane."

"She's talking to her."

"No, she's not. You're being paranoid."

No. She wasn't. Stieg knew what Erin had done. The same thing she'd done to him when he was unknowingly sitting with the Four Horsemen. She let the She-elf *see*.

The skill taught to her by Betty had somehow cleared the She-elf's mind. Sort of.

The prince was right. She was still insane, but something told Stieg this might have been the insane she'd been for a long time.

Dark Elves weren't known for their calm natures.

The She-elf grabbed Erin by her throat and got to her feet, lifting the Crow with her. The move seemed to calm the princess down and she relaxed back into her throne.

With one move, the female tossed Erin into the back of the cage and ran toward her, screaming. Erin caught hold of the She-elf's arms and slammed her into the bars. Fully caught up in the action, several guards leaned in to yell encouragement, and that's when both females moved.

Erin turned, lifted her hands, and finally unleashed a load of flames in a wide circle, forcing the guards to drop down or be burned to the bone. While Erin distracted them, the She-elf caught hold of one of the guards and yanked him against the bars three times until blood poured from his head. She reached down and yanked the ring of keys he had tied to his belt. Other guards tried to make a grab, but she was as fast sane as she was crazy.

Seanait charged across the pit. Spears came through the bars. Erin turned several of them to ash, and the others the She-elf deftly avoided by dropping to her knees and sliding across the dirt until she reached the door.

"Stop her!" the princess yelled, getting to her feet. "You fools! Kill her!"

That's when Stieg knew . . . *now*.

Erin stopped her flame in time to see him lift his head and look at her. She'd been afraid that being treated like a dog might set him back a bit. But no. He'd just been waiting for her. She saw it in his eyes. In the way he straightened his shoulders.

And the way he broke the chains that held him.

In one move he got to his feet and turned to face the one who held the leash. The prince.

"*Uathach!*" the prince screamed, calling for his sister, but it was too late.

Stieg gripped the leash and yanked the elf royal forward until he could ram his entire fist into the male's mouth and down his throat. When he yanked it out again, it was covered in blood and he gripped muscle and cartilage in his fist.

The princess wailed in terror and pain, even as more guards and soldiers surrounded her. Even the crowd was ready to fight for her. That is until Stieg threw back his shoulders and unleashed his wings.

In an instant, the crowd's attitude changed and several yelled out, "A Raven! Run! Flee!"

But as some began to run away, Erin stepped out of the cage and with the dark She-elf standing slightly in front of her, Erin unleashed her own wings.

The princess pointed with one hand while gripping a guard's shoulder with the other. "A Crow," she said softly at first. Then, howling, "*A Crowwwwww!*"

Panic set in and everyone was running.

Erin hadn't even done anything yet. *Good Lord*. What had her ancient elders done in the elf lands to gain such a reputation? She just had to know!

The dark She-elf picked a dropped spear off the ground, broke it over her knee, and slammed the point into the first guard who ran by her. With the spear still sticking out of his belly, she yanked the sword from his hand and cut off his head and a good part of his shoulder.

With clear, but brutally cold eyes, she faced Erin. "You ready to kill everyone?"

"Actually, we were just going to leave, so . . ."

The She-elf raised one brow.

"It's just . . . we're kind of on a schedule."

"Do you really think they'll let you go? Do you think *she* will let you go after your Raven killed her brother?"

Erin couldn't help but smile a little. "But . . . he started it."

And for the first time ever, Erin heard Stieg Engstrom laugh.

CHAPTER THIRTY-FIVE

The hall had cleared out except for Stieg, Erin, and the dark elf princess.

"They will not let you go," she continued on, ignoring the shared moment between Stieg and Erin. "Even now, their troops are gathering to strike us all down. You have only faced their guards. Their soldiers are a different thing all together."

"Look," Erin explained, "we have a world to save, so—"

"What do you want, Crow?"

"Want?"

The Svartalfheim princess tossed back her head, long blue-black hair flipping over her shoulder. "Don't play games with me, human. Every Crow wants something."

"We need transport. Fast transport. Horses or something equivalent."

"To get back to Midgard, where you belong?"

"To get to Corpse Shore."

The She-elf's eyes widened. "And they thought *I* was insane all that time. Why would you go there? Nidhogg will not welcome you, Crow."

"It's my only option."

"Then you have no option at all. But . . . it's a deal I will make. Help me get out of here alive and I will see that you have what you need so you can die a violent and bloody death that you most likely deserve at the claws and fangs of Nidhogg."

"And thanks for that!" Erin laughingly replied, in her best *one day I plan to kill you but right now I'm pretending we're best of friends!* Betty imitation. It was kind of brilliant. Definitely entertaining.

Erin faced Stieg, her fake smile dropping, her laugh abruptly ending. She didn't need to fake any of that with him, which he appreciated. "You all right?"

Stieg blinked, once again surprised by the question. "Am I bleeding?"

"Not that I can tell."

"Ooooo. . . kay."

"Just answer the fucking question!"

"I'm fine."

"You sure you're up for this?"

"What's happening right now? I don't know what's happening!"

"I'm bothering to care," she snapped. "Enjoy it while it lasts."

"Oh. Okay. Well . . . thank you for that. Uh . . . and I'm fine. I was just waiting for you to make your move."

"How did you know I actually had a move?"

"Because you're a Crow," the dark elf cut in with a nasty sneer. "Once I knew what you were, I knew my revenge would be written in the blood of my enemies in the annals of history."

Erin glanced at Stieg but what did she expect him to say? What was there to say to any of that?

"Look, lady," Erin began, "I'm a Crow, but that doesn't mean I'm any worse or—"

Erin suddenly grabbed the princess by her arm and pushed her toward Stieg. He automatically moved her behind him, using his body to protect her, while Erin used her nondominant hand and caught the arrow that had been flying toward them.

Annoyed, because Erin was in the middle of talking and she hated being interrupted, she used her other hand to unleash a line of flame that turned the archer elves into screaming balls of fire, tearing down the hallway and disappearing into the castle.

"—or better," she continued on, "than any other warrior."

Princess Seanait pushed past Stieg and Erin with a, "Yes, yes, I see that. Now, do you mind if we get my bloody revenge underway?"

"She's so pushy," Erin complained to Stieg once the dark elf was already across the room.

"What do you expect? She's a princess."

"So? I'm from Staten Island."

Stieg shook his head. "I really don't know how to respond to that."

The uppity dark elf princess had been right. The guards had moved back and the troops had moved in, but they didn't attack right away. They could be heard down a long hallway, waiting around the corner.

"You need weapons, Raven," the princess told Stieg.

"I'll get some."

"When? When our souls have left our bodies?"

"Up-itty," Erin muttered.

"We'll get you out of here," Stieg promised. "It's what we do."

"It's what Ravens do," Erin clarified. "Crows just kill everyone in our way. So make sure you watch where you step."

Stieg's big hand covered Erin's entire face. "She's just kidding," he said while he pushed her back. "We'll take the lead." He pulled his hand away from a giggling Erin and softly warned her, "Stop fooling around."

"I can't help myself. She brings it out in me."

"We have bigger issues right now than your love of fucking with people."

Stieg was right. Getting out of the castle would be tough and even getting out of elf territory basically impossible, but their friends were still depending on them.

"You're right. Let's go."

He started to turn away, but stopped and looked back at her.

"What?" Erin asked, thinking something was wrong.

Stieg leaned in and kissed her.

She immediately responded, her arms looping around his neck, the blades still held in her hands. She didn't realize until that very moment how worried about him she'd been. Kissing him, feeling his body against hers, knowing he was—at least at the moment—alive and safe meant more to her than she'd thought anything could.

So lost in that kiss, Erin didn't appreciate in any way the dark elf princess leaning in and growling, "Are you two camp whores done?"

When Stieg pulled away and saw the tip of Erin's blade pressed against the royal's throat—right by that big artery too—he chuckled and gently chastised, "*Erin*."

Stieg came around the corner and grabbed the first two elves who charged. He smashed one's head into the stone wall until he'd bashed his brains in. The other he choked at the same time until his eyes bulged from his head and blood poured from his pointed ears.

The shock of the elves' comrades wore off quickly and their leader yelled for an attack.

Stieg ignored the command and bent down to retrieve the swords the men still had clutched in their hands. Before he could stand, he felt the air shift as Erin leaped over his back, her blade slashing, cutting through an elf's head before he could even raise his weapon.

She spun away, stabbed another elf in the heart; spun back and as she moved into a crouch, disemboweled a red-haired elf.

His entrails slithered out of his body and across Erin's arm, landing on the floor.

Stieg slashed the sword one way, cutting an elf from his shoulder to his opposite hip. The other sword he swung back and up, taking the head of another soldier.

As Princess Uathach's troops pushed forward, Princess Seanait came around that corner. She held a sword in one hand and a dwarf-made axe in the other that she'd pulled down from the wall. With a scream that still made her sound completely mad, she charged into the fray, slashing, hacking, and dismembering her way through. In the tight hallway, the floors became slippery with blood, which both Erin and Seanait used to their benefit.

Seanait slid under legs, castrating her enemy's troops as she slipped by. Erin avoided weapon attacks by dropping into splits and attacking from below. Her blades left a string of swiftly killed elves who probably never felt a thing until they hit the ground.

Stieg did what he could to clear the way until he reached the back door Seanait pointed out to them.

He started to go through, but Erin caught his arm and pulled him back. She handed her blood-drenched blades to him so that her hands were free. Placing her palms together, she closed her eyes. Small flames popped between her fingers and when she pulled her hands back, she held a large ball of flame that grew bigger by the second.

Stieg put his arms around Princess Seanait, turning them both away. Erin unleashed that flame and he felt the heat as it exploded that part of the building. Heard the screams of the elf troops on the other side of the wall, burning to death or getting crushed under an avalanche of stone and marble.

He released the dark elf and watched her expression change from fascination to horror. It was the expression people got when they realized that some little redhead had taken out half a castle building with her flame. That was power.

"Are you a witch?" Seanait asked Erin in awe.

"No. But Skuld did tell me I was saucy."

They worked their way through the remains of the castle wall. Bodies, weapons, and shields littered the courtyard. Some elves were crushed by falling stones. Others were still smoldering.

Still, there were more troops to contend with. Archers, specifically. They stood on the western battlements with their bows aiming down.

"How fast are you?" Erin asked Princess Seanait.

"You've seen."

"Good." She glanced at Stieg. "Then run." She slammed her foot against the edge of a shield. It flipped up and she snatched it out of the air before crouching down and using it to shield her body as arrows rained down on them from above.

A few feet away, Stieg's shield barely hid his much-bigger-than-an-elf body.

More elves ran out on the east side of the battlements, arrows already nocked.

"Shit." Erin moved so her back was to Stieg's and her

shield protected them from the east, his from the west. But they couldn't keep this up for long.

"Flame?" Stieg called out.

"Not without exposing an artery."

"Shit."

Erin was thinking they might have to take a chance and unleash their wings, but she didn't know how they would do that and not get shot down. Before she could do something rash and stupid, the rain of arrows slowly came to a stop.

Erin peeked over the top of her round shield and saw the archers staring down. At first, she believed them to be staring at her and Stieg. But they weren't. She looked over her shoulder. Dualtach stood in the rubble, his gaze examining everything.

"We're fucked," Stieg muttered.

He might be right. It was one thing to not like Princess Uathach, but quite another to betray your own kind. Although Erin had never felt like part of anything until she'd joined the Crows, she was still risking all to protect the human race, despite the fact that she found most people pretty goddamn ridiculous.

Dualtach focused on a spot in front of Erin.

She moved the shield enough to see what he was looking at. She sniffed. *Oil.* There was a puddle of oil in front of her. A puddle that came from . . .

Her gaze moved up until it reached the base of the east battlements where the elves stood. And there, with a hole in the bottom from a piece of flying stone, stood a barrel of oil.

"Get ready," she warned Stieg before flicking the finger of her right hand and sending a tiny spark at the puddle. It hit the mark, flame swirled in the oil, and moving fast, tore back toward the barrel.

The elves stared only a moment before they made a crazed run for it.

The fire hit the barrel and Erin screamed at Stieg, "*Go!*"

They kept their shields up because the archers on the west side began firing again, but when they neared the north battlements, Erin and Stieg unleashed their wings and took to the air just as the casket exploded. The power of it sent them spinning over the west battlements and out into the surrounding forest.

The blast was so strong, Erin didn't know if she was right side up or not. She didn't know anything, couldn't do anything but go with it.

She hit the ground and rolled down a small hill until she slammed into something strong enough to stop her.

Panting, Erin flopped to her back and ended up staring into fangs the size of her feet. "Oh, shit, we're back in Jotunheim." She sighed, despairing that she'd never get away from goddamn giants.

The thing above her roared and Erin punched it. Just on principle. She'd been through a lot.

It whimpered and took several steps back.

"Oy!" a deep voice snapped. "Watch your hands."

Erin turned over onto her stomach, placed her hands down, and pushed herself up. She could see what was standing so close to her.

Turned out it was an entire army.

"Oh . . . shit."

Stieg heard a roar and snapped awake; he'd been briefly knocked out when he'd landed on the ground. Worried about Erin, he stood, fell, and stood again. It was not pretty or graceful, but it was the best he could do under the circumstances.

Finally steady, he blinked several times to make sure he wasn't seeing a thousand of everything. He had that happen once when he drank that expensive tequila at Kera's welcome party. Only then it was thousands of Valkyries in bikinis and it was perfect.

What he saw now, however, was not that. Sadly.

But to be honest, he was fucking fed up and probably had a concussion, which led him to do something very Viking. Using the one sword he still had, he cleared off the arrow shafts littering his shield, opened his arms wide in challenge, and bellowed, "*You wanna fight? Then come on!*"

He felt a tap on his arm and turned to see Erin gazing up at him.

"Whatcha doin', buckshot?" she asked.

"Dying with honor?"

"Or we can hold off on that until we have, like, no other options?"

Stieg's head hurt so all he could ask was "Options?"

"Like negotiations?"

"Oh. Yeah, okay."

"I thought you'd already negotiated," a deep voice boomed.

Stieg winced. "Mind lowering that voice, dude?"

"With them?" the male elf demanded, dismounting from his catlike beast. "You negotiated with *them*?"

"It's been centuries, you old bastard. It's not like I had a choice," Princess Seanait snapped.

"Don't bark at me, evil demon child!"

"You left me there!"

"They said they'd kill you if I didn't!"

"You're here *now*!"

"I was told to be here! *But now I wish I'd ignored the message!*"

"Hey!" Erin roared. "Do you mind?" She dug her hand into Stieg's hair and tugged until he put his head on her shoulder. "His head hurts. Think we can take it down a notch?"

The elf male sneered. "I can't believe you made a deal with a human, Seanait."

"Not a human," she smirked. "A Crow."

Stieg jumped when the troops suddenly lowered their spears and went into combat positions.

"Okay," Erin said, her smile so wide Stieg could feel it against the top of his head. "I need to *know* what those other Crows did when they came here to cause *this* reaction. 'Cause I gotta tell ya . . . I'm lovin' it!"

"She saved my life, old bastard, and I promised I'd get her and her Raven lover out of here."

"And a Raven?" the dark elf male whined.

She snarled. He snarled back.

"I'm guessing this is your father," Erin said.

"What do you think?"

"I am King Tiarnach of the Svartalfheim," the dark elf said. "And I am in your"—he sucked his tongue against his fangs in obvious disgust—"debt for saving my daughter."

"It was our pleasure," Erin lied.

"Now we must go inside this castle, kill everyone, then roast and eat the remains of Princess Uathach, our vanquished enemy."

Stieg's head snapped up at those words, but Erin quickly pulled him back down, stroking his hair.

"No," she told Stieg. "This is not our issue. We have other issues."

"Would you like to join us?" the king offered. He turned to Stieg. "You're a Viking and she's a Crow. "There will be much raping and pillaging. Enough for everyone."

Erin's hand slapped over Stieg's mouth before he could say a word.

"As appealing as that offer is to a *female* of any species," and Stieg could hear the barely controlled anger in her voice, "King Tiarnach, we must respectfully decline."

He shrugged big shoulders. "There will be boys there for you, if that's what you're worried about."

Erin made a strange little squeak in the back of her throat. A sound Stieg didn't think he'd ever heard her make before.

"I really need to go," Erin told Princess Seanait. "*Now.*"

The princess motioned to the troops and a minute later an elf walked forward with two large creatures already saddled and ready for travel. "Food and water are already attached to the saddles."

Erin pointed at the animals. "What the fuck are those things?"

"You said you needed transport."

"I was thinking *horses.*"

The princess, the king, and the troops laughed.

The king finally said, "Silly little Crow. *Ride* horses? We eat them."

"Unless you mean centaurs," the princess suggested. "But we eat them, too."

"Okay," Erin said, wiping one hand against another before throwing them up in the air. "I'm out." She walked over to one of the animals. It was enormous, with giant fangs. And didn't appear remotely friendly.

Even worse, Erin didn't really get along with cats. A few times stray cats on the street had actively stalked her as if they'd recognized the bird within.

She leaned close and said to the black-furred beast, "Don't give me any shit, and you and I will do just fine."

"Wait," Princess Seanait called out. She held her hand out to her father and snapped her fingers. When her father did nothing but stare at her, she lifted her hand until it was right under his nose. "Give it to me, old bastard," she snarled.

"I should have drowned you at birth like your mother told me to."

"Which was one of the reasons I cut off her head. Now give it to me."

"They don't need it."

"And if they stray into your brother's territory?"

With a surprisingly dramatic sigh, he reached under his armor and yanked off a chain, slapping the necklace into his daughter's hand.

She gave it to Stieg. "If anyone questions you before you get to the dwarves, show them this. It should protect you."

"Thank you, Princess Seanait. King Tiarnach."

"Good luck," the king said, turning back to his travel beast.

"You'll need it," Seanait muttered before mounting her own animal.

Stieg grabbed the reins of one of the animals and he walked with Erin into the woods. They heard the troops marching toward Princess Uathach and her subjects, but they didn't turn around or try to intervene.

Stieg didn't get involved because he knew there was nothing to be done except risk their lives, which they were already doing too much of as it was.

And Erin didn't intervene because she didn't like any of the parties involved and she was probably hoping they'd wipe each other out.

He didn't really blame her, though. These elves were assholes.

Erin abruptly stopped and Stieg heard her talking to someone. He went around to the other side of the animal and found her talking to the witch.

Dualtach handed over the Key and the map. "I knew you could hide the weapons, but not the hand. If they saw the hand, they would have found the map and everything else."

"No problem." Erin tied the Key to her saddle and returned the map to her back pocket. "Are you going to be okay?"

"I'll be fine. King Tiarnach would never risk killing a witch." He grinned. "It brings bad luck."

"Thanks for your help."

"And thank you for making things entertaining."

Erin again grabbed the reins and led her beast toward a clearing, but before, she got too far, Dualtach called out, "One more thing, Crow."

She stopped and looked at him over her shoulder.

"For a human, you've been . . . I won't say smart, but *crafty*. If I were you, I'd keep that up."

Erin gave a nod and moved on, Stieg right behind her.

When he was close, he said, "Ever notice that even their praise still manages to be insulting?"

"It's like dealing with that aunt at Thanksgiving who really doesn't like you, but doesn't want your mother to notice, so everything she says is passive aggressive." Reaching the clearing, Erin stopped. "All I can say is that if I had the power, I would set Alfheim and Svartalfheim on fire and let the whole *motherfucking thing burn*."

"Erin?"

"Yeah?"

"You will *never* be the passive-aggressive aunt."

"Oh, no. I'd be the fully aggressive aunt."

CHAPTER THIRTY-SIX

Erin and Stieg rode through the night and all the next day, leaving the royal nightmare behind them. When the sun went down again, they finally had to stop. Luckily, they found a river where they set up camp beneath some nearby trees. While he built a fire, Erin removed the bedrolls from their saddles and unrolled them.

She was about to sit down when Stieg asked, "What do we feed them?"

She had no idea until the beast she'd been riding roared and pawed the ground impatiently.

She really wished the elves had given them horses. Whatever these cat things were, they smelled awful and tended to spit. It was disgusting. But, even Erin had to admit, they were fucking fast. Faster than horses and with a lot more stamina.

"I have no idea," she admitted. "But with those fangs, I'm doubting grass."

"We could let them search out their own food," Stieg suggested.

"And what if they don't come back? Mine hates me."

"She really does."

Erin watched the beasts and noticed that they kept pulling toward the river.

She walked over and took Stieg's mount—she wasn't going near hers unless she was riding the bitch—and led him to the water. He sniffed and sniffed and then dashed forward.

Erin hadn't been expecting that so when he jerked forward, she went right into the water, face-first. She dropped the reins and turned over. Stieg's hands grabbed her waist, lifting her out.

It wasn't *his* laughter that bothered her, though. It was the goddamn cat's! At least, she was guessing that wheezing sound was laughter as the giant beast rolled onto her back.

"Are you okay?" Stieg asked.

"I'm going to kill her."

"We need her."

"I'll walk!"

Burying his head against the back of her neck, Stieg held Erin so she couldn't get away and do what she was threatening to do.

"I still hear you laughing," she told him.

"Sorry. I'm so sorry."

"Bastard." But she was laughing, too.

Stieg's mount seemed oblivious. Too busy hunting enormous river fish, killing the things with his fangs and tossing them onto the shore so he could share them with the other beast.

"I'm tired," she finally admitted.

"Let's get some sleep."

"No. Not yet. First . . . I want a bath."

He gestured to the river. "Milady, your bath awaits."

They removed their clothes and took them into the river with them, soaking them to remove the copious amount of blood from their recent battles. As they cleaned their clothes and themselves in the shockingly but wonderfully warm water, they talked. Just talked. Like regular people. No discussion about gods and Vikings and Ragnarok and ass-kicking nuns. Just a regular conversation between two regular people.

Well . . . sort of regular people.

"You were on an episode of *Cops*?"

"Yeah," Stieg grudgingly admitted.

"Why?"

"I was in a car."

"Uh-huh."

"And they pulled us over."

"You gave them attitude?"

"Not until they frisked me. And the more they tried to get me to submit—"

"The more defiant you were."

"Pretty much. It changed everything, though. One of the Raven elders is a hardcore *Cops* fan. He saw me on the episode and they made it their business to track my ass down."

"Did you throw those cops around like stuffed toys?"

"Yes."

Erin laughed. "I love it! I've gotta find that episode when we get home!"

"You can see it online, and Siggy has it on DVD."

"What's the video called online?"

"Depends who posted it, but mostly *Big white boy on meth beats up cops*."

Erin laughed harder. "That's the best!" She wrung her clothes out. "Here. Give me your stuff."

He handed his things over and she got out of the lake, taking the time to carefully place the clothes on branches.

When she returned, he warned, "Those won't be dry by morning."

"No problem." She held up her dripping wet hand and Stieg

watched flames wrap around her fingers. "I've got a trick for that, but it's a faster process if the clothes aren't soaking wet."

"You really like your flames, huh?"

"They make me feel like a superhero."

Snuffing out her flames, Erin grabbed his hand and closely examined the metal cuff he still had on his wrists. "We should have had that witch take these off you."

"These are made by dwarves. I'm not even sure Odin can remove them."

"Well, we have to cut through Nidavellir anyway. We'll see if they can help."

"It's not a big deal."

"It is to me. It was bad enough you were dragged here, but then you were treated like an unruly pet by elves. I feel totally guilty. And I don't usually feel guilty."

"Maybe that's because you're in love with me and you don't want to see the man of your dreams suffering."

"Really?" Erin asked, dropping his hand. "You're turning my own bullshit against me?"

They dried off by the pit fire and ate some of the dried meat and bread that Princess Seanait had given them.

What kind of "meat" they were eating, neither asked. It was something they didn't want to know. But other than the mystery meat, it was an enjoyable evening.

Erin couldn't remember the last time she'd had an enjoyable evening with any man. She had them with her sister-Crows all the time but those were different. True, they were sometimes naked at the time—some of her sisters were real comfortable being naked whenever and wherever—but they were women.

Other than sex, men didn't really hold much interest for Erin. She found them kind of annoying and easier to torment than to actually have a conversation with.

But Stieg could hold his own with her. More important, when he didn't know something, he didn't pretend he knew something. She hated that as much as a guy who couldn't shut the fuck up. A specific Erin pet peeve so well known by the other Crows that those with chatty boyfriends went out of their way to ensure they never left the poor guy alone with her unless they *wanted* him taught a lesson. Something she was more than happy to do for her sisters.

Erin finger-combed the tangles from her hair and, since she was naked anyway, looked over her wounds. She had a few but nothing she was too worried about. The beauty of being a Crow—fast recovery.

Deciding she was basically fine, Erin stretched out on her bedroll and began to fall asleep. Until Stieg stretched out next to her. She slapped her hand against his chest to halt him and said, "I'm not fucking you."

"I know," he replied with a yawn. His arm slipped around her waist and he settled in beside her, his face pressed against her shoulder.

"If you know, what are you doing?"

"Trying to sleep, if you'd shut up."

"We're both naked."

"And?"

"Don't have condoms."

"And?"

"And why can't you sleep over there?"

"Because I want to sleep here, beside you."

"I'm not fucking you."

"Is there a reason you keep saying that, Erin?"

"Just making sure we're clear."

"We're clear. Can I go to sleep now?"

"Stop pretending you're above it all," Erin told him. "And is actual cuddling necessary? Can't we just lie next to each other?"

"Sleep, woman!"

"No need to yell, Mr. Bitchy."

The beasts woke Stieg up when the sun was barely peeking over the mountains. They made sounds that he took to mean they were hungry, so he dragged himself over to them, yawning and scratching his head, and removed their bridles so they could get their breakfasts out of the river. They hadn't tried to get away last night so he didn't think they'd bother now, which was good because he was in no mood to run after them.

Erin was still asleep, and he settled in next to her, his hands behind his head.

She turned toward him, her arm over his chest, her jaw pressed against his shoulder.

Stieg breathed in deep. If the elves weren't such assholes, he actually might enjoy living here, but humans were clearly not welcome in the lands of elves and that was all he needed to know.

Erin softly snored and Stieg smiled a little until he felt her hand slide down his chest, past his abs, and finally wrapped around his cock.

"Uh . . . Erin?"

She made a little sound in the back of her throat and her hand tightened, but she still didn't wake up.

Now Stieg blew out a breath. "Erin?"

Her grip tightened even more.

"Erin!"

She snapped awake. "What? What's wrong?"

"Remove your hand or move your hand. Those are your two options at the moment."

"What?"

He nodded toward his groin and her gaze followed until she laughed.

"Oh!" She pulled her hand away.

Not exactly what he was hoping for, but . . . whatever.

"Sorry," she said around giggles.

"You did that on purpose," he accused.

"No, I didn't. When I'm asleep my hand has a will of its own."

"Guess I should be glad you didn't set Jackie on fire."

"I do not set things on fire unless I—" She blinked and leaned back to see his face better. "Jackie?"

"Jackie the Man."

"You call your dick Jackie the Man?"

"You're trying to tell me that you, Erin Amsel, don't have a name for your pussy?"

It took a moment but, after propping herself up on her elbow, she finally admitted, "Lady HappyKitty. She purrs when she's petted."

"You have a tagline?" Stieg asked, laughing. "*Seriously?*"

"Lady HappyKitty deserves a tagline. She's given me so much pleasure over the years."

"No wonder cats hate you."

Erin went suspiciously quiet and stared down at him, her lips pursed as she looked him over.

"What are you doing?"

"Thinking."

"That's not your thinking face."

Erin snorted. "I didn't know I had a thinking face."

"You do. But what I'm looking at now is your plotting face."

"Well, I was just thinking—"

"You said no sex. Or to paraphrase you, you're not fucking me."

"Look at you, knowing the word *paraphrase*."

"I expect the Silent and the Protectors to think we're stupid, but you broads should know better. And be careful about throwing stones from that glass house."

"Look, all I'm saying is that in the light of day, now that I'm not so exhausted and pretty much healed up . . ."

"We still don't have condoms, and with our luck we won't die here, we'll just end up going back home with you knocked up with some fucking elf baby."

"I love how guys think condoms are only to protect against pregnancy, but I can't have that conversation with you right now."

"Because safe sex lectures are so hot."

"I'm just suggesting that before we get up and face the day, we have other things we can do."

Stieg grinned and wiggled his eyebrows.

Erin rolled her eyes. "First off, that's an exit, not an entry, so you can get that idea right out of your head. And, again, don't make me pull out the safe sex lecture."

"I like how you use it as a threat."

"The beauty of me," she offered with a toss of her head, "is that I can make anything pleasurable or absolute torture. The question is . . . how much do you irritate me?"

"If you asked me that a week ago, I would have said a lot. But I sense I've charmed you in our time together."

"Not really, but it's cute you think so." Keeping her eyes on his face, she lowered her hand again and wrapped her fingers around his cock.

"I think you're just using me to satisfy your sexual needs, Amsel."

"I am."

He shrugged. "Yeah, okay."

He had Erin on her back before she could blink.

She didn't know what was going on with her. She was so determined last night not to be bothered, but she woke up this morning needing him. That had never happened before.

If it was just sexual, she could take care of herself, but it wasn't just sexual. Not anymore.

Of course, she wasn't about to admit that . . . ever.

Instead she pulled him close and kissed him, her hands moving over his shoulders, down his back. Instinctively, she began to open her legs to him, to lock her ankles behind his back, but he pulled away with a grunt.

"You're a woman of mixed emotions. You're driving me nuts."

"It's a gift. You know . . . to me."

That's when he spun her around and she saw his dick hard and waiting. She would have been put off by the move if he hadn't already buried his mouth against her pussy, his tongue circling around her clit before lapping at it, then circling. Fingers slid inside her and Erin moaned. Then he abruptly stopped.

"What are you doing down there?" he demanded.

"Nothing but enjoying myself."

"Yeah. I know. Get to work, woman."

"Am I really the only one who notices our size difference? Some positions may be beyond our capabilities."

He gripped her by the hips and lifted her up, eyeing the space from where she was and where his dick was, and yes, there was a good amount of distance between the two. "Dammit."

Erin laughed. "Hold on." She wiggled away from his hands and sat on his chest, facing away from him. She wrapped her fingers around his dick once again and held it. Then, she took her time sucking the entire thing into her mouth.

Stieg placed his hands against her back, sliding his fingers up and down her spine; the cold metal of the cuffs on his wrists lightly brushing her skin.

Enjoying the feeling, she happily sucked his dick a few times before pausing to run her tongue from base to tip and back again. She sucked on the head only, her hand stroking the shaft. Then went back to sucking the entire thing.

Stieg's fingers began to grip her waist, his hips rising off the ground. She could hear his moans and it made her want to get him off. It felt like nothing else in the world mattered but doing that.

She deep-throated all of him—not easy, the guy was obnoxiously big—and swallowed a few times to contract her throat muscles. His moans turned to hard panting and his grip on her tightened. She sucked him harder, her hand around the base until every muscle in his body tightened and he came hard in her mouth, nearly choking her.

Erin wiped her mouth with the back of her hand and grinned, but Stieg suddenly yanked her back until her pussy was on his mouth and he was sucking the life from her.

God, she was already wet. Getting him off had made her hot and wet. Nothing else could turn him on more. He didn't even bother to turn her around. He just used his tongue to toy with her clit and slipped two fingers inside her pussy, stroking back and forth while his tongue teased and played.

Erin squirmed on top of him, her hands braced against his abs, her hips rocking back and forth against his mouth. He moved his fingers around inside her until her hips almost jerked right off him. Using just one finger, he stroked that spot while sucking on her clit.

Her entire body began to vibrate, the toes resting by his shoulders curling, her muscles tightening. Then she exploded, her groans echoing through the trees, her entire body shaking until she crashed on top of him.

She rolled away, the two of them staring up at the sky.

"And a good morning to you, too!" she announced to the world, making Stieg laugh again.

CHAPTER THIRTY-SEVEN

With the help of the map Tyr had given them, Erin and Stieg made their way through Svartalfheim with few problems, only needing the king's necklace twice, and the need to kill once.

Kind of a relief considering what they'd already done.

The mountainside that was the doorway to Nidavellir, the land of dwarves, was not guarded in any way. Nor was there even a forest around for guards to hide in.

Erin and Stieg stood outside the open mountainside for a good thirty minutes, just staring at it.

"Are they really not worried? You know, about intruders?"

"Apparently not." Still mounted on his beast, Stieg looked around. "Are we just going to sit here or are we going to go?"

"We have to go. We're running out of time and I'm not sure how long it'll take us to get to the Land of the Dead."

They led their beasts toward the exit, but when they were a few feet away, the animals balked, rearing back, refusing to go any farther.

"Guess we're on foot from here," Erin said, dismounting and removing everything from the beasts. They even took

off the saddles and bridles so the animals could roam free
until other elves took them in or they made their way back
to their home.

With weapons at the ready, Erin and Stieg entered the
dark cave, but still . . . nothing. No guards. No soldiers.
Nothing protecting the entrance into Nidavellir.

Erin stopped. "What are we doing?"

"Being cautious . . . ?"

"I'm so bored by that."

"I *really* wish you'd gone to that appointment for the
ADHD testing."

"Come on. Let's just go."

"Erin—"

"Come on! It'll be fun!"

"*No.* It will not be fun. It will be dangerous."

"Don't you want to live on the edge?"

"I'm hanging with you. I'm already on the edge."

She took a few steps forward and raised her hands, unleashing a wide circle of flame and lighting up the entire
area. Pulling her hands back, she turned to Stieg and said,
"Oh, shit."

They stood at what he guessed was the *top* of a set of very
narrow stairs that led down and down until they could no
longer see them. Unlike entering elven territory from Jotunheim, there seemed to be no mystical doorway that would
simply take them to the next world. Instead they'd have to
walk down the long, narrow set of stairs with no handrails.

"I can't express to you how much I *don't* want to do this,"
Erin muttered, staring down.

"That makes two of us." He thought a moment. "Maybe
we can fly."

"We'll have to wait on that. All I see around the stairs is

darkness. We can't fly into complete blackness. Who knows what we'd fucking hit." She was right, of course. Although the fact that they couldn't see into the darkness surrounding the stairs meant that it wasn't normal either. She even sent down a ball of flame and it was simply swallowed up rather than lighting the area.

Erin rubbed her hands together. "Let's just do this." Again, she was right. They didn't have time to delve into their phobias.

"I'll take the lead," he said, but Erin's arm shot out, halting him.

"So the guy with no flame and no flame protection should get in front of the woman *with* flame?"

"When you put it like that . . ." Stieg stepped back and gave a small wave toward the stairs.

Erin walked to the top of the steps and let out a long breath. Then she started walking. Stieg gave her a moment to get ahead and followed.

The entire time neither spoke as they walked down except to say when a break was needed. Then they sat on the step they were standing on and took that break, which was less for physical strain than an emotional one. After ten minutes or so, they carefully stood back up and started again.

It was one of the most unpleasant experiences Stieg could remember having. Even their time with the elves hadn't been as bad. Because this was just . . . hell. And it felt like it lasted for days, terrifying because they had no concept of time. Except for the stairs being strangely lit, there was no other light. No sunlight. No moon. No torches. Nothing.

Even worse, there was the occasional sound of what he could only describe as *scuttering*. A word he was positive he'd never used in a sentence. But that's what was coming from the stone walls.

Scuttering.

And the knowledge that something could come out at them from the darkness did not help the situation in any way. Especially when the last thing one wanted to do was jump suddenly.

This was not the place for any sudden movements.

But they kept going. They had to; they had no choice.

Erin stopped. Stieg assumed she was ready for another break, but she didn't sit. She didn't move forward. She just stood there.

"Erin?"

"It stops."

"The stairs?"

"Everything. There's like two more steps and then nothing but dark." She shook her head. "I don't know what to do."

That was something he'd never heard Erin admit before, which meant she was really stressed out. Not that he blamed her. The mystical doorway between Jotunheim and Svartalfheim had been a swirling vortex, scary but also active. Like jumping into a raging river. It gave the illusion he might have some control. But *nothing*? He didn't know what to do with *nothing*. And clearly neither did Erin.

"So what are our options?" Stieg asked.

"We could stay here forever."

"Seems a tad illogical. We can go back up the stairs. See if Dualtach can help us."

"Dude . . . back up those stairs? Are you high?"

"You have dancer's legs," he teased.

"I do. But I'm not about to walk back up those fucking stairs."

"Then we don't have any other options."

"Okay. You're right."

He watched Erin stand there, taking in deep breaths like she was about to run a marathon.

"Erin Amsel."

"What?"

"You're a Crow."

"Yeah?"

"And I'm a Raven."

"Your point?"

Stieg went down two steps until he stood right behind her. "And we were chosen by gods. Not to worship them, but to fight for them." He wrapped his arms around her waist and lifted her up until she was trapped against his chest.

"Stieg Engstrom, what the holy fuck are you doing?"

"We are Vikings." He held his screaming woman tight and jumped into the black.

"Stieg! You mother . . ."

"—fucker!"

Báraldur heard the screamed curse and looked away from the sword he had in the fire. He sighed. "Dammit." Leaving the weapon in the fire, he walked to his front door and yelled out, "Vikings!"

Báraldur's wife came in from the stables and gazed down at the pair who'd burst uninvited into their home. "You picked this gods-forsaken place," she complained, "and then you bitch when they come through the bloody door."

"The rent was cheap, wasn't it?"

"You're cheap."

"Just get them up."

"You get them up!"

But the pair didn't need any help, because they got up fighting. The man using his arms to block his face from her blows and the woman calling him every horrible thing in the book.

"You do that to me again and I'll cut your legs off!"

"We had no choice!"

"Fuck you!" She was only a foot or so taller than his wife, but she was skinny. A wisp of a thing.

The man also stood, but he kept growing.

For a moment, Báraldur thought he might have been wrong. Maybe the man was from Jotunheim. They never came this far, the giants, but there was always a chance. *Life* was chance.

Thankfully, the growing stopped and he realized that what stood before him, arguing with the woman, was a man, not a giant.

"I should set you on fire!"

"I had no choice, Erin! You were just standing there!"

She roared and turned away from him but stopped quick when she saw Báraldur and his wife. "I'm . . . I'm sorry. We thought we were alone."

"Yes," the man said, "we—"

"No one's talking to you!" the woman barked.

The man threw up his hands in frustration.

Báraldur saw his wife bow her head, hiding the smile on her lips.

"You're from Midgard," Báraldur noted. "Land of the humans."

"Yes," the man answered. "And we need to get to Corpse Shore."

The woman faced the man again. *"Why don't you just fucking announce it to everybody?"*

"Are you just going to keep yelling at me?" he yelled.

"Yes!"

Báraldur's wife, unable to stand the fighting another second, went to the woman and took her hand. "Come, girl. Let us get you some food and water from our kitchen."

"I'm not hungry."

She gazed up at the red haired woman. "But you will come nonetheless or I'll make sure we are seeing eye to eye for the rest of your life. Understand my meaning?"

"Yeah. I do."

"Then come." Báraldur's wife led the woman away.

Once they were gone, the man said to Báraldur, "The situation we were in . . . I had to do *something*."

"I believe you, Viking. But I don't think she gives a fat fuck."

CHAPTER THIRTY-EIGHT

Annalisa waited while the orderly unlocked the door to the room that held Jace's false prophet ex-husband. They were going to send out a challenge tonight to the Carrion and wanted the false prophet to be secured someplace where they had immediate and unquestioned access to him.

She'd come after hours, paperwork for the transfer signed by officials that would keep most of the pain-in-the-ass doctors from questioning too much.

The orderly opened the door and Annalisa walked in.

"All right, Mr. Braddock . . ."

Instantly Annalisa noticed two things. Jace's ex didn't automatically complain that he was called *Pastor* Braddock, and the room was really dark.

Braddock didn't like the dark. Probably because that's when the Crows tortured him. When it was dark.

She turned toward the orderlies to ask if they knew where Braddock was, but they closed the steel, reinforced door in her face.

"That can't be good."

Two Carrion emerged from the shadows and walked toward the center of the room.

"Yeah." Annalisa sighed. "Not good at all."

Karen struggled to keep her phone to her ear with her shoulder while shoving papers into her bag. "I'm asking you guys," she begged the fellow shifter on the other end of the phone, "to help. We can't pretend this doesn't affect us. It affects everyone."

"Look, Karen, I don't know what you want me to say. You were told a long time ago that if you wanted to associate with those people—"

"One guy! He's my best friend." She closed the bag, clipping it shut.

"It doesn't matter. He's not one of us and he's not that human, so we don't see this as our problem."

Karen clenched her jaw in frustration, quickly realizing her fangs had come out.

This was why she had so little to do with her kind. They were humans who could shift into wild animals, but the Nordic Clans were the freaks? Then again, maybe it had nothing to do with the current Nine Clans.

"Is this about the wolves?" Karen asked her contact.

"Don't be ridiculous."

"Really? Am I really being ridiculous?"

As long as the world had existed there had been shifters. Of every race, religion, and species. The ones considered the most volatile were the wolves that, it was said, had descended from the Nordic god Loki. For centuries, they were part of the Nine, just like the Ravens. But they were hard to control and had become known for killing and eating entire towns when the mood struck them. Eventually, they were kicked out of the Nine and the Crows took their place. Something the wolves had never forgiven the Crows or the Clans for.

Although Loki's wolves had no say or sway among the Vikings, they still had pull among the shifters.

Rushing to the door, Karen grabbed the doorknob. "Look, I know the fucking canines can be difficult, but I really wish you could—" She opened the door, and they were just coming down the hall toward her. Leathery wings out. Big bodies moving.

Karen slammed the door shut, could hear them running now. Running toward her.

"Karen? Karen? What's going on?" she heard from her phone before she dropped it and ran to the closet. She yanked that door open and grabbed Stieg's stupid goat, which she'd taken in after a highly upsetting call from Vig, even though the thing hated her and hid in the closet almost the entire time she was home.

Hefting Hilda under her arm, she ran toward the balcony, hearing them bursting into the room behind her. Karen didn't even stop to open the glass doors. She went through them, using her body to protect the screaming Hilda.

She leaped up on the railing and jumped, landing on the ground and rolling until she was on both feet. People around her were screaming, ducking to avoid the flying glass.

Karen ignored them all and ran. That idiot, screaming goat still in her arms.

Billy stood outside the door while the patients in the other room screamed and howled. The crazies always knew when something was off. He looked at Scott, his "partner in crime" as the nurses liked to call them. "Dude, we shouldn't have done this."

"Shut up." Scott hit one of the doors with his fist and yelled out. "*All of you shut up!*"

But no one shut up. It just kept going.

"The nurses are going to come."

"Who? Darryl? He's sleeping in the break room downstairs and Delores is out for her dinner break. So shut up!"

"She's a doctor!"

"And they'll think that nut Braddock did it and ran. We'll be in the clear."

Billy knew why Scott was doing this. For the ten grand they'd been offered. But Billy hadn't found out until tonight that part of the deal was leaving the doctor in that room alone with those . . . freaks. So pale. Almost green. And like their skin was . . . flaking. Decaying, even.

It was weird!

The horrible noises coming from Braddock's room ended and the other patients didn't just calm down. They stopped. They stopped everything. It was like they were waiting.

Scott pointed at the door and Billy stepped back. "Fuck you. You do it!"

"Pussy," Scott shot back. After waiting a few more seconds, he walked to the door and pressed his ear against it. "I don't hear anything," he whispered.

"You sure?"

"Positive."

Billy inched closer but still didn't put his head against the door.

Finally, frustrated, Scott pulled out his keys and unlocked the door.

It was hard to see in the poorly lit room, but Billy couldn't miss the male head in the middle of the floor.

"I don't see her," Scott said, kicking the damaged lab coat she'd been wearing aside. Her stethoscope lay ripped apart and tossed on the bed.

"Let's get out of here," Billy said, turning toward the door.

A hand gripped his throat and Billy let out a panicked squeal. Scott jumped back, but before he could react, another male head hit him in the face, knocking him to the floor, his screams setting off the other patients.

The doctor stood in front of them. She was covered in something black and green; her hands were sticky with it. Billy could feel it on his neck. What really terrified him was the doctor herself. She wasn't panicking. She wasn't angry. She definitely wasn't scared. She just gazed calmly at him with those cold eyes.

He saw eyes like that every day when he had to check on the patients that the docs had diagnosed as sociopaths. Men and women who would never get out of this place unless it was to go back to prison for the rest of their lives.

Scott struggled to his feet, and when he finally stood, he suddenly swung at the doc with the blade he always had hidden on him. In case the patients got a little out of hand.

But the doc, her eyes never moving off Billy, caught Scott's wrist and twisted. The blade hit the floor, but before Scott could bend down to get it, she released Billy and flung out her free hand, hitting Scott in the throat.

Billy thought it was a lame attempt to punch Scott, but something splattered across Billy's face, nearly blinding him. Scott dropped to the ground, eyes wide open, his skin torn, blood pumping out of his throat and dripping all over the floor.

She held up the hand she'd hit Scott with, right in Billy's face so he could easily see it. He watched the talons— because that's what she had—retract back into her fingers, disappearing beneath skin and normal human nails.

Shaking, Billy stared at the doc.

"Well, that could have gone worse," she calmly told Billy. "Those dudes are hard to kill. Luckily, there were only two and I'm not prone to panic." She stepped closer to him.

"Now . . . tell me everything, Billy. And I won't spend hours tearing you apart. But lie to me . . ."

She held up her forefinger . . . that talon back.

The doc didn't finish her threat, but big black wings eased out of her back and Billy screamed.

He screamed and the other patients joined in.

Kera had barely stopped the SUV in front of the Ravens' main house before Jace jumped out and ran up the stairs. Yanking out the keys, Kera followed her friend, catching up to her just as they made it to the kitchen where the Ravens had Karen, a blanket around her shaking body. She was still human, but her eyes were a weird yellow color and her fangs peeked out from beneath her gums.

The girl was terrified.

"Oh, my God, Karen!" Jace said, stopping in the middle of the kitchen and staring down at Stieg's friend. "Are you okay?"

"Do I *look* okay?" The shifter's voice was no more than a growl. "They came to my apartment, Jace. *My fucking apartment!*"

"I'm so sorry," Jace said. "But I'm really glad you're okay."

"She saved Stieg's goat."

The two women gawked at poor Siggy, who had the goat in his lap and was rubbing its belly like a puppy.

Karen's hands clenched into fists. "If you bring up that goddamn goat one more time . . ."

"I don't know why you're angry. Stieg would be really glad to know you were watching out for his best friend."

"You keep talking, and I'm going to mark all over this house!"

"What happened?" Kera asked Josef, deciding not to get involved in this particular fight. She had enough to worry about.

"Like she said. A couple of Carrion came to Karen's apartment tonight."

"For Stieg?"

"We don't think so." Josef stood, motioned to his chair.

Jace sat down and tried to comfort Karen, but the shifter wanted none of that. In fact, she hissed at poor Jace like a caged house cat being dragged to the vet.

Josef stood next to Kera, his back to Karen and the others. "You understand why they did this?"

"To kill our only connection to other shifters?"

"We know other shifters, but none that will help. Only Karen could have made that happen for us."

"Okay. Um . . . do me a— Shit." Kera pulled her cell phone from her back pocket and answered. After listening to the conversation at the other end, she disconnected the call and took Josef by his arm, pulling him out of the kitchen. "We have a problem."

"I sensed that."

"Annalisa went to the mental hospital to get Braddock so we could secure him at our house, but he's gone, and the orderlies were paid to lock her in his room with two Carrion."

Josef's eye twitched a bit. Just like it did when he was about to get into a fight with Chloe. "Okay."

"I guess what I'm not sure about," Kera admitted, "is what all this activity means."

"I'm sure nothing good."

Leigh stood in the Bird House hallway glaring down at her phone. She swore, yet again, if she survived the upcoming apocalypse, she was *so* going to break up with her boyfriend. He was such a dick!

A knock at the front door stopped her from sending out a string of curses. Knowing it would set her boyfriend off and wanting to be all-in for that particular fight, she went to the door first, but didn't open it. None of them did anymore. Not since Erin got shot in the head by one of Pastor Braddock's minions.

Instead, Leigh stood on the opposite side of the door, hand on the doorknob, and slowly eased the door halfway open before she stopped, blinked, and closed the door again. Turning off her phone, she went down to Chloe's office and knocked on the door.

"Come!"

Leigh leaned in. Chloe, Tessa, and Betty. Perfect. "You guys busy?"

"What's up?" Chloe asked.

"I need you at the front door."

"Are you okay?"

"Just . . ." She waved at them.

"It's not more cult people coming to kill us, is it?"

"No."

The three women glanced at each other, then followed Leigh back to the front of the house and, after a breath, opened the door.

The Carrion had nailed a naked male body to it, runes burned into his chest.

"Huh," Betty said.

Tessa clasped her hands in front of her, both forefingers pressed to her chin. "Please tell me that's not one of our, uh . . . guys."

"Too small to be a Raven or a Protector." Betty went up on her toes and tried to see something on his back. Not easy . . . again, the man was nailed to the door. "It's one of the Silent."

Chloe winced. "Are you sure?"

"He . . . the body, has Vidar's rune branded on the shoulder."

"Think it's Brandt?" Tessa asked.

Chloe pulled her phone from the front pocket of her jeans

and looked up a name in her CONTACTS. She put the phone to her ear and suddenly let out a breath. "Brandt! Hi. Uh . . . are you guys missing anybody? You are. Notto. I see. Uh . . . we think he's been nailed to our front door. Well, we're not positive because, um . . . no head. Yeah . . . yeah . . ."

Betty stepped past the doorway, paused, and leaned back in to casually announce, "Found the head."

Tessa went outside, returning a moment later and mouthing to Chloe, *Notto*.

"Okay," Chloe went on, clearly feeling horrible about all this, "we have a confirmation. It's definitely Notto. Uh . . . yeah. Sure. You guys come over . . . whenever . . . to . . . collect him." She cringed. "Okay. Bye." She disconnected the call. "Well, that was terrible."

"It's like kicking a puppy," Leigh complained, staring at Notto's remains. "I mean, the Silent are basic fighters, but they're not . . . us, ya know? They're politicians. Not exactly a challenge."

Leigh pointed at the runes branded on Notto's chest. "What do these mean anyway?"

Betty crossed her arms under her breasts. "You know that challenge we were going to give to the Carrion tomorrow to help lure Gullveig out in about three days when Erin will be back with the sword if she doesn't get killed within the Nine Worlds?"

"Yeah."

"Well . . . that schedule's been moved up to just before dawn"—she glanced at her watch—"in about eight hours."

"But Erin thinks she has several more days."

"Yeah." Betty closed the door, Notto still attached to it. "But she doesn't."

CHAPTER THIRTY-NINE

"You know, over the years, I could have killed him. Now I realize I *should* have killed him."

Arnóra placed a plate filled with last night's meats on the table in front of the stranger. "I've said that more than once myself and yet my husband lives. Even worse, the longer he lives, the more the children become attached." She poured a mug of mead. "What's your name, girl?"

"Erin."

"I'm Arnóra." Elbows on the hard wood, she leaned against the table and studied the human, Erin, as she picked at her food. She was calming down. Probably feeling a little bad about yelling at her man.

"You ain't no Viking, girl."

She didn't even flinch, those green eyes of hers flicking up to Arnóra's face, a small smirk on her lips.

"Vikings would turn a girl like you into a slave," Arnóra went on. "Maybe they already did with your ancestors. And now you've come back for vengeance. In the name of them . . . and the god Skuld."

The girl chewed her food, her gaze locked with Arnóra's.

No, this one wouldn't back down. This one wouldn't give up.

"Ain't that true . . ." Arnóra whispered, ". . . Crow?"

The dwarf sat him down next to his workbench and, after removing the metal cuffs those bastard elves had placed on him, put a horn of mead in Stieg's hands. "Name's Báraldur."

"I'm Stieg Engstrom."

"Engstrom? Heard tales of that bloodline. Not a friendly lot."

"Wouldn't know."

"That your woman?"

Stieg opened his mouth to reply, but it sort of hung there until he shook his head and said, "I have no fucking idea."

"Yeah. Females get like that sometimes. Makes me miss the days my old Da told me about when they used to kowtow. But one of 'em picked up a sword during a battle and all that changed. Ain't been right since. She a shieldmaiden, your girl?"

"Sort of."

"And what are you?"

"A Viking, like you said."

"A human—a *living* human—doesn't make it this far without the powers only a god can give." The dwarf sized him up. "You're big enough to be a Giant Killer but if you were that, you'd still be in Jotunheim getting stomped on by giants. Your woman ain't no Holde's Maid and she don't look like she ever fought no bear, so she ain't Isa. If you were Claws, you'd still be among the Elves 'cause they got oceans aplenty. You ain't smart enough to be a Protector—"

"Gee. Thanks."

"—and not arrogant enough to be one of the Silent."

The dwarf held up seven fingers. "There are always nine

Clans, Viking. And with only two left that makes you a Raven. And that woman . . . alone in the kitchen with me wife . . . a Crow."

"We're not here to hurt anyone."

"Then what are you doing here?"

"It's complicated."

The dwarf pulled a chair over and sat in front of Stieg. "All right," he said, "who fucked up and started Ragnarok again?"

"Nidhogg will suck the marrow from your leg bones while he talon-fucks what's left of your corpse."

Erin gawked at the She-dwarf. "That's a lovely sentiment. Thank you."

"Just warnin' ya. You're better off goin' home."

"I go home, everybody dies. So that's currently not an option for me. I at least have to try."

"So what do you need from me and mine?"

"Nothing, really. This is just where we ended up once we hit the bottom of those goddamn stairs."

Arnóra chuckled. "Say what you like about them stairs, girl, but at least they tell me what I'm dealing with."

"I don't understand."

"Do you know how many start down them stairs? Not as many as the ones who turn away. And the ones who do go down . . . they eventually go back up before they even get halfway. So the fact you made it *this* far, and you ain't lookin' for gold and magical weapons you can show off to your friends or try to rule the world with . . . says to me, you've got what me dear Ma called 'determination.' Not only important when making weapons but when surviving this group of worlds we all live in." The She-dwarf slammed a large, wide blade on the table.

"What's that?"

"The blade I was going to use to kill you when I realized you were a gods-damn Crow."

"You know, we're really quite nice. The Crows."

"No, ya ain't. But you are determined. And I like that. So I'll help ya."

"You will?"

"Yeah. I can get you food, weapons. For your travels. I won't bother with clothes, though. We ain't got nothing to fit you two. But at least enough food to get you where you need to go."

"Wait." Erin scratched her forehead. She suddenly had a headache. A very bad headache. "Enough food?"

"Yeah. Food to last you until you get to Nidhogg."

"How long does that trip take from here?"

"We don't usually travel that far. No one wants to go to Corpse Shore. It's a disgusting place. So"—she glanced off, counting in her head, before announcing—"twenty-three days."

Erin shot up out of her seat. "What? *Fuck!*"

They met in the middle of their dwarven hosts' home.

"Twenty-three days?" Erin snarled.

"I know," Steig replied. Apparently they'd both gotten the bad news from their hosts at the same time. "I know!"

"What are we going to do?"

"Maybe we can get a message to them."

"To do what?"

"Hold back on the challenge. To wait it out until we get home."

"It won't matter. In twenty-three days—or, in this case, eleven and a half days *earth* time—Gullveig will be back at full power. That happens, I won't be able to get near her, no matter what weapon I'm fucking using. She'll just think and be gone before I can get close."

"Fuck."

"Fuck!"

They began pacing around each other.

"So what do we do?" Stieg eventually asked. "What do we do?"

"I don't know, but there's gotta be something."

He faced Erin. "I'll call to Odin."

"For what?"

"He can help."

"He had his chance to help. Over and over. And you know what? He didn't do shit! Why would that change now?"

"Call to Skuld then." Before Erin could disagree, Stieg added, "Why don't we call for both?"

"Now you're just talking crazy."

"Then what do we do?"

Erin paced away, stopped, faced him. "We go back."

"*What?*"

"We've still got the Key. We open the doorway here, using the spell and runes that Inka showed me and we go back to our Clans. And we fight by their side. We *die* by their side."

Stieg stopped and gazed at her before adding, "With honor."

"With honor."

They moved toward each other, meeting in the middle again. Right arms bent at the elbow, they clasped hands, committing to their decision.

It was the most profound moment Stieg had had until he heard Báraldur behind him sigh and mutter to his wife, "Good gods . . . Vikings."

Still clasping Stieg's hand, Erin looked at their hosts. "What does that mean?"

"You Vikings," Arnóra explained. "It's like you think you only have two options. Follow original plan or die in battle."

"There's another option?"

"Yeah."

Erin pulled away from Stieg and faced Arnóra. "And you're just telling us this now?"

"I didn't have a chance before! You started cursing and stormed off to offer death as an option to your minigiant there."

Erin took several steps toward Arnóra, but Stieg yanked her back. "We really don't have time for you to flip out here," he reminded Erin before focusing on Arnóra and Báraldur. "What can you do for us?"

"Not us. Torfinna. She runs the docks."

"Wait. A *boat* can take us to Nidhogg?" Erin asked.

"Close enough."

"And you're just telling us this?"

"Again," Arnóra yelled back, "you ranted and walked away! *You didn't give me time to tell you anything!*"

CHAPTER FORTY

Arnóra and Báraldur led Erin and Stieg through the town of Jórunn. It was clear they were inside a mountain, but it didn't feel like the walls were closing in or they were horribly trapped. Everything was so wide and expansive that Stieg felt comfortable. You know . . . except for the way everyone stared at them. And followed. While armed.

Every male and female dwarf carried a weapon. Nice ones, too. Deadly ones.

It was strange, though. The tallest barely reached Erin's shoulders, but Stieg had no delusions that those who followed him and Erin were anything less than mighty warriors. They could use the weapons they made as well as any Viking.

Understanding this, he did nothing to unsettle the dwarves. He simply followed Arnóra and Báraldur and kept his gaze forward.

He wished he could say the same for Erin.

Because she just stopped right in the middle of the street, turned at the waist, and screamed out, "Hah!" with her hands thrown up. Like "jazz hands."

And she did it for absolutely no reason that Stieg could see!

The dwarves behind them stepped back, not to move away so much as to ready themselves for battle. Weapons raised, bodies tense.

Snarling, Stieg snapped at Erin, "What is *wrong* with you?"

She couldn't answer him, she was laughing too hard. So hard she had to lean against him to stay on her feet. One hand covering her mouth. Eventually tears flowed.

Slowly, the dwarves lowered their weapons and one She-dwarf in a chain mail dress leaned in, placing a soft hand on his forearm. "Poor, lass. She gone mad then?"

Stieg took a few seconds before answering. He wished he could say that what they were witnessing was days of stress coming out in human hysteria . . . but that would be a lie. Erin Amsel was Erin Amsel. There was no madness in her, just insanity, which might sound like the same thing, but to him it wasn't.

"I'm sorry," he lied. "She's been under a lot of stress."

"Poor wee thing. She does look half-starved. Don't ya feed her, boy?"

"She's actually well-fed. Where we come from, she's considered *curvy*."

"Ohhhh," the dwarves said in unison, and the She-dwarf in the chainmail dress patted his shoulder. As if to say, "Good lad. Make her feel better."

Stieg was feeling pretty good about himself until he realized that Erin was no longer laughing. She was just standing there . . . staring at him.

"What?"

"Curvy? Did you just call me curvy?"

"Yeah. I like curvy."

"Uh-huh."

"I'm sensing by your cold-blooded stare and lack of words . . . I've done something wrong."

* * *

Erin passed small houses and big dogs and a lot of forges.

Good Lord, how many carcinogens were released into the atmosphere from so many forges *inside* a cave?

"You're not talking to me," Stieg wisely noted.

"Nothing to say."

"Really? Because I feel like you want to say something."

"Nope."

"This is the curvy thing, isn't it?"

"Is it?"

Arnóra and Báraldur stopped in front of a small house with the door open and the two gestured with their hands. Erin walked in, ducking to clear the doorway.

An old She-dwarf sat in a stuffed chair with her leg up on an ottoman and a pipe in her mouth. She glanced up and smiled around the pipe stem, gazing at Erin the same way Betty had when Erin had first met her.

"It's the Crow," the She-dwarf said, laughing a little.

"Have we met?" Erin asked, because the dwarf acted as if they had.

"Nah. Sit."

Erin grabbed a sturdy wood chair, but the She-dwarf suddenly said, "Don't try to put your big fat ass in that. Sit on the floor."

Shocked, Erin's back straightened and the old bitch burst out laughing.

"Just kidding, Crow." She motioned to the stone walls of her house. "Sound travels 'round here. Even I know what *curvy* translates to where you come from. So sit your fat ass down. It'll be fine. Nice thick chairs, they could even handle one of my big ol' hogs."

Erin sat down and resisted the urge to strangle the old bitch.

"You, too, Viking," the She-dwarf yelled out the doorway.

Stieg had to bend at the waist to get into the house and he did end up sitting on the floor. It was the only way he fit in the place among all the books, the altar, and the three pigs. Big ones, too. At least two hundred pounds each.

The sight made Erin crave bacon.

"Name's Torfinna."

"Can you help us get to Corpse Shore?" Erin asked.

"For what?"

"Torfinna," Arnóra said from the doorway. "Just help 'em. For me and Báraldur."

The old She-dwarf puffed on her pipe. "If you want to get to Corpse Shore, Crow, then start walkin'."

"We need to get there faster than that."

She banged her pipe on the table beside her to clear it, then packed it with more tobacco. "Why? Because you think you and that sword can save your friends?"

Erin locked her gaze on the She-dwarf. "How do you know any of that?"

"Dock life. You learn things."

"Don't lie to me."

"And you better watch your tone."

"How about," Stieg cut in, "we all discuss this calmly. Especially," he said close to Erin's ear, "since we are seriously outnumbered."

Erin briefly closed her eyes. Took a moment to get control. "Okay," she finally said, feeling much calmer. "So, Torfinna, what can you tell us about the sword?"

"The sword might be able to do the job ya need. But you, fatty, wielding it, can't."

"See what you started?" Erin snarled at Stieg.

"I said *curvy*!"

"In LA, it's the same goddamn thing."

"*We're not in LA!*"

"It's about power, ya see," Torfinna went on, ignoring Erin and Stieg. "And you, Crow, ain't got enough for it."

Erin looked at Stieg. "We're gonna need to get that fire giant, aren't we?"

"*No*. You combine that sword with Surtr and you will get Ragnarok." Torfinna put the pipe in her mouth and lit it. Took a long drag, held it, then released it right into Erin's face.

Erin gritted her teeth, but managed not to beat the old dwarf to death. She had to admit . . . her restraint made her proud.

"But you do need extra power," the She-dwarf continued.

"Then I'll get some. But first I need you to get us there."

Relaxing back into her chair, Torfinna asked, "What have you got for me?"

"Got for you?"

"We're dwarves, Crow. We bargain. What have you got to bargain with?"

Erin pulled one of the Vig-made blades from her holster and held it up.

Torfinna leaned in, studied it. "Nice work, but I have me own forge."

"Of course you do."

"Like the hand."

"I need the hand."

"A Carrion hand? What ya need that for?"

"To get home, so I can be unhelpful and fat apparently."

Stieg rammed his fist against the ground. "I said curvy!"

Desperate to end this—he could handle one Erin but not two, and he had two right now—Stieg asked, "What kind of things are you looking for, Torfinna?"

Please don't say souls. Please don't say souls.

"What about that thing around her neck?"

"Thing around her—"

Stieg remembered what the dark elves had given him and Erin to get through Svartalfheim.

"The necklace," he prompted when Erin appeared confused by the request.

"Oh, yeah." Erin pulled the chain over her head and held it up in front of Torfinna.

The old She-dwarf squinted, closing one eye.

"Yeah. All right." She snatched the necklace from Erin's hand.

"Come on then." Torfinna tried to get up out of her chair but . . . yeah.

Stieg stood, slammed his head, ignored both females laughing at him, bent down, and grabbed Torfinna's hands, helping her up.

"Thanks, Raven," she said, still laughing. She walked past him and out of her house.

By the time he and Erin followed Torfinna back outside, only Arnóra and Báraldur remained.

Stieg faced the pair who'd helped them. "Thank you both."

"You're welcome, Raven," Arnóra replied, grasping Stieg's forearm with her hand as he grabbed hers. "And good luck to you."

Báraldur reared back a bit when Erin held her arm out, like he was afraid she would stab him or something. When he realized that wasn't it at all, he took hold of her forearm and smiled. "Good luck to you, Crow."

Stieg and Erin followed after Torfinna, but he glanced back and noticed the pair were just standing there, watching them go, and appearing really . . . sad, which made what they had to do next seem kind of terrifying.

*   *   *

"Why does everyone in the Nine Worlds seem to hate the Crows?" Erin asked Torfinna.

Stieg threw up his hands and mouthed *What the fuck?*

"What?" Erin asked out loud. "It's not like we don't have time to get that question answered, considering how slow she's moving."

The dwarf stopped and faced Erin.

"What?" Erin asked again. "It's true. But you're old, so . . . you know."

"They don't tell you new Crows, do they?" Torfinna asked.

Suddenly, Erin knew the old dwarf couldn't care less about the insults, which was kind of annoying since she was trying to get back at the old woman for constantly calling her *fatty.* "Tell us what?"

Torfinna started off again, but as she walked, she talked. "The first Crows were all slaves. Very angry slaves. Skuld only picked from the angry. Back then, they could travel to whatever world they wanted to. The Nine Worlds were open to all. But the Crows didn't just go to explore the new worlds open to them. They went in to steal and to slaughter"—she glanced at Erin over her shoulder—"everyone. They considered it practice. Training, I guess you'd say. They stole weapons from us. Pets from the giants that they turned into pit fighters. But the elves . . . they had special use for the elves—dark and light.

"You see, the Crows had their own witches back then and they liked their magic . . . cruel. Their chosen witches usually were the angriest of the group. The elves were used for their magical properties. The Crows would take them back to their world, keep them captive, and tear bits of them off as they needed. They kept them alive in their nests for as long as they could. It got so bad that the decision was made to close off the worlds. No more easy access for anyone human. If you wanted in, you had to work for it, which meant not enough power could be worked up to send an entire kill squad of Crows in; only one or two at a time.

"Now it's true enough that one or two Crows could hold their own against a troop of warriors without much effort, but an entire army? Of elves? That's when things turned, and the elves started hunting the Crows for sport. Taking their wings for trophies. But not just the Crows, all humans. The Valkyries. The Protectors. If they ended up in the wrong place at the wrong time, they faced a dark end. Many say it was because of the Crows. That they started it."

Erin laughed and both Stieg and Torfinna stopped and gawked at her.

"No, no," Erin quickly said. "I wasn't laughing at . . . I mean, that's a horrible thing, what happened, and I wasn't laughing at *that*. I'd never laugh at *that*. It's just . . . *they started it* is kind of my thing. So I thought that was kind of . . . funny." She cleared her throat and waved her hand forward. "Why don't we, uh . . . keep going? That way?"

Torfinna headed off but Stieg stared at Erin for a few seconds longer before shaking his head and following the dwarf.

"Yeah," Erin muttered to herself before falling in step behind them. "That was awkward."

Stieg gazed out over the expansive river that cut through the cave. He hadn't been expecting the *karve*—a smallish old Norse longboat—tied to a dock, several dwarves loading weapons and other goods onboard.

"They'll get you to Corpse Shore from here."

Erin glanced at Stieg, and then asked Torfinna, "No offense, but why can't we just fly?"

Smirking around her pipe, Torfinna walked to the karve

and clapped her hands at one of the dwarves. "Toss me a chicken."

And . . . he did, which was weird.

Torfinna brought the chicken to Stieg and held it out to him. "Take it," she ordered.

He did, but he wasn't really comfortable with a live chicken in his hands. He wasn't raised on a farm.

"Now throw it. High. Over the water."

"Can't you just tell us—"

"Do it."

Stieg didn't want to, but the damn thing had started to peck at him and he just wanted this over with. So he did as Torfinna ordered and shot-putted the poor chicken out over the water.

Since chickens couldn't fly, he waited for gravity to take over and the chicken to fall to its watery death, but that never happened. Something, he wasn't sure what, leaped out of the water and snatched the chicken from midair before disappearing back into the black depths of the water.

"You fly over that, you won't last two minutes," Torfinna explained. With a smile, she added, "They can go higher, too. Clear to the top if they have to."

"You had to kill a chicken to show us that?" Erin asked.

"You seem like the type who needs to see why something won't work. You just ignore talking."

Erin looked like she was about to argue so Stieg said, "She's right. Let it go."

"This boat is fast and can you get you to Corpse Shore in about ten minutes. You could fly around the river, but that'll take you only half as long as walking. And you don't have that much time."

"Well," Erin began, "how many days are you talking about because—"

"You," Torfinna said, looking directly at them both, "don't have that much time."

Stieg and Erin exchanged glances and Erin asked, "What are you telling us?"

"I'm telling you, the battle that you so desperately need to get to . . . is about to begin. *Now.* And I'm willing to bet gold, Crow"—Torfinna let out a sad sigh—"that the only thing you'll ever be able to do is watch your sister-Crows die. But at least they'll die with honor."

Sadie Monroe sat at the red light in her boss's black BMW, while her boss yelled at her over the speakerphone because she was taking longer than ten seconds to get from San Fernando Valley to West Los Angeles.

"It's not like it's rush hour traffic!" her boss went on.

"I'm on Sunset," Sadie promised.

"Where on Sunset?"

"The 405 overpass. I'll be at the office in—"

"You better have my cappuccino order."

"I do!"

"And it better be right this time. And hot!"

Sadie stuck her tongue out at the dashboard, wishing she had the balls to do that to her boss's face!

"I don't hear a *Yes, ma'am. It's hot!*"

"It's hot! I promise it's—" Sadie stopped talking and leaned in, squinting at a spot a few hundred feet away from her. She watched, fascinated, as something—a man, maybe, but with big leather wings—flew down from the sky with another screaming man in his arms.

Was someone shooting a movie or something?

"Sadie? Are you listening to me?"

"There are two men on the overpass."

"Oh, God, is there another jumper? If you see him jump, don't you dare stop to give the police a statement!"

They didn't jump. The one with the . . . well, the wings, stood on the fence that prevented people from just randomly throwing themselves off overpasses. He held out the other man—who was screaming and hysterically crying—with one hand, which meant he was really strong.

"What the hell . . . ?"

"Sadie, what's going on?" For the first time Sadie heard something akin to concern in her boss's voice.

"I . . . I don't know."

Just as the sun began to rise, Sadie saw something flash. "Oh, my God! He's got a knife."

"Sadie, get out of there. Get out of there now!"

"He's not near me," she said, taking out her personal phone to record the whole thing.

"He could have a gun or something."

The man with the wings raised the knife into the air as he screamed out something. She rolled down her window but couldn't really hear him.

"Sadie, what's happening?"

"There's a couple cop cars. I think it's almost over."

The cops got out of their cars and pointed weapons at the winged man, ordering him to get down. But the winged man ignored them, still giving his speech, yelling out to the sky. Then . . . he just dragged his knife over his hostage's throat.

"Oh, my God! He killed him! He killed the guy!"

The cops started shooting, bullets riddling the winged man's body, but it was like . . . nothing. He barely moved. Just kept holding the hostage's body over the 405 Freeway, shaking him so that every drop of blood from his throat drained out of him.

Sadie didn't understand. What was happening?

She could still hear her boss calling her name, but her voice was fading and everything was going white and . . . and . . . and . . .

Önd tossed the false prophet's body away and jumped down from the bridge to the road below. All the vehicles and humans were gone now, caught between this world and another. Time itself had been stopped. Only those with the power, those who knew the truth of this world and all the others, knew what was happening.

The rest—the sheep—if they were lucky, they would never wake up.

Önd threw his arms wide and let out a roar. A call of challenge to all those brave enough to face him and his troops.

"Hey!" a female voice responded and Önd opened his eyes to see a single Crow standing alone on the freeway. Her wings out, a rune-covered axe in her hand. The War General. Although, he'd never give her the respect due such a title. She was nothing but a worthless Crow. "Are you the only one, slave?" he asked. "The only one to face me?"

"Didn't you know? Crows never fight alone."

They came up behind her. Clan after Clan. The Crows. The Ravens. The Isa. The Silent. Protectors. Holde's Maids. The Claws of Ran. The Giant Killers.

And, on nearby hillsides, on their winged horses, the Valkyries waited to take those who died in battle to Valhalla.

Önd stretched out his arms and his own army strode up behind him. The Carrion. The Mara. Giants. Hell demons. Trolls. And fallen angels sent by Lucifer himself. He had double the army and the Clans knew it. He saw color drain from many of his enemies' faces. "Well?" Önd demanded of the War General. "Have you nothing to say, slave?"

"You can stop calling me *slave* . . . bitch."

Önd's gaze narrowed on the Crow, locking every detail of her face into his memory so he could find her and kill her himself. But then a Crow dropped from the sky and landed on Önd's back, her blade immediately buried into his neck.

"Hey, dead thing!" the War General yelled out. "Ready for a fight?"

Önd reached over his shoulder and grabbed the slave by her hair, throwing her off. He yanked the blade from his neck and tossed it. It didn't kill him, but it did hurt.

He hefted his sword and called out, "Come, slaves! It's time to learn that your place in this world is *ON YOUR KNEES!*"

CHAPTER FORTY-ONE

The boat ride would have been amazing . . . if Erin wasn't in a full-blown panic. Of course, Stieg quickly noticed, her panic wasn't like everyone else's. She didn't scream. She didn't cry. She didn't curse. She simply stood, strong legs braced apart, arms crossed over her chest. Gaze locked dead ahead.

That's how Stieg knew she was panicking. She wasn't making jokes. She wasn't talking a mile a minute. She wasn't even complaining.

He had to admit, a panicking Erin was as terrifying as a raging Jace. Because what they were willing to do when they were like that could destroy entire universes.

As the boat cut through the water easily, the dwarves avoided her like she had the plague. Stieg stood by her side but didn't speak to her or touch her. He knew she didn't want any of that.

She didn't need pity; Erin needed results. Say what you want about her mouth and her attitude but she always got results.

"We're almost there," the dwarf captain told him. "Once you're on shore, you'll want to head northeast to find what you're lookin' for."

Stieg nodded. He knew immediately when they'd moved from Nidavellir to the Land of the Dead. They were no longer inside a mountain but everything around them was gray. The sand on the shore, the sky above them, the water the boat cut through. All gray.

The boat pulled up to the land and Erin was already moving, jumping into the water and walking to shore.

"Take care, lad," the captain called after him. "And watch your back."

Jace used her shield to block the sword aimed at her head and swung her arm back to cut the throat of the Carrion easing up behind her.

Someone kicked her in the face and she hit the ground. A Mara immediately crawled onto her chest, pressing her fingers against Jace's head. Images and memories of her time with her ex-husband flooded her and she felt like she was back there. Trapped there. With him. In misery and despair, unable to get out.

Rage tore through her and she dropped her shield and blade, so she could wrap one hand around the back of the Mara's head, and grabbed her chin. Jace twisted and the Mara's neck snapped. Then screaming, Jace slammed the Mara's body onto the ground, placed her knee against its chest, and began trying to pull the bitch's head off.

As she struggled, the ground beneath her shook. Jace lifted her head and watched the giant stomp toward her. He was a mile or two off, but she didn't care. She dropped the prey in her hands and unleashed her wings, taking to the air. Screaming, she charged, zooming past Crows and Ravens and Carrion. She neared the giant and pulled the blade holstered to her side.

She wanted to kill him. She had to kill him. She would kill him!

Hands caught her around the waist and yanked her out of the giant's path. "Nope," Ski said from behind her as he carried her away from her prey.

Normally Ski would never get between any Crow and her prey, but when Bear pointed out where Jace was headed, he knew he had to step in. She was in a rage, which meant she wasn't being her most logical self. At least not as logical as he needed her to be when it came to giants.

But Ski would never think of taking Jace away from the actual battle. They needed her and her rage. So, instead, he found a large group of hell beasts who'd cornered a group of Silent and dropped her right in the middle.

Jace landed hard on one and tore the throat out of another with her talons.

Confident she was where she needed to be, Ski turned and flew back toward the giant, who was about to stomp on some unsuspecting Isa.

"Giant Killers!" Ski called out.

Freida and her warriors charged forward, using their mighty hammers to attack the legs of the creature. Ski landed on the giant's nose and jumped to his cheekbone. The giant tried to swat him away, but Leigh dove in and slammed her talons in the middle of the giant's palm. The giant screamed and closed his hand, but she dashed out before he could crush her in his grip.

"Blade!" Ski yelled and Maeve tossed him a sword she'd picked up from the battle. He shoved it into the giant's eye, ripping it out of the socket.

Blood poured out, nearly drowning him. Ski took to the skies when the giant began to swing wildly. Freida crushed the giant's Achilles tendon and another Killer who'd climbed the giant's leg crushed his kneecap.

"*Nine Clans, move!*" Ski bellowed as the giant toppled over, nearly taking out the nearby J. Paul Getty Museum building, which would have been a tragedy.

He and his brothers loved that museum.

They walked about five minutes, but Erin knew as soon as they hit Corpse Shore because of the smell. The smell of decomposing flesh. She'd smelled it before during her years as a Crow, but never like this.

They'd only gone a few more feet before Erin was forced to cover her nose and mouth with her hand and Stieg dry heaved into the sand.

"Oh, God . . . Erin."

Shivering, her need to vomit getting worse, she slowly faced Stieg, saw what he was looking at. She didn't have words for what she saw. The gray, boring ocean the dwarves had taken them across was now filled with rotting corpses. Some had already been partially eaten. Others were simply decaying in the overcast sun above. That's where the smell was coming from—the bodies.

The horror didn't end there. The corpses that undulated in the surf were definitely dead, but they weren't gone. Their souls were trapped in those bodies and, as punishment for their past transgressions, that's where they'd stay.

Erin could hear them calling out for help. For release. Begging for the nightmare to end.

She and Stieg had made it. They were in Náströnd. Corpse Shore.

"We have to go," she said, ignoring the cries of those already dead and the smell that just wouldn't go away.

"Erin—"

"No," she told him, wanting him to understand there was no discussion. "We keep moving. We keep going, no matter what."

"Okay," he said, but his voice sounded weird and his gaze was locked on something past her shoulder.

"There's something behind me, isn't there?" she finally asked.

Stieg nodded.

"Is it Carrion?"

Head shake.

"Nidhogg?" she asked hopefully.

Another head shake.

"Something I need to kill?"

"One of us does."

She started to turn around, but Stieg again shook his head. "Please don't move," he practically begged. "Trust me. Just don't move."

"I have to move eventually."

"Just stand . . . there."

Stieg's wings eased out of his back. Slowly. Quietly.

Erin waited, tense.

"*Now!*" Stieg bellowed.

Erin dive-rolled forward as he flew at her. Once she got back to her feet, she grabbed her weapons from her holster and turned. Stieg had tackled what had been coming up behind her.

She really didn't know what it was. It wasn't human. Or even once-human.

Purple and gray, the thing had reptile-like flesh. Even worse, it had a prehensile tail, the end of it like a talon that dripped something dark purple and ominous. It was creeping up to stab Stieg in the face.

Erin charged the thing, but as she was diving toward its back, hidden twelve-inch black spikes sprouted from its spine, as if it sensed her coming. She dove over them instead of landing on the thing's back and rolled to her feet.

"Erin, run!" Stieg ordered.

She ignored him and kicked at the thing's head. Still holding Stieg down, it looked up at her.

Erin saw those eyes—like a lizard's—and she immediately thought, *Nope*, and shoved her blades directly into both its sockets.

Squealing, it fell off Stieg and Erin held her arm out so he could pull himself up.

The thing lay on its back, screeching and kicking and turning itself in a circle.

"Kill it," she ordered Stieg, unwilling to hear any more of that.

Stieg grabbed the thing by its head and twisted hard until he'd turned it 360 degrees.

Dropping it to the ground, he straightened. "There are more," he told her flatly.

"Yeah, I know. We need to get moving."

"No, Erin. I mean . . . there are *more*."

Whirling around, Erin saw a row of lizard things standing there, waiting for them. They stood upright, like men. Some had weapons in their scaly claws. Apparently it wasn't just their tails that were prehensile.

Erin allowed herself to despair. Her shoulders and head dropping; eyes closing; the air sadly easing out of her.

She let herself have that moment for all of fifteen seconds.

Then she lifted her head, screamed in rage, and charged.

Kera ducked the mace aimed for her head and swung her axe up, catching the Carrion between the legs. He dropped to his knees and another Crow, who'd gotten one of the flint blades from the Carrion's brother, sliced off his head.

And yet, as they battled on, all of them trying to make this last as long as possible in the vain hope that Erin and Stieg might suddenly appear, there was still no sign of Gullveig.

And every time another Clan member fell in battle, Kera felt it as acutely as if it were she. As if she'd taken the blow. As if she was the one dying in a pool of her own blood.

Kera ignored that feeling, though. She had to or they would all be dying in their own blood.

Erin continued to go for the eyes, but her timing had to be impeccable. A second too long moving her blade, and a secondary lid shut closed and that thing was like steel, so the tip of her blade bounced off it.

Stieg occasionally used a weapon retrieved from the lizard things, but mostly he snapped necks or ripped off legs. His biggest problem was avoiding those damn tails, so Erin tried to cut them off when she could because whatever leaked out of them burned holes in the sand.

Of course, all this was well and good and nothing they hadn't done before. Fighting things they'd never seen before until someone or everyone was dead.

That was their job.

The problem, though, was that the lizards just kept coming. Every time Erin thought they were finally cleared, more would come over one of the gray hills. Or dig themselves out of the ground.

Finally, when more came running at them, Stieg pushed Erin away. "Go," he ordered.

She didn't want to leave him but knew she had to. She had no choice. With her blades clutched in her hands, she turned and ran down the beach, leaping over bodies, ignoring the hands grasping for her. She wished she could say she'd gotten used to the smell, but that would be a lie.

That horrible, disgusting odor did help with one thing, though Erin knew she was going in the right direction because the farther she moved away from Stieg, the stronger the scent became. Nidhogg, she knew, would want to stay where the meat was.

And there was so much meat. The number of waterlogged bodies grew exponentially the farther down the beach she went.

As she kept going, Erin kept spitting in a weak attempt to get the vile taste out of her mouth, and rubbing her watery, stinging eyes with the back of her hands. None of it helped. Suddenly, a gnawed-on leg bone landed in front of her. The marrow had been sucked clean, but there were some traces of flesh still on it.

Erin stopped and, desperately trying to blink away the pain, she turned and . . . there it was.

Nidhogg aka Malice Striker.

She wouldn't even try to guess how big he—she guessed it was a *he*—was. Fifty feet? One hundred? One thousand? Erin didn't know. He was covered in pale gray scales that matched the dull gray of this land. Two white horns rose from his head and darker gray spikes went from his neck, down his spine, to the tip of his tail. He had a long silver mane that spread around his body like a silken sheet. Sharp blue eyes stared down at the victim near one of his front claws.

That corpse was screaming.

Nidhogg placed one talon across its chest to hold it in place while he took his time with his free claw ripping the other leg off. He lifted the leg and opened his snout, revealing fangs. Rows of fangs. And he ate that leg like Erin ate a chicken leg, which made her wish for the first time ever that she had become vegan.

Erin debated how best to do this. She only knew what

she'd learned in the flippin' *Poetic Edda*, and it wasn't the kind of information she needed when trying to manage a person or a god.

Wait. Was he a god? Or just a dragon. Or were dragons gods? Wait. No. Tyr said the dragons had their own pantheon, which meant they weren't all gods. Right? She gritted her teeth in frustration. See? She had more questions than she had fucking answers. And while she was trying to manage this, her friends were dying!

On the verge of throwing one of her blades at Nidhogg's head and yelling *Give me that sword, whore!*, Erin spotted him.

He scrambled down the nearby root of the World Tree, his little body running across the sand; leaping from body to body, bone to bone; gleeful as always.

Erin ran toward him. He didn't see her. He'd probably never, in the eons he'd been alive, had anyone race toward him while in this place. So when she reached down and scooped him up in her hands, he began to put up a fight.

Legitimately concerned with disease, Erin squeezed her hands together and warned, "Bite me and I crush these fucking bones like matchsticks. Make a sound and I'll tear off your little feet."

Ratatosk immediately calmed down and Erin dodged behind the World Tree's giant roots. She waited for a moment and when she heard no cries of alarm, she opened her hands and looked down at the squirrel and messenger of the gods. "I need your help," she whispered.

He chittered back at her and, for the first time, Erin understood his chittering perfectly. "What do you mean no?" She gasped. "Don't you threaten me, little fucker."

He went on for a bit, explaining how he wasn't supposed to get involved in anything. His job was to bring messages.

That was all. And even as he went on, she could hear him striving for the appearance of innocence. Like a check kiter talking to a cop after he's been caught red-handed.

"I don't want to hear it. You're gonna help me, or I swear by all that is holy, I will stalk your ass, whether it's in this life or the next! And we both know that I'm the crazy bitch who will make that happen. Don't we?"

Ratatosk nodded his small squirrel head.

"Good. Now come on!" She looped back around the tree root but froze when she came face to fang with Nidhogg. Startled, Erin dropped the squirrel and Ratatosk took his opportunity to run, making a beeline right to the dragon's front leg and up his body, disappearing in his hair.

Nidhogg's two front claws were crossed and his ten-thousand-foot-long tail—okay, she didn't know if it was *that* long—slithered around to scratch the top of the dragon's head with the tip. His right talons drummed against the hard sand as he gazed down at Erin.

Finally, Ratatosk reappeared from under Nidhogg's mane and made himself quite at home on top of the dragon's head, right next to his left ear.

The staring between all three of them went on for a bit longer than Erin wanted, but she was having a very hard time finding her voice.

"Is there something I can help you with?" Nidhogg asked, all gentlemenlike manners and what sounded like a strong British accent, which seemed weird since he was supposed to be Nordic. Plus, the dragon could speak. Like a human being. His lips even moved.

"Helloooo?" he tried again. "Anyone home? Because you don't look dead, so you *really* shouldn't be here."

Ratatosk whispered something in Nidhogg's ear.

"A Crow?" Nidhogg said, laughing. But when Erin didn't

laugh along with him, he fell silent, his blue eyes narrowing. "Is what he says true? Are you a Crow?"

"The tone of your voice makes me uncomfortable answering that."

He growled, his long body uncoiling. It was like watching a giant snake move except Nidhogg had four legs and could speak. "There are no Crows allowed on *my* territory."

"This is actually Hel's territory if we're going to nitpick. I can see the entrance to Helheim from here—"

The growling became worse and Erin raised her hands, palms out. "Let's not get angry."

"Too late."

"No, no. I just . . . I need five minutes of your time."

"For what?"

"Your assistance in an important matter."

"My assistance? You, a Crow, need *my* assistance."

She blinked and the dragon moved in, his nostrils painfully close, his hot breath on her skin.

"Do you, insignificant Crow, understand who and what I am?"

"I do. But that doesn't change that I . . . I . . ."

The dragon reared back when Erin's words faded off.

"What's wrong with you?" Nidhogg demanded, looking over his shoulder, then back at Erin. "You truly don't seem like someone who'd shut up. So why have you?"

Erin shrugged. "No reason. And," she quickly added when she watched Ratatosk begin to chitter in Nidhogg's ear, "whatever he's telling you—he's lying."

"Why do I doubt that?"

Stieg heard the dragon speaking to Erin again and he eased away from the dune he'd hidden behind.

Yes, he'd finally killed all those lizard things. And, if he hadn't been so incredibly stressed out, it would have been fun. But he'd taken two swords, went on a good ol' Viking rampage, either beheading or disemboweling all his victims, then came right here to find Erin.

At least she'd seen him. Stieg knew that much, and he could tell she was not having much luck with Nidhogg.

It seemed that what Erin had said was true. Absolutely *everybody* hated the Crows. Even dragons that spent their entire day eating filthy, stinky corpses, which could not be an enjoyable job.

However, the one thing Erin did have—with the help of Ratatosk—was Nidhogg's entire focus and attention. They'd have to use that to their benefit.

"You know," he heard Erin say, "I won't say that Ratatosk is lying on that one, but I wouldn't say that I tried to *yank* Odin's eye out. I merely tried to . . . gouge it out."

"What's the difference?"

"Intent."

Stieg quickly moved away from the trio until he could run without worrying too much about Nidhogg hearing him. Their biggest challenge was the size of the dragon. His tail alone was over a hundred feet long and Stieg just couldn't seem to get past it.

But Stieg kept going. He didn't reach the end of the tail, but he did find the entrance to a cave. Runes surrounded the stone opening and he prayed he was right. That this was Nidhogg's home. Or, at the very least, where he kept his horde.

Stieg ran inside, already freaking out about how far he'd have to go to find any of Nidhogg's treasure, but he turned a corner and slid on gold coins, crashing face-first into a pile of jewels and precious metals that easily filled the entire chamber. He pushed himself to his hands and knees and scrambled across the pile, stopping to dig random holes in the hopes of finding the sword. But it wasn't working. He stopped. Stieg was panicking.

He couldn't panic. He remebered what his brothers had always taught him. *Panic will get you killed faster than anything.*

Sitting back on his heels, Stieg closed his eyes, took in a breath, let it out. After a full minute, he opened his eyes and began to *think* rather than react. "It's not Nidhogg's sword," he said out loud. "It's the fire giant's sword. Whom he will aid during Ragnarok . . . which means he'll keep it in a place of—"

Stieg ran over the horde to the other side of the cavern, through a narrow tunnel, and into another, well-lit chamber . . . His hands began to shake, his eyes naturally averting at the intensity of the powerful weapon. Even hung on the wall, the sword blade was bright with burning flames. It had to be several hundred feet long.

Thankfully the hilt was closest, so he didn't have to walk the entire horizontal length of the chamber. He took a minute to recall the words Inka had taught Erin to obtain the sword, while he'd stood there listening. He'd never been so grateful to have constantly shadowed her before she'd been about to leave on her quest.

He recited the spell and waited for it to do . . . whatever it was going to do.

And what did it do . . . ?

Stieg grinned and reached down to pick up the five-foot, non-glowing sword from where it had fallen.

Now he just needed to figure out how to get him and Erin out of here.

"It's true," Erin admitted, her glare for Ratatosk and Ratatosk only, "I did once steal Idunn's apples and then—"

"she cleared her throat—"sat back and enjoyed the gods' getting old and freaking out about it. But, in my defense—"

"She started it?" Nidhogg asked lazily, his giant head resting on the palm of his front claw.

"You know, *I* am the innocent party here."

"What did Idunn do? Look at you funny?"

"No. I just didn't like her tone. Like she's so above me."

"Is that your issue, puny human? That Idunn—a *god*—considers herself above *you*? The descendent of a slave?"

"We all have our gifts."

"And yours is?"

"Charm."

Nidhogg exchanged bewildered glances with Ratatosk, who now sat high and safe in the roots of the World Tree.

"Wowwwww," the dragon said.

"And I gotta tell ya," she told him in no uncertain terms, "I'm not appreciating your tone at the moment, either."

"Am I hurting your feelings? Your cold, hard, Crow feelings?"

"*Tone.*"

Behind one of the dunes Erin saw Stieg again. He held up a very small—for a giant, anyway—uninspiring sword. But the way he excitedly gestured at it, she could only hope that it was Surtr's sword.

Pointing to the left—both Nidhogg and Ratatosk turning to look—and tossing the Carrion hand past Nidhogg's right side so that Stieg could run up and grab it, she said, "I know you probably don't have an actual . . . bathroom. But is there a spot I can go and take a—"

"Why are you here?" he asked, surprising her.

"What?"

"Why are you here?"

Erin's usually active mind went blank. It had never occurred to her she'd end up having a conversation with the dragon, so she hadn't bothered to come up with a backstory. "Ummmmm . . . why wouldn't I be here?"

"Because this is Corpse Shore. That is, as indicated by its name, filled with"—he gestured with his talon—"corpses and a smell that I can tell is not your favorite."

"I'm just tired."

"Uh-huh. Why don't you just tell me what you're up to?"

"I'm not up to anything. You're a mighty dragon. Who *wouldn't* want to meet you?"

"Everyone. Because I *am* a mighty dragon and I eat corpses. So no one really just . . . visits me."

"Well . . . I do. We have a lot in common."

His laugh was short and harsh before he reined it in. "This I must hear." He glanced at Ratatosk. "You want to hear, yes?"

Ratatosk chittered agreement and Erin thought about cutting his tiny little rat head off!

"Please," the dragon said, with a wave of his claw, "tell me what things we have in common. I can't wait."

Shit. "We both . . . uh . . . love the beach."

"Uh-huh."

"And, uh, we enjoy being on our own when at the beach." She could see Stieg waving at her in the distance, trying to get her to get out of there.

"But," she went on, "we still love good conversation." She pointed at Ratatosk. "We both think he's just a rat with a fluffy tail."

"Anything else? Because so far, your choices are exceptionally weak."

Erin snapped her fingers. "We both have a way with flame!" She blinked and asked, "You are a fire—"

"Yesss. I'm a fire dragon."

"Exactly! I also have the gift of flame. A little something extra from Skuld."

"I see," he said, still sounding incredibly unimpressed. She had the feeling that if she didn't impress him, he was going to eat her. For eternity. That was not something she wanted to experience.

But she didn't think she could impress him. So she went with flattery and self-deprecation.

"I mean, you are a fire dragon, so much more mighty than I could ever be," she went on, desperate, "I mean, that must be so awesome. The power of your fl . . ."

His head tilted a bit. "The power of my . . . what?"

"I'm . . . I'm sorry?"

"You are trying to use flattery on me in the hopes that I won't tear you apart, limb from limb, and then suck down your marrow like a fine wine."

"No, it . . . it wasn't flattery. You really do have the gift of fire. Much more powerful than mine," she said, finally feeling intense excitement.

"It's a gift for you, Crow. It's just part of me."

"So much a part of you that you and Surtr are . . . buddies?"

"I can't say that. No one is really buddies with Surtr. He's actually quite the asshole. But, of course, being a dragon and basically *made* of flame, I can come and go from Muspellheim. You know, when one gets bored with the screams and terrified begging of the condemned, one will often head to a Muspellheim pub for some ale. If one is so inclined."

"Uh-huh."

"I wouldn't suggest you go there. You may be able to make little flame angels in the snow or whatever, but you walk into Muspellheim and you'll be turned into ash before you even realize that you're on fire."

"Uh-huh."

"Oh, come now. No need to fret so. I don't have to make your death torturous."

Erin raised her forefinger and, while holding it up for Nidhogg to see, she walked around him until she was past his shoulder. "There's something else we have in common."

He sighed. "And that is?"

"Wings. See?" She unfurled her wings, let them stretch out from her back. "Cool, right?

"Small. They're very small bird wings."

"Well . . . compared to you, I'm like a hummingbird. But hummingbirds are fast."

He snorted. "So you're going to make a run for it."

"No. At least, not until I tell you that while I was keeping you busy out here, my Viking boyfriend was stealing Surtr's sword. Oh, and uh"—she snapped her fingers like she'd forgotten something—"fuck you!" Then Erin spun around and flew like everything depended on it.

Because everything did.

Standing on the freeway billboard so she could clearly see the battle, Kera sent more troops to head off a squadron of Lucifer's minions. She couldn't believe that bastard was involved. And no one had warned her! Even now she could see the Four Horsemen looking out over the battle. They'd known Gullveig had involved the king of hell, and it would have been nice if they'd bothered to warn her or Erin. Somebody!

Thankfully there'd only been three giants, and the Giant Killers had made quick work of them with the help of anyone with wings.

The trolls, however, were a bigger problem. Well . . . not bigger, per se. But not as quickly taken out and there were considerably more of them.

A Carrion landed behind her, and Kera turned and hacked

its head off with the axe that the goddess Freyja had given her. Her axe did not originally have that ability, but Vig had broken down one of the Carrion's weapons and merged the flint from their blades with Kera's. It had been phenomenally effective.

Once again, Kera looked over the battle, hoping to see a bouncy little redhead with a big mouth, but so far nothing. Nor any shifters, so that hope was dead in the water.

Still worse, poor Erin didn't even know things had changed. She thought she had days left. This battle would not last for days. Kera wasn't sure it would last for another fifteen minutes. The eight Clans were holding their own but for how much longer, she didn't know.

"Freida!" she yelled to the Giant Killer's leader. "The trolls! Get the trolls!"

Kera saw some of the Mara suddenly appear behind her sister-Crows who were busy fighting demons. "Annalisa! The Mara!"

Annalisa, grinning, took the rest of Kera's Strike Team toward the Mara. The woman loved dealing with the Mara. When they tried to torment her with her own memories or nightmares, it never seemed to go well for them. Kera didn't actually know what her sister-Crow did or what those demons saw, but the reversal had sent many a Mara screaming into the night.

Seeing that the Killers needed some help with the trolls, Kera turned to signal to the Ravens.

"Rolf! Help the—"

Arms around her waist cut the rest of Kera's words off and the Carrion snatched her off the billboard sign she'd been standing on and carried her to the other side of the freeway before tossing her onto the grassy shoulder near an exit.

She rolled and stopped on her back. That's when the Carrion leader landed. His big legs straddled her, with a blood-covered sword in each hand, the tip of one pointed right at her throat, his leather wings out and beating against his back.

"Hello, slave." He grinned. "I have great plans for you."

Everything was ready. Stieg had created the circle, written all the runes in the sand. And the Carrion's hand sat in the middle of it all, just as Inka had instructed.

Now he just needed Erin.

Holding the sword against his chest, Stieg paced back to the top of the dune, hoping to see that Erin had finally finagled herself away from Nidhogg and that she was almost . . .

He let out a relieved smile when he saw her flying toward him. But then he heard that roar and that giant shadow began to cover him. He leaned to the side—although he didn't really have to—and yeah . . . that was Nidhogg . . . *chasing* Erin.

"Go!" she screamed at him. "Go, go, go, go, *GO!*"

Without any other options, Stieg ran back down the dune, quickly said the words Inka had taught them and watched the circle turn into a mystical doorway.

"*Stieg*," Erin yelled, closer than ever. "Just *gooooooooooooo!*"

So he did—and gods help them all.

CHAPTER FORTY-TWO

Kera hit the ground, with Önd on top of her, ramming his fist into her face. She grabbed his arms, pushing him back. She brought her legs up between them and kicked, throwing him off. Rolling over, she scrabbled on hands and knees toward her axe, avoiding the stomping, kicking feet around her.

Kera had reached her weapon, her fingers wrapping around the handle, when she was grabbed by the ankle and flipped over.

As she was dragged back, the axe still clasped in her grip, she swung at Önd but he caught her wrist and stomped on her other hand, pinning it to the ground. He began twisting her wrist even as he burned her flesh with his touch and Kera could feel the bone breaking.

She rammed her foot into his groin, and the leer on his face changed into a grimace.

Önd leaned down, his mouth open, fangs dripping. Kera tried to yank her arms away but he held on tight, coming closer and closer—

The bear tackled him right off her, its thousand pounds knocking Önd to the ground and nearly crushing him in the process.

Kera sat up, mouth open. They came onto the 405 Freeway in a blur of fur, claws, and fangs. Their roars and growls beginning to drown out the war cries and curses.

A black panther leaped in front of Kera, slapping away another Carrion before turning into Karen—*Oh, my God! The lovely, lovely Karen!*—and, standing tall, she faced Kera. "Are you okay?"

Kera nodded and took Karen's outstretched hand.

"Your wrist," Karen noted, concerned.

"It'll heal."

Karen studied the crowd of fighters around her. "No Erin? No . . . Stieg?"

"Not yet. But they also think they have three more days, so . . . *Karen, move!*"

Kera shoved the woman hard, pushing her out of the way as Önd came back, the claw marks from the bear that had attacked him going from his head to his feet.

He swung his sword down, trying to cut Kera in half. She dove to the side, rolling until she reached her axe. She picked it up in time to block his next blow.

"Do you really think you can kill me, slave?" he asked, pushing her back with his weapon. "When I'm done with you—"

Betty came at him from the side, ramming her blade into his gut. Annalisa slammed her blade into his neck. Maeve wrapped a rope around his throat and yanked him back.

Kera, now able to move freely because Maeve and the others had him, hefted her axe, loosened her shoulders.

She stood in front of him. "When you're done with me what . . . dead thing?"

Kera swung her axe under and up into his groin, and the Carrion's scream echoed out over the battle. She yanked her weapon out, hefted it again, and swiped it across, taking his head.

Once he was on the ground, Kera tossed her axe to Alessandra so that she and their sister-Crows could hack into the Carrion leader, tossing pieces of him away in the hopes he'd never be re-assembled by Hel.

Karen, still in human form, stood behind Kera. With her hands clasped in front of her, she said, "I see why Stieg kept me away from you guys."

Kera turned to talk to her, maybe make her feel a little better, but Karen suddenly took in a sharp breath and her entire body went rigid. She quickly shifted back to cat and faced north, angrily hissing.

And Kera knew.

"Clans! *She's coming!*" Kera called out to the others.

The ground shook and the sun grew brighter, seeming to turn everything around them gold.

Gullveig appeared on the far side of the overpass. She wasn't in her Rodeo Drive gear, but that could have been because she couldn't fit into it. In her goddess form, she towered over the freeway and the battle. The only thing covering her naked body were thousands of gold necklaces and strings of pearls; diamonds, rubies, emeralds woven into her hair. "Kill them!" the goddess laughingly screamed out. "*Kill them all!*"

"Kera!" Chloe called. "What do we do?"

No Erin. No sword. But this would be their only chance.

Kera looked up at the hills again. The Four Horsemen still sat up there, waiting.

"We fight!" She unleashed her wings and flew up over the battle so her sister-Crows could hear her. "*Crows! We fight!*"

The Valkyries still watched from the hills opposite the Four Horsemen. Like vultures, the four waited for the battle to end so they could feed on the souls of the dead. They watched but did nothing.

Just as her Valkyrie sisters were doing, Katja Rundstöm realized as she watched her brother Vig fight with his Raven brothers. And now, Gullveig had made her appearance, but the key figures the clans had counted on—Erin and that damn sword—had not. Even if she and sweet Stieg weren't dead, there was no guarantee they'd arrive on time. None at all.

"Does this feel right to anyone?" she finally asked her sisters.

"We have our orders," Sefa repeated. She'd been repeating it for the last twenty-four hours, but Kat could tell it was bothering her leader. Killing her even.

"I agree with Kat," one of her Clan sisters said from the back.

"We choose from the slain every day," Kat reminded Sefa. "We choose the most honorable. The ones who *fight*. And if we have nothing else to lose . . ."

Sefa closed her eyes. She was loyal to Freyja. They all were, but unlike the Crows, the Valkyries didn't question their god. They'd never had a reason to, but this was different.

Finally, Sefa pulled her sword from the holster that hung off the saddle of her winged horse and held it up in the air. "Valkyries! To battle!"

They struck at Gullveig. Again and again, but nothing touched her. She just laughed, her voice booming out. Her hands knocking them all back.

Even when the Valkyries on their winged horses, the Ravens, and the Protectors joined in the strike, nothing harmed her. Nothing.

But Kera refused to give up. She'd never give up. Instead she did take a quick break on a nearby hill, trying to think of next steps.

Brodie, panting at her side, gazed up at her, waiting for her orders.

She patted her dog's neck.

"If I told you to run, *ordered* you to run," she asked the dog, "would you?"

The bark Kera got back was so vicious, she immediately got defensive. "I was just asking! No need to snap, Bitchy McGee!"

Brodie stopped snarling at her and abruptly stared down at the ground. She seemed . . . jumpy. Like the old Brodie. The one Kera had found abandoned and alone on the streets of Los Angeles.

"Brodie? What's wrong?"

Kera crouched down beside her dog, her arm around her dog's middle. The pit bull began to dance from foot to foot. A weird sort of hop thing that Kera had never seen her dog do.

What was happening? Had she lost her mind? Was all this too much for her sweet dog?

But then Kera felt something wrap around her ankle and it wasn't Brodie's tail.

Crow weapon raised, Kera looked over her shoulder, to see—

"Erin! Oh, my God!" She reached down to hug her poor battered friend, who was lying flat on the ground, her face, arms, neck . . . everything Kera could possibly see was covered in bruises and open, seeping gashes. She was like a walking wound.

Yet, despite all that she'd clearly been through, she was still the Erin Kera knew, loved, and barely tolerated on her best day.

"Where's the cunty whore god?" Erin asked, her voice sounding raw.

"On the freeway."

"Freeway?"

"The 405. The fight ended up on the 405."

"You challenged the Carrion to a fucking battle on the 405?"

"No, the Carrion challenged *us*," Kera explained while pulling Erin to her feet. "And don't chastise me, Amsel. Do you know what we've been through waiting for your—oh, my God! *What is that smell?*"

Kera slapped her hand over her mouth and nose and dry heaved.

Even Brodie skirted away from Erin.

"Cut me some slack," Erin complained. "I was just hanging out on a beach with a bunch of corpses."

"Dude, I'm not sure that's a good enough excuse."

When Brodie began coughing, like she was trying to dislodge something from the back of her throat, Kera sent her to get Chloe and Tessa.

"Did you get the sword?" Kera asked, her hand still over her mouth.

"Yes, you fucking drama queen." She held up . . . a big knife? At least not a sword for a giant.

"What the fuck is that thing?"

"Surtr's fire sword."

"That looks like something Vig cleans fish with. There's no way that is going to work on her."

"Would you just trust me?"

"No!"

Chloe and Betty landed, but both immediately backed away from Erin.

"What is that funk?" Chloe demanded.

"Can we table this discussion 'til later?" Erin asked,

pushing past them so she could carefully study what was happening on the freeway.

Betty shook her head but, unlike Chloe and Kera, she didn't bother to cover her mouth. "I have to tell ya, sweetie, I've only known two or three actors who've ever smelled that bad before."

"I can't believe you've found *any* who smelled that bad."

"You didn't hear it from me, but some actors do not bathe on the regular."

"So what's the plan, stinky?" Chloe asked.

"Well, the first thing you're going to do is stop calling me 'stinky.' And second, we need to distract Gullveig."

"Why?" Kera asked. "So you can poke her with your little stick?"

"Stop trying to turn me on, Watson."

Erin waved at someone below and Kera saw that it was Stieg. She let out a relieved sigh, then felt guilty as hell because she hadn't asked about the man. That should have been the very first thing after making sure Erin was okay!

But to be honest, she was still shocked that Erin had made it back. She'd thought asking about Stieg would just be pushing her luck.

Erin faced Kera and the others. "We need a distraction."

"I'll do it," Chloe said.

"No," Betty cut in. "None of you girls are sacrificing yourselves. I've grown much too attached to all of you. I'll handle it."

"Betty, you can't!"

Betty snorted. "Oh, I'm sorry. Did you really think I was going to sacrifice myself? I thought you bitches knew me better."

The Elder Crow took off, flying over the battle until she reached the other side and landed by one of the Aisling twins; Kera still didn't know which one was which.

It had been Chloe's decision to put the twins nowhere near each other during the fight. A strategy that Kera had completely agreed with. The girls were fierce fighters but when they were near each other . . .

"Oh, she's not going to . . ."

But she was. Betty sent one twin to challenge the Carrion troops who protected Gullveig; and, after tracking down the other, sent that poor girl to challenge the demons who just happened to be loitering around Gullveig.

"Guys," Kera protested, "we can't—"

Erin looked at the ground, her abrupt reaction cutting Kera's words off.

"Oh, God," she whispered, "he found us." Erin moved past Kera and waved again at Stieg.

"Who found you?"

"It's complicated. I just need you to trust me," she said, her wings lifting her off the ground. "And when I tell you . . . everybody run."

Chloe watched Erin fly off. "I don't know about you, Kera . . . but I really don't like this."

Kera understood that. Especially when the ground beneath her feet moved. Hard.

"Chloe . . . ?"

But Kera only realized how bad this had suddenly gotten when the shifters, still in their animal forms, turned tail and ran. Out of nowhere. With no warning. And for no obvious reason.

Yet the one thing Kera had learned a long time ago from life with her dog and watching a lot of *National Geographic* documentaries . . . wild animals didn't do anything for no reason. They only did things to survive.

"Man," Chloe observed, "we are *fucked.*"

* * *

Gullveig was about to leave. The battle wasn't over by any stretch, but none of these humans offered her any real challenge, nor did they interest her in any other way either.

So why sit here? Especially when there was a sale at Neiman Marcus!

"You bitch!"

Gullveig thought someone was directing that hysterical sounding scream toward her. She searched the crowd to find whoever was attempting to challenge her. She'd kill them and then go get some shoes. Rumor was, if you got there early enough, *thirty* percent off.

Who could beat that deal?

But the ones yelling . . . they weren't talking to her. They were talking to each other.

At first, she thought she might be seeing some witch trickery, but no. This wasn't witches. These were twin Crows. How odd. How did that even happen? Did they die at the same time? What twins died at the same time?

The twins yelled at each other, slapping away the Carrion trying to kill them, before turning on each other. It was like throwing two cats in a bag. There was no elegance to their fighting. They didn't use weapons. They simply tore into each other like wild animals.

Finally! Gullveig was entertained!

"Move! Now!" Kera screamed from the top of the small hill where she stood with Chloe. "Everybody! Go!"

At first, Ski thought Kera was calling a retreat. Clans didn't call retreats . . . that's why they always ended up in trouble. But he felt something. Underneath him. Something moving.

Something was coming and it was coming fast.

"What's going on?" Bear asked from beside him.

"I don't know . . . but I think we should listen to Kera."

Ski reached down and grabbed Jace off her latest victim. He carried her off the freeway, ignoring her Berserker screams. He landed next to the Crows and some of his Protector brothers. "What's happening, Kera?" he asked, his arms around a struggling, screeching Jace.

"Erin's back," she said with less enthusiasm than he expected.

Jace stopped fighting and her red Berserker eyes locked on Kera. "Erin's back?" she asked, suddenly rational. "And Stieg?"

"Him, too."

"Then why aren't you happy?" Ski asked.

She pointed. "Because of *that*."

It began right in the middle of the freeway, before the Sunset Boulevard exit. The asphalt fell in and the sinkhole widened, spreading out until it reached across all the lanes.

The white horns came up through the earth first, followed by claws that landed on the part of the freeway that hadn't been destroyed yet.

From the depths of the World Tree that thing emerged. And it just kept coming.

Jace pulled away from Ski, her eyes instantly going back to their beautiful blue color as realization dawned and Jace said what they were all thinking . . .

"That crazy bitch brought Nidhogg here?"

The twin Crows continued to fight, neither seemingly able to kill the other. So fascinated by it all, Gullveig barely noticed that pinprick against her chest. She looked down and saw the tiny little knife sticking out of her skin. It didn't even get past her breastbone.

Laughing, she spotted the Crow hovering in front of

her. "What the fuck is this, slave?" She pointed at the tiny weapon. "Is this supposed to destroy me? Is that what you got me out here for?"

The Crow ignored her and called out, "Inka!"

A Holde's Maid chanted a spell from a spot beneath the Four Horsemen—*Wait. When did they get here? Tacky Christians. When I rule, I think I will destroy them first*—and the tiny weapon exploded into a sword made for giants. When flames erupted from the blade, she knew it was probably Surtr's sword.

"So that was your plan?" she asked the redheaded Crow. "To use Surtr's sword to destroy me? Bitch, you don't have the power for that."

The Crow grinned. "Oh, I know."

Spinning away from her, the Crow threw her arms out wide and screamed out, "What are you going to do about it, pussy? *What are you going to do?*"

Gullveig had no idea who the woman was yelling at. "Poor thing. You've snapped, haven't you? I don't know who you're talking to, slave. I'm over here."

The Crow faced her again and placed her tiny human hands on the hilt of a sword meant for a giant. Not even *a* giant but *the* ultimate giant. Surtr, himself.

Did she really think she had a chance in Helheim of—

"You treacherous little whore."

That voice. That wasn't the voice of a human. Gullveig lifted her gaze and rage ripped through her. *Nidhogg.* That little bitch had brought Nidhogg. *To challenge me?*

The little twat brought a dragon to a goddess fight? "You useless, stupid bitch," Gullveig mocked.

"Yeah, yeah," the redhead replied, her hands still on the weapon. "And you're a motherfucker!"

Gullveig would be insulted by that but to be quite truthful, she didn't know who the little bitch was talking to.

* * *

"What the hell is Erin doing?" Vig asked. Now standing off the damaged freeway, he waited by his sister, a large group of Giant Killers, his Raven brothers, and a few Crows.

"Doing what she does best," Betty answered. "Acting like a complete and utter dick."

Kat pulled off her winged helmet and scratched her head. "What kind of plan is that?"

"The only one she has left," Stieg softly replied.

Kera grabbed Jace before she could fly to Erin's side, wanting to protect her like she always had before.

"Kera, she can't!"

"We have no choice, sweetie," Chloe explained because Kera couldn't. She could barely manage to hold onto Jace. "Erin has no choice."

Erin closed her eyes and waited. She waited for flames to engulf her; destroy her.

But she was ready. She was ready to die . . .

She just didn't think she'd have to wait this long.

Erin opened one eye, trying to peek, and Nidhogg's enormous head was very close. Disturbingly so. But he was just staring at her. He wasn't doing anything.

"Well?" she pushed.

The dragon chuckled and leaned back, half his dragon body buried in the hole he'd come from.

"Sooo . . . you want me to clean up your mess for you. Is that it? That's why you lured me up here? To help *you* and these genetic failures called humans?" He shook his head. "No. No way. You're on your own."

"You're scared, aren't you?" Erin asked. "You're frightened."

The dragon winced, his scaled face way more animated than she'd actually thought would be possible. "Is that really the best you can come up with?" he asked, sounding a little sad. "I mean . . . seriously?"

"Look," Erin snipped back, kind of fed up, "I've got this borderline migraine that's not going away; this smell from your shitty, corpse-filled home is filling my entire nasal cavity and the back of my throat; I'm probably permanently scarred now from that fight with those goddamn elves and, let's be honest, I'm much too pretty to have permanent scars. It's like fucking up the Mona Lisa."

The dragon moved back a bit, his maw briefly dropping open before he said, "You're not serious."

"Hey! This is a half-million-dollar face."

"Only half-a-million?"

"If it were worth a million, I'd have my own TV show and a clothing line. Because that's how *awesome* I am. I'm putting up with all you godlike, giant bitches because apparently no one else in this goddamn universe can possibly get rid of this little slit!"

Gullveig—the fiery sword still sticking out of her chest and apparently forgotten—pointed at herself. "Are you talking about *me*?"

"And none of that," Nidhogg shot back, "is my problem. Fix this shit on your own."

"You know what? I'd really like to do that. If I could, you giant lizard, I would! But according to dwarves who insist on calling me fatty—"

"Well . . ." Gullveig began.

"Shut up," Erin snapped before turning back to Nidhogg. "I can't. So yes, I came to you. I lured you up here. I did what I had to do, just so I could get this goddamn shit over with.

If for no other reason than so I can go home, sit in the TV room, and watch really bad reality TV. Maybe eat enough mac and cheese until my thighs and ass are as big as yours. I am *fed up*. So, yeah, in answer to your fucking question, that's the best I can do. Accuse you of being scared of this worthless little twat!"

"Well, listen up, little girl—" the dragon began

"Excuse me?" Gullveig cut in. "You're fed up with me, slave? Really? *Do you know who I am? Can you even conceive—*"

"Does she know she still has that sword in her chest?" Kera asked Ski.

"I don't think so. I think she's too angry."

"I am a *goddess*." Gullveig continued ranting while Erin and Nidhogg stared at her. "I have seen things and lived and destroyed and created more than your tiny brains can ever hope to imagine. You think this dragon can destroy me? He's a lizard. The lowest. Slithering around on the ground—"

"Actually snakes slither. Lizards have legs, so . . ." Nidhogg tossed in.

"But you're not lizards, right?" Erin asked, appearing quite interested.

"No. Now it is true that we both have scales, but dragons are vastly different. To put it in terms humans might understand, you could say that what separates dragons from lizards is that dragons have opposable thumbs."

"That's not a thumb," Erin said, pointing at his front claw.

"It's like a thumb."

"Not really."

"Why are you arguing with me? I, mean, how many dragons do you know that you can just run around, arguing about them like you know my kind?"

"I'm just saying—"

"Yes, but you're saying it wrong!"

"Fine," Erin snapped back. "You have claw-thumbs. Happy now? Does knowing you have claw-thumbs make you happy?"

"You see, this is what I mean. You pick and you pick until you make me crazy. Is that what you want, human? To see me crazy?"

"I've already assumed you're crazy because you live around a bunch of corpses like it's normal."

"*I get hungry!*"

"Hey!" Gullveig bellowed. "I am talking! *Do you know who I am?*"

"How many times is she going to ask that?" Kera wondered aloud.

"Too many times for that dragon," Jace said, shaking her head. "This is not going to end well for her. Not at all."

"I am," Gullveig went on, "the most important thing in this universe. And I am going to destroy everything that you love or hold dear. I will make you watch while I tear and render and decimate—"

Kera watched as Gullveig ranted, lost in her threats and narcissistic rantings. It was like watching one of those on-set, behind-the-scene videos of an actor losing it on some unimportant camera assistant.

The difference, though, was that Gullveig wasn't an over-paid actress with an Oscar under her belt, and Erin and Nid-hogg did not work for her.

A realization that pair had already come to.

The left side of the dragon's snout curled in disdain and he finally looked down at Erin, motioning to the sword Gull-veig had not removed from her chest yet.

Erin placed one hand on the hilt of the sword. She was about to place the other, when Nidhogg held out one, long, black talon.

Gripping it, Erin noted, "I'm trying not to freak out at the fact that my entire hand can't completely wrap around the tip of your talon."

Now the dragon grinned, showing fangs that were the length of some Vikings Kera knew. Big ones.

The dragon threw back his shoulders and took in a breath that had trees swaying and Kera digging in her feet, feeling like she was about to be sucked into an air vent.

There was a pause . . . the only sound that any of them could hear was that of Gullveig . . . still ranting.

Nidhogg's head jerked forward and flames so powerful and bright and hot burst out of him that everyone was forced to scramble farther away, hiding behind nearby pillars or buildings. Whatever was necessary.

When the flames stopped, Kera quickly stood and saw that . . .

Well, that nothing had changed.

Nidhogg still stood there with his claw out, Erin was still holding the tip, and Gullveig was still ranting with a sword through her chest.

"Wow," Chloe said from beside Kera. "That bitch really can't die."

Erin finally opened her eyes and Kera watched the overwhelming disappointment spread across her face when she saw that Gullveig was not dead.

Knowing they were completely out of options, Kera prepared to call a retreat. They would need to get ready for Ragnarok. It was coming now.

On the other side of the freeway, Kera watched Death's black horse rear up on its hind legs and horse and rider turned and trotted off. Death's three brothers following.

"Guys . . ." Kera said, almost afraid to believe that—

In mid-rant, Gullveig looked down at Surtr's sword. The

blade was still covered in flames, but now the flames were spreading. From weapon to goddess.

She gripped the hilt and tried to pull the sword from her body, but it wouldn't budge.

"No," Gullveig said, panicking. "*No!*"

Nidhogg looked at all the Clans and offhandedly remarked, "If I were all of you . . . I'd probably run."

As the flames began working their way through Gullveig's body, her entire being started shaking, her screams vibrating everything for miles.

Erin flew back, trying to get away from her, still unable to stop staring.

A claw wrapped around her and she was pulled into Nidhogg's chest as he turned away.

The very air around them exploded with heat and light and tornadolike winds. All Erin could do was burrow closer to Nidhogg and wait for it all to be over.

Something licked Stieg's face and he had to say he was very happy to realize it was Brodie Hawaii. Because only a dog should lick his face like that.

When he sat up, he thought maybe he was in Valhalla, but then he saw a billboard for a shitty rom-com torn from its moorings and lying on the ground.

He was still alive.

"Erin." Stieg jumped to his feet, unleashed his wings, and went up—

Nidhogg was standing over him, with Erin on his shoulder.

Ignoring the dragon, Stieg flew at Erin, grabbing her into his arms and holding her tight.

"Awww," Nidhogg mocked as they kissed. "Young love."

"Shut up," Erin shot back. She dropped her head on Stieg's shoulder and he felt her smile against the bare skin of his neck. "Just shut up."

"Human," Nidhogg said. "Next time you need my assistance . . . I suggest you ask rather than piss me off. I could have just as easily sucked your entrails out like noodles rather than help you. Understand?"

"But I'm so much better at pissing people off. It's a gift. Like being double-jointed. Or being good at math."

With a sound of disgust, he gestured them away with a flick of his claw. They unleashed their wings so that they hovered over him as the dragon backed up into the hole, one of his horns nearly shearing off the top of the Getty Museum. Stieg heard a collective gasp of panic from the Protectors and he rolled his eyes in disgust. *That* was their big concern? Losing a stupid museum?

Nidhogg slowly disappeared until, for a moment, all they could see of him were his nostrils. Then they too disappeared deep into the earth.

And that's when the world began to move beneath them.

"Earthquake!" someone cried out.

"No!" Inka yelled. "The holding spell! It's ending! Grab your dead, dying, and wounded! Retreat! Now!"

Stieg and Erin separated, each helping their own brethren remove themselves from the freeway. They had less than a minute to get themselves out of there before everything returned to the world as it had been.

Sadie Monroe sat at the red light in her boss's black BMW and quickly realized something was . . . different.

"Sadie?" her boss demanded from the other end of the phone. "What is happening?"

Sadie shook her head. "Uh . . . I don't know." She leaned forward, trying to get a better look through the windshield. "That man must have jumped." Although that didn't sound quite right. "I mean the cops are just standing there looking down on the 405. And I think there was an earthquake. Oh, my God! There's so much damage!"

"Good Lord! Get out of there, girl! Before the cops make you a witness or a building falls on you or something else ridiculous!"

"But—"

"If my cappucino's not hot when you get here . . . there will be hell to pay. Understand me?"

"I'll be right there."

Sadie disconnected the call and, praying that the cops were too busy to notice, she blew off the red light and drove through the intersection, horns blaring at her, some people cursing.

"Sorry, sorry!" she yelped, cringing when a van almost clipped her.

"Stupid bitch!" someone yelled.

"You don't understand!" she screamed back. "My boss needs her cappucino! Or the world will end!"

Honestly, these people had *no* idea what she went through on a daily basis.

They hadn't moved in minutes, standing unseen near the Getty Museum. None of them able to do anything but stare. Finally, Odin turned to his brethren and said, "That crazy bitch brought Nidhogg up here."

"You picked her," Freyja sneered.

"I didn't pick her. *She* picked her."

Even though they couldn't see it, they all knew Skuld grinned behind her Los Angeles Rams hoodie. "I did," she admitted. "And I'm fabulous!"

"So who won the pot?" Thor asked.

"I don't think we had a listing for *crazy bitch brings Nidhogg*," Tyr noted.

Freyja looked down at the scroll. "No, we don't."

"I guess Skuld wins then," Holde complained.

"No. She only said that Amsel would come back. She didn't say she'd survive the battle."

"Damn," Thor said to the Fate. "Talk about no loyalty."

Skuld shrugged. "I have to admit . . . I underestimated my girl."

"Holy shit," Freyja announced, looking up from the scroll, "Idunn wins. She said she'd survive."

They all turned to the goddess holding her basket of golden apples.

"What?" Idunn asked.

"You hate her," Freyja reminded her.

"Yes. And I've wanted her dead. We all have. And yet the bitch *still* lives. How could she *not* survive?"

"Huh," Odin said, shrugging. "She's got a point."

CHAPTER FORTY-THREE

Erin didn't know how long she'd been asleep. She was pretty sure it was days. It felt like days anyway.

It was the screams, though, that finally woke her up.

She scrambled up in her bed, ready to do battle to protect her sister-Crows . . .

But these weren't her sister-Crows. They were goats. Like ten of them.

Erin looked around. This wasn't her bedroom, either. The last thing she remembered was taking a shower because no one would come near her until she did. Even Jace who'd tried to hug her but just kept saying, "I . . . I can't. I'm sorry, but . . . *I can't! You smell!*"

So Erin had taken an unreasonably long shower, scrubbing like she'd never scrubbed before, and then lay down on her bed "for a little nap." That was the last thing she remembered.

Until the goats.

She had no idea where she was but she had on shorts and a T-shirt so she felt comfortable leaving the bedroom—the goats trailing her—going down some stairs, and out into what she guessed was the backyard.

That's where she found Stieg . . . feeding more goats.

She threw her arms wide. "What have you done?"

He pointed at Hilda, who was next to him. "You said she needed a herd."

"You could have taken her to a goat farm."

"But she's my goat. Why should I give up my goat?"

"Okay, but you could have just gotten *two* more goats. They would have been a small herd but it would have probably done the same thing."

He looked down at the goats waiting for food. "You didn't tell me all that."

"At the time I didn't think it would matter, but I'm sure you can find other homes for them all."

"Well, I'm attached now."

"Oh, God." Erin turned away to go back to the house.

"Your mother called."

Erin froze, her eyes closing. "She called me *here*?"

"Yeah. They tried you on your cell, of course, but it kept going to voice mail."

"Any idea how she got this number?"

"Guess one of the Crows gave it to her."

"Uh-huh." Erin faced him again. "What did you two talk about?"

"She said her and your father would be visiting in about two weeks. They were going to stay at a hotel, but I said they could stay here."

"Here? With you?"

"With us."

"We're an *us*?"

"As far as your mother's concerned, we're practically married."

"How many times have you talked to her while I was asleep?"

"Just a few times."

"A few . . ." Erin let out a breath. "Okay."

"I like her."

"I don't care."

"She says she likes me, too. She says I sound like a very nice boy."

"You're doing this on purpose, aren't you?"

"Just a little."

"I should have let the world burn," she muttered.

"What?"

"Nothing."

Deciding she couldn't deal without some much needed coffee, Erin went back into the house.

As Erin stared at the coffeemaker, silently willing it to make coffee faster, she heard a tap at the kitchen window. It was Ratatosk sitting on the little ledge.

She pushed open the window. "What do you want?"

It chittered at her and Erin—much to her growing horror—realized she understood him as she'd understood him on Corpse Shore. At the time she'd believed that to be a one-off sort of thing.

Now she knew. She'd understand Ratatosk forever, and he'd enjoy driving her nuts.

"Funerals?" Erin nodded. "Yes. Of course. We'll be there."

Ratatosk chittered again.

"Yes, I answered for Stieg, you little shit, because I know he'd go." Erin gasped at what he said next and was reaching for him when he jumped off the ledge and walked away. He should have moved faster, though. Hilda charged and butted his squirrel ass, sending him screaming a good fifty feet away.

"Good girl!" Stieg called out to his goat.

Knowing that Stieg had sent Hilda to handle Ratatosk . . . well, maybe she didn't mind so much if her parents stayed here. With Stieg . . . and her. With them.

Oy! Whatever.

She slammed the window and went to get her damn coffee.

The gods, for once, did something. They provided the longboats that held the Nine Clans' honorable dead.

While the youngest of the Crows sang a very sad but lovely version of "California Dreaming," the Clan leaders and Kera, War General, lit the ships on fire with large torches.

The gods stood off to the side in silence, giving their unspoken blessings as the Valkyries pushed the boats out into the water and the Claws took them out to sea where they would burn through the night.

There were no tears. No rage. Just acceptance and the knowledge that they would be seeing their brethren again in Valhalla.

As each Clan passed the Crows, they all stopped a moment and nodded at a surprised and clearly uncomfortable Erin.

Then the gods passed and each, in his or her own turn, did the same.

The Ravens passed by the Crows last and Stieg winked at her, giving her one of his rarely seen smiles before flying off with his brothers.

Her sister-Crows then surrounded Erin, Kera the first to wrap her arms around Erin and hug her close, Jace quickly taking her place, whispering against her ear, "I'm so glad you took a shower." Erin laughed as Betty kissed the top of her head and Chloe threw one arm around her shoulder and smiled at her with something like pride.

"You, Erin Amsel, are the biggest pain in the ass. And don't ever change."

Erin laughed but before she could tell them that wouldn't be a problem, Brodie jumped up and slathered her tongue across Erin's face, making her gag in disgust.

"Oh, my God," Kera snapped, "get over it, bitch. You spent an entire day with funky corpses. I doubt a little dog slobber is that overwhelming for you."

EPILOGUE

It was an all-Clan party in the heart of Yosemite. Not only were all the Clans there, but so were the shifters who'd fought by their side.

The drink was flowing, the food was good, and everyone seemed to be having a great time. But Erin wasn't in the middle of it like she usually was. So Stieg "borrowed" Brodie and had her track the Crow for him.

He found her deep in the Yosemite woods, perched on a boulder looking down on the party below.

After patting Brodie on the head and sending her back to the others, he flew up to the top of the boulder and landed beside Erin.

She hadn't said much since the funerals. He had the feeling she'd been overwhelmed by it all. No one, especially Erin, ever expected her to be revered by the other Clans. But she was and would be until Ragnarok did finally come. She'd risked everything to get that sword and to end Gullveig. And she did it without once thinking about herself or what could happen to her if she failed, because failure had not been an option.

But she hadn't failed and it was time to realize that and

move on. If for no other reason than he knew that just getting rid of Gullveig didn't mean the end to the work the Clans did. Instead, it probably meant more. A vacuum had been left, and there would always be someone else, whether god or human, who'd desperately want to fill it. It would be up to their Clans to prevent that.

Still, they had tonight and a pretty good party.

"You okay?" he finally asked when she refused to say a word.

"Sure."

"I think we should take your parents to Disneyland."

Erin looked at him. "What?"

"When your parents come, we should take them to Disneyland."

"Why?"

"Because it's fun. I've been there. I had fun."

"We're not taking my parents to Disneyland."

"Fine, but we have to do something with them."

"I'd suggest Vegas, but I'm worried they'll gamble all their money away and be forced to move in with me."

"We have room. If they don't mind the goats."

"My mother will mind the goats. And I never said I'd stay with you for good."

"So you're leaving?"

"I didn't say that, either. I mean, Jesus, Engstrom, with every look you give me you're asking me for commitment and I don't do commitment. I can't even commit to the car-pool lane when I have four other people in the car and yet you want me to commit to a long-term relationship with you."

"Is that what's been bothering you?"

"What did you think?"

"I don't know. I thought it was the recent reverence of the Clans."

"Oh, please," she scoffed. "That won't last. By next week

Freida will be calling me a whore again, I'm sure I'll pop Lindgren in the mouth for something, and Kera will irritate the living fuck out of *everyone* with one of her goddamn clipboards."

She let out a breath. "But *you*."

"I get it."

"You do?"

"Sure. You're in love with me and there's nothing you can do about it."

She turned and faced him. "What?"

"But it's all right."

"Is it?"

"Yeah. I love you, too."

"Gee," she replied flatly. "Great."

Stieg leaned in, pressing his forehead against her temple. "I looooooove you," he said again, trying to sound like a foghorn.

"Stop," she said with a laugh.

"Love, love, love, love youuuuuuuuu."

Laughing harder, Erin looked away. "Bastard."

Erin didn't know what she was going to do. She hadn't expected to survive any of this, much less get a man out of it.

But every time she thought that she was dead where she stood, that her Second Life was over for good, there was Stieg Engstrom. He always had her back and she always had his.

That was something she couldn't just walk away from. No matter how much the whole idea of being part of a couple terrified the hell out of her.

Going face-to-face with dragons? Eh.

Destroying a goddess? Whatev.

Waking up every morning for the rest of her Second Life to that ridiculously gorgeous, goofy face!

God—or, you know, whoever—help her.

She grabbed his hand. "Come on."

"Where?"

"To the goddamn party. I haven't had my two drinks yet and there's a ton of people down there who sadly do not have a two-drink minimum and are just ripe for the torture. And who knows when I'll get a chance like this again?"

She pulled him off the boulder and they easily landed, their wings helping them.

Erin started to walk toward the party, but Stieg tugged her back until she was in his arms and he kissed her.

She wished she could say she didn't kiss him back. She wished she could say that she felt nothing for him. But she loved him. Despite not wanting to, she loved him.

So when he finally pulled away from her, she snarled, "Bastard," and then led him out of the woods.

When they reached the party, Karen jumped into Stieg's arms, hugging him tight. Then she hugged Erin.

She definitely didn't have a two-drink minimum and it seemed that tequila was definitely her thing. But Erin didn't mind. Karen and her shifter friends had saved their ass. They'd always be welcome at a Crow party from now until the end of time.

They didn't feel like yelling over the music so they just hugged and Karen went back to dancing.

Erin climbed on Stieg's back, her legs over his shoulders, her hands buried in his hair. He moved through the dancing crowd, taking the beer Vig shoved in his hand and scratching the head of a happy Jace who was dancing with Ski . . . and her puppy Lev. Because, *of course* she was.

Brodie flew around them before diving into a gaggle of drunken Crows, and Erin playfully punched Kera in the shoulder . . . which quickly turned into a fistfight but Stieg kept moving.

Then something went weird.

It started with Brodie. She suddenly grabbed Lev out of Jace's arms and carried the puppy away by the back of the neck. At the same time the shifters stopped moving. Their bodies just froze in mid-grind. And, in seconds, every one of them had shifted into whatever animal they were and began to back up, all of them snarling and snapping.

A few seconds later, the earth rumbled, everything shaking.

"Earthquake!" someone drunkenly called out, laughing. "Hold on, everybody!"

Erin backflipped off Stieg's shoulders and moved through the crowd until she found the Crows huddled together.

Jace, now standing between Erin and Kera, shook her head. "I don't think this is an earthquake, guys."

Erin knew her sister-Crow was right even before the Half Dome, a Yosemite icon, split in half and an explosion of rock and dirt shot out over them.

Everyone ducked and waited. When they could look again, he stood on the left side of the split rock.

And, in the silence that followed, they heard Inka whisper one word.

"Loki."

Laughing, the god spread his arms wide and Loki's Clan of wolf shifters tore down the mountains toward them.

Erin pulled out her blades, cracked her neck.

Kera, still in her role of War General, stepped forward. She had her axe at the ready and her wings out.

She looked back at the Nine Clans and, with a roar that would impress any Viking, Kera bellowed, "*Kill all of them!*"

HOT AND BADGERED

It's not every day that a beautiful naked woman falls out of
the sky and lands face-first on grizzly shifter Berg Dunn's
hotel balcony. Definitely they don't usually hop up and
demand his best gun. Berg gives the lady a grizzly sized
t-shirt and his cell phone, too, just on style points. And then
she's gone, taking his XXXL heart with her. By the time he
figures out she's a honey badger shifter, it's too late.

Honey badgers are survivors. Brutal, vicious, ill-tempered
survivors. Or maybe Charlie Taylor-MacKilligan is just
pissed that her useless father is trying to get them all
killed again, and won't even tell her how. Protecting her
little sisters has always been her job, and she's not about
to let some pesky giant grizzly protection specialist with a
network of every shifter in Manhattan get in her way. Wait.
He's trying to help? Why would he want to do that? He's
cute enough that she just might let him tag along—that is, if
he can keep up . . .

CHAPTER ONE

What had she been thinking? Using the "Ride of the Valkyries" as a ringtone? Because that shit waking a person up at six in the morning was just cruel. Really cruel.

And, as always, she'd done it to herself.

Charlie Taylor-MacKilligan slapped her hand against the bedside table next to the bed, blindly searching for her damn phone. When she touched it, she was relieved. She had no plan to actually get out of bed anytime soon. Not as hungover as she currently was. But she really wanted that damn ringtone to stop.

Somehow, without even lifting her head from the pillow she had her face buried in, or opening her eyes, Charlie managed to touch the right thing on her phone screen so that she actually answered it.

"What?" she growled.

"Get out," was the reply. "Get out now."

Hangover forgotten, Charlie was halfway across the room when they kicked the door open. She turned and ran toward the sliding glass doors that led to the balcony. She'd just made it outside when something hot rammed into her shoulder, tearing past flesh and muscle and burrowing into bone. The power of it sent her flipping headfirst over the railing.

"What do you think?" the jackal shifter asked.

Sitting in a club chair in his Milan, Italy, hotel suite, Berg Dunn gazed at the man holding up a black jacket.

"What do I think about what?" Berg asked.

"The jacket. For my show tonight."

Berg shrugged. "I don't know."

"You must have an opinion."

"I don't. I happily have no opinion on what a grown man who is not me should wear."

The jackal sighed. "You're useless."

"I have one job. Keeping your crazed fans from tracking you down and stripping the flesh from your bones. That's it. That's all I'm supposed to do. I, at no time, said that I would ever help you with your fashion sense."

Rolling his eyes, the jackal laid the jacket on the bed and then stared at it. Like he expected it to tell him something. To actually speak to him.

Berg wanted to complain about this ridiculous job, but how could he when it was the best one he'd had in years? Following a very rich, very polite jackal around so that he could play piano for screaming fans in foreign countries was the coolest gig ever.

First class everything. Jets. Food. Women. Not that Berg took advantage of the women thing too often. He knew most were just trying to use him to get to Cooper Jean-Louis Parker. Coop was the one out there every night, banging away at those Steinway pianos, doing things with his fingers that even Berg found fascinating, and wooing all those lovely females with his handsome jackal looks.

Berg was just the guy to get through so they could get to

the musical genius. And, unlike some of his friends, being used by beautiful women wasn't one of his favorite things.

It was a tolerable thing, but not his favorite.

"I can't decide," the jackal finally admitted.

"I know how hard it is to pick between one black jacket and *another* black jacket. Which will your black turtleneck go with?"

"It's not just *another* black jacket, peasant. It's the difference between pure black and charcoal black."

"We have a train to catch," Berg reminded Coop. "So could you speed this—"

Both shifters jumped, their gazes locked on the balcony outside the room, visible through doors open to let the fresh morning air in.

Another crazed female fan trying to make her way into Coop's room? Some of these women, all of them full-humans, were willing to try any type of craziness for just a *chance* at ending up in the "maestro's" bed.

With a sigh, Berg pushed himself out of the chair and headed across the large room toward the sliding glass doors. It looked like he'd have to break another poor woman's heart.

But he stopped when he saw her. A brown-skinned woman, completely naked. Which, in and of itself, was not unusual. The women who tried to sneak into Coop's room—no matter the country they might be in—were often naked.

What stopped Berg in his tracks was that *this* woman had blood coming from her shoulder. The blood from a gun wound.

Berg motioned Coop back. "Get in the bathroom," he ordered.

"Oh, come on. I want to see what's—"

"I don't care what you want. Get in the—"

The men stopped arguing when they saw him. A man in black military tactical wear, armed with a rifle, handgun, and several blades. He zipped down a line and landed on the railing of their balcony.

Berg placed his hand on the gun holstered at his side and stepped in front of Coop.

"Get in the bathroom, Coop," he ordered, his voice low.

"We have to help her."

"Do what I tell you and I will."

The man in black dropped onto the balcony and grabbed the unconscious woman by her arm, rolling her limp body over.

"Now, Coop. Go."

Berg moved forward with his weapon drawn from its holster. The man pulled his sidearm and pressed the barrel against the woman's head.

Berg aimed his .45 and barked, "Hey!"

The man looked up, bringing his gun with him. Gazes locked, fingers resting on triggers. Each man sizing the other up. And that was when the woman moved. Fast. So fast, Berg knew she wasn't completely human, which immediately changed everything.

The woman grabbed her attacker's gun hand by the wrist and held it to the side so he couldn't finish the job on her. She used her free hand to pummel the man's face repeatedly.

Blood poured down his lips from his shattered nose; his eyes now dazed.

Still holding the man's wrist, she got to her feet.

She was tall. Maybe five-ten or five-eleven. With broad, powerful shoulders and arms and especially legs. Like a much-too-tall gymnast.

She gripped her attacker by the throat with one hand and, without much effort, lifted him up and over the balcony railing. She released him then and unleashed the biggest claws Berg had ever seen from her right hand.

Turning away from the attacker, she swiped at the zip line

that held him aloft, and Berg cringed a little at the man's desperate screams as he fell to the ground below.

That's when she saw Berg. Her claws—coming from surprisingly small hands—were still unleashed. Her gaze narrowed on him and her shoulders hunched just a bit. She was readying herself for an attack. To kill the man who could out her as a shifter, he guessed. Not having had time to process that he was one, too. Plus, he had a gun, which wouldn't help his cause any.

"It's okay," Berg said quickly, re-holstering his weapon. "It's okay. I'm not going to hurt you."

"Yeah," Coop said from behind him. "We just want to help."

Berg let out a frustrated breath. "I thought I told you to get into the bathroom."

"I wanted to see what's going on."

Coop moved to Berg's side. "We're shifters, too," he said, using that goddamn charming smile. Like this was the time for any of that!

But this one rolled her eyes in silent exasperation and came fully into the room. She walked right by Berg and Coop and to the bedroom door.

"Wait," Berg called out. When she turned to face him, one brow raised in question, he reminded her, "You're naked."

He went to his already packed travel bag and pulled out a black T-shirt.

"Here," he said, handing it to her.

She pulled the shirt on and he saw that he'd given her one of his favorite band shirts from a Fishbone concert he'd seen years ago with his parents and siblings.

"Your shoulder," Berg prompted, deciding not to obsess over the shirt. Especially when she looked so cute in it.

She shook her head at his prompt and again started toward the door. But a crash from the suite living room had Berg grabbing the woman's arm with one hand and shoving Coop across the bedroom and into the bathroom with the other.

Berg faced the intruder, pulling the woman in behind his body.

Two gunshots hit Berg in the lower chest—the man had pulled the trigger without actually seeing all of Berg, but expecting a more normal-sized human.

Which meant a few things to Berg. That he was dealing with a full-human. An expertly trained full-human. An ex-soldier probably.

An ex-soldier with a kill order.

Because if he'd been trying to kidnap the woman, he would have made damn sure he knew who or what was on the other end before he pulled that trigger. But he didn't know. He didn't check because he didn't care. Everyone in the room had to die.

And knowing that—*understanding* that—did nothing but piss Berg off.

Who just ran around trying to kill a naked, unarmed woman? his analytical side wanted to know.

The grizzly part of him, though, didn't care about any of that. All it knew was that it had been shot. And shooting a grizzly but not killing it immediately . . . always an exceptionally bad move.

The snarl snaked out of Berg's throat and the muscles between his shoulders grew into a healthy grizzly hump. He barely managed to keep from shifting completely, but his grizzly bear rage exploded and his roar rattled the windows. The bathroom door behind him slammed shut, the jackal having the sense to *now* go into hiding.

The intruder quickly backed up, knowing something wasn't right, but not fully understanding, which was why he didn't run.

He should have run.

With a step, Berg was right in front of him, grabbing the gun from his hand and spinning the man around so that he had him by the throat. He did this because two more men in tactical gear were coming into the suite from the front door.

Using the man's weapon, Berg shot each man twice in the chest. They both had on body armor so he wasn't worried he'd killed them.

With both attackers down, Berg refocused on the man he held captive. He spun him around, because he wanted to ask him a few questions about what the hell was going on. He was calmer now. He could be rational.

But when the man again faced him, Berg felt a little twinge in his side. He slowly looked down . . . and found a combat blade sticking out.

First he'd been shot. Now stabbed.

His grizzly rage soared once again and, as the intruder—quickly recognizing his error—attempted to fight his way out of Berg's grasp, desperately begging for his life, Berg grabbed each side of his attacker's face and squeezed with both hands . . . until the man's head popped like a zit.

It was the blood and bone hitting him in the face that snapped Berg back into the moment, and he gazed down at his brain-covered hands.

"Oh, shit," he muttered. "Shit, shit, shit."

The other intruders, ignoring the pain from the shots, scrambled up and out of the suite. As far away from Berg as they could get.

Someone touched his arm and he half-turned to see the woman. She raised her hands and rewarded him with a soft smile.

That's when he calmed down. "Shit," he said again, holding out his hands to her.

She stepped close, held his wrists, studied the blade still sticking out of his side. She then examined the wounds in his chest. Unlike the intruders, he hadn't been wearing body armor. The bullets had hit him, had entered his body, but he was grizzly. Even as a human, you had to bring bigger weapons if you wanted to take down one of his kind with one or two shots.

Berg knew, just watching her, that she was going to help him. She was going to try. But she was in more danger than he was, and she needed to get out of here.

"Go," he told her and she frowned. "Seriously. Go."

He pulled his hands away from her, went to his travel bag and took out a .45 Ruger, handing it to her. "Take this."

Her eyes narrowed again as she stared up at him.

"I get the feeling you need it more than me," he pushed. "Just go."

She took the weapon, dropped the magazine, cleared the gun with one hand before shoving the loaded mag back in and putting a round in the chamber.

Yeah. The woman knew how to handle his .45. Maybe better than he did.